THE WOLF VS THE SHADOW FAE

THE HIDDEN CITY SUPERNATURAL SLEUTH

LAURETTA HIGNETT

Editing by Cissell Ink

Book Cover by Atra Luna Graphic Design

First Edition 2025

CAST OF CHARACTERS

Daphne Ironclaw — Our hero, an optimistic, unhinged wolf girl. Currently even more unhinged than usual because her boyfriend got abducted, and she has some mysterious memories beginning to surface (spoiler alert: it's the Evils).

Romeo Zarayan — The Warlock, High Priest, Lord of Shadows. Romeo is still missing, presumably abducted by his kin, the Shadow Fae.

Dwayne — A law unto himself.

Dacre Sagwood — A handsome witch from the Sagwood coven and a foster father.

Ruby and Samuel — Dacre's foster kids, both talented little witches. Keep your eye on Ruby, she's a firecracker.

Myf — Formerly a mysterious, agoraphobic, Welsh pantry-dweller, now a seriously depressed, pantry-dwelling dragon shifter.

Lennox Arran — Lion shifter and the Alpha Shifter of Philadelphia. Potentially Daphne's half-brother, which is icky considering Lennox has been trying to get Daphne into bed forever.

Monica — Daphne's boss, the manager of the Otherworld department of the CPS. Monica is ninety-nine percent made up of caffeine.

Judy Sagwood — Daphne's colleague, the office bitch. Becoming increasingly insufferable and still weirdly addicted to yogurt.

James — A hardworking colleague.

Louisa — The lovely woman from the DMV that Dwayne keeps hitting on whenever he's bored.

Prue — An old friend. See Bad Bones: The Blood & Magic series for more on Prue.

Countess Ebadorathea Greenwood — A sorceress with a terrible (and deserved) reputation. She makes a great woodfired pizza, though.

Christopher Jupiter — the oldest Jupiter brother and Worst Person Alive. Which is bad news for Daphne; she still thinks he's dead.

Lord Brackin Pesh of Gloom — A high fae lord and Daphne's old master. Dresses like a pirate and has some odd kinks. Brackin is the spare to the Pesh family title and is the dastardly younger brother of Lord Bron Pesh of Gloom.

The Scorch — A mystery!

Former King Monton of Dusk — he's actually dead but worth mentioning. Monton ruled the Kingdom of Dusk before being killed in a hunting accident a couple of decades ago.

Former Queen Carissa of Dusk — Monton's wife. Carissa reluctantly stepped up to the throne after Monton's death but stepped down again immediately.

King Ronus of Dusk — The head honcho of the Kingdom of Dusk. Formerly the Duke of Nightfall, Ronus took the throne of Dusk after the former King died and Queen Carissa stepped down.

Queen Talia of Dusk — Ronus's wife, former Duchess of Nightfall.

Steven — A brownie servant.

Maeve, the Winter Queen — Hoo boy, watch out for her.

Lord Fandoine — One of the twenty-three fae warlords that Daphne escaped from when she was lost off-world in her late teens. Like the other twenty-two warlords, Lord Fandoine locked Daphne in a tower with the intention of marrying her the next day.

THE BRIDES

Princess Nyla of Spring — The favorite to win the Bride Trials. Blonde, beautiful, bloodthirsty, and an arrogant bitch.

Princess Glorina of Dawn — A crafty brunette beauty.

Princess Saoira of Autumn — A glorious redhead with a passion for giving TED Talks on the environment in Faerie.

Princess Ember of Sandstone — the daughter of the former Queen Carissa and stepdaughter of the former King Monton. A sweet little psychopath.

Lady Sybell of Nightfall — A sexy, raven-haired, red-lipped woman with hidden depths.

Lady Brisa of Frost — Platinum hair, icy eyes, cold heart.

Lady Winnara of Gale — A crack shot with a blow dart, Lady Gale has silver hair and pearly skin.

Lady Meena of Bloom — A blonde beauty, a little out of her depth.

Lady Bork — an ogre, and my personal favorite of all the brides.

ONE

"I really do appreciate you coming out here, Daphne." The handsome witch gave me a brilliant smile as he handed me a big mug of coffee. "I'm sorry if it's turned out to be a waste of your time."

Stab him.

I ignored Brain-Daphne and smiled back. Dacre Sagwood really was a very conventionally good-looking man, giving Handsome Prince vibes—tall, broad-shouldered, twinkling blue eyes, a masculine square jaw, and a dimple in his chin. His thick head of honey-blond hair was swept back off his proud brow.

It wasn't a glamor. He really did look like that.

"Thank you," I said, nodding graciously. "And I'm sorry, too, for the inconvenience. I didn't mean to interrupt your home-schooling session. You have a lovely home, Mr. Sagwood."

It was a nice place. Three story, dark brick, balconies on every story, a wide covered porch, and pretty white rose bushes out front. Like a lot of old-world witches, the Sagwoods seemed to favor a Victorian Gothic aesthetic.

Even Dacre was dressed in a pristine black three-piece suit. The rooms were dark-paneled, lined with portraits of snooty ancestors, and packed with antiques, but the whole place was very clean. Not a speck of dust anywhere.

We're wasting time. We've wasted too much time, Brain-Daphne continued her almost incoherent muttering inside my head. *It's been two weeks already. We need to stab this guy and go. Girl, let's go!*

Dacre Sagwood sat in the winged armchair opposite me in their living room, framed by his two children sitting on ottomans on either side of him. Both children were smiling serenely. "That's okay," Dacre replied. "We can get straight back into it once we're done. And don't feel guilty, Daphne," he added, meeting my eyes. "I understand how mandatory reporting works. I'm grateful there are O-CPS officers like you who take every report seriously. No matter how erroneous they might be."

I smiled, nodded, and took a sip of my coffee.

Asshat, Brain-Daphne snapped. *What the fuck does erroneous mean?*

I didn't know.

We should make it a rule we have to stab anyone who uses unnecessary words like that, she snarled. *Anyone that uses the word egregious, too. I still don't know what that means. Let's just stab him and go, babes. Let's go, let's go, let's go...*

We couldn't agree on anything at the moment, and it was so hard to concentrate with her screaming in my head. I kept my smile plastered on my face and tried to ignore her. Brain-Daphne was going through a rough time right now. My internal survival mechanism was currently behaving like a pit bull in a meth frenzy.

"I appreciate your patience, Mr. Sagwood," I said, my voice shaking a little. "This will only take a few minutes, anyway. I just have to ask you a few questions, and I'll be on my way." I pulled out a notebook from my backpack, moving stiffly in my motorcycle leathers. The ride out to Somerton had taken just under an hour, and it had done nothing to calm the turmoil within me.

It had been almost two weeks since Romeo had disappeared. When Holly called to tell me he'd vanished on the way into the Otherworld court, I rushed there to check it out. The scent of the fae almost knocked me unconscious; it was like a punch to the sinuses.

There was no other explanation. His kin had come for him.

I knew they would. There was nothing the royal high fae were more obsessed with than their bloodlines—both rigorously maintaining them and cutting off diseased branches. I knew the Shadow Fae were going to be a problem eventually; I just didn't realize how soon things would come to a head.

And now the worst had happened, and I was paralyzed with fear and tortured by indecision.

Flicking through my notebook, I tried to find the list of questions I was supposed to ask Dacre Sagwood. The form was here somewhere. And the initial report... Where did I put it? Clearing my throat awkwardly, I gave him an apologetic look. "I'm sorry, Mr. Sagwood. Please just give me a moment."

"Oh, that's quite alright. Take all the time you need, Daphne."

The boy next to him gave an odd squeak. Dacre Sagwood smiled down at him fondly and patted his knee. "Relax, Sam. We'll be done soon, and you can get back to playing."

Sam grinned at his foster father. His smile looked forced. He didn't seem to believe Dacre at all.

Family. You can't live with them, can't kill them.

You can, my brain said snippily. *You killed yours. And Romeo is probably trying to kill his bio family right now. Or they're killing him. Or torturing him.* She gnashed her teeth. *Let's go there and beat them to the punch. Murder frenzy. Kill them all.*

Except I couldn't get there. And right now, nobody was helping me.

At first, everyone expected Romeo to come home all by himself. I was the only person who seemed to understand how hard it was to even survive in Faerie as a mortal, let alone get home if you didn't have a World Key.

The fae diplomat had already declined to intervene, calling it a private family matter. Asherah wasn't even swayed by the fact that it was her fault Romeo had been stolen by the Shadow Fae in the first place.

A painful week crawled by with no word from him. Romeo's covenmates had grown desperate enough they launched their own rescue mission. But they wouldn't even entertain the idea of taking me with them. It was far too dangerous, and they were too scared I'd get hurt.

Or, more accurately, they were scared of what Romeo would do to them if I got hurt. Like most people, they still underestimated me.

I soon realized they had no idea what they were doing anyway, so I stopped asking them to help, and just smiled and nodded when they told me about their stupid plans. At this rate, they wouldn't even be able to get out of Philadelphia, let alone make it to Faerie.

I snapped back to attention as Dacre Sagwood waved his hand graciously towards me. "Please, go ahead," he said. "And feel free to ask the children anything you want." His smile grew conspiratorial. "We have no secrets here."

"That's good." I glanced at the children. Ruby, the girl

4

on Dacre's left, was twelve years old, with dark skin and very curly dark hair scraped into little puffs on either side of her head. Samuel, the boy, was ten, with white skin and huge flashing hazel eyes.

Neither of them looked like Dacre, because neither of them were his biological children. They were foster kids, orphans of the Great Suffocation. Ruby had been in a local group home since her mother had died. Samuel had been accidently placed in the human system when his own mom passed on and had only been transferred to O-CPS last year when he manifested his magic.

According to my files, the children had been fostered by Dacre and his wife Jessica for almost eight months, and they'd applied to adopt them.

"Is your wife around, Mr. Sagwood?" I asked him.

"She is away for work, I'm afraid," he said, shrugging in a helpless manner. "She is incredibly busy this time of year."

"Of course."

I'd done a little research on the couple already. Dacre wasn't originally a Sagwood. He was from Chicago and had married into the Sagwood coven through Jessica, the daughter of the coven's High Priest. Jessica was a partner at an accounting firm in the city, and, from all accounts, she was a workaholic with two feet planted firmly in the human world.

It was shallow to even think it, but Jessica and Dacre seemed like a very mismatched couple, looks-wise. I'd checked out Jessica's work profile on her company's website, and she had a very round face, a ruddy complexion, and pale hair scraped back into a bun so tight it made her huge eyes bulge out of her head.

I could have asked Judy, my colleague at the O-CPS

office, for more gossip about the couple. Judy was a Sagwood—a third cousin of Jessica, in fact—but Judy was a giant bitch, and I preferred not to have to deal with her if I could help it.

In fact, Judy would normally be working on this case herself. While our assignments were supposed to be random, Judy generally picked up anything witch-related in Philadelphia, if she did anything at all. But due to the fact that I was almost vibrating out of my skin with anxiety, desperate to keep moving, and begging for things to keep me occupied, I'd already blown through my entire caseload, so I was now picking up anything new as soon as it came in.

My brain whined. *We should go. We should go now.*

No, I told her. They all asked me to wait. No, they'd begged me to wait.

I really had no choice. If I had to go to Faerie by myself, I'd have to find a portal first, and I knew more than anyone how hard it was to find one when you were looking for one. I also knew how dangerous it was to throw yourself head-first into the unknown. It was more likely I'd find myself in some hellish underworld dimension instead of in one of the Royal Courts of the Shadow Fae.

The safest way to get to Faerie was to use a World Key, but I needed a strong witch to make one for me. The strongest witch I knew was the sorceress, Countess Ebado-rathea Greenwood. She'd promised to help me, but said I'd have to wait for a few days.

Prue had also begged me to wait. She explained she had to do some research first. She played the guilt card and even managed to get Chloe on speakerphone to remind me of how devastated everyone had been when I disappeared off-world as a kid.

I didn't care. I just wanted Romeo back. But I couldn't charge off by myself to find him.

Of course we can. My brain threw up an image of me jumping into a portal and stabbing a bunch of magical creatures on the other side. She was really anxious. *See?*

Even Dwayne told me to cool my jets. He hated Faerie, so I knew he wouldn't want to come with me. Besides, his psychotic girlfriend would probably descend into another jealous rage and kill me for real this time.

My brain bristled. *We can't waste any more time. Time moves differently in Faerie, remember? By now, it could be months for him. He could be dead.*

Romeo wasn't dead. I still had the crystal necklace he'd given me. It was the first thing I'd reached for when Holly told me he'd disappeared. When I placed the crystal on my palm, it had stood straight up with the point in the air, confirming he wasn't in the mortal realm anymore. It had glowed a couple of times, indicating he was in danger, but it hadn't gone dark. Romeo still lived.

We will go and find him, I promised my brain. But I have to trust my friends. They'll come through for us.

You have too much faith.

I have to have faith.

Babe, if I don't get an outlet soon, I'm going to explode.

It had been too long since I said anything. Awkwardly, I flipped a few pages in my notebook. "I'm sorry, Mr. Sagwood." I shot a look at Ruby, smiling serenely at me from Dacre's left, and took a little sniff. I did the same for Samuel, and almost sneezed. His witchy wax-and-herb scent was very strong for a kid. "I just have a couple of questions." I met Ruby's eye. "You're all up to date with your homeschooling?"

She nodded. "Yes."

Dacre smiled at her fondly. "Ruby's a very smart kid. She gets her schoolwork done quickly every day."

"That's good. And you, Samuel?"

His voice was a little croaky. "Yup. I mean, yes, ma'am. I do my schoolwork with Ruby first thing every morning."

"What did you have for breakfast this morning, Samuel?"

His serene smile wobbled slightly. "Uh, oats. Overnight oats," he added pointedly.

"And you, Ruby?"

"I had oats too." Her tone was more confident.

Okay, good. Everyone was telling the truth.

I'd already done all my sight reports. The kids both had their own rooms, which were clean and tidy. Both children looked a little thin, but they could be naturally wiry. Ruby wore a pretty blue dress with puffy sleeves and knee socks, and Samuel wore knee-length shorts and a cotton shirt. There were no visible bruises or marks on either of them that I could see. "As I said, this is just routine. We have to investigate every report."

That wasn't actually true. Any other day, this report might have been shelved as low priority, or even just discarded completely, but I had too much time and energy on my hands.

"I suppose it was just one of the old gossips from the coven who reported me." Dacre chuckled. "None of them like the idea of me adopting outside of Sagwood."

My smile grew tight. It was a human report, actually. An elementary school teacher had filed it, and once the children were identified, it was passed over to the O-CPS office. Apparently, the teacher had spotted both children at the market and had become concerned for their welfare. Samuel had fainted, and Ruby was consoling him after he woke up.

They both reassured the teacher they were fine and happy. Samuel even went so far as to say he'd been faking it; he was just trying to get Ruby to buy him candy. But the teacher was suspicious and managed to glean enough information from the children to identify them before they rushed off. In the report, she emphasized that she only filed the report because her intuition was screaming at her.

I knew what that felt like. And I was so glad I'd come. The thought of a serious case of child abuse slipping through the cracks just because we didn't have enough resources to check everything out made me feel sick.

The alternative was sitting on our hands, vibrating out of our skin with anxiety, and moping around waiting for him to come home, my brain said sulkily.

Hush, I told her. We might get that outlet you've been hoping for.

Dacre leaned forward, catching my eye. "I know it sounds awful, but some of the women in my coven are awful busybodies. I don't suppose you can tell me who made the report, can you?"

"I'm afraid not," I said, giving him a rueful smile. "But, Mr. Sagwood, you can rest assured I've ticked all the boxes here today. Ruby and Samuel look happy and healthy, and you appear to be doing a good job as a foster parent."

He exhaled with relief before dramatically catching himself. "Forgive me, Daphne, it's just such an emotional roller coaster. I don't know if it's in our file or not, but Jessica can't conceive, and this might be my only chance to be a dad. I don't mind admitting it, but I think it's a good thing you can't tell me who made that report, because I think I might kill them if they ruin this for me. Ruby and Samuel are precious." His eyes shone. "I can't lose them."

All true. Everything he'd said was true—there was no skip in his heartbeat, no bead of sweat on his forehead.

"I understand completely, Mr. Sagwood." I gave him an understanding smile and turned to the children. "Ruby, Samuel, thank you for your time. Would you mind waiting

9

in the kitchen for a moment? I'd like to talk to your foster father privately for a moment."

Both of them immediately got up obediently and walked into the next room, closing the door firmly behind them.

Nice posture. When was the last time you saw a kid walk like that?

Dacre Sagwood gave me a brilliant smile. "I'm glad that we could—"

"Shush." I held up my finger, as I dug into my backpack. I drew out a little pyramid of crystals and twigs and placed it on the coffee table in front of me.

He frowned. "Wh—"

"Quiet." I met his eyes and gave him a hard stare, before returning to position the little crystal structure.

Dacre frowned. "I'm sorry, Daphne, but—"

"What part of quiet don't you understand?" I nudged the little pyramid left a little, trying to get it into the zone.

He stammered for a second. "I'm sorry?"

I glanced up again and raised an eyebrow. "You put on a good show, Dacre. Not a word of a lie in anything you said, huh?"

"Of course not." His eyebrows pinched together. "Why would I lie? I've got nothing to hide."

"You wouldn't lie. Not to me, anyway. As for having something to hide... I guess we'll see about that, won't we?"

Just like the teacher who made the report, my intuition was screaming at me, too. It had been since I walked in the door.

I moved the little charm around on the table, pointing the crystals towards the kitchen, and tuned it the same way I might tune a radio. "I've come to understand something about the covens here in Philadelphia, Dacre," I said quietly, listening for any whispers or heavy breaths of the children next door. "The Jupiters were monsters. The Sweetgrass coven are elitist assholes. And the witches of Sagwood are crafty." I nodded towards the crystal pyramid on the table. "I actually got this idea from a Sagwood witch. My colleague Judy uses this listening spell whenever I have a meeting with our boss, Monica. It pissed me off so much I ended up stealing it off her desk."

A little to the left... I could hear small lungs breathing. There. I glanced up and met Dacre's eyes. "I bet you heard somewhere that I'm good at telling when someone is lying, huh?"

"Daphne, no." He shook his head, his expression devastated. "I would never—"

"I have to hand it to you. You covered all your bases. You know I've got a good nose. I can hear your pulse skipping when you lie, so you didn't lie. You know I'd be able to sniff out a glamor, so you didn't bother covering Samuel's pale cheeks or the dark circles under Ruby's eyes. I bet you didn't realize I can smell increased levels of cortisol in someone's blood, though."

He blinked. I watched his pupils zip left and right quickly.

"Oh, there it is. You get it now. Those two children you are fostering smiled happily and said all the right things, Dacre. But both of them are absolutely terrified."

He took a quick breath in, shuffling forward on his seat. "Of course they are," he said, holding out his hands in a beseeching gesture. "They're scared you're going to take them away from me. I've given them what they've been missing their entire lives, Daphne. Their parents weren't wealthy; you know that from your file—that's why they died in the Suffocation in the first place. They didn't have the resources to get to safety."

That was true. Both kids were raised by poor single

moms who were forced to work normie jobs just to pay the bills. Both of them died coming home from work when the Suffocation was at its worst.

Dacre took a deep, shaky breath. "And now, they've both got rooms of their own. Toys, books. They get the best education. Of course they're scared. They have so much trauma from losing their parents in the first place, Daphne. They know who you are and what you do. They're terrified you're going to take them away."

I paused for a second, watching him carefully.

Huh. Well, that's logical. He might be right.

Except I knew deep down it wasn't true. Intuition was funny. It wasn't logical, and it wasn't a conscious thing. It was the result of all the clues that I unconsciously registered at heart-level.

And right now, my heart was in control. My brain had lost the plot, though.

I opened my mouth, but a soft whisper brushed through the room, so I closed my lips quickly so I could listen.

Ruby's voice. "It's going to be fine, Sammy," she whispered. "Please don't cry. We did everything perfectly. Don't worry, she'll be gone in a minute."

Samuel let out a sob. "But we've used up a whole hour of our work time today. He's going to make us stay up until midnight so we can finish the quota. If we don't finish..."

Ruby let out a soft sigh. "If he doesn't give us food today, we'll just eat the dandelions out in the yard again."

Wow. Brain-Daphne let out a whistle. *I didn't see that coming.*

I did. Overnight oats sound lovely, but it's just gruel.

Okay, babes. I'm on board. Let's do this.

The children fell silent again. I fixed Dacre with a look and raised an eyebrow. "What quota?"

12

Dacre's brows pinched together. He exhaled a confused breath. "I don't... I don't know what they're talking about. I swear."

His pulse skipped a beat.

"Liar," I snorted. I decided to keep the follow up questions for later and listened to the kids again.

Samuel let out a little whimper. "I wish we could go back to Bellevue."

"Bellevue is gone, Sam," Ruby said firmly. "We can't go back. You need to accept it. Sarah and Jackie are dead."

I frowned, confused. Bellevue was the group home both kids had been in before they'd been fostered by Dacre and Jessica. It was a great little home, actually. Sarah and Jackie were lovely witches who adored kids. Neither of them belonged to a coven, and both women were devoid of all the exclusionary elitist bullshit and political maneuvering that came with large family coven life. I'd gone to check on a kid there only four days ago, in fact, and Sarah had given me a box of fudge to take home.

Myf, my depressed dragon shifter roommate, had thrown it in the trash.

I pointed at the man sitting stiffly across from me. "Did you tell those kids that Sarah and Jackie were dead?"

Dacre's generically handsome face tightened in rage. His eyes flickered for a second. He was thinking. Hard.

I held up a finger—Ruby was still talking, and I wanted to listen to her.

"I'm going to get you out of here one day, Sammy," she said. "I promise. We'll run away and never look back."

Sammy whimpered again. "He'll find us. He said he'd always find us."

That's what they all say. My brain snorted. *Don't bother running, you'll die out there alone, nobody will ever love you like I do, you owe me, if you don't do this, I'll kill the only person you've ever loved, I put a roof over your head, the least you can do is spin me some gold out of this hay...*

All this hit a little too close to home. My heart started thumping loudly in my chest. In my head, Brain-Daphne cracked her knuckles, getting ready for action.

"I promise you, Sammy," Ruby said, her voice shaking. "I'll get you out of here one day. Now, be quiet like a mouse, okay? Let me listen to what's going on in there. She'll be gone soon, and we can get back to work."

Across from me, Dacre's hands were starting to twitch, his eyes darting from side-to-side. I stood up, in case he made a move, and fixed him with a hard look.

Dacre held up his hands. "Listen—"

"You took two traumatized children out of a happy group home to use as slaves."

"No!" Dacre shouted. "Of course not! I *saved* them."

"From what?"

He stood up, drawing himself up so he towered a full head above me, and thrust out his chest. "They're orphans." His voice quivered with emotion. "And they're just being dramatic because I'm making them do their schoolwork. The quota is their assignment tasks for today, and they're just sulking because I won't give them candy for breakfast. I've given them everything, Daphne! I took them out of an awful group home and gave them this beautiful house."

He's really laying it on thick, isn't he?

My lips thinned. He really was.

"I just want to love them." Dacre let his voice tremble. "Bring them back in here and ask them yourselves. They'll tell you. They're happy here."

I stared at him for a moment. I was sure, but I needed concrete evidence.

Get the girl, Brain-Daphne suggested.

It was a good idea. My heart told me she could handle this. While Ruby was sitting next to Dacre earlier, I saw something in her eyes that I recognized. Defiance. Determination.

"You'll see," Dacre said passionately. "I love those children like they're my own."

I took a deep breath. "Okay, I'll ask them."

He sagged with relief. "Thank the goddess."

I called out. "Ruby? Can you come in here, please?"

The door swung open, and both children marched obediently into the room. "Not you, Sammy. You can wait in the kitchen." I didn't want Samuel to see this. But, if this went the way I thought it would, Ruby would want to watch.

"Hey, Ruby. I just have one more question for you." I walked over and dropped to one knee so I could look her in the eye. "Are you happy here?"

"Of course. I love Papa—I mean Dacre." She looked down at her feet. "Sorry, I know I'm not supposed to call him that yet." Her eyes grew misty. "But I hope that as soon as the adoption goes through, I'll be able to call him Papa."

Damn, this girl is a far better liar than you ever were.

I let the silence hang in the air for a moment, waiting until she looked up at me again. Then I locked eyes with her, reached behind my back to the hidden sheaths under my shirt, and pulled out one of my Orion blades. Ruby's eyes widened as the dull metal glittered strangely in the light. Her heart started to flutter, and she took a step back from me.

I spun the blade on my palm. "Sarah and Jackie aren't dead. I saw both of them only a couple of days ago. Dacre lied to you."

Ruby froze.

"Whatever else he told you was probably a lie, too," I

continued. "He's not powerful. Dacre is only an in-law of the Sagwood coven; he's not even on the leadership team. And Jessica works in the human world, because she doesn't have much magic."

It was an educated guess. An echo-location stab in the dark. I shrugged idly. "Dacre probably only found that out after the wedding. His father-in-law doesn't even like him." That was also a wild stab in the dark, but if this guy was well-liked, he'd be part of the Sagwood coven hierarchy already.

Behind me, Dacre gasped dramatically. "No! That's not true!"

Ruby watched me carefully. She didn't move. She was listening.

Good. I gave her a gentle smile. "Whatever he's said to threaten you, it's a lie, too. He's using fear to control you."

I remembered exactly what that was like. I'd been in Ruby's position too many times before. I knew what it was like to be terrorized into compliance. As a kid, it had happened so often that I got burned out from it. There wasn't much I was scared of anymore.

In fact, there was only one thing I was scared of, and that was never seeing Romeo again. But my heart knew I would find him.

I *had* to find him.

With effort, I tore my thoughts away from Romeo and focused on the little girl in front of me. "Dacre has no power," I whispered to her. "I can take both you and Samuel out of here right now, and he can't do anything about it. Not now, not ever."

Doubt flickered in Ruby's eyes for a split second.

She thinks he'll kill you if you try it, my brain snorted. *She's worried about us now.*

I caught that, too.

16

Behind me, Dacre let out an audible sob. "This is so awful," he cried. "I would never hurt these children. I love them! Please tell me this is a joke. Please tell me that this is some kind of hazing thing you do to prospective adoptive parents, and you're only testing us."

Ignoring him, I leaned closer to the little girl and gave her a wink. "I mean, he *could* try to fight me. I'm sure he's told you he'll kill anyone who tries to take you away, right?"

She didn't say anything, but her eyes flicked towards Dacre for a split second, then to the tall plinth in the corner, where a fat orange goldfish swam in a perfectly round fishbowl.

Ah, of course. The old "threaten to hurt the innocent pet" trick. My old dark elf master used to whip my favorite racing erlyn whenever I was disobedient. I could handle being whipped myself, but it always destroyed me to watch my beloved pet being tortured in front of me.

Ruby needed more reassurance. "I don't know if you've heard of me," I said quietly. "But I'm the one who killed the nestmaster Zofia. I beat the Alpha Shifter into submission —both of them—and I killed Wesley Jupiter. I killed his son, too." I shrugged. "It was easy."

Ruby's eyes glowed. Her mouth dropped open. Almost there. She just needs one more little push.

"Dacre Sagwood's powerless," I continued. "In fact, I could gut him like a pig right now, and I wouldn't even have to fill out any paperwork."

Behind me, Dacre howled. "Ruby—"

The little girl's face hardened. "Stab him."

Dacre gasped. "Ruby!"

Yesss, get it, girl!

"He only took us from the group home because both of us have manifested magic," Ruby said, her eyes flashing. "None of the other kids in the home have manifested. He

17

walked in and said he was looking for beautiful children to adopt and create a perfect family, but he made sure to scan us to test our magical potency when Jackie wasn't looking. Our case worker told us we were lucky that he wanted us. But he forces us to make charms to sell on his website."

My mind was officially boggled. *Whoaaaa,* she breathed out. *Girl, it's usually me that's right about this stuff. You really nailed it.*

Ruby spoke quickly, relentlessly. "Sammy and I work fourteen hours a day to make love potions and luck charms, and if we don't make our quota, he doesn't give us any food. He told us that Bellevue burned down and everyone died." She jerked her chin towards the fishbowl in the corner. "You see that goldfish? He says that it's his last foster child, and she disobeyed him, so he turned her into a goldfish. Sometimes he takes it out and lets it flop on the carpet for a minute."

A surge of fury tinged my vision red.

"He also said that if we tried to escape, he'd turn Sammy into a fish. Dacre told me I'd have to watch Sammy flopping on the floor, gasping for air, for as long as he found it amusing. There's more—" Her eyes suddenly widened in alarm.

I knew it was coming. I'd put my back to Dacre on purpose, so he'd feel confident to attack. I caught the quick inhale of air and a swoop of hands, and a pungent bloom of foxglove, even before Ruby cut herself off.

Dacre was about to throw a curse.

Moving wolf-fast, I whipped around. Time slowed. Dacre had his arms outstretched with a foul-smelling leather pouch in his fingertips. His eyes blazed hot with fury.

Instant rot curse. Oooh, that's a nasty one.

The curse was already flying. I spun on my knee, grabbing Ruby at the same time, whipping her out of the way in case the leather pouch hit her, and rolled her along the ground. Using the momentum, I threw myself into a spin on the floor, knocking Dacre's legs out from under him. He landed with a smack on the floorboards, making an *oof* noise.

The pouch hit the sofa behind me. It pulsed, the fabric grew instantly damp and let out a rank smell, and within half a second, it rotted away in front of my eyes.

Brain-Daphne let out a whistle. *Ew.*

I flipped myself to my feet and walked over to where Dacre lay on the floor, groaning.

Ruby got there first. Letting out a furious scream, she pulled back her foot and kicked him in the stomach.

Dacre doubled over, gasping for air.

"Eight months," Ruby shouted. "Eight months!" She pulled back her foot and kicked him again, jabbing him in the back, right in the kidneys. For a little girl, she sure kicked hard. "You beat us and starved us for eight months, you mother*fucker!*" Her shiny patent leather shoes sank into his groin.

This wasn't right. I held up my hand to stop her. "Ruby."

She paused, panting heavily.

"Honey..." I said softly, shaking my head. "No." I paused. A painful, tense silence rolled through the room. "It won't help," I told her. "I promise you, Ruby. If you kick him like that, it will only hurt you."

She glared at me, her chest rising and falling furiously, her nostrils flaring. Betrayal shone in her eyes.

Huh. What's her deal?

Her expression confused me, until I played back my own words in my head and chuckled.

"Oh. No, I don't mean that metaphorically," I said. "I

meant it literally. Your shoes aren't protective enough to kick him like that. You'll only do damage to your toes. You might even break them, and broken toes are a bitch to heal because you can't put them in splints."

I grabbed a hefty brass candlestick off the mantle and handed it to her. "Here. Use this."

CHAPTER

TWO

I took the goldfish with me. For some reason, I couldn't let the poor thing stay in that house. Dacre and Jessica hadn't had any other foster children, so I knew it wasn't really a little kid. But for all I knew, Jessica Sagwood was as sadistic as her husband. I had no intention of leaving an innocent creature in this house.

While the kids were packing their bags, I called Levi to let him know what I'd found. As Romeo's deputy, Levi was responsible for all witch-related crime in Philadelphia.

The poor guy cursed when I told him what had happened. "Fucking Sagwood. The whole lot of them are like villains in a Dickens novel."

"I already took care of everything, Levi," I said. "I called it in, the Enforcer went to talk to Jessica at her office, and he sent his deputies to pick up Dacre. They just left."

Otherworld Enforcement didn't mess around—they rolled the bleeding, moaning witch into a spelled bag, zipped it up, and threw it in the back of a wagon. "They're taking him straight to the Otherworld court now. You can head down and decide what to do with him or just leave him to rot in a cell." The penalty for most major crimes was death, but I wasn't sure where Dacre would fall on the scale of major and minor crimes.

I could have killed him myself. I probably should have, but it wasn't my vengeance to take. After leaving him bloodied and unconscious, Ruby declared she wanted him to live so he could suffer for a bit longer, and she bounced off to pack her bags.

Levi sighed wearily. "Thanks." He paused for a second. "Are you doing okay?"

My jaw clenched involuntarily. "No."

"Look, you know how sorry we are, Daphne. I know you want to come with us. It's just... Faerie is a dangerous place."

"I know." There was no point telling him, *again*, that I knew the place intimately, because I'd been stuck there for years. I was used to being underestimated.

Levi was silent for a second. "Of course you do. It's just... me and the guys... we're a team and we work really well together."

He's saying that we'd just mess everything up. My brain snorted. *Bunch of morons.*

"We're going to get him back, I promise you that. We've got it all figured out. I've almost finished the World Key, and we just have to charge it. Micah is compiling the intel we need on the geography of the Inbetween so we can find our way around, and Brandon is sorting out munitions—"

"That's cool, Levi," I interrupted. Charging a World Key took immense amounts of magic, the geography of the Inbetween was incomprehensible and totally unmappable, and mortal guns didn't work in Faerie. In fact, I'd seen a goblin sell a Kalashnikov as a tomato stake. Romeo's coven had absolutely no idea what they were doing, and they were too arrogant to listen to me. Romeo was the only one who knew what I was capable of.

Panic clawed my chest for a second. I put my hand on my heart and forced myself to take a breath. My fingers found my quartz crystal necklace, and I clutched it compulsively.

Romeo was still alive, and I'd find him.

But what if he doesn't want to come back? What if he's on his vengeance mission, and he's hell-bent on killing all the Shadow Fae? What if he's getting married off to a sexy fae wom—

I clenched my teeth so hard, I heard one of my teeth crack. Oh my god, brain, shut the hell up!

"You just stay here and relax," Levi blathered on. "We've got it covered. I wish I didn't have this mundane Coven shit to deal with at the same time."

I made a non-committal noise. I was glad his workload was slowing him down. If he actually got his World Key finished and charged, it was more likely he'd end up in a lower-dimensional underworld than Faerie.

Levi huffed out a bitter laugh. "Sorry, I'm just feeling sorry for myself. We put the weight of the world on Rome's shoulders, and now that he's gone, it's too much for us to handle. There's no one else like him in the Otherworld. We need him."

"I know," I said.

It had only been two weeks, and the covens of Philly were already getting restless. Romeo was such a formidable figure in witch society, and the threat of his punishment was usually enough to keep the covens in line. I could only imagine what they'd do if they found out he was gone.

"We'll get him back, Daphne."

I gnawed on my lip for a second. "Yeah, you will. Hey, when you finish your World Key, bring it over so the countess can look at it, would you?"

"Oh, I don't think that's necessary—"

"Please? You don't want to end up in Helheim by mistake, believe me."

"I know what I'm doing," he said stubbornly. "I've read a bunch of grimoires."

Pigheaded moron. "Come on, you're refusing to take me with you; this is the least you can do to make up for it. I'll worry about you otherwise, Levi. Just let her look at it. Please?" I didn't want to hurt Levi's feelings, but the countess would relish it.

"Fine," he sighed.

"Great." Ruby and Samuel walked back into the room. "I gotta go, Levi. Stay safe." I hung up.

CHAPTER

THREE

Ruby's bag was so heavy she had to drag it along the ground behind her, and it clunked suspiciously, like she had the family silverware stuffed in there.

I nodded approvingly. "Good idea." Rummaging around in the drawers in the sitting room, I found a jeweled letter opener, a diamond tennis bracelet, a stack of fifties, and a handful of change, and I shoved all of them into Samuel's bag.

We hustled downstairs and got into a cab. I would have to swing back and pick up my bike later.

Samuel burst into tears when we got to Bellevue. It was almost as if he wasn't going to relax until he saw proof Dacre had been lying to him, and his nightmare was over. Sarah and Jackie both walked down the steps of the old building when we pulled up in the cab. Samuel flew out as soon as we stopped and buried himself in Jackie's arms.

Brain-Daphne watched them, uncharacteristically pensive. *I wish someone had saved us like that.*

"Someone did," I said out loud. "Don't you remember what Chloe did for me?"

I mean in Faerie. And in the dark elf world, and in the Swamplands, or in the Norse world, or Hellenic realm... When we were enslaved a bunch of times.

"That's why we do this. Chloe saved us first, and we had to learn how to save ourselves. Now, we save other kids."

WE HAVE TO SAVE EVERYONE!

The voice screamed from within me, and it hit me like a truck. For a moment, my vision went blank, and I shuddered violently. "What was that?"

No idea. Brain-Daphne was just as surprised as I was. *It obviously wasn't me. I know I've been absolutely out of my gourd lately... Oh, man, don't tell me we're fracturing our personality again*, she whined. *There's too much going on in here as is.*

"No," I mumbled, frowning at the ground. "It didn't feel like part of me, it felt like... a memory hitting me. Something from a former life, maybe."

Brain-Daphne giggled maniacally. *Oh, yay. More childhood trauma resurfacing!*

We'll deal with it, I reassured her. We always do.

I got back in the cab, carefully positioning the goldfish bowl on my lap, and put my earbud in so I could keep talking to myself without looking crazy. "I think this case is messing with some old trauma. I suppose it was bound to happen." I exhaled heavily. "When the countess and Prue come through, we'll head to Faerie—"

If the countess and Prue come through.

"*When* they come through," I emphasized through gritted teeth. "We're going to be heading somewhere that holds some pretty bloody memories for us. I guess I'm just preparing myself for the slaughter."

Slaughter? My brain nudged me. *That sounded dark. You okay, babes?*

I'm fine.

26

Ha. No, you're not. But I like this new version of you.

"It's not new. It's the same old me." I sighed. "Still Heart-Daphne. But now the man who takes up the biggest space in my heart has disappeared, so I guess I'm a little bloodthirsty."

That's usually my wheelhouse.

"You don't have exclusivity to bloodthirstiness, you know. Especially when my heart is being threatened."

Fair enough. But if you're going to be bloodthirsty, you need to dispense with the guilt trip afterwards. Be the sweet little psychopath you've always been.

"I can handle myself. I can find Romeo, face my old demons, and keep a firm grip on my mental health."

She paused for a beat. *Sureee you can.*

I exhaled wearily. "I had to learn to trust you during the whole Bella debacle. Now you have to learn to trust me. My friends will help me; I know it."

She was quiet for a long moment. *What if they don't? What if Dwayne has just waddled off to shag his girlfriend in some other far-flung city? What if Prue was lying, and she's actually returned to D.C. to that hunky husband of hers, and she's happy that Romeo has disappeared? What if the countess is just stringing us along, and she has no intention of helping us travel to Faerie with a World Key?*

"They're my friends." I ground my teeth. "I trust them. And you have to learn to trust me."

I wish my voice hadn't shaken when I said it.

CHAPTER
FOUR

J udy screwed up her nose when I walked in holding the goldfish bowl. "No snacks in the office, Daphne."

I smiled at her. Judy was a miserable bitch hell-bent on making my work life unbearable, but I couldn't help feeling sorry for her. "It's not a snack, Judy. Even if it was, you are literally double-fisting two pots of yoghurt right now."

"Yoghurt isn't a snack," she hissed. "It's a way of life! And if that thing's not a snack, then it's a pet, and they're prohibited in the office."

"It's not *my* pet." I set the bowl down carefully on my desk. I had no idea what I was going to do with it. My heart told me to bring it with me.

Judy harrumphed and abandoned her game of Minecraft completely so she could focus on me. James, my lovely hardworking colleague, wasn't in the office. A quick glance into my boss's glass cage told me she was in, but hard at work, pacing back and forth behind her desk jerkily like a malfunctioning robot and talking nonstop into her headset.

Judy curled her lip, looking at the goldfish with obvious

scorn. "If it's another emotional support animal, you couldn't have chosen a worse one. Fish are stupid."

I decided to change the subject to distract her. "I picked up that report that came in for Dacre and Jessica Sagwood's foster kids."

Judy frowned. "That? Why would you even bother? It was just a silly human busybody with too much time on her hands. Like you," she added pointedly. "There was no reason to go rushing around there. There's plenty of paperwork here to keep you occupied. I could have told you that it was a waste of time."

I took off my heavy motorcycle jacket and placed it on my chair, sighing with relief at getting rid of the weight. Everything felt so heavy these days. "Turns out, it wasn't a waste of time. Dacre Sagwood is now cooling his heels in the Otherworld lockup."

Judy mouthed, looking exactly like the goldfish on my desk. "Why?"

"Because he was using those kids as sweatshop labor. He'd deliberately chosen them and put them to work making spells. Your covenmates were slavers, Judy."

Judy went pale. "No. You must be lying. You're just trying to justify your paranoia—"

I unclipped my body cam from my shirt and waved it at her. "You can check if you like. He attacked me when I exposed him."

"But..." Judy shook her head slowly. "Jessica Sagwood hasn't.... Her father... he's..."

"The Sagwood High Priest? I know." I peered at her. "And Jessica Sagwood hasn't *what?*"

Judy seemed uncharacteristically nervous. "She's... she's not around."

I smell gossip. Poke her. "What does that mean?"

"She... she..."

I fixed her with a hard glare. "Spit it out, Judy."

Judy paused for another minute and licked her lips. "She hasn't been seen at rituals in a long time. Nobody has seen Jessica in months."

"She's missing? Why didn't anyone report it?"

Judy gathered herself, pulling on the air of superiority she usually wore. "It's coven business," she snapped.

"So, you just covered it up?" I shook my head, confused. "I don't get it, Judy. She's your third cousin, right?"

"Look, Daphne, you're an outsider. You don't understand how things work in a coven."

I exhaled heavily. "I don't think I *want* to understand it. It sounds like a terrible coven to belong to if you give up on your members when they disappear!"

"It's not like that."

"What is it like then?"

"Jessica was a bit of a magical dud," Judy spat out through clenched teeth. "Her father was embarrassed by her. He was forced to be content with the fact that she did well in the human world—"

"Did *well?*" I gaped at her. "Jessica is a partner in a big accounting firm. She's an enormously successful woman!"

"That doesn't mean anything to the Sagwood coven or to her dad. He married her off to a handsome witch from a Chicago coven—"

"Who turned out to be *evil*," I said through clenched teeth. "Enslaving children for *forced labor*."

"But—"

"You work in *child protection*, Judy!"

For the first time since I met her, Judy looked shaken. Her face went pale. "We can compensate the kids. Nobody needs to know. We can smooth everything over—"

I slammed my hand down on the desk. "You're *not*

covering this up, Judy. I honestly can't believe you're saying these things!"

She stared at me, inhaling heavily through her nose. "It's coven business."

"It's not anymore! Not since Dacre Sagwood fostered two covenless children and turned them into his slaves!"

My heart had started to thump out of control. I had to stop, clutch at the crystal around my neck, and take a deep breath to calm down.

It was family business. Coven business. Cover it up, don't say anything, they're not a bad person, they've been kind to me, I've never had that experience before, they're a pillar of society...

"Dacre's not really a Sagwood," Judy said sulkily. "Jessica's dad thought the match was a good idea at first, since she didn't seem interested in any other witches. He pushed her into it, but since then, he's decided Dacre is a bit of a cad. He's an outsider."

That wild stab in the dark hit the bullseye, huh?

I glared at Judy. "He's a Sagwood. He married into your coven. You welcomed him with open arms. He hasn't been expelled, even though it appears his wife has gone missing, and nobody has asked where she is."

"Well, Dacre said she had some emotional issues and went to 'find herself.' But she's been gone for a long time."

"How long?"

She hesitated. "Seven months."

"And nobody said anything?"

"He's very charming." Judy squirmed under my harsh stare.

I let the silence hang in the air for a second. "Nobody knows where she is?"

"No."

"So, your coven sister went missing, and nobody has

seen her for seven months. Nobody cared enough to ask any questions, because she didn't have much magic, and her father was a bit embarrassed by her, anyway. And her husband is *so* handsome and *so* charming. He took two little kids from a happy foster home to use as *slaves*, Judy!"

I had to turn away; I couldn't look at her anymore. My heart hurt. My breath came in shallow pants, but I couldn't stop it, I couldn't make myself calm down. This world was filled with pain and suffering, with despair, and I felt like I was flailing around in the pitch black, trying to save everyone. I was so tired. It hurt. It hurt so much. The darkness was everywhere. It was inside me.

I had to save him. I had to save Romeo. I knew it in my soul, and not just him, but everyone. The whole world was in danger... no, not just the world, but *worlds*, all the worlds, if I don't do something now—

I HAVE TO SAVE THEM ALL!

My heart stopped. Everything went black.

The scream echoed in my head, almost splitting it in two. I doubled over, panting.

My brain kicked me. *Bitch, snap out of it! Push it down. Whatever the fuck is coming up, we need to push it down. We're not breathing. We need to breathe! Bury it. Now!*

No. I couldn't. I needed to face it. It was time. My lizard survival brain was screaming at me to push it all down so I could survive the tsunami of darkness rearing up inside of me...

No. Not now, not anymore. It was time to face what I was.

What the fuck are you talking about? Brain-Daphne screamed at me. *Face what?*

In my mind, I screamed back, I don't know!

"Daphne?"

Monica's voice pulled me out of the darkness. I lurched

back to reality almost violently. My brain took advantage, and Spartan-kicked the rest of the writhing darkness into the void inside me, squashing it back down.

I took a shallow breath. "Yes?"

"Are you alright, hon?" Monica was wildly aware I was absolutely messed up in the head, but since I was doing the work of a team of twelve O-CPS officers right now, she was willing to ignore the fact I was teetering on the edge of total insanity.

"I'm fine." I stood up and took a deep breath in. "I'm okay. Sorry, Monica, I think I—"

She beamed at me. "Great, great, that's a good girl, now that you're here I just wanted to let you know I got your report about the Sagwood kids, nasty business, that, I'm glad you hauled that rascal Dacre in," Monica rattled in her machine-gun way. "You seem to have burned through every single outstanding case we have in this office, so whatever exercise routine you're doing or skincare regime or your diet or whatever, keep doing it, Daphne, because you're on fire, haha." She paused for a second to flash a grin at me. "Take a couple of days off, dear, in fact, take the rest of the week, recharge yourself. Oh, and by the way, there's someone from the DMV out in the human office asking to speak to you."

Monica was giving me emotional whiplash. It took a second for her words to sink in. "Someone from the DMV?" I frowned.

Uh oh. This doesn't sound good.

No, it didn't. It didn't sound good at all.

CHAPTER
FIVE

I held on to the crystal around my neck as I made my
way out to the human CPS office. Fear made Brain-
Daphne short-circuit. *That little breakdown was obviously due to fear about the big guy—*

It wasn't. It was something else.

Let's go now, my brain hissed. *We can jump on a plane
to Castlemaine and leap through a portal and find our way
there.*

We have to wait, I told her, gritting my teeth. We have
to have faith. My friends will come through for me. We'll
find him.

As soon as I saw who was waiting for me, I huffed out a
relieved breath. A short, curvy Black woman with tight
iron-gray curls, a gray polo shirt, and a DMV badge waited
by the human reception desk. She wore dark glasses that
covered most of her face and stood still, staring at nothing
in particular.

She wouldn't be able to see me coming. Not with her
eyes, anyway. She smelled like warm milk, nutmeg, and
cinnamon sugar, which was weird.

Wait, no. She was drinking a pumpkin spice latte.

Where the hell did she get that from? It was spring; they stopped serving those months ago.

Underneath the woody-sweet smell of the latte, I caught a hint of her real scent—ozone, dew, rock, and water. The smell of the cosmos. Sometimes when I was busy in meetings and he was bored, Dwayne liked to waddle downstairs and head across the street into the DMV to flirt with this woman.

I hadn't known she was an Oracle before he told me.

I should have realized she was something. Dwayne always had a thing for overpowered women. Not that she was physically powerful, of course, in most respects, she was practically a mortal.

But this pretty older lady was unfathomably powerful. She could see the future.

Oracles appeared in every culture, in every religion, in every single realm, in every universe. They came in many different packages, and, for lack of a better understanding, they were often given the vague title of Mouthpiece of the Gods. Dwayne had joked that if Asherah got jealous of him flirting with another woman, at least the Oracle would see her coming.

She smiled as I approached. I veered left a little until I was in her line of sight—not for her benefit, but for mine, and immediately felt guilty for being ableist. "Hello," I said politely. "I'm—"

"Hello, Daphne," she said, smiling. "It's nice to finally meet you. Dwayne says such lovely things about you."

This was a nice change from having his girlfriends trying to attack me every ten seconds. "That's nice."

"I'm Louisa," she said, holding out her hand.

I shook it. "Dwayne has told me lovely things about you, too."

Her grin widened. "He's a rascal, isn't he? I must admit I

enjoy him very much, Daphne. It's nice to interact with someone who can surprise me."

I chuckled awkwardly. "I suppose his nature makes him unpredictable, huh."

"Sure does. He's fun." She toasted me with her take-away cup and took a leisurely sip. "Mind you, any other time in history, I'd be gently suggesting he pop through a portal and find somewhere else to play for a while. He creates a big blind spot in my vision." She let out a little sigh. "I can't tell if it's meant to be there or not."

I frowned. "I don't understand."

"Neither do I." She grinned and took another sip of her pumpkin spice latte. "Do you understand how my kin and I work?"

"Not really, "I admitted. "I know you can see the future."

"Possible futures," she corrected. "We see the stones tossed in the pond of the universe and watch the rings ripple out in every direction. We see where the waves are most likely to hit. The tapestry that the fates weave... we see the wool while it's spun and dyed, so if a thread is colored red, we can predict what bloody scene it will be used for."

"Right." I nodded.

"But we don't just tell the future. We're the keepers of this universe, Daphne. When all the waves start to head in the same direction, the balance is tipped. And if nothing is done to correct it, it can lead to total annihilation."

I nodded politely, not sure what to say. "That sounds like a big responsibility," I managed.

The Oracle shrugged. "It's not that bad. Normally, it just takes a little nudge here and there to get things back on track—to make sure the waves flow back and forward at a steady pace, and nothing gets drowned when the scales tip. If that darling God of Chaos hadn't been messing with my vision, I would have seen your Warlock getting taken by his kinfolk a little too early, and I would have done something to ensure they didn't get a chance to ambush him."

I frowned. "What do you mean, 'too early'?"

"He wasn't ready." She shrugged. "And you weren't with him. Unfortunately, because of Dwayne, I didn't see the pattern in the fabric being woven until it was too late."

Gahhh. Too. Many. Obscure. References...

"I should have canceled Romeo's driver's license," Louisa said. "Without ID, he wouldn't have been able to get past security in the human court, and he wouldn't have been ambushed on the way to Otherworld court."

My brain growled. *Dwayne. Goddamnit.*

"Oh, no." Louisa shook her head. "Don't blame him. He muddied the waters, yes, but I have a feeling that the water is supposed to be muddy right now."

I nodded politely. "Okay."

"Forget Dwayne." She let out a huff of exasperation, clearly seeing I wasn't getting it. "The least destructive ripple would have been the future where you were with the Warlock when he was taken. He needs you desperately, Daphne."

She paused, and took a sip of her latte. "When a world has been unbalanced, it must be corrected, or the results can be catastrophic. I'll give you an example. There is too much order in this realm right now. Authoritarianism is on the rise, because the Beast of Bakkanon went on a tyrannical rampage through Faerie when he woke up, and that energy has vibrated through to our world. But the Beast is dead, the fae he enslaved have been freed, and this realm has Dwayne, a small god of chaos, carefully redressing the balance."

"I don't—"

"Get it, I know." She sighed. "It's so hard to explain. But

it's all about balance. You are the sunshine to Romeo's storm. You should have been taken together. Without you, the storm is going to rage out of control. And, on the other side of that coin, you need him. He's the only one who knows exactly what you are, and he's going to help you understand it."

Something dark wriggled within me. "What am I?"

"You're not supposed to understand yet."

That's good, because I don't understand a goddamn thing this woman is telling me right now.

She grinned. "You're an optimistic girl, Daphne, and it's a lovely trait, but you'd be surprised at how often optimism leads to hubris. And the gods kill mortals for their hubris."

That dark tendril within me wriggled again. *What the fuck is that?* "I— I—"

Louisa huffed out a breath. "Look, Daphne. I'm here to do the job I should have done two weeks ago. I'm nudging the ripples back on the right path. All you need to know is that the balance in Faerie has been upset, and a path has been created that will lead in ever-decreasing circles straight downhill to total annihilation." She took another leisurely sip of her latte and smacked her lips appreciatively. "Mmm. I know it's cringe, but I love these things. If all existence ends, then I'm going to miss pumpkin spice lattes."

I took a quivering breath in. "Louisa, this is all a little obscure and worrisome..."

"I don't mean to scare you, Daphne. Things are probably going to be okay in the end. The water is so muddy, I can't really tell. With all that said, I do know for sure that you have to go to Faerie, and you have to go there *now*, or else it could mean the end of our whole universe very soon."

"*What?*" My heart skipped a beat. "But how? And—"

38

I cut myself off abruptly as Judy thumped past me. The Oracle's revelations were so earth-shattering, I almost forgot I was at work. It was a good thing we were chatting in a corner away from the reception desk. If any of these humans were close enough to listen to us, we'd be getting some serious side-eyes by now. Judy stomped over to the waiting room and jerked her thumb imperiously at a young girl.

Witches. Judging by their coloring—white, with blonde hair and tiny noses—they were probably Sagwood witches, just like Judy. I stifled my sigh. I was getting suffocated in Sagwood today.

The young girl wore jeans and a pretty cashmere sweater and looked incredibly sulky. Her designer suit-wearing mother seemed terribly embarrassed to be in a CPS office. She kept fingering her pearls compulsively.

I waited until they'd walked past me, and I turned back to the Oracle. "Sorry, Louisa. Can you elaborate on that last point a little? What's going on in Faerie, and how is it going to destroy the world?"

"Romeo is going to destroy the world."

"*Romeo* is?" I exhaled heavily. He wouldn't. Romeo wouldn't do anything to risk the fate of any world. "How?"

She wrinkled her nose. "It's complicated. There are many moving parts, and I don't know how any of them connect. I can only see the forces pushing down the end of the scale and the inevitable outcome if it continues. Right now, there are too many players pushing on one particular tipping point." Louisa's tone became layered, multi-tonal, and grew in resonance. "But I will tell you right now, if you don't go soon, and things play out as I see them currently, then Faerie will be destroyed, and then nothing will stop the mortal realm falling to the same fate."

Ooh, this didn't sound good.

Louisa held up her fingers. "Two things I know for sure. There are two push points, Daphne. Romeo is one. You are the other. Romeo has to open his heart." She leaned close and lowered her dark glasses. Two luminous white eyes stared right into me. "And you have to trust yours."

Is she talking to me?

"Yes, lizard brain," the Oracle said. "I'm talking to you."

Wow. That's mean. I've been doing a great job.

My gut churned. I already had enough to worry about. "Can we get back to the whole world annihilation thing? What can I do to stop it?"

"Exactly what I said. Go to Faerie." She shrugged. "Just be you. Forget your brain, follow your heart."

Fuck off, my brain whispered. *I'm important.*

I licked my lips nervously. "I don't understand..."

"You don't need to understand. Not yet, and not ever. You don't even have to realize what you are. You just have to be... you. Trust yourself."

Louisa's watch beeped. It sounded so ominous, I froze, waiting for a monster to crash through the walls.

The Oracle sighed, tossed her empty latte cup basketball-style into the trash can in the corner—a three-point shot—and tapped her cane on the ground. "Okay, I've gotta bounce. My break is over. I have to get back to work. Good luck, Daphne. Just be yourself, okay? Go save the world. Don't fuck it up."

CHAPTER

SIX

I couldn't concentrate on anything after that. The Oracle had spooked me and confused me like crazy, but one thing I heard loud and clear.

Trust your heart, my brain grumbled. *Not particularly helpful, is it?*

"It is helpful," I mumbled under my breath, too stressed to keep my response internal. "And it's what I've been trying to do. I just keep second-guessing myself, and it's tearing me apart. You're not helping me with that, you know."

We've never been in love like this before! Brain-Daphne gnashed her teeth. *I know I'm losing my noodle, babes, I just can't help it. I need to save him, and I need to save everyone.*

"I need to save them all," I echoed gloomily. What the hell was that voice inside me? And why was it now starting to scream?

I rubbed my chest absently as I walked back through the busy human Department of Human Services. "I'm just so damn confused. Nobody wants me to go to Faerie. Nobody will help me get there, and they're all telling me to wait. And now, an Oracle is telling me I need to go *now*."

41

Loud voices were coming from inside the Otherworld CPS office. I hurried back inside, my curiosity piqued.

The young girl and her mother were shut in the meeting room with Judy, and they were all yelling at the top of their lungs.

"I'm telling you right now, that thing out there isn't real!" the girl shrieked.

"Constance, stop it right now," her mother said, her tone imperious. "You're embarrassing me."

"I'm embarrassing *you*?" The girl's voice went up through three octaves. "You dragged me in here!"

"I had no choice," her mother replied. "Ever since you manifested, you've been uncontrollable."

"Uncontrollable? Just because I'm pointing out every single strange thing I see? Because I don't turn a blind eye to all the injustice in the world?"

"Constance, you need to calm down." Judy's tone was cold. "Your mother is right. You have to respect your elders."

"Why?

I heard both Judy and the girl's mother gasp.

"You've given me no reason to respect you," the girl said. "You've given me a million reasons to *not* respect you. Don't come near me, or I'll scream." A chair scraped back. "I know there's cameras in here. I'm sure your boss would love to review the footage and see what happened for herself."

Brain-Daphne was short-circuiting. *Stab Judy, stab the mom, save the girl. Save Judy? Take the girl home, put her in the pantry, feed her pizza.*

A tense silence gripped the room for a moment, then the girl spoke again, "Something has changed in our coven, and it's not just the Great Suffocation. We've gone from caring about everyone, to caring about witches first, to only

42

caring about ourselves. You're so focused on keeping up appearances to the outside, you haven't noticed that the inside is *rotting*."

"Constance, sit down," Judy commanded. Her voice shook.

"No." The chair scraped again, and footsteps stomped. "I'm not delusional. I'm not a doormat. I'm not going to sit here and let you insist that everything is okay. I'm going to show you." The meeting room door banged open, and the pretty young girl marched out, pulling a handful of sparkling black dust out of one pocket.

Oh, shit, is she coming this way?

Constance's eyes sparked. "I'm going to show you what that thing really is!"

What thing? What thing?! Is she talking about us?

My pulse thudded. I needed to make a decision. My brain shrieked. *Tackle her! Punch her in the face! She's going to do something terrible!*

The young witch stomped across the office. She was heading straight for me.

Stop her!

I was paralyzed. Just like I'd been for the last two weeks. Paralyzed by indecision. My brain forced my fingers to twitch around my blades. My heart told me to stay still and let it happen.

The mom rushed out of the meeting room with Judy hot on her heels, their expressions horrified.

Constance threw a handful of dust in the air, barked out a string of power, and wove her hands around each other. She pushed a huge punch of blackberry-flavored magic towards me and screamed. "Reveal!"

Bitch, stop her! We have to stab her!

I threw myself on the ground and rolled underneath my desk.

There was a crash of breaking glass, followed by a rush of water that ran all over my desk. Someone panted frantically, trying to catch their breath.

A naked leg hung off my desk. Who the hell was that?

Constance turned around, her eyes blazing with triumph. "See?"

Silence gripped the room for a long moment. Her mother fainted, crumpling on the floor with a thud.

Judy's mouth fell open. She stammered uncontrollably. "Jessica?"

CHAPTER

SEVEN

L ater, I caught a cab back to Dacre and Jessica's house so I could pick up my motorcycle. I broke every single traffic law on the way home, then circled back around the greater Philadelphia area and did it all again, fantasizing that Romeo, wherever he was, might sense that I was endangering my life and would pop back to stop me.

I could almost hear him in my head. I knew what he would say. Daphne, he'd say, his voice vibrating with barely contained rage, you ride like you want to die. Do you want to die?

Right now, I kind of did. The turmoil within me was tearing me apart. It felt unbearable.

The Oracle said I had to trust myself... but how? How could I trust my own judgment when my brain and my heart were at war? How could I even think straight when there were so many uncertainties, so many variables? My heart desperately needed Romeo back. My brain was worried he didn't want to come back. My brain wanted me to throw myself through a portal and go find Romeo now. But my heart told me I had to wait and trust that my friends would come through and help me. My brain craved violence and destruction; my heart felt a strange sense of shame at the idea of killing *anyone*. The uncertainty and indecision felt visceral, like sandpaper on my skin.

Eventually, it got dark as the late afternoon morphed into evening. Once the police helicopters trained their spotlights on me, I gave up trying to make myself feel better and made my way back to the Hidden City.

The weather seemed to mirror my indecision; it couldn't decide if spring was here or not. This morning had started bright and cheerful, but now it was dusk, and a harsh wind had sprung up from the north, plunging us back into winter's icy grip. Freezing air whipped through the parking lot in the Devil's Pocket.

I wheeled my bike through the brick wall entrance, shivering, my head down, only to run into more of the same icy blast on the other side. The weather in the Hidden City mirrored the outside world, so the City was dark and cold. The wind howled through the trees, whipping the branches into a frenzy. Nobody else was around—no creatures scuffling through the woods on either side of the path, no residents walking home. The lack of people felt ominous. Apocalyptic.

I hurried towards the East Tower, keeping my helmet on to drown out the howl of the wind. Even through my leathers, I was freezing. Desperate to get indoors, I got back on my bike and started the motor. Normally, I hated riding through the city—it was dangerous since there was a good chance a kid could pop out on the path in front of me—but there was nobody around, and I was filled with the urge to move fast while I knew where I wanted to go.

Indecision. It was killing me.

On my left, between the East Tower and the West, a building crew had started on my passion project—The

Hidden City Kids Drop-In Center. One of the project managers had asked me something about the layout a week ago, and I'd frozen, unsure what to do. I wanted to ask Romeo what he thought, but he was gone, and the builders had gone onto other projects while they waited for me to make a decision. The ache in my chest threatened to punch a hole right through me.

We were getting better, my brain whined. *We were starting to trust ourselves again. We were getting more confident. No hesitation, no regrets, and we trusted ourselves. And now the big guy disappears, and we're back to square one. No, it's worse. We never used to be this bad.*

I knew that.

Brain-Daphne shivered miserably. *Do you remember how we used to be? Before we split in two?*

I did remember. Indecision was never a problem then. She showed me a multitude of scenes from all the realms I'd lived in.

We were a total badass. We could be that again.

I don't know how, though.

What the hell happened to us?

I thought about it. Romeo disappearing was a big factor, but it had happened before that. Was it Troy? I'd been so wrong about him. Lennox Arran, too. Now, I didn't trust my own judgement anymore.

If I didn't trust my own judgement, how could I save them all?

Okay. Who the fuck are you talking about? Who is this "all" that you have to save?

"I don't know," I said out loud, my voice muffled in my helmet. "I'm missing something. I just don't feel like I can trust myself because I'm missing something really important."

What, though?

I rode my motorcycle directly into my storage garage and, shivering uncontrollably, climbed the steps to the first floor. One of the light bulbs had blown in the atrium, and it was very dark, the shadows deep and sinister.

The wind screamed outside. A sudden rattle made me jump out of my skin.

I looked, finding the source of the noise, but my heart didn't stop pounding. A window had been left open at the back of the building, ostensibly to let the grouches in so they could clean overnight while they were active. The window was vibrating in the wind.

I stared up at it. Would the grouches even come in on such a dark and stormy night? I dithered for a moment, wondering what to do. The indecision had crept into every part of my life.

In the end, I left the window open and listened to it rattle in the wind as I walked towards the elevator. Each creak and clatter made me flinch more and more, until, unable to bear it any longer, I ran back and closed it.

The ride up to my apartment was slow and miserable. The cold seemed to have sunk into my bones. I reached the forty-fourth floor and couldn't even bring myself to be happy that there were no dead bodies on my doorstep or knives stuck in my peephole.

The last few months had been rough. No wonder I was such a mess.

Wearily, I knocked on my door and called out to Myf. "It's me. I'm home."

She didn't reply.

Guilt swamped me. Myf had been quiet lately. I figured since she wasn't drinking anymore, she was just in introspection mode. I wasn't sure what to do, so I left her alone. "I couldn't decide what to bring home for dinner, Myf, but we can order pizza," I called out again.

There was no answer. I cracked the door open and walked in.

My apartment felt cold. Empty. A strange desolation washed over me. Dwayne hadn't been here for days, and his comforting endless-void scent was rapidly dissipating.

There was a note on the table. Sharp spiky letters filled the page. There were holes in the paper where she'd pressed too hard, and the pencil had ripped right through.

YOU SAID *you'd help me. I believed you. But you don't give a shit about me. You left me here all alone, all by myself, while you ran off with your boyfriend, and now you barely even talk to me. You knew I was hurting, but I was always the last person you cared about. Considering everything—what I am, how long I've been with you, how dangerous the beast inside me is—I should have been the first person you took care of.*

Well, you know what? I found someone who cares about me. Someone who cherishes me, and he's going to take care of me from now on. Because I've finally faced the truth. You never gave a crap about me, Daphne.

I CRUMBLED the note in my hand and burst into tears.

Myf was right. I'd dithered over what to do with her for too long. I didn't know how to help her, so I let her fester in my pantry, drinking herself into a stupor every day, and all I could do was keep telling her she was safe, she'd be okay, we'd get her help.

But she was right. I'd done nothing to help her. I'd promised her, but I'd done nothing beyond scheduling her some therapy sessions with Cindy, my colleague. Myf was overwhelmed with trauma after a lifetime of being pulled between two ancient warring factions—the Welsh

Guardians, who worshiped dragon shifters as gods, and the People of the Claw, who wanted to enslave her, brainwash her, and use her as a weapon and sell her to the highest bidder.

I figured the only person that might have any understanding of what she'd gone through was Cindy, who'd been enslaved once upon a time because her poop was a powerful aphrodisiac. Like Myf, Cindy used drugs and alcohol to numb the pain of the trauma she'd been through. The most I could do to help Myf was arrange some therapy, which Cindy hadn't gotten to yet because she had a backlog of addicts to work through first. Nobody else could really get to the root of her problems, because nobody could relate to what she'd gone through.

That's not really true, my brain said tentatively.

I took a shallow breath. A sick feeling writhed in my gut as we both unpacked and examined that thought.

My brain laid it all out. *We've been sold to the highest bidder a few times. We've been used as a weapon. We've been threatened with awful things, like forced breeding and forced marriage. We know what it was like to be reduced to an object—a hole, a womb.*

Oh, no...

We've even been worshipped in one or two realms.

I never thought about that before, but it was true. I'd been considered a goddess in a couple of different worlds I'd fallen into—mostly tiny realms where I was a giant. I knew how uncomfortable it was. How much it messed with your psyche. The expectation, the confusion, the pressure. The feelings of intense unworthiness.

The realization hit me like a brick to the head; the shame was sickening.

I could have done something to help her. I could relate

to Myf perfectly. I just didn't, because I never used drugs or alcohol to numb the pain.

No. We just buried it all.

Fuck. I had. That's exactly what I'd done. I'd shoved it all down and pretended it didn't exist. At least Myf screamed and cried and sobbed about her pain. I just ignored it.

There was even that memory Romeo had removed that had caused me enormous pain. With a smile, I told him we'd worry about it as soon as the mnemosyne ran out of juice.

I'd buried it all down. And because I had, I'd forgotten who I was.

Myf was right. I could have helped her. Now it was too late. I'd failed. She was gone. My knees gave out, and I crumpled to the ground and curled up into a little ball and sobbed as if my heart would break.

I should have saved her.

For a long time, I felt nothing but deep sorrow. Guilt, remorse, sickening, churning. I'd failed Myf, because I was too worried about my own stupid problems.

I was crying so loudly, I didn't hear a thing. Not until the door smashed in.

CHAPTER

EIGHT

My front door splintered, cracking in two, and half of it smacked open. Creaking on broken hinges, it dropped to the floor with a loud clatter.

I barely flinched. I knew who it was, anyway. Dwayne honk-chuckled a little sheepishly. **Oops. Put a little too much sting in that one.**

I buried my face in my hands. The tears wouldn't stop. The pain wasn't easing up, and I wouldn't let it. I deserved to feel like this.

I'd forgotten who I was. And now everyone was paying the price.

Well, this is deja vu, or what? Dwayne sauntered into the kitchen. **Last time I caught you sobbing on the kitchen floor, it was because of that asshole Jupiter boy. I know you're not crying because of him, because you took care of that one, right? You took the long way around, but you got him eventually.**

He was trying to make me feel better. It wasn't working.

I suppose you're sad because of the big guy getting abducted by the fae, huh? He stomped over and climbed into my lap awkwardly, crushing me with his weight. He nuzzled me with his beak. **Don't worry, baby girl. We'll get him back. Or we'll get you another boyfriend. Maybe a couple of them, so we've got some spares. You do seem to have a penchant for stabbing your boyfriends.**

"It's not that." My nose dripped, and I wiped it with the back of my hand. "I mean, yeah, it's because he's missing. But it's Myf. She's gone."

Dwayne snorted. **Is she? Good ridd—** Seeing my face, he cut himself off. **I mean, that's very sad. So *very* sad. Why did that miserable flying cow leave?**

I sniffed and wiped my cheeks. The tears just weren't going to stop. "She was a vulnerable young girl, Dwayne." I hiccupped. "She left because I wasn't helping her."

You were. You gave her a safe space to stay, and you made sure she was fed, and you tried to keep her sober. You put up with all her whining. You arranged therapy for her. What else were you supposed to do?

"I– I could have empathized with her—"

Bollocks. Dwayne let out a hiss. **That girl doesn't need empathy; she needs a kick in the pants. She's only focused on herself.**

"I know what she's going through, though. I went through almost exactly the same trauma she did. I understand exactly how she feels, so I—"

Oh, yeah? Dwayne cut me off. **So, what were you doing at her age?**

The edges of my vision suddenly blackened. That scream echoed through my mind again. *I have to save them all!*

It only took a second, but it felt like hours. Then, the heavy weight on my lap moved, smacking me in the crotch with a clawed foot. I flinched and returned to the present.

Well, little one? Dwayne's face reared out of the darkness. **What were you doing when you were Myf's age? Were you crying in a cupboard, downing stolen whiskey, and moaning about how sad you were?**

I blinked and tried to focus. "I... I don't know. I don't know where I was at seventeen, actually." My memories were so jumbled, it was hard to put them in order. "Anyway, it's not the same. We had different experiences—"

You had it a lot worse. Dwayne's voice was blunt in my head. **A *lot* worse. You didn't choose to go through all that pain and suffering, but every single choice you've made since then has made you the goddess you are now.**

I took in a small, surprised gasp of air. Dwayne had never said anything so nice before. Calling me a goddess was overkill, though. Some of the constriction in my chest eased.

Myf is making her choices now, and you're not responsible for them. You've done everything you were capable of doing to help her. She'll become what she wants to become.

I took another deep breath, feeling a little better. Dwayne wasn't often the voice of reason. In fact, he was never the voice of reason.

And, he added, **I'd be less worried about her leaving, and more worried about who she's with now.**

"Oh, no." I grimaced, resting my head on Dwayne's silky neck. "She's gone to the shifter compound, hasn't she?"

He shrugged. **Probably. She has wanted to ever since she met him. You know that.**

I'd warned Myf all about Lennox. I told her everything about him, but she'd gone anyway. Goddamnit. I struggled with Dwayne's weight for a second, trying to get him off me so I could get up. "I have to—"

54

He shoved me back down. **Not today, baby girl. You need to let that flying, spicy-breathed cow make her own mistakes.** He grinned at me, showing all the spikes on his tongue. **Anyway, are you ready to go?**

"Where?"

To Faerie. Duh.

I hesitated for a second, confused, and frowned at him. "You can't go."

Why not? He tilted his head. **I thought you wanted to go rescue your boyfriend.**

"I do. And according to Louisa, I have to go rescue him. But—"

Oh, you spoke to Louisa? She's a sweetheart, isn't she? Fabulous boobs.

"You can't come with me, Dwayne," I said. "Asherah will kill you. More importantly, Asherah will kill *me*."

I don't give a fuck about her. Dwayne's eyes narrowed, and he let out a furious hiss. The switch in mood almost gave me whiplash. **Don't mention that ignorant hussy to me ever again.**

"Uh..." I mouthed for a second. "Why?"

We're over. Done.

"You broke up?"

I broke up with her. He curled his lip, glaring furiously into the distance.

"Because she tried to kill me and Romeo?" I prompted.

Dwayne frowned, glancing at me. **Uh, no. That was just a misunderstanding, and she wouldn't have actually killed you anyway. She was just being dramatic.**

I waited a second, but he didn't elaborate. "So why..."

I don't usually make serious misjudgments when it comes to the women in my life, little one—

A snort left my nose before I could stop it. At his glare, I sandwiched my lips together.

55

Dwayne arched an eyebrow at me, but after a moment, he continued, **Asherah is *not* the woman I thought she was.** He bristled. **Our values are not aligned. We don't agree on the fundamentals of existence. I can't be with a woman who doesn't understand me, little one.**

I hesitated, trying to put it all together. "Okay. Did she, uh, try something outside your boundaries?"

I didn't think Dwayne had any boundaries.

He let out a honk-grunt. He really was angry. **It's not that.**

"What is it, then?"

Asherah's been really weird lately. I knew she'd like Scorpion-Prue, I mean, that's why I ordered Prue to go in and flirt with her in the first place, to distract her and calm her down. But ever since that battle by the lake, Asherah's been dropping little hints, making little comments that made me think she was trying to—his eyes narrowed—**change me.** A little snarl built in the back of his throat, a dangerous, cute little rumble.

I wasn't sure where this was going. "Change you? How so?"

Dwayne whipped his head around to face me, his pitch-black eyes glowing with rage. The snarl erupted. **Asherah had the *nerve* to suggest that a giant scorpion with laser beams for eyes is the ultimate form for a god of chaos.**

I gasped. "No."

Yes. He let out a little hiss and spread his wings, the barbs on his tongue glinted malevolently in the light. **She actually said that. It proves she doesn't get me. She's not the woman I thought she was. She's just a silly girl who doesn't understand anything.**

"Oh." Suddenly, I understood perfectly. Asherah wasn't just wrong, she'd insulted him by even suggesting it. "She hurt your feelings."

You're damn right she hurt my feelings. A scorpion with laser beams for eyes isn't chaos; it's destruction. I wouldn't fit into that form at all. I'm much bigger than that, and this form is the only one on this plane of existence that suits me. The fact that Asherah can't see that is insulting to both of us.

I exhaled wearily. It made sense to me. Dwayne was much bigger than mere destruction.

So *obviously* I'm coming to Faerie with you.

The tight feeling in my chest eased a little. I wouldn't have to go alone. I put my arms around him, burying my face in his silky white feathers. "I'd love for you to come with me, Dwayne, I need all the help I can get. Louisa told me that if I don't find Romeo soon, the whole world could—"

Dwayne cut me off with a slash of his wing. **Oh, I'm not coming to help you rescue your boyfriend.**

"You're... not?"

No. He turned and glared dramatically into the distance. **I'm going to the Winter Court to fuck Asherah's mom.**

CHAPTER
NINE

I opened my mouth and closed it again. Then, I swallowed. "Okay."

Dwayne turned, saw my face, and chuckled awkwardly. **I mean, you don't really need my help. But I'll come and keep you company while you go gallivanting around the old fairy mound to find the big guy.** He clenched his wing into a fist. **I swear by all that is unholy that while we're there, I'm going to find the Winter Queen, I'm going to seduce her, and I'm going to shag her into the next dimension.**

I paused for a second and blinked. "Oh-kayyy."

Not that your thing isn't important. He shrugged. **It can be a double mission.**

"Sure."

So... He waved his wing impatiently. **Let's go.**

Suddenly, I felt so tired. "I wish it was that easy."

It is. Let's go.

"I'm waiting for the countess," I said. "And for Prue. I need a World Key to get to Faerie, and the countess promised she'd make me one. And Prue said she needed to find out something about the Court of Inbetween first. She said it was very important—"

Go ask her now. She's back.

I flinched. "Prue's back?"

Yeah. Got back a couple of hours ago, actually. While you've been boo-hoo-hoo-ing on the floor, her and the countess have both been next door drinking margaritas.

You've gotta be fucking kidding me. I scrambled to my feet, my heart thumping in my chest. "What? They're both here?"

Yeah, of course. Dwayne stomped over to the broken front door, ripped it off his hinges with a short tug of his beak, and waddled out. I followed him into the hallway and watched him kick the countess's door open. He padded inside.

"The door has a handle, sir," Ebadorathea Greenwood's voice held a touch of disapproval. "While I do love your little visits, you should know that I have to replace that lock every time you kick my door in."

I followed Dwayne inside. The countess had magically enhanced her apartment, making it look like a medieval castle by extending the walls, decorating it with ancient stone and tapestries, and raising the ceiling until it was vaulted with exposed beams. Priceless antique furniture was scattered around—an ancient chaise-lounge that used to belong to Marie Antoinette, an ottoman that looked suspiciously like it was made of human skin, and a delicate writing desk with Dutch swear words carved into it were a few highlights.

"There you are, Daphne, dear." The countess stood in her enormous kitchen, emptying a bottle of tequila into a blender. "You took your time." She tossed the empty bottle behind her. It vanished into thin air.

Prue—as gorgeous as always in skintight jeans, a cherry-red crop top, with her hair pulled up into a messy bun—stood next to her, cutting up limes. She grinned and waved her knife at me. "I was wondering when you'd get off work."

"Prue." I rushed towards her. "Finally. I've been freaking out."

"I know you have." She gave me a firm hug. "And I'm sorry. Look, I get it, I can't talk. I'm the first person to throw caution to the wind and rush off to save the world without the proper preparation." Pulling back, she gave me a fond smile. "But I'm glad you listened to me."

I gave her a weak smile. "Because I trust you."

"A lot of people would say you're a fool for trusting the Daughter of the Beast," she said, her tone a little bitter. "Then again, I suppose you regularly put your faith in a god of chaos, so you're used to listening to your heart. Well, you did the right thing, because hoo boy, have I got some information for you!"

"You do?"

"Yeah, I do. This will change the whole trajectory of your little rescue mission," Prue said, cutting another lime.

Okay, my brain sighed. *I'll give you this one. You keep telling me that I need to listen to you more, and I guess you're right. Wonder Twins, activate, I guess.*

The countess dusted off her hands. "I'm out of orange liquor. I'll be back in a second."

I held out my hands as if to grab her before she disappeared. "Countess—" She bustled off. I watched her go and blew out an exasperated breath. "She told me to wait, too. What the hell am I waiting for?"

Don't worry about them. I'm all you need. I only need a couple of minutes to get my things, Dwayne said. **Then we'll be good to go.** He waddled off out the door.

"Well, you're not waiting for me anymore," Prue said, squeezing the lime into the blender. "I got what I needed." She gave me an apologetic glance. "The first thing I need to tell you is that I can't come to Faerie with you."

I nodded. "I hadn't expected you to be able to. You've only just returned from Delaware. I imagine that Max wouldn't like the idea of you running off on another dangerous rescue mission so soon."

"It's not just that. Even if he was okay with me going with you"—she grimaced—"we'd need to infiltrate the Inbetween, and unfortunately, I'd be a liability."

"Oh."

"I asked around with my fae contacts, checking on the collective mood in Faerie, just to see how they felt about me." She glared at the chopping board. "It appears that the whole 'daughter of the Beast' thing is still an issue."

"I understand." For me, this all happened a long time ago, when I was a little kid, but for Prue, it was only a couple of years. I remembered all the stories, though.

Prue's biological father was the Beast of Bakkanon, the one Louisa the Oracle had mentioned earlier—a high fae warlord born with a unique power. He underwent some serious family trauma that festered, eventually turning him into a genocidal maniac, who tried to devour the magic of every creature in every surrounding realm, including the mortal realm.

Prue's mom managed to subdue him for almost fifty years. When he awoke, Salozar Winterbourne—the local DC Fae Diplomat and the Beast's former right-hand man—made the ultimate sacrifice to subdue the Beast so he could be killed.

Salozar had been desperately in love with Prue. He'd died in Prue's arms, and she hadn't quite got over it. I'd always found that part of the story heartbreaking.

Everyone in Faerie knew the part Prue had played in getting rid of the Beast. The current antipathy was more to do with the fact she'd behaved like a tyrant during the Great Suffocation. She'd been so desperate to save the magical creatures from being choked to death, she often forcefully deported fae expats and halflings, throwing them into portals whenever she was able to.

As a consequence, it undid almost all of the goodwill she'd amassed by killing the Beast of Bakkanon.

Prue sawed another lime in half with unnecessary violence. "I know you don't like to talk about it much, but you spent a lot of time in Faerie, didn't you?"

"Yeah, a lot." Years and years, in fact. At the time, I had no idea where I was, and there was a good chance I'd bounced back and forth from Faerie to other realms all the way through to my late teenage years. It was only later, as an adult, after I read all of Aunt Marche's books and talked to all the halflings and expats in Castlemaine, that I pieced some of it together.

Prue gave me a hard stare. "So you know what you're getting yourself into."

I gave her a firm nod. "I do."

"And you know how to get around? You understand how to navigate Faerie?"

I let out a humorless bark of laughter. "Of course not."

"Good." Prue smiled. "You get it."

Faerie wasn't just one place, it was many places, and it was almost impossible to comprehend in a geographic sense. In fact, Faerie existed outside the realm of understanding in a lot of ways.

There were things you could comprehend, such as the two main courts, which we called Winter and Summer. They were more than that, though, they were rest and alertness, life and death, rebirth and decay, day and night. The royals of these courts were so astonishingly powerful it was probably more accurate to refer to them as gods.

And, like most gods, they were capricious, uncaring, and revoltingly selfish.

For example, Maeve and Titiana weren't remotely interested in what the Beast of Bakkanon had been doing at the height of his reign of terror, and neither had done anything to stop him. The Beast hadn't been from any royal court, instead, he was a warlord from a region that bordered the court of Dusk and Autumn, closer to the Wastes, where he eventually built his castle.

The Inbetween was a lot more like us, the mortal realm. The magic was less strong because it was diluted with its opposite.

Faerie didn't cycle through the seasons like our world did. Instead, each region embodied an aspect of either the seasons or the cycle of day and night. Winter on one side, Summer on the other. Everything else was The Inbetween.

As well as the Wastes and the Wilds, there were four small royal courts in the Inbetween. All of them had an affinity depending on how close they were to Summer or Winter. In my head, I translated the Inbetween courts to Dusk and Dawn, Autumn and Spring. The reality was far more complicated, but I liked to think of it in simple terms. The Shadow Fae—Romeo's kin—came from the court of Dusk.

"I'm sorry I can't be there." Prue ran a slice of lime around the rim of a glass and dipped it in salt. "I was hoping they'd understand about the Suffocation, but it looks like I'm still persona non grata," she muttered.

"You did what you thought was right," I said, watching out of the corner of my eye as Dwayne waddled back in with what looked like a military duffle bag in his beak. The bag clunked suspiciously. He tossed it into the middle of the countess's living room and stomped off again.

"Yeah. Nobody likes their choices taken away from them." Prue exhaled heavily. "I'm okay with being the bad guy. But it means I can't come with you to Faerie on your little rescue mission."

The countess returned with a fancy glass bottle filled with orange liquid. "I cannot come with you either, dear. I wish I could."

Ha. Liar.

The countess wrinkled her nose delicately as she splashed some of the orange liquor into the blender. "Honestly"—she gave an elegant shrug—"I am left with little choice but to stay here. I have a waxing appointment tomorrow. I'll get charged a cancellation fee if I try to reschedule it now."

I bit my tongue. The countess was being flippant on purpose. She was no Oracle, but she was a competent Seer, and I knew she'd thrown bones to determine Romeo's fate and mine. There was a reason she was staying away.

"That's okay," I said to her. "You're doing enough by making the World Key."

The countess paused in the middle of dripping some syrup into the blender and frowned. "I'm sorry?"

I peered at her. "You have been making a World Key for me, haven't you?"

"A what?" Her expression cleared, and she let out a little chuckle. "Oh, I made that a few days ago." She turned away, rummaged around in a coffee canister, and took out a little silver amulet.

"Countess!" I gaped at her. "I thought you needed time to finish it!"

"Oh, no, dear." She laughed. "World Keys don't take long. The hardest part is imbuing them with enough power.

You'll be happy to know I sacrificed one of my favorite soul ties to do that." Holding out her arm, she hitched up the sleeve of her scarlet gown, showing me a heavily tattooed arm, and flipped it over. A big patch near her wrist was bare. "You're welcome," she said pointedly.

"Thank you," I said automatically. "But..." I shook my head, unable to contain my frustration. "You told me I had to wait! You said you needed more time."

"No, Daphne. *You* needed more time," she said, her tone haughty. "I don't. I am exquisitely efficient."

Dwayne stomped back into the room, this time hauling a camouflage-printed tent bag. He tossed it on the pile and marched back out the door.

I refocused. "Time for what?"

She arched her eyebrow at me. "Time for *you* to pull yourself together." She tossed a handful of ice cubes on top of the mixture and hit a button, and my response was lost in the roar of the blender.

I took a deep breath, trying to calm my nerves. *So, we waited for two whole weeks, leaving Romeo potentially in danger, while Prue tried to figure out if she could come with me or not?*

Trust, I told her. We have to have faith and trust.

While I waited for the countess to stop blending, Dwayne hauled four more bags into the living room, grumbling under his breath the whole time. Prue caught my eye and mouthed at me as Dwayne stomped back out. "What is he doing?"

I gave her a nervous smile. "He's coming with me."

"Is *that* why he's hauling supplies into the middle of the room?" Prue rolled her eyes and groaned dramatically. "He's coming to Faerie with you on what will most likely be a very delicate diplomatic rescue mission? Why don't you

65

just go ahead and throw a live grenade into a fireworks factory, Daphne?"

I ran my eyes over the piles of camo-printed bags—clearly stolen from some military facility somewhere—and sighed. "I suspect there are a few grenades in that bag, yes."

Prue cut another lime, hesitated, and pointed her knife at me. "You know the vibrations of Faerie are going to mess with him. I don't know if you remember this, but when Chloe went missing and got stuck in Faerie, Dwayne was the scourge of the fae underworld for two whole weeks."

"I remember," I said. "But he didn't do it on purpose. He got lost. They thought he was a dragon."

"Because he grew to the size of a bus and kept eating soldiers."

"The underworld made him peckish," I said pathetically. "He's coming with me, Prue. I don't think I have any choice in the matter. He's, uh, got an important mission of his own."

"I don't think I want to know." Prue sighed.

"Yeah, you don't. Now, *please* can you tell me what super-important information you found that's going to rock Romeo's world?"

She dumped her knife, grabbed her purse from the counter, rummaged around inside of it, and held up a small, leatherbound book. "You need to give this to Romeo. He has to read it. I've marked the important pages." She flicked the bright multi-colored tabs that jutted out of the notebook.

I stared at the battered old leather. It smelled ancient. "What is it?"

"A journal." She gave me a look. "You can read it if you want to, but it's very personal. It's about Romeo, and it might upset him."

I took it from her, keeping the journal closed. I didn't really need the warning. Considering I knew he was part-fae before he did and made the deliberate decision not to tell him, I owed it to Romeo to let him read it first. "I'll make sure he gets it."

"And give him this." She passed me a small, blue marble. It tingled in my fingers. "The journal is written in High Fae. In case he doesn't understand what he's reading, I've trapped some of my words into a charm to give him a little explanation of everything. Like a recording."

I knew how to read the High Fae script. For some reason, I didn't remind Prue of that. "Okay."

"He'll know how to unlock the charm." Prue made a face. "He might need to listen to a friendly voice after reading that journal," she said, sounding uncharacteristically uncertain.

I squinted at her. "Is it... is it bad?"

"No. Maybe," she admitted. "Sometimes the truth is painful, especially when your whole worldview gets upended. I'm not sure how he's going to react."

I opened my mouth to let out a weary sigh. Just then, the smell of stone baked bread, basil, and melted cheese hit my nose, and my mouth instantly watered. The countess bustled in holding a massive cutting board with a giant authentic Italian pizza on top. "It's almost time!"

"While I agree with you that it's always a good time for pizza," I said, "where did you get that from? That smells... authentic."

"I installed a woodfired oven out back," she said.

"Out the back of *what?*" We were on the forty-fourth floor, and there were no balconies. The windows didn't even open more than a few inches.

"Never you mind." She shimmied further into the room. I expected her to place it on the counter in the kitchen, but instead, she walked into the living room and slid the cutting board onto an antique side table. She pointed at it. "There you go, dear."

I shook my head. "But—"

"Now, eat." She gave me a commanding stare. "You'll need sustenance."

Suspicion pricked me. I gave a cautious whiff, but all I could smell was fragrant tomato sauce, mozzarella cheese, fresh herbs, and delicious carbs. It smelled amazing.

Dwayne marched back into the room. Even his glare softened when he spotted the pizza. **Save me a slice, baby girl.** He tossed another bag onto a pile by the door and waddled out again.

The countess walked back to the kitchen, picked up the blender, and tipped some margarita into a glass. I looked at her, then at the pizza.

It smelled so good. And I was starving.

I darted over to the living room and picked up a slice, marveling at the crisp base, the delicate scent of the fragrant fresh basil, and the stretchy pull of the mozzarella. I bit into it and chewed, my eyes rolling back in my head with pleasure.

It was heavenly. The base was the ideal texture, crunchy, chewy, satisfying. The cheese was smooth, and it stretched deliciously.

It was only after I swallowed my first bite that I registered the zing of a ward activating.

I sighed, took another bite, chewed, and glared at the countess. "You trapped me in a warded circle, didn't you?"

Prue took a swig of her margarita. "Told you that would work. Carbs really are her only Achilles heel."

I swallowed my mouthful. "You lured me into a trap with pizza. Like I'm in a goddamn Looney Tunes cartoon."

The countess gave me a smug smile and toasted me with her cocktail glass. "Yes, dear, I did."

There was no point being mad with them just yet. Not while the pizza was still hot. I finished one slice in silence, using my toe to peel back the antique rug under my feet. The countess had drawn the circle on the flagstones underneath in chalk. I eyed the runes she'd used with interest. "You don't want me to go." It was the only logical explanation. "You're trying to keep me safe."

"Oh, no, dear." The countess chuckled like it was the most absurd thing in the world. "On the contrary, you have to go. Not just yet, though."

I furrowed my brow while I demolished another slice. As soon as I was less confused and upset, I'd ask her for the recipe and demand access to her pizza oven. "What's the point, then? I can get out of here easily, you know." I took another bite. "It's just a hard ward. I only have to concentrate a little, and I'll be able to buzz right through it."

She smiled. "It's just for protection."

Despite the pizza, I huffed, suddenly exasperated. As much as I told myself I was used to it, I hated being underestimated. I especially hated being underestimated by people I thought were my friends. "Protection?"

"Yes, dear."

We don't do ourselves any favors, my brain said hesitantly, as if she were suddenly realizing something. *It's not like we've demanded respect lately. We don't even ask for it anymore. I mean, you haven't killed Judy yet. You haven't even threatened her, and she totally deserves it. You didn't even make a fuss when Romeo's coven refused to entertain the idea of taking us with them.* She hesitated. *Remember how we used to be?*

Barely. My memory had holes in it. And the person I'd become was falling into those holes and drowning. Romeo had thrown me a lifeline, because he saw me. He saw what I was capable of.

He was the only one who did. And now he was gone.

We used to command respect. No, we used to demand it. We forgot who we were.

Frustration made me shout at Brain-Daphne out loud. "I don't need an epiphany right now!" I jabbed a finger at the countess and Prue, standing in the kitchen. "And I *don't* need protection!"

The countess's eyebrows rose. "It's not for your protection, dear. It's for ours."

I frowned. "For yours?"

"Don't worry." She took a leisurely sip of her margarita. "It's just a precaution."

My heart started pounding. An awful sick feeling churned in my stomach. "A precaution against what?"

A strange noise pierced the silence. Something started beeping very loudly. "There it goes..." Prue murmured. "Right on time."

I frowned. "What—"

All at once, the memory hit me, and darkness swallowed me whole.

CHAPTER

TEN

I *have to save them all...*

Death and despair, hunger and pain. Poverty, hatred, war. They rampaged through the realm and devoured everything in their path, eating away at the people and turning them into diseased wretches, into *them*, into the evils. They grew and spread like a cancer, mutating everything pure and good into the worst things that this universe could imagine.

Something soft brushed my cheeks. **Daphne?**

The darkness receded a little. A crack of light crept in. With it came understanding.

The light was hope, and I wasn't there anymore. I wasn't stuck inside the jar Zeus had created, rubbing up against the impure manifestations of everything foul and unholy in this plane of existence. I wasn't watching from up high, a giant, watching the devastation Zeus planned, all unfolding before me.

I was home, in the mortal realm, lying on the floor on the countess's antique rug with a slice of margherita pizza still in my hand.

My fingers clutched the slice as if it were a lifeline.

"Daphne? Daphne, can you hear me?"

I could hear everything. There was a whole world inside me, packed with every single evil thing you could imagine. It was stuck in the box of my soul, and it had always been there. Screams echoed in my head, memories of the tortured, agonized cries of the innocent as the evils descended on them.

I'd picked up the whole world, and I'd devoured it before the evils could spread.

They were still here.

A tentacle wriggled within me. Despair. Pain.

Shove it down.

...No.

You have to! Shove it down now!

I felt my heart thud.

No, I told my own brain. Not this time. Not ever again. I can't do that anymore.

As soon as I had that thought, a strange feeling of conviction gripped me. It felt so foreign, and it gave me so much relief, I felt my heart expand. It wiped out that doubt, that lingering indecision within me.

Brain-Daphne screamed at me. *Are you sure? Are we sure we can handle this?*

I'm sure, I said to her. I can't forget what I am. And I won't forget ever again.

Are you sure sure? Like, positive?

Oh my gods, yes, I'm sure.

...Okay, I trust you. Bitch, you better be right!

I felt her sink back into me, into my psyche. The inky-black tentacle wiggled again, waving at me. I visualized myself standing on the edge of the ocean of darkness, watching the evils try to reach for me. Raising my chin, I held out an arm, extended my finger, and flipped it off. *I'm not stuck in there with you anymore. You're stuck inside me. And you're not getting out.*

I know what I am. And I'm never going to forget it ever again.

That silky feeling brushed over my cheek again. It tickled a little. I twitched.

A woman whispered. "Daphne?" It was Prue.

I cracked my eyes open. Dwayne's face came into focus first. He loomed over me, staring me right in the eye. He looked furious. Prue crouched behind him holding a bag of frozen peas against one cheek.

I blinked and caught a glimpse of the countess all the way back in the kitchen, dumping the rest of the margarita into her cocktail glass.

"The mnemosyne," I croaked. "That was what you were waiting for, wasn't it?"

"Yes, dear," the countess sang, dropping a candied lime slice into her glass. "Your darling Warlock was overly optimistic as to how long that pomegranate could hold such a vile memory. Even with an arcane tool sealing it in, it was never going to last any longer than a few weeks."

I remembered everything now. I remembered the reason why Romeo had taken the memory. Christopher Jupiter had seen the evils inside me, and he wanted them. The memory was causing me so much pain, I couldn't function properly.

Thank the gods he was dead.

The mnemosyne wasn't a permanent solution, because memories can't be permanently removed. The weight of them could be held in a surrogate living thing for a brief period. "Two weeks ago, Romeo told me it had about a month left."

"And time moves differently in Faerie." The countess scowled at me from the kitchen. "Did you really want to risk it expiring while you were gallivanting around what might be dangerous territory? The shock of it might have sent you over the edge." Her face softened. "Here, you have a safe space, and you have time to process everything. You have time to pull yourself together."

Brain-Daphne stirred. *The countess makes a good point,* she said grudgingly. *I'm not sure if we could have handled both the epiphany and the memory hitting us without that pizza.* She showed me an image of her getting a tattoo of a slice of pizza surrounded by a holy corona. *It saved us.*

"Besides," the countess continued. "It has been beeping like a smoke alarm with a low battery for days now. Goddess knows that if I had to listen to that wretched ear-splitting *peep* noise for any longer, I might lose my mind." She cracked open a new bottle of tequila and tipped it into the blender. "And you, my dear, are crazy enough for the both of us."

"I'm not going to argue with that." *We're going to get better, though. Now that we remember who we are.* My eyes flicked back to Prue. "What happened to you?"

Prue lifted the bag of peas, showing me her face. The skin on her cheekbone was split—a nasty gash ran underneath her eye, and the skin around it was already swollen and bruised. "Dwayne punched me in the face," she explained.

I gasped. "Dwayne!"

And I'd do it again, Dwayne said, strutting over to the pizza next to me. Someone had obviously placed it close by while I was unconscious, like a delicious emotional support foodstuff.

Dwayne pecked at a slice. **It's not my fault I got a little startled and threw hands. Wings.** He shrugged. **Whatever. My point is, nobody told me anything. I come in**

here, and you're convulsing on the floor. He scowled. **You're lucky I'd already packed my Glock.**

My gaze swung back to Prue. I'd never seen her injured before. I wasn't sure she could even *get* injured. Her body wasn't really real; it was just a manifestation.

"Can't you, uh, manifest an unbroken cheekbone and unblacken your eye?" I asked her.

"I could, but I feel like I deserve it." Prue sighed wearily. "Look Daphne… in my defense, none of us knew what to do. When you came home to Castlemaine, and it became obvious that something apocalyptic had happened to you—you have the ravaged remains of a destroyed world and every evil that exists trapped inside you, for God's sake. What were we supposed to do? I mean, *obviously* therapy didn't work out. But I remember telling you it was probably best if you tried to forget the worst parts. Shove it all down. And you did." She looked ashamed. "I thought it was a good idea. Chloe forgot who she was, and she was really damn happy for ten years."

"Until she wasn't." I met her just after she regained her memories. I lived with her for a while, and I got to hear her screaming in her sleep.

"Well, yeah. It's a Band-Aid solution." Prue turned and glared at the countess.

The countess stared back at her. "Why are you looking at me like that?"

"Because you used to regularly pull that memory out of Daphne's head while she was asleep and shove it in semi-ripe fruit, your grace," Prue said, her tone reproachful.

"Did I? That doesn't sound like me." She turned on the blender, rocking it vigorously.

Prue sighed again. "My point is, obviously it wasn't a good way to deal with such a horrifically traumatic event. Especially because that event *literally* lives within you."

75

"You don't have to worry," I muttered. "They can't get out. They're stuck. The only person who can open the box is Pandora, and Pandora doesn't exist anymore."

Prue gave me a patronizing look. "That's not the way time works, Daph—"

"I know it's not linear. Prue, I've lived in countless dimensions where time meant nothing, and a few where nothing else existed *but* time."

"Sorry." She hesitated and waved her hand. "I know you hate it when people underestimate you. I don't know why we keep doing it."

They keep doing it because we let them. In my mind, Brain-Daphne put the finishing touches on her Holy Pizza tattoo. *Not anymore.*

I took a deep breath and it felt good. "I'm sure in some plane of existence Pandora is still real. But she's not in this one, not after I came along. She was destroyed along with her home when the evils escaped the first time. I'm the box now, and I can't be opened. Nobody can do it."

The countess pursed her lips. "Didn't that stupid Jupiter boy try?"

"Christopher Jupiter had the dumb idea to try to summon Zeus so he could make another Pandora. But Zeus wasn't even the one who made Pandora in the first place," I explained. "Hephaestus was the one who made her. And it doesn't matter anymore, because Christopher Jupiter is dead, the Hellenic realm is too far away, and the only Star Door we know of has been destroyed. These evil bastards are stuck inside me for as long as I live."

In my mind's eye, Brain-Daphne stood at the edge of the sea of darkness, flipping off the inky-black tentacles.

Prue took the frozen peas off her cheek. "And then what? What happens when you, uh, aren't living anymore?"

"When I die, they'll cease to exist. The evils won't survive transmogrification." I said it with such certainty, such clarity, because I knew it for a fact. *Hoo boy, this newfound sense of conviction feels nice.* "Zeus created them, but he didn't create them as concepts. They're personifications of evils that already existed; they were just supposed to swamp our mortal realm with their essence and destroy it. Personality doesn't exist beyond the physical realm. When my spirit is severed from my body, my soul will carry them into the aether, and they'll cease to exist."

The darkness within me bristled angrily. Ha. I was right.

Prue nodded thoughtfully. "That's good news." She peered down at me with her good eye. "You sure you've got a handle on it?"

"I'm sure." I stood up and stretched. "And honestly, Prue... I've never felt better. I feel whole again." For the first time in... I didn't know how long. I felt whole.

We *feel whole.*

I grimaced. Way to ruin the mood, brain.

The countess clapped her hands. "That's enough lying around, dear. You better get moving, because from what I saw in the smoke and in the pattern of the bones, you don't have much time."

CHAPTER

ELEVEN

I t wouldn't be the best idea to race into Faerie wearing my Professional Business Shirt under my motorcycle leathers, so I took a moment to run back to my apartment and get changed. I chose sturdy, lightweight fabrics in dark colors, a mix of combat gear from one of our latest skirmishes—cargo pants, an undervest with armored plate inserts, a moisture-wicking dark gray shirt, thick socks, and my toughest, most comfortable pair of boots.

It was best to travel light when moving through Faerie, so I only packed one small backpack with a spare shirt, pants, a flask, granola bars, matches, a small hacksaw, one change of underwear and two more pairs of thick socks.

The socks were important. When you were wet, cold, hungry, bruised, scared, and sad, there was nothing that put you in a good mood better than a soft, dry, cozy pair of socks. It was the little things that mattered.

I jogged back to the countess's apartment to find Dwayne's pile of bags had turned into a mountain in the middle of her living room.

I nudged one of the bags with my foot. "You know none of the explosives will work in Faerie, Dwayne."

He glowered at the bags. **Oh, yeah. I forgot about that. Napalm?**

I shook my head firmly. "No."

No? Smallpox blankets, then? Anthrax-filled greeting cards? He kicked one of the bags; it clunked. **Cauldron of boiling oil, perhaps?**

I stared at him. "No."

He sighed. **I guess we can just take the trebuchet. It's in the garage downstairs.**

"We're *not* taking a trebuchet, Dwayne."

Fine. But we're taking the beer. He tapped his wingtip on a giant crate.

"We're not taking the beer."

Fae beer makes me gassy—

I glared at him. "I'm not carrying it. I'm carrying *you*, remember?" None of us had any idea how to make a World Key for a small god, so I'd have to hold him in my arms while we travelled.

Fine, he huffed. **But if I get bloated and float away in the breeze, don't say I didn't warn you.**

Prue pulled me into her arms and gave me a tight hug. "Don't do anything I wouldn't do."

"I won't." It was an inside joke. There really wasn't anything Prue wouldn't do.

"Best of luck, dear," the countess said. She tiptoed over and patted me awkwardly on the head then tossed the silver amulet at me. "You know the drill."

The countess, at least, had never underestimated me. A grin stretched my lips. "I do."

I'd done this before. Hold the intention of your destination in your mind, slap the shiny side of the World Key on your chest, and say the magic word. "Do you have any other gifts for me?" I asked her. "A glowing sword? A magic cloak? Long lasting Elvish bread?"

She huffed, offended. "For goodness sake. I made you a pizza, child. Take the rest of that with you."

Dwayne had eaten the rest of it. I thought for a moment. "Actually... Do you have a cloak? It doesn't have to be magic. It might be a while before I can steal one, and I look like Combat Barbie right now. I'm going to stick out like a sore thumb."

"Urgh." She rolled her eyes, stalked out of the room, and came back immediately holding a dark green woolen cloak in her hands. "I want this back. It's Gucci."

"Thanks." As I hoped, it covered my whole outfit. I wrapped it around myself and took a deep breath. "I think I'm ready."

Good. Dwayne let out a low honk-growl. **Let's go fuck a Faerie Queen.**

I raised my eyebrows and gave him a look.

He chuckled awkwardly. **I mean, let's go find your boyfriend.**

CHAPTER
TWELVE

Travelling by World Key was infinitely more comfortable than tumbling through natural inter-dimensional rips—the tiny tears in the fabric of our reality. I squeezed Dwayne to my chest and kept my eyes closed as I hurtled through time and space. Fireworks exploded behind my eyelids. The pressure on my skin was so intense, I almost blacked out.

After a split second of pure agony, the pressure vanished.

The first thing I noticed was how hard the ground underneath me was. Hard and spiky, like I was lying on a bed of nails. I blinked my eyes open.

"This can't be right." At first, I thought I might have gotten my intention wrong. The sky above me was too bright for this side of the Inbetween. I should have landed in the Kingdom of Dusk.

I rolled over so I wasn't looking directly at the sky anymore. No, it wasn't *exactly* too bright, it was just too yellow. It should have been more orange-red toned. Had I come to Dawn by mistake?

My newfound conviction glowed like a flame in my

chest. No, I had come to the right place. If I was good at anything, it was holding an intention.

I sat up, still clutching Dwayne to my chest. He'd buried his head underneath his wing for the journey. He yawned. **Are we there yet?**

"We're here." In a newly harvested wheatfield, in fact. The spiky things underneath me were hard, dry stalks of grass.

I stood up. Bare, rolling hills stretched as far as the eye could see. Behind me, the shape of a town shimmered in the distance. Everything seemed so... dusty.

Awkwardly, knowing he might be unsettled by the increased levels of magical energy in the atmosphere here, I held Dwayne close, giving him a comforting hug. "Are you okay?"

I'm fine.

I eyed him carefully. He seemed okay. Dwayne was the same size and shape, at least, which was a small mercy. "You're sure?"

Well, I could use a drink, he said pointedly. **If only I had some beer.**

"Well," I said slowly. "If I got the location right, there should be a tavern on the edge of that town over there."

Fabulous. He hopped down out of my arms. **Let's go.**

I shouldered my bag, and we started walking. The ground under my feet was harder than it was when I was here last, and the air tasted drier than I remembered. We hiked up and down hills, making our way to the little town farther to the east.

As we got closer, I could see some of the more distinctive buildings and make out their unique architectural shapes—swooping arches, towering spires, and vaulted ceilings. The buildings weren't exactly large; they were thin, tall and spiky—anything to cast as long of a shadow as possible.

Dwayne gestured with his wing. **Is that Dusk?**

"Not exactly." I waved my arm in a circle around my head. "All of this is the Kingdom of Dusk." I pointed at the town. "That is a regional town on the outskirts of the City of Dusk.

He frowned, glaring into the distance. **So, where's the City? We should hurry and find the big guy now. I've got a Faerie Queen to seduce.**

"It's hard to explain, because geography in Faerie works on vibes rather than a strict directional sense, Dwayne, but to simplify things"—I inhaled the air, tasting the atoms on my tongue—"the City of Dusk is over there." I pointed to my left. "It doesn't feel exactly the same as it did when I was here last. But then again, I don't actually know when I was here last. It could be decades ago."

And which way is the Winter Court? Dwayne's voice in my head was deliberately casual.

I gave him a brilliant smile. I was just happy he wasn't turning into a giant and dive-bombing the townsfolk. The chances of Dwayne ever getting to the Winter Court were almost nil, and the chances of him banging Queen Maeve were even less than that. I admired his determination, though. "It's not in any particular direction," I told him. "To get there, you've got to follow the chill in the air and give in to the weariness in your bones."

Chilly air, big boner. He nodded. **Got it.**

We walked for what felt like hours. The sun—still too yellow in the sky for my liking—was setting behind us as we made our way into the outskirts of the town. We hopped over a rickety fence, crossed another two dry fields, and vaulted over a stone wall, finally finding the main road leading into the town.

"In the common tongue," I said, waving, "This town is called Gloom."

Huh. Looks pretty cheerful, if you ask me.

"That's the thing." I paused and frowned. "It shouldn't be. All the towering spires and vaulted arches are meant to create long shadows. This town is in Dusk, remember? They're supposed to *love* shadows. It doesn't look very shadowy anymore." I narrowed my eyes, peering ahead. "Maybe it's because it looks like the town has been painted recently."

That might be it.

I pointed up ahead. Like most feudal towns, the whole thing was ringed with a high stone wall with heavy iron-studded doors that could be slammed shut and barricaded in case of an attack. The doors I could see were wide open. That wasn't unusual. What was unusual was the color of the stone archway around it. "That archway used to be natural dark stone. Now it looks like someone has taken a can of whitewash to it."

Huh. Well, it's really messing with the aesthetics.

Now that I was sure where we were, my hand compulsively reached for my crystal necklace, still buried between my boobs. I brought it out and placed the crystal on my palm.

The point twitched and swung left. I exhaled a relieved breath. "He's here. And he's in the City of Dusk, like I thought." I kept walking, heading to the Gloom town gates.

Why aren't we heading straight there?

"We wouldn't make it past the city watch. They don't let unescorted common fae enter the city unaccompanied; they're not going to let a mortal girl and a psychotic goose just wander inside," I explained. "We need a nobleman to take us there, and we need help infiltrating the castle so we can get to Romeo." My eyes narrowed on the town of Gloom. "And I know just the man to take us there."

The road grew a little busier as we made our way into the town. Fae creatures of various shapes and sizes emerged from their homes and went about their business —tiny black-and-gray moth-fairies fluttered on diaphanous wings, stout little goblins with bulging tummies stomped around, and huge ogres with stained tusks glowered menacingly at nothing in particular.

The locals, though—the common Dusk fae—all wore heavy cloaks with large hoods pulled deep over their faces. I noticed one fae woman wearing a huge gray bonnet that almost obscured her face completely. Then, I saw another one exactly the same. Then another one.

It made me weirdly uneasy. "When I was here last," I whispered as we walked over the cobblestones, "It wasn't in fashion to obscure your face, in fact, it was considered rude. But everyone here is hiding their faces."

I wasn't sure when I was here last, though. The fashion might have changed. In Faerie time, it might have been half a century since I'd been here. Although, apart from the freshly whitewashed stone buildings and arches and the yellow tint to the skyline, everything felt familiar. And now that I thought about it, fashion might change but culture rarely did.

The streets grew more crowded as the sun finally dipped below the skyline. We headed uphill, passing a row of stores set under deep porches, a saddlery, a butcher, baker, and candlestick maker. As full darkness fell, I noticed that the common folk kept their hoods pulled low, and nobody took their bonnets off. It made me feel uneasy.

Are we there yet?

"No. Sorry, sir."

We crossed a river towards the bigger stone dwellings

on the far edge of the town. I hoped my mark still lived there.

Brackin Pesh, the Slum Lord of Gloom. He could get me inside the City of Dusk to find Romeo. I'd make him.

He wasn't the ruler of Gloom. Brackin Pesh was the younger brother of Lord Bron Pesh, the Duke of Gloom. The duke was never here—I'd only ever seen him once the whole time I'd been stuck here, in fact—but Brackin never left the town. He treated Gloom like it was his own personal playground and liked to pretend he was its ruler instead of his brother.

The duke's official residence was a dark stone manor house that backed right up against the shadow of the mountain. I could just see it now. The sun set behind it, so it was always in shadow.

His little brother's house was further down the hill, now brushed with a fraction of the sun's fading light. Brackin's house was only two levels, and smaller, cave-like, made of dark stone with deep sunken porches ringing each level.

Where Lord Bron was a typical haughty, snooty high fae who looked down on everyone, and anyone he considered beneath him, Brackin Pesh was, to put mildly, a slimy piece of shit. He hadn't received the moniker Slum Lord of Gloom for nothing. The younger brother by at least a century, his mother, a lady-in-waiting to the old Queen of Dusk, had thought she was doomed to only produce an heir and not a spare. When Brackin emerged, she treated him like a miracle child and spoiled him rotten.

Where are we going?

"There." I pointed to Brackin's house up the hill. "I'm going to check in on an old enemy and see if he can help me."

Don't you mean check in on a friend?

86

"I said what I said." I sighed roughly as we trod up the hill. "I might have to bargain with him, though. He's a weasel and doesn't do anything unless it'll make him some money. It might cost us." I shuddered as I imagined what he'd ask for.

Ignoring the deep, elegant, recessed porch, I took a detour around the side of the house and knocked on the servants' entrance.

The door cracked open, and a plump woman wearing an apron and one of those deep bonnets pulled low over her face answered. "Yes?"

I recognized her. "Hello, Mottie."

"Daphne?" She tilted her head back, trying to see me better from underneath her bonnet. "Is that you?"

"Yes, it's me."

"You look different."

"I'm older. Is Lord Brackin home?"

"No." Brackin's housekeeper replied. "Now, piss off." She slammed the door shut.

I sighed. I really didn't expect less of her. Mottie, a local common fae woman, had always been a bitch. She wasn't fond of Brackin, but then again, she wasn't fond of anyone.

Mottie hadn't lied, though—most of the time, the fae couldn't lie, but they generally twisted the truth in so many knots and dressed it up in so many layers of misconception and misunderstanding that it felt like a lie. Mottie had given it to me straight. Brackin wasn't here.

I exhaled wearily. What now? I'd have to find him.

Dwayne looked up at me. **She seems nice.**

"She's a bitch," I told him. "That was Lord Brackin's housekeeper. For a bit of background, when I was in my early teens, I got swept up by one of Brackin's less legitimate work crews on the edge of the Wilds. He likes to send his men out there to see what he can get, and find useful

87

things to sell and trade, y'know? Sometimes, those things are people."

Dwayne frowned. **Oh.**

"Technically, slavery is forbidden here," I explained. "Just like back home. And, just like home, if you're a young girl—an off-worlder—all alone, with nobody to advocate for you, and you've got a scary man with a powerful title telling you that he owns you now, and you must do what he says, well..." I shrugged. "I spent six months here under his thumb with him as my master, doing anything he needed me to."

Dwayne had gone very still. **Anything?**

"No, it wasn't as bad as it sounds," I reassured him. "I wouldn't come here if it was. Mostly, I was a runner, fetching his food and drink, collecting his rent money, his bribe money, his bookie money. I kept really quiet. He scared me, of course; he threatened me with all sorts of horrible things. He didn't do anything sexual to me, though." My cheeks warmed a little. "He has a... thing."

Dwayne frowned. **What kind of thing?**

"He's... he's into tickling."

Tickling?

"Yeah. He liked getting tickled, and apparently, I'm not good at it. No common fae or anyone vaguely humanoid is good at it, according to him. He kept a harem of mothpixies." My cheeks burned along with the fury in my belly. "Mothpixies drink salt water. At night, Brackin would sit in his sauna until he was all sweaty, then he'd go into their apiary, take off his towel and get them to flutter all over him with their wings until he..." I grimaced. "You know."

Dwayne's expression was unreadable. **Huh.**

"Mothpixies aren't exactly intelligent, but they're sentient creatures. He used them for his own sexual gratification." I gave a shudder. "It's disgusting. Anyway, eventually I realized what kind of man he was. It took me exactly six months to figure out he was just a lazy, greedy coward, and I could take him down with one hand tied behind my back, even as a young teenager. He was doing all sorts of illegal things—the slavery, for one."

So, you stabbed him and ran away.

"No, I told his mom. I mean, yeah, I stabbed him, *then* I told his mom. She'd been wondering why he wouldn't choose a bride and give her grandchildren. I pinned him down, naked, in the apiary, took his mother in to show her, and told her everything. Luckily, she listened to me."

I suppose you did stab her son.

"Well, to be fair, she wanted to stab him herself when she realized why he'd been avoiding matrimony. The moth-pixie thing is incredibly embarrassing for their whole family. And this was before I got my Orion blades, so unfortunately it didn't kill him. He lived, and his mother was forced to face the fact that her spoiled-brat son was a scummy slum lord and a creepy sexual deviant."

I had hesitated to kill him back then, which wasn't normal for me. Lord Brackin had a silver tongue, and he'd been very convincing. He'd scared me so badly, I hadn't put a foot out of place for the whole time I was here.

But now, I was glad I hadn't killed him. If anyone could get me into the City of Dusk, it was him.

"Come on," I said. "I'll ask around, see where he is. I'll find him, talk to him, and see what it will take." A desolate feeling rushed through me. Bargaining with the fae, especially a silver-tongued devil like Lord Brackin, was both dangerous and exasperating.

We walked back down the hill and made our way through the town, watching the townsfolk rush everywhere. Dusk went on for hours here—the last hints of the sun were slowly draining from the night's sky, turning the horizon from brilliant oranges to vivid reds and purples, with a deep midnight blue right overhead, but the people were still wearing their bonnets and hooded cloaks as if it were midday.

Dwayne was getting bored. **Where did you say that tavern was?**

"It's—" I caught a pair of eyes flashing underneath another deep gray bonnet, and my pulse quickened. A human face, with Orbiter human eyes. A young girl.

"Come on." I changed direction abruptly and hurried after her.

Who is she? Dwayne padded along beside me, his feet making tiny *pat pat pat* sounds on the cobblestones. We weaved through the townspeople, ignoring the odd snarl and grunt as various creatures tried to get my attention, snaked through two alleyways, then entered a narrow street lined with strings of lights ringing back and forth overhead and traders setting up stalls on either side.

We rushed into the market. "I don't know who she is," I said. "But she's a human girl. Humans don't just wander into Faerie, Dwayne. They're usually stolen."

I was talking to myself. Dwayne had disappeared. He couldn't have gone far, though, and he seemed stable enough, so I focused on the human changeling girl. She turned off a few stalls ahead of me, ducking into a narrow alleyway.

I didn't follow her. I didn't have to. The familiar scent of fabric dye and misery hit my nose, and I groaned. "I know this place," I said out loud.

It was a sweatshop. I'd spent a few months in there sewing aprons until my fingers bled. When I took Brackin down, he was forced to close this sweatshop, because the rest of his "employees" decided to run while they still could.

Looks like our mark has rebuilt his empire. Brain-Daphne cracked her knuckles.

I fumed for a second. Goddamnit. Now I'd have to crack his skull, *then* try to talk him into taking me to the City of Dusk.

Getting inside the palace was going to be the hardest part of this whole mission. I'd never been there before, but I knew security was rock-solid.

Brackin was my only way in. The bastard had a slick tongue, but it might abandon him if he had bruises all over his face and my knife to his back.

I fumed for another long moment, then followed the human girl to the sweatshop. Halfway down the alleyway, I found the brittle oak door and tried to turn the handle. It was locked.

I kicked it. The lock smashed, the door flew in, and I marched inside.

CHAPTER

THIRTEEN

A chorus of feminine screams greeted me.

The sweatshop looked almost exactly like it used to. Twelve desks lined the room, six on either side, with an aisle in between. Each station had a roll of fabric, a pedal-powered sewing machine on it, and was worked by a person in a deep bonnet. Most of the figures were curvy and feminine, but there were a few with more masculine shoulders and sturdy chests.

I couldn't see any faces. Why were they wearing the bonnets here, inside?

I jerked my head towards the door. "You can go."

Silence. Everyone sat still, frozen in place.

"Go on." What were they waiting for?

"Uh..." A woman stood up. "Our shift has only just begun, ma'am."

"You don't have to stay for a second longer. You're free now."

"You mean our debts are paid?" A young creature scrambled to her feet. "Our ledger is out of the red?" Her voice was squeaky.

I stifled a groan. Lord Brackin had obviously upped his

manipulation game. "You have no debts. Whatever Lord Brackin has told you, it's wrong. You can all leave. You're not slaves any longer."

There was a beat of silence. A deep voice sounded from a station across the aisle. "But... we're not slaves."

I frowned. "You're stuck in here, working for no pay. That's called a slave."

"We're working for potions." The girl I'd followed in— the human girl—stood up from her station. "We're not slaves. Slavery is outlawed here, ma'am."

She'd clocked me as a mortal realmer, but she spoke using the common fae tongue. I pointed at her. "You're a human."

"Yes, a changeling," she said.

I narrowed my eyes. "Did Brackin take you?"

"No. Of course not. I've been here my whole life. My fae parents feared they'd created a monster when their own baby tried to pull my mother's nipples clean off and hit my father with a chair, so they travelled to the mortal realm through a mushroom circle and swapped her for me. My parents love me, ma'am."

That sounded bad. I raised my brows. "What happened to their fae child?"

"She lives in Chicago." The girl shrugged. "She's made her fortune in the professional wrestling circuit."

Okay... I pointed at her. "So, you're not a slave."

"No, ma'am." She shook her head firmly.

"Why are you here, then? This is a sweatshop."

"We work for Lord Brackin. We can't leave."

I thought a little clarification was needed here. "He pays you?"

The girl hesitated. "No, not exactly. We're working off our debts."

That cunning bastard. Brackin was obviously too scared

to try to manage another slave ring, so he'd found a work-around. Loan sharking made no sense, though. It was a cultural taboo to loan money here, and Brackin wasn't that stupid. "What debts?"

"Our healer debts," she explained. "Lord Brackin holds our debt markers. We're working off what we owe him."

"Owe him for *what?*"

"For anti-burn."

It took me a second to translate the fae word the girl had used into English. "What anti-burn? You mean like a potion?"

"Yes. Lord Brackin holds the market on anti-burn potions," the girl said. "It's far too expensive to buy outright because it's in high demand, and it's got a short shelf life. My mother was so badly burned when the scorch rampaged through town early last moon, so we had no choice but to negotiate with Lord Brackin for the cure." Seeing the confusion on my face, she continued, "We all have to commit to working a half-moon for every vial of anti-burn he provides us."

Yeah, that didn't help. What the hell was the scorch?

"I can't quit," the girl went on, looking a little worried. "If I do, he won't give me any more anti-burn if I need it."

I huffed out a breath. *I think I got it. The scorch was a fire, obviously. Brackin is holding meds. He's set himself up as a pharmaceutical company, and he's charging exorbitant amounts or demanding labor in lieu of payment. That rotten bastard.*

While I glared furiously into the distance, the girl tentatively sat down and started running a square of gray fabric through her sewing machine. A faint waft of cortisol drifted to me. These people were scared. But, I suspected, not of Lord Brackin.

The bonnets. The scorch. Anti-burn. The strange yellow tint to the sky. Something fishy was going on.

I could ask these sweatshop workers more questions, but, like poor Ruby and Sammy, I suspected that keeping them from their work would only make them more anxious. It wouldn't be fair to interrogate them.

Besides, I had some furious energy to expend.

I needed to find Brackin.

CHAPTER

FOURTEEN

I stomped around the town of Gloom for an hour, wondering what to do. I had no idea where Dwayne had gone, I had no place to stay, and I had zero idea what the hell was going on in this damn town.

My gut twisted painfully. I was starving, too. I wanted to save the granola bars in case I got stuck out in the wilderness, so I decided to get some food. I followed my nose, heading to a tavern near the town's entrance, picking a couple of pockets for some fae coins on the way.

Full night had fallen now, but the atmosphere was still a little tense. Nobody lingered in the streets, everyone rushed with somewhere to go, and everyone kept their hoods and bonnets on.

I pushed open the door of the Toad's Hole and walked inside. This old bar was over two hundred years old last time I was here, and it was built to last. A cacophony of scents hit me as I entered—a strong waft of weed-smoke, a punch of gamey roasted meat, and various creatures' feral body odors.

I made my way over to the bar and ordered the only thing they served that I would be able to stomach right now

—a vegetable pottage and a crusty roll of bread. A craggy-faced common fae man stooped over the bar and grunted rudely at me. Before I could place my order, a familiar voice hit my ears.

Male, mature but not old, with the smooth, resonant tones of the High Fae. He was begging in a way that sounded incredibly familiar. "Please. Please, sir, I beg you..."

I jerked. It was the Slum Lord of Gloom, Brackin Pesh himself, I was sure of it.

I'd found him.

Spinning around, I looked through the crowd. Brackin was a tall man, generically beautiful, ethereal and angelic in the manner of the High Fae—perfect cheekbones, pore-less skin, pointed chin, and big, expressive flashing eyes. It took me a moment to find him, because I'd been expecting him to be at least a head taller than all the other people in here. After ducking through the crowd for a moment, peeking through the gaps of the patrons, I finally caught a glimpse of his face in the back of the tavern by the booths.

Instead of the soft tunics and glittering flowing capes that other fae courtiers wore, Brackin Pesh favored more sturdy fabrics in darker colors—a leather vest over a billowy black shirt, tight, tan-colored breeches, shiny knee-high black riding boots, and a long leather duster with the high collar turned up, framing his face as if it were a price-less work of art. He dressed more like a pirate than the son of a fae Duke.

And, for some reason, he was on his knees. Fists clenched together, a pleading expression on his face. "Please, my Lord... sir..."

What the actual fuck is going on?

Adrenaline pulsed through me. Lord Brackin was obsessed with his appearance. The only people he ever deferred to was his older brother and his mother, and I'd

97

never heard him call anyone "sir." My senses heightened; I tasted the air carefully, moving more discreetly through the crowd and trying to see what was going on without drawing any attention to myself.

What powerful force was here in the bar right now? What kind of dangerous entity would bring Brackin to his knees—

Oh.

I straightened up and marched over.

Dwayne sat in the booth on a pile of cushions, regarding Brackin on the floor with a lordly expression. A giant mug of ale and a big steaming pie sat in front of him. He lifted his magnificent white head and grinned at me as I approached. **You took your time. It's not like I've been looking everywhere for you, little one.**

"You haven't! Dwayne, I've walked the length and breadth of this whole town, you were nowhere to be seen!"

Yes, that's what I said. I said it's *not* like I've been looking everywhere for you.

I managed to stifle my exasperated huff. "Sir, you snuck away while I was mid-sentence."

I assumed you were talking to yourself.

That's a fair point.

Thanks, Brain. Jerking my head towards Lord Brackin, now with his forehead touching the floor, I asked, "Did you beat me to the punch?"

Dwayne let out a dirty chuckle. **Oh, I haven't punched him.**

"Just one more time," Brackin whispered, lifting his handsome head from the floor. "Please, my Lord..." He saw me, and his eyes widened. "Little Daffodil," he breathed out. "Is that you?"

I reached down and hauled him to his feet. "Yes, Brackin, it's me."

"What are you doing back here? I thought I granted you your freedom." He tried to sink back down to his knees.

I grabbed his arm and pulled him up again. "No, your *mother* granted me my freedom, because slavery is forbidden."

He waved his hand. "Semantics. Water under the bridge, and all that. I learned my lesson. Nice to see you, Little Daffodil. You will have to excuse me, but I'm a little busy right now." He attempted to kneel again.

I held him upright. "Lord Brackin, what the hell are you doing?"

He struggled in my grip, trying to drop back down to his knees. "I'm worshiping a god, that's what I'm doing."

Dwayne gave a regal nod. **That's right. Bow down, bitch.**

Good gravy, what the hell was going on now? This made no sense. Dwayne, as usual, cloaked his essence behind his form. Most people didn't realize what he really was, but they could sense he was a bit more than what he appeared, and it was enough to make most people wary.

It wasn't like him to flaunt his true nature. In fact, he never did it. I shot Dwayne another look. He was still cloaking. I hadn't even smelled him when I walked in.

The Slum Lord pulled his arm out of my grip and lowered himself again. I heaved out a sigh. "Brackin, stand up."

"No." He sank to his knees and held out his shaking hands towards Dwayne. "My Lord. I will do *anything*...."

I groaned and reached out to grab a handful of Brackin's jacket so I could haul him to his feet again.

Just then, I noticed a suspicious substance seeping through the front of his lace-up breeches. I dropped my hands and backed away as if he were radioactive. Ew. "Please don't tell me that's what I think it is."

Brain-Daphne wrinkled her nose. *Oof. It is.*

Suddenly, it all made sense. I threw my hands in the air. "Are you kidding me, Brackin?"

"A god of desire has walked into my life," Lord Brackin whispered, his voice dreamy. "A god of sensual seduction. A god of ultimate satisfaction. Ohhhh, my..." He exhaled a long breath and shivered.

Ew.

I shot Dwayne a look. "Sir. Really? Here? In the Toad's Hole tavern?"

I wanted to see if tickling really was a thing. Turns out, it is. Dwayne shrugged. **Less surprising to me is that I'm *really* good at it.**

I edged a little further away from Brackin.

I've never seen anyone come that many times in a row, Dwayne honk-chuckled. **He should be dead of dehydration by now.**

"Just one more time," Brackin pleaded. "I haven't been touched like that in decades. Not since—" His eyes flicked towards me, and he cut himself off.

Dwayne waved one of his wings. **Old fancy-pants here likes my feathers.**

Brain-Daphne, who was a lot kinkier than I was, pursed her lips. *I'm unsure how to feel about this.*

I knew how I felt about it. Extremely grossed out and totally exasperated. "Brackin Pesh, get your butt into that chair. *Now.*"

"No." He fell back to his knees. "I must worship my god—"

My patience evaporated. I grabbed him by the hair, yanked him to his feet, and threw him into the booth.

He cringed away. Not from me, but from Dwayne. "Please forgive me, my Lord," he stammered. "This changeling wretch knows not what she does!"

"For the last time, I'm not a changeling wretch," I snapped. "I'm a wolf shifter. Dwayne's my friend. I brought him here. We're on a mission to find someone important." *And possibly save your whole world.*

Brackin Pesh's eyes darted from me to Dwayne. "You brought him here? You brought this mighty sex god to my hometown?"

"Yes," I sighed. "Now, look at me, Brackin. I need you to answer some questions."

After a moment, Brackin turned to Dwayne and bowed his head. "Would it please you, Sir, if I spoke to Little Daffodil, the changeling wretch? Would you grant me your favor?"

Dwayne bowed his head regally. **Knock yourself out, weirdo.**

"Thank you, my Lord." It was a moment before Brackin tore his eyes away from Dwayne. "Well. My dear, you *have* aged." His nose wrinkled in distaste.

"Please focus, Lord Brackin." I took a deep breath and settled into the booth next to Dwayne. "Listen up. I need you to get me into the City of Dusk."

"No." Brackin shook his head abruptly. "Impossible."

I frowned. "Why? It shouldn't be impossible. Can't we just go in with me as your maid or something?"

"Nobody can travel to the City right now, Daffodil. Not without scouts, guards, and powerful mages cloaking the entire party. The roads are too dangerous."

"Why?"

He looked at me as if I was stupid. "Because of the Scorch."

"Okay." I leaned back in my seat. "What the hell is the Scorch?"

"What do you mean, what is the Scorch?"

Brackin stared at me for a second, bewildered. "How

can you not know? Have you just dropped out of the sky, Daffodil?"

"Yes." I eyeballed him steadily. "That's exactly what happened, Brackin. I've spent the last five years back home in the mortal realm."

He looked intrigued. "What is it like there, in the mortal realm? Is that where you found my Lord Godfeathers, here?"

"Just answer the question. What is the Scorch?"

Brackin's expression grew uncharacteristically apprehensive. It was a second before he answered me. "It's a plague," he whispered. "In the form of a great screaming white bull. The Scorch is a plague that has beset our lands of late, Daffodil. It is a white wraith that screams in out of nowhere, burning everything in its path."

I frowned. That didn't really clarify anything for me. I'd never heard of anything like that before. But it might explain one other mystery for me. "So that's why the locals are wearing those bonnets, then?'

Brackin nodded. "It is one reason, yes, although a flimsy bonnet will provide little protection against the fire of the Scorch." He let out a sigh. "In truth, the atmosphere here has grown harsher of late. The shadows used to provide us with succor, but they are not as healing as they used to be. Now, we create our own shadows to linger in." He shrugged half-heartedly. "The bonnets have become the fashion in all of Dusk."

And he was cashing in by getting slaves to sew them. Another mystery poked me. "Why are you painting the buildings white, then?"

"Oh. Bron's wife did that." He screwed up his face in distaste. "She wanted to brighten the place up."

I thought about it. That didn't make much sense. Brackin's older brother was married to a lady from the

Court of Spring, but she would have adapted to the darker side of the Inbetween automatically when she came here. I'd never seen her—she spent all her time at court in the City of Dusk. "She doesn't live here, though, does she?"

Brackin laughed. "Gods, no. She sent her trades to do it. For what it's worth, I don't like it at all, but it doesn't affect the depth of the shadows. No." His expression grew somber. "Something else is doing that."

"What do you think it is?"

He hesitated for a moment. "The Inbetween has become... unhealthy. And the Scorch is a symptom of the disease."

The Oracle had said there was imbalance. *Faerie has become unbalanced.* And apparently, Romeo might make it worse.

"Do you know what's causing it?" I asked him.

He shrugged and settled back into his seat, crossing one leg over the other. He was becoming more comfortable, but every now and then, his eyes would shoot over to Dwayne, as if making sure Dwayne wasn't going anywhere. "'Tis a slow tip of the scales, Little Daffodil," Brackin finally said. "Too slow for our Seers to see the exact cause. But one key factor has been the line of succession in the Court of Dusk. The line was broken, you see, and the magic of the throne has been weakened."

I racked my brains, trying to remember who sat on the throne of Dusk. "King Monton has ruled Dusk for hundreds of years, though."

But Brackin shook his head. "King Monton was killed in a hunting accident years ago, along with his young son, the heir."

I vaguely remembered hearing about that. Brain Daphne groaned and put her head in her hands. *Politics. I fucking hate politics. Especially fae politics. It's worse than advanced algebra.*

We've never done advanced algebra.

Because we hate it.

Brackin was still talking, so I focused back on him. "After King Monton and his heir were killed, his wife, Queen Carissa reluctantly took the throne, but there was some sort of uprising in the court, and she abandoned her claim. Her child, Princess Ember, was passed over, as she was not Monton's blood. Monton was her stepfather. Eventually, King Monton's younger brother, the Lord Ronus Wintermade, stepped into the breach and took the throne of the Kingdom of Dusk."

I narrowed my eyes, trying to access the treasure-trove of information stored in my memory banks. "Lord Ronus. He was the duke of..."

"Nightfall," Brackin supplied.

I nodded. Nightfall was a region a little closer to Winter than the City of Dusk. "Go on."

"Ronus Wintermade and his wife, Talia, have been the King and Queen of the Court of Dusk for many years now. And, from what my brother tells me, they've been fair and firm lieges."

"Right." I nodded at him. "So, what's the problem? Why is the balance upset and this Scorch rampaging through the Inbetween?"

"Ronus and Talia are both old and unable to bear children. The line of succession has been broken. They have no heirs, and the people are worried that Dusk is falling."

I'd lived in Faerie off and on for a long time, and I liked to think I understood how the magic of this realm worked. I couldn't imagine why the balance of the whole of Faerie would be upended by the fact that there was no firm line of succession on any royal throne.

One King dies, someone else steps in. It didn't really matter who it was, as long as they embodied the spirit of their Kingdom. And they didn't massacre their people or invade the neighbors, of course.

"No heirs?" I dug deep into my memory. "I remembered hearing that Ronus and Talin had a huge family. Didn't they have lots of children?"

"Eight. All are dead."

I whistled through my teeth. "How?"

Brackin shrugged. "Four died centuries ago in war—old skirmishes with the Seelie on the other side of the Inbetween. Two were killed Off-World. The Scorch got the last two."

A tingle of intuition hit me. "Like... was it an assassination?"

"No, Little Daffodil. The Scorch has been rampaging for a decade now, and King Ronus was trying to figure out what it was. You have to figure out what something is first, then you know how to kill it."

A smile touched my lips. I remember Romeo saying that to Marie not that long ago.

"Ronus charged his sons with uncovering the mystery of the plague that had been tormenting the Inbetween. His last remaining heir died during a reconnaissance mission to the Wastes. They thought the Scorch might have come from there. Well, they found it, but it killed them."

Eight kids, all dead. I'd heard that Ronus and Talin were good rulers, which was rare in Faerie, where the royals tended to be selfish and bloodthirsty. I felt sorry for them.

A weird tapping noise caught my attention—Dwayne had finished his pie, and his beak was clanging on the bottom of the tin. With a start, Brackin leapt to his feet, swiped another pie out of a passing gnome's hands, placed it reverently in front of Dwayne, then backed into his seat.

"So that's why I cannot escort you to the City of Dusk, Daffodil," he said, reluctantly returning his gaze to me. "There is a plague rampaging through the land, and, more often than not, it is burning the Shadow Fae to ash whenever we attempt to travel. We haven't even been able to send a candidate to the palace for the Bride Trials," he said sulkily. "My townsfolk of Gloom were disappointed we could not put forth a representative for consideration."

My intuition poked me again so hard I felt like it had drawn blood. "Bride Trials? The Court of Dusk is holding a Bride Trial?'

"Yes, that's correct. It's all very exciting. Apparently, Queen Talia found someone that could be considered a suitable heir to the throne. A bastard child, rumors say. The king and queen are unsure which one of their children sired him, but he has been tested, and he is their direct kin."

Holy shit. Holy fucking shitballs.

Goosebumps broke out all over my body. "Really?" I croaked.

Brackin nodded, flagging down a serving woman. "You'd be interested to know this, Daffodil. He's from the mortal realm. A changeling child, just like you."

You've gotta be kidding me.

Romeo.

FIFTEEN

I t was several minutes before I could form coherent thoughts. In the meantime, Lord Brackin got himself a huge flagon of ale and gazed soulfully across the table at Dwayne, who was demolishing his fifth game pie.

It couldn't be. It couldn't be Romeo they were talking about.

It could. He doesn't know who his father is. There's a good chance one of the Princes of Dusk went on Rumspringa, banged his way across the mortal realm, knocked up the Jupiter heiress, then skedaddled back to Faerie to avoid having to pay child support.

This isn't going to endear him to his Fae side of the family. He already wants to kill his dad.

If it is him, then we just got confirmation that his dad is dead.

Maybe Romeo will leave it at that.

Brain-Daphne let out a harsh bark of laughter. *No, he's not going to do that. He's going to kill someone.*

Now I knew why the Shadow Fae had stolen Romeo so quickly. They needed him. He was the last remaining heir to the Throne of Dusk.

Maybe we shouldn't give him that journal. He might go nuts and kill them all.

I'd been worried that might be the case. The journal Prue had given me was sitting in Ziplock bags for water-proofing purposes. Suddenly, it felt like it was burning a hole in my back. We don't know what it says, I told my own brain.

Well, she said, using a duh voice, *maybe we should read it.*

I'd already betrayed his autonomy enough. Besides, it wouldn't change anything for me, only for him. I had to get it to him.

I swallowed the huge lump in my throat. "So, uh, this... newfound Prince of Dusk."

"The Prince of Shadow," Brackin corrected me. "It's a traditional title for the heir. He won't be Prince of Dusk until he's married, but he's already been given a title when he was confirmed as the heir." Brackin made a sour face. "My brother tells me he's a very handsome fellow for a crossbreed. But he won't be confirmed as the Heir until he marries. The line of succession requires stability, so he must be bound in matrimony to a suitable candidate, and quickly, so the Court of Dusk has arranged a Bride Trial."

Brain-Daphne suddenly growled inside of me.

"It's taking place three days from now," Brackin continued. "And all other business with the Court has been suspended. So, not only can we *not* go to the City of Dusk because we will get incinerated by the Scorch on the way, but we will be turned away from the castle automatically once we get there. Only Trial participants and sponsors are allowed to attend Court right now."

I swallowed again, trying to clear the lump in my throat. The Shadow Fae had stolen my boyfriend, and they were hellbent on marrying him off to the first royal fae woman who came along.

Brain-Daphne had turned feral within me. *Read the journal, find Romeo, help him kill them all...*

Faith and trust, I reminded her. I've got this.

I knew what a Bride Trial was. When one member of the ruling class in Faerie had an eligible child ready for marriage, but they had no firm suitor in mind and too many interested parties, sometimes they would throw a festival to screen the potential brides. Every town and municipality were invited to suggest a candidate. It was good for fostering a sense of patriotism in an unsettled kingdom, and the common folk loved the idea of someone from their town marrying a royal High Fae.

The only problem was the death toll. During the Trials, the potential brides were tested on everything it took to become a royal—etiquette, manners, diplomacy, resilience, magical potency, artistic talent, and, of course, the ability to beat someone else into a bloody mush.

The Bride Trials were a dating game show and a fight to the death—sort of like a cross between The Bachelor and The Hunger Games.

During the talent portion, you were allowed to juggle iron spikes and fling them at your opponents. During the diplomatic testing, it was expected you should be able to skillfully prod someone to declare war on a rival town.

In the end, there was usually only one bride standing. If more than one survived, the King and Queen chose the winner. The royal court would advise them, and a fair and loyal liege would listen to their court, because of course, if they didn't, there was always a good chance they'd get stabbed in the back and overthrown at some point in the next few centuries.

Fae politics. Good gods.

I took a deep breath and gave Brackin a hard stare. "You have to take me there."

109

He drained his flagon, threw his head back, and laughed. "Daffodil," he said, shaking his head. "There's no chance."

Time to get heavy. I let a growl slip out from my lips and pulled out one of my Orion blades. "You have been taking advantage of your people."

He still looked amused. "No, Little Daffodil. I've been helping my people."

I pointed one of my blades at him. "By charging exorbitant amounts for potions they sorely need!"

"There's no need to be dramatic." He rolled his eyes. "They cost me a fortune to make. I'm not a charity. You can put that little pointy thing away, changeling wretch. I'm not risking my life to travel to the City of Dusk right now."

"Brackin Pesh," I growled, waving both blades at him now. "I'm not joking. You'll take me, or I'll be sticking one of these through your shoulder and pinning you to the floor like last time. Except this time, the blade will poison you."

His grin faltered. He hesitated for a second, thinking, then gave a careless shrug. "No," he said firmly. "There's no choice in the matter. You are being foolish. You can stick me with those pretty knives if you want to, Little Daffodil, but if I try to take you to the City of Dusk, the Scorch will render the flesh from my bones in a far more painful manner. Even if we made the journey into the City without dying, we won't get into the Court."

I thought frantically. "What if we *could* get in?"

He cocked his head. "Pardon?"

"You said that Gloom couldn't submit a candidate for the Bride Trials because of the Scorch. Well... What if you had one? They'd let us in then, wouldn't they?"

"Technically, yes." He wrinkled his nose. "We don't have one, though."

I shrugged. "I'll do it."

110

He reared back. "What?!"

Brain-Daphne echoed him, *What?*

"I'll do it," I told Brackin. "I'll be Gloom's candidate."

Girl! Are you insane? It's a death sentence!

I shushed her. We don't have to actually do the trials. We just have to get in, find Romeo, get him out of there, and bring him home.

After a long moment, his outraged expression melted, and Brackin began to laugh. "You? A little changeling girl? *You* want to submit yourself for the Bride Trials for the chance to wed the Prince of Shadow? Ha!"

His laughter was a little insulting. "I know all the rules," I said. "The potential bride doesn't have to be Fae-born. In a Bride Trial, the aristocracy say they don't even care about the species of the entrants, in fact, they make a point of wanting to diversify the gene pool."

It wasn't true in practice—the King and Queen would only ever choose a high fae princess. But they billed the Trials as a chance for any commoner to win the heart of a prince. "I know for a fact that one of the towns will probably enter a troll because they're hardy enough to survive the slaughter."

"You can't." He chuckled. "There's no way, Daffodil. You don't live here. The candidate must be a resident of Gloom."

"I *was* a resident. You kept me prisoner here for six months—that's longer than the required three-month residency for admission to the Trials." I smiled. "I've just been on an eight-year vacation. Now, I'm back."

Brackin hesitated for a second, then continued laughing. "You won't survive the first day. From what I've heard, princesses from every court have entered."

I hesitated. That was serious. I eyed him, keeping my blades up and pointing at him. "Even from the main courts?"

He shuddered. "Gods, no. Maeve and Titiana do not bother with us at all; they barely tolerate our courtier's presence in their own courts. The princesses that have entered are all from the Courts of the Inbetween."

Okay. It was bad, but not too bad. The idea of going up against twelve different versions of Asherah was unthinkable—I wouldn't last a heartbeat.

Who are you kidding? We probably wouldn't last very long against the minor Fae princesses, either. Not in any of the Trial categories.

Royal fae children spent hundreds of years learning to rule. Without exception, they were razor-sharp diplomats, ruthless manipulators, vicious, merciless fighters, and, unfortunately for me, they were usually stunningly, overwhelmingly beautiful. The royal court in particular favored beauty over a lot of other values. The princesses would kick my ass and serve face at the same time. And I'd be competing with them for Romeo...

A pinch of jealousy stabbed me.

Brain-Daphne sent a vicious kick right into my temple. *Don't be stupid. He got abducted, remember? Do you think he wants to do this?*

Mentally—because I was still holding both Orion blades pointed at Brackin—I held the crystal between my breasts and brought back that titanium-strong feeling of conviction within me.

I was right. I was sure of myself, and I was sure of Romeo. He loved me. I had to save him.

Or we have to save them from him.

And, again, I didn't have to actually compete in the Bride Trials. I just had to get to the City of Dusk, find Romeo, and get home.

"Yes," I told Brackin firmly. "I want to be Gloom's candidate for the Bride Trials. You have to take me to the City of Dusk now."

He eyed me back, still smiling. "No."

"You have to." I jerked the blades. "I'm not kidding around, Lord Brackin."

"You can't threaten me, Daffodil." He shrugged languidly. "I'm as good as dead if I take you."

This negotiation was going nowhere. I had nothing to offer, nothing to bargain with, and apparently, I couldn't even threaten him. "Please?"

He laughed. "My dear, I'm only entertaining you now because you came in the slipstream of my Lord, the Godfeathers—"

Brain-Daphne rolled her eyes so hard, it gave me a lightning migraine.

"—And he gave permission for me to speak to you." Brackin's attention drifted over to Dwayne, now sticking his head right in his flagon and sucking it up as if his whole neck were a giant straw. A gurgling sound indicated the flagon was empty. Dwayne straightened up and let out a thunderous burp.

Brackin's eyes unfocused with lust. He slid down in his chair a little, obviously about to sink down on his knees again.

"Hey!" I jabbed both blades in his direction, nudging his leather vest. "I'm *not* kidding. I will kill you, Brackin! You know you're not popular in this town, so I don't think anyone is going to stop me from stabbing you in the gut right now."

In fact, there were two goblins at the table next to us who'd started a little cheer, encouraging me to get on with it. The craggy faced bartender had even started a slow clap.

Brackin Pesh pursed his lips, staring at me. "Then I will

die with a smile on my face. I've been blessed by the god of ultimate pleasure; I already know what Heaven feels like."

"Oh, I don't think you'll be going in *that* direction, you bastard," I snarled.

His smile slid, his expression suddenly growing sad. "In fact, the thought of never feeling his touch again fills me with pain." His lip quivered, and he opened his vest up, exposing his heart. "You might as well run me through now, Little Daffodil."

Fucking drama queen coward.

A growl built in my chest; my frustration was beginning to overwhelm me. I had to get to the City of Dusk, and I had to get there now. And this over-dramatic piece of shit was my only hope. I couldn't think of any other way inside.

My hands started to shake. "Brackin...."

Suddenly, one of my hands was lighter. I flinched, adrenaline pulsing through me. Something had happened, and I wasn't sure what it was.

I looked down. In my right hand, I still held my Orion blade. But in my left hand, I had a single white feather.

My eyes flicked left; Dwayne was holding my other blade in his beak. He'd swapped it with one of his feathers.

Brackin saw it and blinked. His eyes grew big and round. "A blessing," he gasped.

It's hard being a sex god. Dwayne inclined his head regally. **But someone's gotta do it.**

There was a long, long moment of silence. Brackin took a deep, shaky breath, and reached out, taking the feather from my hand.

"If my Lord Godfeathers demands it," he finally said. "I will take you to the City of Dusk."

CHAPTER

SIXTEEN

T dragged him out of the booth by the collar and hurried him out of the tavern. "We need to leave right away. We've got no time to waste."

"Yes, we must hurry," he agreed. "Registration for the Bride Trials closes tomorrow morning, so we must get there before dawn. Tomorrow night is the Commencement Ball. We must gather the essentials," Lord Brackin said as we climbed the hill to his home. "I shall need to get my full courtier wardrobe ready, or Mother will harangue me."

"No," I said firmly. "Just the essentials. We need a horse each, Brackin, and that's it."

"I need my courtly accoutrement," he whined. "I must look the part."

"You can go as you are. Your brother keeps a residence in the City of Dusk, doesn't he? You can borrow some of his stuff." I pushed him up the hill. "We need to leave now."

"He's taller than me. And... But... The Bride Trials," he said, furrowing his brow and looking down on me as he strode on long legs up the hill. "You can't embarrass Gloom if you are to be our candidate. You have a pretty face, Daffodil, but—and don't take offence—but you are as graceless as a bully-cart, and you dress like a masculine sea hag."

"Oh, that's not offensive *at all.*"

"It's the Bride Trials. You'll need at least eight bespoke gowns, one for each event. Mottie can probably glamor some old curtains to look like pretty dresses for you, and they—"

"Don't worry about it. We don't have time. I'll make do." Dresses were the last thing I was worried about. I just had to get to the Kingdom of Dusk to find Romeo. It almost felt like the closer I got to him, the more I could feel he needed me. Like a storm on the horizon, and I was the shelter.

I'm coming, baby.

"This is going to be humiliating." Brackin pouted. "You are going to make Gloom the laughingstock of the Kingdom, you know that, don't you, Daffodil?" He pushed open his front door and stomped inside. "Morale has been bad since the Scorch started rampaging. With you as our candidate, this town might never recover."

I followed him around while he roared at his two footmen to get ready for travel. Mottie grumpily packed his bags, swearing at me under her breath the whole time. Eventually, we gathered on the cobblestones outside, waiting for the footmen to bring us the horses.

"How long will it take to get there?" I asked him.

"Only one night's travel," Brackin replied. "If we trot, we will get there well before dawn. Although we will need to detour if we see the Scorch on the horizon." He gave me a hostile glare. "There is a chance we will never make it to court. If it senses our presence, it will chase us. We cannot travel during the day, as the day makes it harder for us to see the Scorch coming."

The horses clattered out into the courtyard. I chose the

smallest one, a pretty black gelding with long eyelashes. I was an expert rider, but standard, non-magical horses didn't like shifters. I was probably the only werewolf in history who could actually ride a horse without being thrown off immediately, but they were always a little nervous about me. I patted my horse's nose and murmured a greeting, trying to soothe him and get him used to my scent. He wasn't a Kawasaki, but he'd do.

Dwayne hopped up on his horse—an enormous, snorting bay stallion—and settled down on the stallion's back. **Wake me when we get there, baby girl.** He tucked his head under his wing.

Brackin mounted his own horse, a big dark-gray mare, and swung around to face me. His expression was uncharacteristically serious. "We must ride fast. I was not exaggerating the danger, Little Daffodil. If the Scorch catches us, we are all dead."

I hadn't been that worried about it—I'd been too frantic about finding a way to get to the City of Dusk—but Brackin's fear was a little contagious. "Well..." I said, looking for a bright side. I waved my hand towards where Dwayne was curled up on the massive stallion's back. "Dwayne can fly. He'll be fine."

Brackin brightened. "That is a good point. At least my Lord Godfeathers will endure." Jabbing his heels into his mare's side, we trotted off, one footman riding in front, one behind.

We left the town in silence and followed the road heading west, travelling through the stubbly brown fields, the same way we'd arrived. We passed a handful of small villages, tumbledown shacks, crumbling stone buildings, and rickety roadside stalls selling sad-looking vegetables and spicy-smelling moonshine.

There were more common fae out and about here,

toiling in the fields by starlight, baking on open fires, or making repairs to their shacks and carts. The region of Gloom was much busier after sunset than it used to be. And everyone still wore those bonnets and hoods.

My eyes were good in the dark. I focused hard on my surroundings as the terrain shifted from villages to the rolling hills of farmland, noting the long swathes of dried-out sections that seemed to zigzag over some of the hills. I cleared my throat, getting Brackin's attention. "Is that where the Scorch has been?"

He glanced over at me. "Yes. Several moons ago, in fact. Wherever the Scorch treads its demonly hooves, it incinerates everything it steps on. It will take a year before those fields become fertile again."

After an hour's ride, the rolling hills became dotted with scrub, then, the odd fat-trunked gnarled fae tree appeared, then more, until each side of the road was packed with thick woods. Every so often, we would move through a thin section of cleared forest. Logging or the Scorch? I didn't want to ask. The impact looked catastrophic. I was starting to worry.

If this creature was bad enough that every common fae in the Kingdom of Dusk only worked at night and wore bonnets and hoods while they did it... it must be something to be frightened of.

A billion stars twinkled above like diamonds overhead. It was an awesome sight, but Brackin's fear of the Scorch had settled in, leaving me anxious. What the hell was this thing?

Brain-Daphne stirred. *I've checked all your memory banks, and I've got nothing. It's years old—too old to be a spell of some sort—it would have run out of magic and dissolved well before now. It could be a creature, a beast, or something, but I can't think of anything that suits the description Brackin gave us. The closest I can think of is some sort of Underworld fire demon.*

"That's what I thought, too," I whispered, giving into the temptation to talk to myself out loud. Now that I was back in Faerie, it felt natural, anyway. I'd always talked out loud to myself here. "But creatures from the Underworld wouldn't survive this long in the Overworld. That would be like throwing a chicken into the Arctic and expecting it to thrive."

Creatures from the Underworld have a unique scent, she muttered. *We've been there before, remember? Generally, they all smell similar to jalapeño peppers. If we catch a whiff of this Scorch, we can rule out the Underworld.*

"I don't think I want to get close enough to smell it," I said nervously. "I don't think it's an Underworld creature, anyway." I gnawed on my lip, still thinking. My gelding's smooth footsteps were rhythmic and soothing. Despite my unease, I was feeling sleepy. "I just can't think of what it might be."

Brackin said it's a symptom of the imbalance.

"Yeah, about that..." I frowned. "I remember Prue telling me about the imbalance between the Wastes and the Wilds when her bio dad was on his rampage. It was like... his extreme authoritarianism was stripping more of the life out of the Wilds, the Wastes were growing, and it was throwing the center of Faerie out of balance. Order versus Chaos. And, like the Oracle said, it seeped out to our realm, too." I chewed on my lip again. "I can't remember if Prue mentioned any symptoms of the imbalance. It was just the Beast himself. He was the disease, and he was quite literally sucking the life out of the Wilds."

From what Prue told us, the Beast of Bakkanon considered himself a god because of the ability he had been born with.

I ran with her idea. "Maybe the Scorch is a fae creature

born with some sort of powerful ability, and they've found a way to fuel their power to the point they've turned into a crazed beast. Maybe they consider themselves a god, just like the Beast did." I cleared my throat, calling out louder. "Brackin, how does the City of Dusk deal with the Scorch? Has it attacked the City?"

"It has tried many times," he answered, not bothering to turn around. He kept his eyes glued on Dwayne, who was sleeping peacefully on the stallion trotting next to Brackin. "Especially when the Scorch first appeared in the Inbetween. The City Walls keep the evil beast away, although the stone bears black marks of char and sear. The King and Queen replaced the oak gates with pure iron so the creature cannot burn its way through. But it has not come near the Kingdom in many years."

The horse ahead of us skittered on the path nervously and let out a whicker. Brackin stiffened, sitting up straighter in the saddle.

The woods were dense around us, close-packed. I lifted my eyes up, checking the sky overhead. Was it me, or were there less stars than before?

A tiny breath of wind gusted towards me from the east, and a whiff of smoke hit my nose. My heart began to thump. "Brackin..."

He whirled around in his saddle, staring at the woods around us. "We are three hours from the City gates," he said, his voice trembling. "It could be a bonfire."

"It could be." A tiny hint of burned wood drifted over to me on another gust. "But I think we need to run."

SEVENTEEN

More stars vanished overhead as the sky grew a little lighter. I nudged my horse into a canter, and Brackin did the same. Dwayne's stallion started and took off at a gallop, flying down the road ahead of us and disappearing around the bend.

"My Lord Godfeathers!" Brackin let out a scream, kicked his mare into a gallop, and chased him. "Come back!" His footman raced after him.

I lifted my ass out of the saddle, staying in the canter, and let them go on ahead. I didn't want to blow my horse out. Three hours was a long time to gallop. "What do you think?"

Brain-Daphne inhaled deeply through her nose. *Smells like trouble.*

It really did. Nothing smelled more sinister than something burning, though. Dread coiled in my belly. "Do you think it's chasing us?"

If it is, then it would mean it's intelligent. It's hunting people.

I rode for a minute or two before Dwayne reappeared,

now flying by himself, and swooped next to me, clearly having been woken by his galloping stallion.

I waved to him. "Are you okay?"

Damn horse nearly killed me.

"Something spooked him. I smell smoke, Dwayne!"

He banked left. **Gonna check it out. I'll be back.** He flapped his wings and soared off into the darkness.

I urged my horse into a gallop, watching the night sky nervously. It was getting less dark with every second. More smoke filled my nostrils.

The wind blew from the nor'-east; the Scorch was coming from that direction. I rode on, keeping one eye on the sky as it lightened.

Swiveling in my saddle, I tried to catch another breath on the wind as I rode. A thick waft of smoke—coming directly from the east—hit me, chilling my blood. We were heading directly west. The Scorch had moved behind us. *I think it's chasing us.*

A minute later, I charged around another bend and spotted Brackin and his two footmen, stopped dead in the middle of the road. Brackin held Dwayne's stallion by the reins and was screaming up at the sky. "My Lord! My Lord Godfeathers! Where are you?"

I didn't slow down. "Keep going!" I shouted. "Dwayne is flying above us. The flames are coming from behind us now. It's changed direction."

"It knows we're here." Brackin's eyes widened. "It's coming." He kicked his mare viciously, and we galloped up the road.

Cold wind whipped past us, chilling my cheeks to ice as we rode faster. My heart thundered in my chest, almost in time to the beat of my horse's hooves. I could smell the smoke clearly now, no longer gusting in on the odd breath of wind.

I glanced behind me. The sky on the horizon, just brushing the treetops to the east, had turned orange. "Faster!"

A white rocket flew over me. Brackin and the footmen both screamed in alarm and ducked, but it was just Dwayne.

He circled back and swooped low, dropping words in my head. **It's a demon, alright.** He sounded unusually serious. **Pretty sure it's chasing you. I thought I wouldn't be able to see much through the smoke, but it's bright yellow, glowing like the morning sun. It's burning everything in its path, zigzagging back and forth. Go faster, baby girl.**

I put my head down and urged my horse on. He didn't need any encouragement. A few seconds later, I heard it—the faint crackle of flames.

Turning in my saddle, I watched as a huge tree in the distance burst into flames. Brackin screamed, "It's here!"

I kept riding, swiveling in my saddle, tracing the brightest light behind me as it zigzagged behind us. Whatever it was, the Scorch burned so hot it threw a visible flare into the sky like a spotlight. It swung over the road, back and forth, a mile or so behind, crossing to the left of the road, then the right, gaining on us even though it wasn't running in a straight line. It was damned fast. A raging bull.

"Ride! Ride, you fools!" Brackin screamed, whipping his horse harder.

Up ahead, the woods started to thin out. Narrowing my eyes against the sting of smoke, I saw the forests give way to the rolling hills of cultivated farmland. A second later, I spotted a billion twinkling lights in the west, right on the horizon.

The City of Dusk.

We hadn't made it yet. We were miles away from the

city gates, and a line in the forest behind us burned hot like lava. I glanced back again, watching that flare of yellow light move closer...

I saw it.

My heart stopped in my chest as the Scorch crashed through the burning trees and ran out into the road. There it was. An enormous, thick-muscled, raging pure-white bull. It radiated extreme heat so hot I could feel it on my face from a quarter mile away. It was as if the molten core of a furnace formed hooves and a snout and charged its way into being.

The moisture in my mouth evaporated.

As if it sensed the presence of mortal flesh to burn, it swung back almost immediately, taking the road instead of zigzagging back and forth behind us.

Holy shit it's going to catch us—

Brackin screamed louder. "Ride! Ride faster!" His huge mare kicked into overdrive, sweating hard. His footmen chased him.

I glanced back one more time, narrowing my eyes against the extreme heat. The Scorch was charging us now, head down, horns pointed right in our direction.

It was going to chase us down. The heat was so intense, my skin would melt off before it even got close. It was going to incinerate us, just like Brackin said.

Suddenly, that silent rocket of white flew through the sky, cutting over the road and streaking right in front of the raging bull below. A soft drizzle of yellow rained down.

Dwayne had peed on the Scorch.

The bull skidded to a halt, froze for a split second, then let out a bellow that shook the atoms of my soul. I had to drop my head to clutch my ears; the pain almost overwhelmed me.

Dwayne banked, turning south, and flew off into the unburning woods.

Through my hands, I forced myself to look back, and I watched as the Scorch scraped a bright-yellow hoof on the road. Then, it turned and crashed off into the woods to the south, following Dwayne's flight path.

He'd done it. Dwayne had lured the Scorch away from us.

I held my breath until we reached the gates.

CHAPTER

EIGHTEEN

I was never lucky enough to grace the grandest parts of Faerie. Mostly, I was kept in the kitchens or stables. Or chained up in dungeons or locked in towers waiting for a warlord to marry me the next day.

The City of Dusk was stunningly beautiful. Every building was a miracle of architecture, built in every shade of dark stone ranging from dove gray to slate to the deepest black obsidian. Warm orange and red lights glowed from the rose-shaped stained-glass windows, and flickering candelabra lit up every sweeping balcony. Elegant plazas were packed with grand statues, fountains, towering spires, or arches that reached into the heavens. The air was cool, but refreshingly so, like the sun had just gone down on a very hot day, and all you could feel was relief.

And I was *relieved*. Romeo was here. I clutched the crystal in my hand, feeling it twitch. Since we'd entered the city, the point had changed direction four times. Romeo was close; I could almost feel him.

I would be even more relieved if I knew where Dwayne was, but I had to trust that he'd show up as soon as I found Romeo, so we could all go home together.

"I've never been more embarrassed in my life," Brackin muttered, stomping a few yards ahead of me. "I can't believe they almost didn't let us inside."

The sentries at the gates had laughed, in fact, when Brackin's footman had announced us. They had kept us outside, arguing that all the Bride Trial princesses were already settled in, ready for the commencement of the festival tomorrow. Then, a whole garrison had broken rank and guffawed loudly when Brackin informed the Watch Commander I was entering the Bride Trials as the candidate for Gloom.

"You?" The Watch Commander had sniggered, looking down at us from the ramparts. "I think there is a rule against entering homeless women, my Lord."

Eventually, mindful of the fire lighting up the sky to the east, they let us inside, but the Watch Commander—a hard-faced man with long blond hair, warm-toned skin, icy eyes, and pointed ears—demanded we submit to a full interrogation before we were allowed to make our way to Lord Bron Pesh's quarters. Brackin protested, but the commander was insistent.

"Security is paramount, especially these days, my Lord," the Commander said pompously, not even looking at me. Both men swept into the keep, walking several yards ahead of me. The footmen followed them, and I trailed behind.

Security can't exactly be paramount if they've already dismissed little old me as a threat, Brain Daphne said sourly. *All of them have their backs to me. I don't know if I'm happy about it or not.*

Silently, I agreed with her. I hated being underestimated... but right now, it was probably best if it stayed that way.

My eyes flicked around the sentry barracks as we walked through, taking everything in. Getting into the

City was hard... getting out might be even harder. Every doorway seemed to be guarded by a sharp-eyed sentry. The tingling scent of strong fae wards waved to me from behind closed doors. We passed through several wards on the way to the Commander's office; each time, he dismissed them with a word, and I caught the waft of magic as they sprang up again after we passed.

Tough wards. Lots of eyeballs. Sharp guards. This was going to be *really* hard.

I focused back on their conversation. "... don't care who you are, Lord Brackin, I have been charged with maintaining the safety of these gates. I must be satisfied that you pose no danger to the Kingdom of Dusk before I can allow you to enter the City." He ushered Brackin into an office and walked inside after him. The footmen both walked in first, leaving me to trail in behind them. It was beyond rude. I was being dismissed as a lowly servant.

I examined the Watch Commander's features closer as he marched back and forth behind his desk and ranted about how important he was. His ears were very pointed, and his coloring... he looked more like a high fae from the other side of the Inbetween than one of the Shadow Fae. In Dusk and beyond, in the Kingdoms closer to Winter, most of the people were paler, with darker eyes and hair, but not always. The ears were a dead giveaway, though.

He wasn't originally from the Kingdom of Dusk. But the man was talking as if he'd founded the City himself.

I decided to try a little micro-aggression to take the wind out of his sails. "It's nice that you've learned to navigate your way around such a big city," I cut in, keeping my voice light. "Have you been in the West very long, Commander?"

His bright-blue eyes fixed on me for the first time, and

he stopped pacing and glared at me. "Who are you?" he asked rudely.

Brackin waved his hand toward me, a dismissive gesture. "This is my Little Daffodil. She is"—he glanced down at me, wrinkling his nose—"an old employee of mine. Like I said, she is Gloom's candidate for the Trials."

The Commander glared at me, then turned back to Brackin. "You have to understand how suspicious this looks, Lord Brackin."

"How so?"

"Look at her. She looks like she's been dragged backwards through an ash pit." His lip curled. "She is wearing trousers. The town of Dew sent an ogre princess as their candidate, but at least the ogre is wearing a nice gown." His eyes narrowed on Brackin, ignoring me. "You show up here, last minute, with a ragged, wretched child—a mortal, to boot—and declare she's your candidate? Even for Gloom, that's embarrassing, Lord Brackin. No other municipality would stoop so low. I can only assume malevolent intent."

Brackin was needled. "Gloom is a respectable town—"

"Respectable enough not to offer up a mortal as a candidate. Come on, man. If you don't have malevolent intent, I can only assume she's a prisoner, and you're trying to get rid of her in some sort of bloody, horrific spectacle." His eyes flicked towards me scornfully. "The other competitors will eviscerate her immediately."

"It is not for you to deny us entrance to the Trials." Brackin drew himself up so he was as tall as possible. "I am Lord of Gloom—"

"The second born son," the commander sneered.

"Well, the firstborn couldn't rustle up a candidate," Brackin said testily. "So I did what he could not."

"And *this* is the best you could come up with?"

"You'd be surprised, Commander. Under all that grime,

she's actually rather pretty, and there's a bountiful figure under those masculine clothes." Brackin's gaze fell on me, and he scowled. "And she's feisty. You'll have to take my word for that."

The commander was silent for a moment. "If you insist on embarrassing your town so badly, I must search your things. Then, you can be on your way to your brother's residence."

Two guards stepped forwards and took our bags off the footman. Another guard pulled at my backpack. I itched to keep it on me but relented. I should have expected this.

Relaxing, I let him take the bag, and he patted me down. The hidden sheathes at my back were spelled to avoid this kind of casual inspection, so the guard ignored them, but his hand found the bulge in my cargo pants pocket where I'd stashed my World Key amulet. He pulled it out and held it up. "A World Key, Commander."

The commander took it off him, examining it carefully. He held it up in front of my face. "Is this yours? Or did you steal it from someone?"

"It's a World Key," I said, trying to shove down my rising temper. "World Keys don't work for anyone they're not programmed for."

"I know that," he snapped.

"Then why would I steal it from someone else?"

He hesitated for a second. "Well, then." The commander's expression turned smug. "Were you planning some sort of last-minute escape from your fate in the Trials?"

"Of course not," I said, keeping my voice light to disguise the lie. *Look at you go; you're getting better at lying.*

"Good." He sneered at me. "Because I regret to inform you, girl, that it won't work, anyway. I have multiple layers of portal-blocking dome wards ringing this City. Nothing goes in or out without me inspecting it first." He chuckled, as if he'd foiled my plan.

I know that, dickhead, I could smell the dome from a mile away. Why do you think I've been scoping out the escape routes out of the city?

He laughed again and tossed the World Key back at me, watching my face for signs of discomfort.

I caught the amulet and slid it back into my pocket with relief. This guy was such an asshole. "I would expect nothing less of the Kingdom Watch Commander, sir. I'm sure you take the responsibility of keeping this city safe very seriously." A petty urge overwhelmed me, and I gave in to it. "Although, if you're open to suggestions, if I were you I'd look at replacing the eastern section of the city wall. I noticed the stone there is very shale-heavy, and shale is prone to combustion. If the Scorch hits that wall dead-on, the stone could explode. Then you'd have a burning-hot god-like entity rampaging through this city faster than you can say, 'World Key.'"

The Commander stared at me, the smugness melting. I watched him cycle through scorn, doubt, realization, chagrin, then rage.

Brackin let out a giggle. "She's got you there, Commander. In Gloom, we found coal deposits in our south wall two years ago, and we replaced them immediately. I take no chances with my town's safety."

The Watch Commander turned away and said nothing.

The search continued. A blank-faced guard pulled out my granola bars, my change of clothes, my battered flask, and dropped them on the stone floor, wrinkling his nose with distaste. To my horror, he pulled out the journal, still double-bagged in the Ziplock, and held it up. "Sir." He threw it.

The watch commander caught it and examined it. "What is this?"

I unclenched my jaw. "A journal."

He rubbed the plastic wrap. "Why is it sealed inside this encasing?"

"I don't want to get it wet."

He frowned and rubbed the plastic, trying to figure out how to open the bag. "I must examine this journal to make sure this is not espionage of some sort."

"Don't you dare," I snapped. My fingers twitched towards my back. *If this fucker reads that journal before Romeo, I'll fill him with so many holes, you'll be able to use him as a watering can.* "That journal is personal and private." And it might contain information about Romeo's dad, which could be very valuable information to whoever held it.

The Watch Commander smiled, clearly happy to finally have something on me. "I am within my rights to confiscate anything I deem necessary to ensure this town's safety." He lifted his head, sneered at me, and waved the journal. "I think I will keep this for the duration of your stay." Turning his back to me, he shoved it into a drawer in his desk.

Well, fuck.

"If that seal is broken," I said softly. "I will have your head. I promise you that."

NINETEEN

"This whole thing is a terrible idea." Brackin was sulky. "I still can't believe I let you persuade me to do this, Daffodil."

We stood in a pretty courtyard, waiting for Brackin's grooms to bring our horses back. Or, rather, Brackin stood, and I crouched, because I was damned tired, and my thighs hurt like hell. It had been a long time since I'd ridden anything besides a motorcycle.

Brackin ran his hands through his long black hair, smoothing it back fussily. "And my Lord Godfeathers has since disappeared, so I cannot be soothed by his sensual presence. I'm stuck with you—the *worst* candidate for the Bride Trials in existence." He glared down at me. "You shouldn't have threatened to behead the Commander. That was unfathomably stupid."

I was seriously regretting that, too. I let my temper get the better of me and provoked him. After he locked the journal in his office drawer with a sadistic grin on his face, he frog-marched us down to the Royal Scribe and had me formally registered to enter the Bride Trials.

It was done; I was committed. I was officially the Gloom Candidate.

"There's no escaping it now, girl," the commander had laughed and walked away, leaving us alone in the courtyard outside the Royal Scribe's residence.

Brackin let out a pained sigh. "I was hoping that once we were inside the City, you'd forget about the Bride Trials, and we wouldn't have to bother with this farce."

Me, too.

It's a minor inconvenience, I told myself. I still had hope that I'd be able to find Romeo, get him out of the City, and take him home before the Trials officially started.

That's if he wants to come home.

A little growl escaped my lips. Before, I was firmly of the belief that he was being held prisoner. Then, I suspected that he hadn't tried to come home because he wanted the chance to take revenge on the man who abandoned his mother and left him a penniless orphan.

My mind went in circles, thinking of all the *ifs* and *buts*. Now, there was another doubt niggling at me. What if he didn't want to leave? What if he was staying here voluntarily?

The circle plunged into a spiral. Who would leave this? A glorious Kingdom, two-dozen beautiful princesses about to compete for your hand in marriage?

Nope, we're not doing that. Brain-Daphne nudged me. *We already decided we're not doing that anymore.*

That rock-hard sense of conviction settled back into my heart. That's right. I remembered who I was. Even if I wasn't sure of Romeo—and I was—I was sure of myself. I'd come here to get Romeo back. If he didn't want to leave, it wouldn't be because I wasn't the baddest bitch in all the realms. Whatever was in that journal, Romeo had to read it so he could make an informed decision.

Get the journal, find Romeo, let him decide what to do next.

Try not to die in the Trials, I added in my head morosely.

"My brother is going to kill me." Brackin kicked a potted fern in frustration as his grooms finally appeared, leading the horses. "Let's just get this over with," he sighed.

We mounted our horses again and walked slowly through the city. The horses were exhausted, and, despite Brackin trying to urge his mare into a trot, they were disinclined to go any faster.

The rolling movement of the gelding underneath me was lulling me into a stupor. Even the clip-clop of hooves on cobblestones soothed me, like a hypnotist's ticking clock.

It was getting late by Shadow Fae standards. Here, in the Winter side of the Inbetween, the people slept through dawn and midday and were most active in the late afternoon. In the Kingdom of Dusk, twilight stretched out to last for several long hours, and it felt magical. By the same token, on the other side of the Inbetween, in the Kingdom of Dawn, sunrise felt like it took up most of the day, and they retired before the shadows started to lengthen.

But I was on mortal realm time, and I was so tired, my eyes felt like they'd dried out almost completely—gritty balls in ungreased sockets.

Still grumbling under his breath, Lord Brackin led us through the city, following winding cobblestone paths. Because of the towering buildings and my low perspective, I could only catch a glimpse of the palace every now and then.

The sight of it stole the air from my lungs. Made of pitch-black obsidian, the pointed towers and swooping arches of the palace gleamed and glittered in the soft, warm lights of the city. The crystal in my palm pointed firmly in that direction. He was there.

We rode on, emerged from a tunnel of archways, and reached a sprawling piazza in front of an enormous grand building in the middle-west side of the city. Brackin stopped and dismounted.

I stared up at the dark slate building. It looked a little like a taller, darker, more dramatic version of the New York State Library. "Is this your brother's house?"

He grimaced. "The Lord of Gloom has taken a floor of it as his residence, yes."

Ah, like an apartment. More footmen rushed out to take our horses away, and we walked up the steps, in between two huge black marble statues. "This is not going to be pleasant," Brackin muttered as we walked inside.

Lord Gloom's residence was on the fourth floor. A guard at the door grimaced when he saw us coming. He knocked on the door, opened it, and announced us. "My Lord of Gloom, your brother is here."

A deep voice echoed out towards us. "Brackin?" Lord Bron sounded shocked.

We walked inside. Unlike the rest of the city, which seemed to be furnished in dark colors, deep scarlets, forest green, midnight blues, Lord Gloom's apartment was an odd mix of light and dark—blond wood floors with deep ruby rugs and licorice walls with flowery spring watercolor paintings. The effect was a little unsettling.

A tall man strode out into the hallway. He looked almost exactly like Brackin—very tall, pale skin, huge dark eyes. His chin was slightly less pointed, though, and, unlike Brackin, he wasn't dressed like a pirate. Instead, he wore a deep blood-red tunic embroidered with a delicate black ivy pattern.

Bron didn't look pleased to see his brother at all. He scowled at us. "What the hell are you doing here, Brackin?"

I dropped into a curtsy, determined not to make the same mistake I had with the Watch Commander. I was wildly aware that I was hanging by a thread—I was starving, exhausted, a little scalded from the Scorch, and my thighs hurt so much from the ride here, I was worried I'd never be able to walk normally again. My Kawasaki didn't buck as much as my gelding did. I felt like I'd been gently punched in the vagina for five hours straight.

I needed rest desperately. If Lord Bron threw me out, I'd have to sleep in an alleyway on cold cobblestones.

Agreed, my brain said. *Let's play nice until we can get some rest. Then, stabby stab stab.*

"Hello, brother!" Brackin's too-cheerful tone made me cringe. "I hope you are well."

"Answer my question," Bron said, glaring at him. "What are you doing here?"

Brackin spread his hands, a casual gesture. "Am I not allowed to visit my beloved sibling in his courtly residence?"

"You can disperse with the faux pleasantries, Brackin," Bron growled. "Your presence at court always means trouble."

Brackin gasped. "You insult me, brother!"

Under my lowered lashes, I saw a high fae woman in a gorgeous yellow gown glide out behind Bron. She put her hand on his arm, resting it there lightly. This must be Lord Bron's wife. Her coloring was fair, with thick honey-colored hair and hazel eyes.

"My husband speaks the truth, Brackin," she said. "Whenever you appear, trouble is sure to follow in your wake." Her tone filled with distaste. "I see you have brought

137

a whore with you." She tisked. "And on my new rug, too. How could you, Brackin?"

Ouch.

"This is no whore." Brackin feigned offence. "This is my Little Daffodil. She's—"

"I don't want to hear about your sexual deviancy," Bron cut him off. "Whatever she tickles you with, brother, I don't want to know." He paused. His expression grew thoughtful. "But, for what it's worth, our mother will be glad you are showing interest in a female, at the very least." I could feel his eyes on me. "Is she a mortal girl?"

"Yes, she is."

"Human?"

"Of shapeshifter stock, I believe. Is that right, Daffodil?"

Lady Pesh pursed her lips. "Hmm. A human would be preferable. Shapeshifters are ugly, savage beasts. Stand up, girl," she snapped. "Let us look at you."

I straightened up, clenching my fists to stop them reaching for my blades.

Lady Pesh's hazel eyes felt like hate-lasers. "What sort of shapeshifter are you?"

I met her gaze calmly. "I was a wolf, ma'am. But, due to—"

She waved her hand, dismissing me. "A dog. Fabulous. You've brought a dog whore into my residence. I suppose she tickles you with her tail, does she, Brackin?"

Wow. Bitch.

He gasped, clutching his heart. "You wound me, Lady Pesh."

"Oh, I wish I could wound you. But your mother will not let me. The house of Pesh must have a spare," she said testily.

"Why are you here, Brackin?" Lord Bron stepped closer. His eyes narrowed suspiciously. "In fact... *How* are you here?

The Watch is not allowing anyone to enter the City right now. The Bride Trials start the day after tomorrow. The Commencement Ball will be held tomorrow night, and security has tightened so much, I've heard that even the caterers are unable to get deliveries from outside the city gates."

Brackin took a deep breath. Then, he edged backwards a little. "My Lord and Lady Pesh," he said, his voice trembling. He edged back a little more and waved his hand towards me. "May I present our official candidate for the Bride Trials. Daffodil will represent Gloom."

Silence fell like an anvil.

CHAPTER

TWENTY

The silence didn't last long enough for my liking. I could still hear them all screaming from the drawing room.

Lady Pesh, unable to look at me for a second longer, ordered her brownie maid to take me away to the servants' quarters, and the brownie dutifully dragged me away. Because a brownie must be available to their domestic master twenty-four hours a day, their rooms were designed so that they could hear their master's call, no matter the time of day or night. Consequently, the sound from the drawing room funneled down the hallway, growing, rather than decreasing in volume.

I could hear every word Lord Bron and Lady Pesh said.

"What in the hell were you thinking, Brackin? Why would you bring a mortal shapeshifter girl here and enter her in the Bride Trials?"

"We can fix this," Lady Pesh muttered anxiously. "This news does not have to extend beyond what you told the Watch Commander."

"It's too late," Brackin said. "He forced us straight to the scribe to register her. She's Gloom's official competitor."

Lady Pesh let out a scream. "No! This cannot be. This cannot be happening!"

Brackin's tone turned sulky. "The responsibility of finding a candidate was supposed to be yours, Lady Pesh. You did not fulfill your duty to Gloom, so I did."

Her screech hurt my ears. "Because there is no female in that damned town good enough to even bother considering! There are no high fae women in Gloom, only common fae, for starters. It's better to offer no candidate for the Trials than to offer.... that *thing*. A mortal. A dog shifter!" She let out another scream of rage. "Brackin, what were you thinking?"

Bron let out a bark of bitter laughter. "I know what he was thinking. She serviced him, of course, and in his post-coital fog, she asked him to submit her as a candidate. The changeling girl probably thinks she's got a chance to win the hand of the Prince." He paused. "Or was this your idea?"

"No, it was hers." Brackin threw me under the bus. "Look, brother... what's done is done."

Bron thundered. "We'll be the laughingstock of the whole City!"

"She'll die quickly. It's okay. She'll die quickly." Lady Pesh was starting to hyperventilate. "Perhaps, in a few years, everyone will forget..."

I tuned them out. "I'm Daphne," I said to the female brownie, as she bustled along beside me down the long hallway, moving like a little tank. She wore a long dark-gray smock with a periwinkle-blue apron, another eye watering light-and-dark color combination which I now understood was the result of Lady Pesh's Spring preferences on the house of Gloom. It was odd. Lord and Lady Pesh had been married for decades, and she hadn't changed any house colors before.

The brownie maid shot me a look but didn't bother

replying. Brownie beauty standards were the complete opposite to ours, and this servant—with her piggy black eyes, crooked nose, jagged chin, and her uneven, dry, pock-marked skin—was probably considered a great beauty to her kin. Her whole face looked like a half-eaten apple that had been left out in the sun.

"What's your name?" I asked her, switching from the common fae tongue to her own brownie dialect.

She glared at me for a moment, still walking beside me. A silent struggle went on behind her eyes.

"It's okay," I said. "I understand. Lady Pesh ordered you to take me to the servant quarters, but you heard what Lord Brackin said about me being Gloom's Bride Trial candidate, so you don't know if I'm a servant or a guest of this house."

Brownies lived to serve the household—their masters and guests were treated with almost god-like worship. They were expected to be very rude to everyone else. This female was having a cultural crisis because she wasn't sure how to treat me.

"How about this," I said to her. "You can treat me as a servant while I stay in the servants' quarters. If I get moved to a guest room, you can treat me like a guest, and I won't hold anything against you."

The brownie exhaled with relief. "My name is Steven."

I stifled the huff of laughter before it escaped. "Nice to meet you, Steven. You know what? I have to say, you're probably the ugliest brownie I think I've seen in my entire life."

Steven screwed up her face, her cheeks turned a horrible shade of greenish mauve. She was blushing. "Thank you." We reached the end of the corridor, and she waved her hand towards a doorway. "This way, Daphne."

The servants' quarters were set up like a separate apartment to the main house. We walked into a small living room, bare and austere, with only a sturdy wooden table and a few small goblin chairs. Brownies never sat down, not until they retired for the night.

Within the living room, separate zones had been established for needlework, appliance maintenance, and spell manufacturing—anything that the household might need. The servants' quarters had a small galley-style kitchen where they could prepare their own food. The Lord and Lady would have their own grand kitchen next to their dining room, so that nothing had time to cool before it could be served.

A dozen other brownies and a couple of goblins were scattered around, all working on something. A small male in the kitchen used a ladle to spoon steaming pumpkin soup into a bowl.

My stomach gave a rumble. "God, that smells good," I muttered.

"You may eat," Steven said a little grudgingly. She jerked forward, then stopped herself, before jerking forward again.

She still wasn't sure how to treat me. She didn't know if she should serve me or not.

I put her out of her misery and dropped a quick curtsy, indicating deference to her as the housekeeper, and grabbed myself a bowl out of the cupboard.

The pumpkin soup was bright orange, fragrant with fresh herbs, and very creamy. The first spoonful I put in my mouth, I almost moaned in pleasure. I ate standing up, just like a brownie, while Steven mended a shoe at the station next to me, watching me. A grudging respect shone in her eye.

I finished the soup quickly—both because I was starving and because brownies always wolfed their food down and I knew Steven would approve if I ate fast—then washed my bowl and spoon in the sink, carefully dried both, and put them away.

Through another archway, I could see dormitory-style bedrooms with a row of different-sized cots. A yawn shook me. I was so tired. The smells and sounds in the servants' quarters soothed me so much, my eyes kept rolling back in my head.

Steven seemed to be hesitating. "It's okay," I told her. "I'll take whatever bunk you can give me. I'm really tired, and apparently, I've got a big day tomorrow."

I'd already accepted the fact that I might be forced to show up to the Commencement Ball, at the very least. I still had to steal the journal back and wait for Romeo to emerge from wherever the Shadow Fae were hiding him before I could get out of here.

Steven screwed up her face. "Wait here." She bustled off to the dormitory.

I hope she's going to give us a goblin bed, my brain yawned. *We'll need a good sleep if we have to go to the Commencement Ball. Need to have our wits about us.*

She was right; we'd have to be at our most razor-sharp. The Commencement Ball was the chance for the potential brides to meet and size each other up before the Trials started. It wasn't a test, or a game, or a pageant, like the rest of the Trials. In theory, it was just a chance for the girls to get to know each other.

In practice, the competitors used the Ball to show off their assassination skills. While the competitors were encouraged to kill each other during the Trials, full blood-shed was frowned upon at the Commencement Ball. So, we'd gather in a grand ballroom, eat, drink, dance, and try to kill each other without anyone noticing. More often than not, at least half the competitors were wiped out during the Ball.

Unfortunately for me, Romeo wouldn't be there. The potential groom wasn't allowed to see the brides before the Trials started. Nobody wanted the groom or his parents to set his sights on one candidate, only to find her taken out of the competition before it began.

Hopefully, I'd have time before the Commencement Ball tomorrow to sneak out, break into the Commander's office and get that journal back.

Maybe we should try to get into the palace so we can skip this whole Bride Trial bloodbath, Brain-Daphne suggested. *Wait, no, you're right. Too many wards, too many guards.*

I smiled. Me and my Brain weren't arguing anymore; we hadn't done that since we left.

I really had pulled myself together. My heart, my brain, and my gut were finally presenting a united front, with an iron core of certainty. It had taken a while, but I knew how to deal with the darkness inside of me now. The evils could wriggle and writhe in the cell of my soul all they wanted; they were never getting out. I wasn't stuck inside with them anymore.

I knew who I was. I was the box. I was their prison. And they were never getting out.

I tuned back into my surroundings and watched Steven stomp out of the dormitory, heading towards me. She still looked worried. "The Commencement Ball." Her eyes ran up and down my body, then flicked over my backpack. "Your gown. It will be crumpled in there."

"Uh, no. I don't actually have a gown in my backpack."

"Where is it? I must press it."

I made a face. "I don't have one."

"You don't have a gown?" Her eyes widened. "What will you wear?"

I shrugged. "Honestly, Steven... It's kind of the last thing I'm worried about right now." I assumed that if it came down to it, Lady Pesh would throw me one of her old gowns so I wouldn't bring too much shame on her House, but Lady Pesh was a whole foot taller than me and thin as a rake.

Wrap yourself in a curtain and try to stay alive. Easy.

"You need a gown," Steven said, gnawing on her non-existent lip. "The Lord and Lady are already embarrassed. You're not a guest, so I shouldn't help you. But if you are not dressed properly, they will be even more embarrassed. But they do not like you, so I shouldn't help you. But if you—"

I held up my hand, palm out, to stop her brain loop. "It's okay, Steven. If you feel like you have too much energy to expend tonight, then I would love it if you were to make me whatever gown you think might be suitable." I stumbled through my knowledge of brownie culture. "Don't use any fabric that is earmarked for use for the household. Recycle an old curtain, or some trash, or something like that, and they won't be mad. If the Lord and Lady permit me to wear the gown, then they will be pleased with you. If they don't, you can sell it and give the money to them, and they will be pleased with you."

Steven's eyes cleared, and she nodded. "Yes. I think I do have too much energy to expend." She clapped her hands and barked out a series of orders to another half-dozen little brownies clambering around the servant's quarters. While she instructed the servants, she whipped out a tape measure, wrapping it around my hips and boobs, then she showed me the cot I could sleep in, thankfully giving me a goblin bed rather than a brownie one. It would be much softer, and it would have a pillow. Steven left the dormitory immediately, snapping more orders at the staff in the brownie tongue.

From the sounds of it, I was going to be going to the ball wearing a lovely gown made of pumpkin peel, dried tomato

146

skins, and the scraps from the chimneysweep's new fireproof apron she'd sewn up yesterday.

Better than going nude, I suppose. Brain-Daphne let out a yawn of her own. *Never liked fighting in the nude, did we?*

I was too tired to think about it. The sounds of a working bee taking place outside were so soothing. I took off most of my clothes, burrowed under the blankets and, despite the impending humiliation and imminent danger, I felt myself relax completely.

There weren't too many bright spots in the time when I was lost off-world, but the best ones were always times like this—when I was surrounded by humble, hardworking people, and I was bone tired after doing my absolute best to serve the day as well as I could.

That's all we can ask of ourselves, really, isn't it? my brain said sleepily. *That we always try our best.*

And I had. I'd made it to Faerie, I'd escaped the Scorch, I'd found a way into the Kingdom of Dusk. And tomorrow, I'd get that journal back and survive another day.

TWENTY-ONE

The clanging of a bell woke me. I was warm—almost too warm—and far too comfortable. Automatically, I scanned myself, checking my injuries and finding them almost gone.

Sleep was the best healer. I wanted more.

The softest feathers tickled my bare chest. My arms were full of warmth, like I was holding a downy hot water bottle. It was such a delicious, soothing, comforting sensation, my brain hung up a *do not disturb sign*, let out a moan of pleasure, and snuggled back down, inviting oblivion. Hugging my feathery hot water bottle, I rolled over and went back to sleep.

I let out a little groan as the bell clanged again. My brain poked me. *That's the falling sun bell. It's the afternoon. The household has risen.*

I squeezed my hot water bottle again.

It farted.

And just like that, the floaty bliss of slumber drifted away, replaced by something that smelled like rancid beans.

Morning, baby girl. And don't say it. It's your fault; I told you fae beer makes me gassy.

"Dwayne?" I cracked one eye open. A razor-sharp orange beak, spiked tongue, and one fathomless, black beady eye stared me right in my face.

Despite the smell, I was so glad to see him. I cuddled him harder, squeezing my eyes shut again. The temptation to go back to sleep was almost overwhelming. "Where have you been, sir? I've been worried about you." I yawned and burrowed my face into his silky feathers.

I told you. I've been looking for the Winter Court. Gotta find Maeve and put the moves on her, remember?

"Right." I licked my lips and opened my eyes again. "I thought you might still be running away from the Scorch."

Huh?

I frowned. "Last time I saw you, you were leading the Scorch away from us. That horrifying white bull would have incinerated us."

Cow.

I cocked my head. "Huh?"

It's a cow, not a bull. He winked at me. **I got close enough to check.**

Huh. I frowned. "Everyone said it was a bull. I suppose it was because it had horns... but cows can have horns. Anyway, I suppose the gender of the apocalyptic horror doesn't really matter, does it?" I smiled at him. "You saved us, Dwayne."

Oh. He hesitated. **I wasn't actually trying to lead it away.**

"You weren't?" I was confused. "What were you doing, then?"

Well, after I pissed on it, trying to put it out— which, obviously, didn't work at all—it occurred to me that old Kinky Tickles might start begging me to piss on

149

him, too. I wasn't in the mood for his shit, so I just... took off.

"I see." I pressed my lips together. "I thought you were heroically sacrificing yourself and letting the bull chase you."

Ah, nope. Sorry. He shook his head. **I was just bailing on my stalker. Look, being worshipped is fun for a minute or two, but I was sick of Old Tickle's shit by the time we left Gloom. And you can't blame a guy for having preferences. The tickling was an experiment, but you know I prefer women. Once I find Queen Maeve, I'll be happy for us to wee on each other.**

I yawned again, happy to hear he hadn't defied my expectations and somehow found the Unseelie Queen after all. "The mission isn't going well, I take it?"

He frowned. **I can't find the Winter Court. I looked all night, got frustrated, and thought I might as well come back here and check on you.**

I hugged him one more time and let him go, rolling over. If the falling sun bell had just gone off, it meant I had about four hours before twilight began. I needed to get moving so I could try to get that journal back.

Need some tips, baby girl. You've been there, right?

It wasn't something I liked thinking about, but I didn't say that. I got up and dressed quickly in my spare pants and shirt, noticing that yesterday's clothes were on the little bedside table next to me and had been freshly laundered and pressed. "Yeah." I felt comfortable giving Dwayne some tips, since there was almost zero chance he was going to find the Winter Court anyway. "Remember, it's not in any particular direction. You have to follow the frostbite tingle on the tip of your nose. Follow the intense urge for rest and regeneration."

I tried. But that stupid hot cow threw so much heat,

I couldn't find a chill to follow. And you know how much stamina I've got, little one. I'll try again later. He propped his head up on one wing, sprawling out on my bed. **So, what's up with you?**

"I was forced to enter the Bride Trials," I told him.

What do you mean, forced? I thought you wanted to do that. Isn't that why we're here?

"It was just meant to be a way into the City, Dwayne." I braided my hair quickly and sat down to lace up my boots. "I'm here to find Romeo and bring him home."

Oh, right.

I glanced at him. "I don't suppose you could find him, can you? Maybe get a message to him?"

Dwayne shrugged. **The big guy isn't on my radar like you are, little one. I mean, I could go around, kick open a few doors, ask a few questions, dangle a few guards off towers—**

"It's okay," I said hastily. The last thing I needed was for Dwayne to get captured and held prisoner, too. "He'll be under heavy guard in the palace, anyway. I'll see him when the Trials start tomorrow."

My heart clenched in my chest. God, I missed him so much. Romeo was so close, but still so far away.

I glanced at Dwayne again. It was worth asking. "Do you think you could get into the Watch Commander's office without being seen?"

Dwayne's eyes widened. **You want me to eat *who?***

I sighed. "Never mind. Forget I asked." Stealth had never been Dwayne's strong suit, anyway.

He got comfortable again, snuggling down in the nest of my blankets. **So, tell me about these Bride Trials, baby girl.**

"It's seven events over seven days," I said. "And it starts tonight. First, the Commencement Ball. Tomorrow, we open with the first of six Trials. From what I've seen before, they usually do them in roughly the same order, usually the physical challenges first, to prove that they're strong enough to bear the weight of the crown. Then, once the competition has thinned out, they'll do one-on-one dates and diplomacy stuff." I stood up. "And by 'thinned out,' I mean once most of the competitors are dead."

Sounds like fun. Wait. He narrowed his eyes for a second. **Should I be worried?**

"Sure. But you don't have to worry about me. I can hold my own. And, as soon as I get the journal and find Romeo, we'll get out of here." I glanced out the window, checking the sun's position in the sky. "In fact, I better get moving."

Want some company?

"I'm going stealth mode," I told him, wrapping my cloak around my shoulders. "The watch commander's barracks are heavily warded, so I'm going to have to sneak past the wards." I had no idea how I was going to get in without being seen. I'd have to wing it.

The sound of a brownie running down the hallway caught my attention. "Daphne!" Steven, charged into the dormitory, her eyes wild. "Hurry. They are waiting for you."

"Who is?"

"The Lord and Lady have sent for you. You must see them now." She tugged on my arm, pulling me out of the room.

"Now?"

"Right now."

Damn. There was no point resisting her—Steven had been given an order, and she was going to follow it. She'd knock me out and drag me to her master unconscious if she had to. I'd just have to sneak out after they were done with me.

Steven dragged me down the hallway towards the drawing room. "What do they want?"

"To speak."

"About what?"

"It is not for me to know."

I sighed and let her haul me into the drawing room. I didn't want her to get in trouble.

The afternoon sun warmed the licorice-colored walls of the drawing room a little, but the watercolors on the walls were still an eye-wateringly offensive decor choice, and they did nothing to lighten the oppressively hostile atmosphere.

Lady Pesh and Lord Bron sat stiffly in wingback armchairs. A tea service sat on the table in front of them, and my stomach gave a rumble when I caught the scent of honey-and-cinnamon-scented flaky pastries. Brackin stood in the corner looking sulky, as if he were in trouble.

The Lord and Lady didn't stand up when I entered. They didn't even look at me, they just glared at the fireplace.

Steven dragged me into the middle of the room and dropped a curtsy. "The girl, as requested, my Lord and Lady."

Lady Pesh stiffened, took a deep breath through her nose as if bracing herself for something terrible, and turned her gaze towards me. "Now listen here, girl," she said, her voice icy. "I know you don't understand what you've done, and you are too stupid to comprehend the consequences of your actions. I do not care that you have signed your own death warrant by entering the Bride Trials. What I *do* care about is that your foolish machinations will bring shame to my Lord Pesh's municipality." Her tone vibrated with rage. "You manipulated the Lord's brother and tricked him into entering you into the Trials as Gloom's competitor. Considering everything you have done, you are lucky Lord Bron and I don't send you straight to the dungeons."

She couldn't do anything to me; I was officially registered now. The Royal Scribes would ask questions if I didn't show up to the Ball.

I was well rested enough to risk messing with her a little. I made my eyes big and round. "You want to send Gloom's Bride Trial competitor to the dungeons?"

"That's not what I said," she snapped.

I gasped and clutched my chest. "But what will the Court say? If the King and Queen hear that you entered a competitor and then sent her to the dungeons before they could meet her—"

Lady Pesh whipped her hand up, cutting me off. "Hold your tongue, changeling wretch, or I will rip it from your mouth."

Oh, I'm begging you to try it, bitch, my brain sniggered.

I let out another dramatic gasp. "You'll rip out my tongue? But how will I speak to the other brides at the Ball? I know they will gossip, and I can imagine the King and Queen will want to know why Gloom's competitor can't speak anymore."

Like most palaces, the High Fae court was packed with narcissists and gossips. You couldn't show any weakness, you couldn't put a foot out of place, or the vultures would pounce.

Lord Bron put his head in his hands. "There is no way this will not end badly for Gloom," he muttered. "We will be the laughingstock of the kingdom."

"We have no choice but to make sure the damage is contained." Lady Pesh stood up, faced me, and jabbed a finger in my face. "Now, listen here, girl, and listen well. There is no saving your life now. You are going to die tonight. Considering the harm you have done to Gloom's reputation, you owe us to go quietly, with dignity. So, this is what will happen. You will attend the Ball," she said, her face tight with rage. "You will stay in the background; you will *not* bring any attention to yourself at all. And most importantly, you will die quickly and without a fuss." She arched her eyebrow. "Do you hear me?"

I gave her a brilliant smile. "I hear you." Time was slipping away from me—I needed to wrap this up quickly so I could get the journal.

My fingers brushed the spot where the quartz crystal sat on my chest. *I'm coming, Romeo.*

Lady Pesh shot Brackin a pissed look. "Lord Brackin will accompany you to the Ball, since he was the one who got us into this mess."

Brackin pouted in the corner. He kept his mouth shut.

Huh. That's gonna cause a stir.

My eyes flicked back to Lord Bron, who still had his head in his hands. It was customary for the ruler of the municipality to escort their competitor. The Court of Dusk would definitely talk if the second son performed this duty instead of the Lord of Gloom. It looked like Lady Pesh had weighed the options and decided it was worth the gossip to keep her husband away from the embarrassing spectacle that was me.

I glanced back at Brackin. He met my eyes, and his expression changed to something else, something I couldn't decipher.

"Now go." Lady Pesh waved her hand, shooing me away as if I were a buzzing fly. I turned and hurried out.

CHAPTER

TWENTY-TWO

I hid in the entrance hall for a moment and decided to get out while I could. I needed to get that journal. Creeping down the hall, I wrapped my cloak around me tightly and made my way to the entrance. Pausing, I listened at the door, waiting for the guard to make his rounds as he walked to the window and back again.

His footsteps grew louder, then drifted away. *Okay, now!*

I cracked open the door and peeked out. The guard was walking away from me, heading for the massive row of windows that looked out on the piazza. *Let's do this.*

I'd only taken two steps out the front door when a gnarled hand appeared out of nowhere and grabbed me by the upper arm and hauled me back inside. "No, you don't, miss." Steven tugged me backwards into the Pesh residence. "We've got work to do."

I stumbled on my feet as she dragged me inside. Holy moly, she was strong. "Work?" I spluttered.

"Yes. Hard work. Possibly the hardest work I've ever been given."

Oh, great. "I'm being put to work in the household as a servant?"

Not again, my brain groaned.

"Of course not," Steven snapped. "There is no time."

"What work are we doing, then?"

"We must get you ready for the ball." She dragged me effortlessly back down the hallway.

Oh. Now it made sense. Brownies were freakishly strong when they were under orders. "Did Lady Pesh tell you to get me ready?"

"No. Lord Brackin did. He is being forced to accompany you, and, like Lord Bron, he does not wish to be humiliated."

Goddamn you, Brackin. I itched to stab him. "Where is Lord Brackin?" I asked, my tone sugary sweet.

"He has gone to make arrangements for the ball. Don't worry about him, Daphne. We have enough to worry about with you!" She started to run, dragging me behind her. My heels squeaked on the floorboards.

I gave up trying to move my legs and let her drag me. "Steven, the ball doesn't start for another four hours."

"I know!" A hint of panic thrummed through her tone. "We have barely any time to get ready!"

She shoved me into the servant's quarters, glared at me, then, she put her fingers in her mouth and gave a sharp whistle.

A little tornado of brownies, pixies, gnomes, and goblins whipped through the room, coming to an abrupt halt in a circle around me. Two dozen pairs of eyes assessed me critically.

"Bath first," Steven declared. "Scrub every inch of her skin. Polish her until she gleams."

Uh oh.

A swarm of pixies enveloped me. A thousand tiny hands unlaced my boots, unzipped my pants, unbuttoned my shirt, and unclipped my holsters, and in half a second, I was completely naked. Then, they grabbed my arms and legs and lifted me into the air. I floated, kicking and flailing awkwardly, squeaking in protest, into the bathrooms.

A handful of other servants were already in there, bustling around the sunken pool that served as a bathtub and diverting the little stream that ran through the bathroom to fill up the tub. A wizened old brownie hobbled forwards with a smoked-glass jar, opened it, and tossed a handful of sparkling green dust into the bath. A gorgeous dusky-sweet scent enveloped me—midnight rose, marshmallow, and caramel. A million bubbles erupted from the bathtub.

The pixies flew me over to the bathtub and dropped me. I splashed into the warm water and sank like a stone.

I surrendered. There was no point fighting them. Steven had been given an order, and she'd rather die than fail the task she'd been set. My only option was to cooperate. If I got ready early enough, I might be able to sneak out before the ball and go get the journal.

After I submitted to enduring the most intense grooming of my life, I actually started to enjoy it a little. The brownies scrubbed my skin with a soft brush, removing days worth of grime, then rubbed a mixture of tiny soft beads and foamy cream all over me, exfoliating at least three layers of skin. I shut my eyes when a half-dozen pixies whizzed in with cut-throat razors but didn't feel anything when they shaved my legs.

I lay back and listened to the brownies and gnomes gossip about the trials. The servants had their own ideas as to which competitors had the edge. I listened carefully, picking up some interesting tidbits here and there. Apparently, the former Queen Carissa's young daughter had entered, but she was just a child. The town of Starlight had attempted to register a troll as their competitor, but the troll had gotten bored on the journey to Dusk and knocked her sponsor's head clean off his shoulders. The Duchess of Gale had purchased every single available poison from every apothecary in the city, cleaning out all lethal stock available.

Two young gnomes shampooed my hair, their strong fingers massaging my scalp. It felt so good, I had to stop myself from moaning.

Steven plopped herself into the bathtub to give me a pedicure. While she poked and prodded, scraped and filed, polished and painted my toenails, she whistled a happy tune. "I'm glad you're enjoying yourself," I said to her.

"I like challenges. And I like being efficient. I'm doing two jobs in one, Daphne. Killing two birds with one stone." She grinned at me. "If I do a thorough job tonight, I won't have to groom you for your casket tomorrow."

Cheeky cow. I couldn't help but smile back. "You don't think I'm going to survive the Ball?"

"I've been in service for two hundred years, Daphne," she said, arching my foot so she could see my pinkie toe better. "I've lived through a dozen or so Bride Trials. The females who survive the Commencement Ball are cunning, vicious, cut-throat, magically powerful, and incredibly manipulative." She shot me a look tinged with compassion. "Don't take it as an insult that I don't think you'll live through the night."

"Your faith in me is overwhelming." I laughed.

"For what it's worth, I'll be sad when you die." She sighed. "You are a nice girl. I have never had a guest in this residence who understands and respects my culture and customs like you do."

I smiled at her. "Thanks, Steven. I do my best."

The gnomes tipped a bucket of warm water over my head, rinsing off the shampoo, then, they squeezed out my hair, and began to comb creamy vanilla-scented conditioner into it. It felt so good, I relaxed back into the bath. There was nothing better than having someone else wash your hair for you.

After an hour, a goblin pulled the plug, and Steven ordered me out of the tub. Three brownies approached me holding fluffy green towels and rubbed me dry. It was lucky I wasn't modest, because for the next hour or so I stood in the nude and was waxed, buffed, toned, and moisturized until my skin was soft and shiny.

Steven dithered over what to do with my hair. Apparently, it was the fashion to have it scraped back severely off the face, braided in an intricate pattern and tucked away. And, for the Ball, it was probably safer to do that in case one of the competitors tried to set fire to it.

Steven tapped her finger on her crooked chin, thinking. "Your hair is too nice to scrape back. It's the color of nautical twilight, an official shade of the Kingdom of Dusk. It's really your only advantage in the Trials."

"Thanks, Steven," I muttered.

"It is the only good thing about you, so we must play up this single advantage," she said, whipping out a comb. "Just... stay away from anything flammable." For the next hour she attacked me with a round brush, roping in a dozen pixies to flutter their wings to help blow-dry it.

A male brownie wheeled in a little case and proceeded to do my makeup. Every now and then he'd stop, gag dramatically, and ask Steven her opinion. Steven would look at me, dry-heave, nod, and they'd keep working.

Finally, hours later, I was finished—hair, makeup, pedicure, manicure. The sun was sinking lower in the sky. Steven bustled off to get the dress, the one she'd cobbled together out of fireproof apron offcuts and the vegetable peels from last night's dinner.

We had an hour to go before the Ball started. As long as I got dressed quickly, I could sneak out to the commander's office to get the journal. And with luck, I'd bump into Romeo on the way, and we could get the hell out of here.

Steven swept back into the room. "Here we are." Her arms were full of fabric; it trailed behind her.

I gasped. "Steven! What... Is... *That?*"

She let out a mournful cry. "It was the best I could do!"

It was the most strikingly beautiful dress I'd ever seen in my life. The fireproof apron had been made out of aymander hide—a fire breathing fae lizard with impenetrable onyx reptilian skin. Steven had polished the scraps until they shone like black diamonds, then fashioned them into a structured corset-style top, cinched in at the waist and hugging the hips, before flaring down into a mermaid silhouette and a flowing train.

"It's... it's gorgeous," I breathed out. "The aymander hide... and those *colors!*"

The pumpkin peels and tomato skins had been dehydrated, pressed, and cut into ribbons, and stitched artfully onto the gown in fiery whirls and swirls of orange and red from the gown's mid-thigh all the way down to the hem, trailing onto the train.

"All the colors of dusk," Steven said in satisfaction. "It was satisfying to work with them. They have gone out of fashion of late."

"Oh. That's awesome," I said a little weakly.

"No." She gave me an odd look. "It will be good to remind the Court of who we are." She turned the dress around and showed me where she'd sewn the hidden sheathes at the back for my Orion blades.

"Steven, you're a genius."

"Yes, I am. Those pretty knives are your only other

advantage. I hope you know how to use them." She waved the dress at me. "Let's go."

I stepped into it, and she buttoned me up. The aymander leather had been polished until the scales glittered. The hide was lightweight and hugged me like a second skin, propping up my breasts, cinching me in at the waist but letting me breathe at the same time. Steven somehow managed to find the time to make thigh harnesses to hold extra weapons. I kicked out my legs, testing the limits of the dress and found the high split gave me ease of movement without revealing any hidden daggers.

"This gown does skirt the line of decency," Steven grumbled as she fixed all the buttons. "But my Lady Pesh did say you were a whore, so at least you will be comfortable in the style you are accustomed to."

"Gee. Thanks."

I didn't relax until I'd slid each blade into the sheaths at my back. I relaxed even more when Steven showed me the train was detachable. "If you are cornered, you can take it off and use it to distract your enemies.

"Like a matador with a bull. Good idea, Steven. Thanks." I twisted and turned, then did a couple of squats. If I lived through the night, I was definitely taking this gown back home with me. I'd have to find another bag. Maybe Dwayne would carry it for me. Who was I kidding, he would probably want to wear it himself.

There was a loud, frantic knocking at the door of the servant's quarters. "I'm here, Daffodil!"

I groaned.

"Open up! I have come to the rescue," Lord Brackin called out through the door. "It took me a few hours, but I have found a gown that might be suitable for tonight."

162

Steven almost rolled her eyes. I smirked and pointed at her. "I saw that."

"No, you didn't," she muttered.

"We must hurry. Open up! Steven, open this door!"

Moving slower than I'd seen her, she walked to the door. "Yes, master. Coming, master." She opened it.

Lord Brackin barreled in, almost unrecognizable out of his normal pirate clothes. He wore a scarlet courtier tunic and flowing cape with House of Gloom dark-gold trim. His arms were full of a pile of light-blue ruffles. "It took me all afternoon to find something that might fit you, Daffodil," he puffed. "But I think I've got it." He saw me and stopped. His eyes went wide.

I waited for a moment. "Lord Brackin?"

He stared at me in silence for a minute. "Uh... I'm not sure if you should wear that, Little Daffodil," he said, cocking his head, still staring at me. "Now, you know I'm not partial to your species—or your gender, for that matter —but I know what most males like. And even *I* can tell that it will be... provocative." He blinked, swallowed, and finally met my eyes. "The other Brides will be wearing floaty light-colored gowns like this." He shook the pile of blue ruffles in his arms. "Perhaps it would be safer to try to blend in."

"I appreciate you going to the trouble of stealing me a dress, Brackin—"

"I didn't steal it!" he protested. I shot him a look, and he frowned. "Fine," he admitted. "I stole it."

"I'm trusting Steven's judgement on this one," I told him, walking over to the mirror in the corner of the sewing zone. I climbed onto a little platform and looked in the mirror.

Holy cow, I did look sexy. My hair was loose and bouncy with a sweeping side part, the strands falling seductively over one eye and tumbling in soft waves down my back. My bare shoulders shone with a pearly luster, highlighted perfectly by Romeo's necklace, the black leather cord and luminous clear crystal pointing towards my breasts. The shining black leather corset with the fiery sunset colors made me look exactly like a warrior princess of the Kingdom of Dusk.

Brackin cleared his throat. "Perhaps you could add some feathers?"

I turned around and glared at him.

CHAPTER

TWENTY-THREE

B rackin and I travelled to the ball in the Pesh family's carriage. Eight guards accompanied us, three in a carriage ahead, three at the rear. Two more sat up front with our driver, a sour-faced goblin. It felt like overkill.

"Please take the road around the city wall," I told the driver as a footman helped me step inside the carriage.

I'd changed my plan to sneak into the Watch Commander's office. Now, dressed like a legitimate contender for the Bride Trials and someone not to be dismissed, I had a good chance of bluffing my way inside. All I had to do was get into that office. With a little distraction and sleight of hand, I'd be able to pick the lock on the desk drawer.

If all went to hell, I could just knock the Watch Commander out, take the journal, and head to the ball. The Commander struck me as a man who wouldn't raise the alarm because he'd be too embarrassed about getting smacked around by a girl like me.

This is a terrible plan, my brain moaned.

Yes, it is.

We're getting desperate.

We've always been desperate.

I'm glad you agree.

"You know, you never actually told me why you're here, Little Daffodil," Brackin said, glaring at me. "At first, I assumed you were back to ruin my life again. But now, I'm starting to think you're here to ruin someone else's life."

"Why I'm here is none of your business, Brackin," I said shortly.

"You certainly seem hellbent on ruining my brother and his wife." He pursed his lips. "They are faking illness so they don't have to attend the ball."

That was controversial. I arched my brow. "Aren't they worried about what the Court will say?"

"Yes." He gave me an odd look. "That's why they're not coming. I don't know why I have to spell this out for you, Daffodil, but they're too embarrassed to be seen with you. They hope to distance themselves as much as possible."

"I know that." I sighed. "I mean, aren't they worried that they'll offend the King and Queen by not attending?"

"Oh. No, they're not. Well, Bron is concerned," he amended. "But Lady Pesh is unbothered by the idea of causing offence. She is under the impression that King Ronus and Queen Talia may not be sitting on the throne for much longer, anyway."

I frowned. "Because of the broken line of succession, right? But that's why they're holding the Bride Trials, isn't it? Marry off the heir, and the throne will be stronger."

He chuckled humorlessly. "Nobody believes this new heir will restore the balance, Daffodil. Harsh light and heat have crept into the Court of Dusk, and it's making us all uncomfortable. The Scorch is the symptom of a deeper disease for which there might be no cure. It is obvious the King and Queen have no clue how to fix it. We are all losing faith."

166

I gnawed on my lip, thinking about the Scorch. I still didn't know what it could be. It felt important that it manifested as a female, though, but I couldn't put my finger on why. I pondered it for a minute, then saw we were getting close to the city gates.

"Stop here, please," I called out to the driver.

He didn't. We didn't even slow down.

"Hey." I kicked Brackin gently with my foot. "Get the driver to stop. There's something I have to do."

"He's not going to stop." Brackin looked resigned. "He won't take instruction from either of us. He has been ordered to take us directly to the palace for the ball."

My brain growled. *Let's jump out.*

Yes. No, wait.

Oh. Brain-Daphne got there first. *Of course. The Pesh guards will stop us. Fuckers.*

I looked to Brackin for confirmation. "The guards aren't here to keep me safe, are they?"

"No, they are here to make sure we go straight to the ball so you cannot escape. They've also been ordered to toss your corpse in the river on the way home," he added unnecessarily. "Bron and Lady Pesh will not risk us embarrassing them any further. They want this ordeal over with as soon as possible."

I watched through the carriage window as the sentry buildings disappeared in the distance. "Damn it," I hissed through my teeth. There goes my chance at getting the journal tonight.

I needed that journal. Prue was adamant that Romeo needed the information contained in it as soon as possible. I was so close to the palace now, so close to seeing him, and even though I knew he wasn't allowed at the ball, I got the feeling that if he saw me, he'd drag me home without it.

And I'd let him.

But something was going on here in the Inbetween. The Oracle had seen it—that's why she sent me here. Something was causing the imbalance, and if it continued, all of Faerie could be destroyed.

She also said that Romeo might do something to destroy it if I didn't get here quickly.

Goddamnit, why couldn't that pumpkin-spice latte bitch actually give us some details.

Some of the puzzle pieces were beginning to slot into place, though. I already assumed the journal belonged to Romeo's mother, Gwendolyn Jupiter. Prue probably got her hands on it through her own mother, who used to be a High Priestess of Washington D.C, a woman who had her own reasons for collecting everything she could that mentioned the fae. I bet Aunt Marche inherited it when she took over as High Priestess and kept it, not knowing what it was.

Prue had read everything in Aunt Marche's library. She would have put all the pieces together and realized it was Romeo's mother's diary, and she'd written about her lover —Romeo's biological father, who we now knew was a prince of the Kingdom of Dusk—before she disappeared. The journal might contain information about the imbalance or even the Scorch.

We should have read it. No, no, you're right. My brain sighed. *It's not for us, it's for him.*

I stifled my smile. I loved how we were on the same page again.

She kicked the hefty iron core of conviction in my psyche. *That's because of this baby. We know who we are, and we know what we're capable of. We're always right, and we're never wrong.*

"You're smiling." Brackin stared at me. "I thought you would be more upset about the guards thwarting whatever you were trying to do."

Just then, I realized he was holding his arms firmly over his torso, as if he was shielding himself. "Don't worry, Brackin," I sighed. "I'm not going to stab you."

He exhaled in relief. "Good." Straightening up, he relaxed back in his seat and slung one leg over the other. "I shall endeavor to enjoy my evening, knowing you're not going to kill me on the way. And hopefully you will refrain from killing me on the journey home."

"According to your brother and his wife, I won't be travelling with you on the way home," I said flippantly. "Aren't the guards going to toss my corpse in the river?" I'd already started forming a vague plan to ditch the Pesh family and disappear into the City as soon as I could slip away from the Ball.

Brackin opened his mouth and shut it. Then, he opened it again and took a deep breath. "For what it's worth, Daffodil, I think they're underestimating you."

I hadn't expected that. I cocked my head. "Really?"

"Of course."

"I was under the impression that you thought I'd die quickly, too."

"Daffodil, please." He wrinkled his nose. "I know what you're capable of. You're as vicious and bloodthirsty as any of the princesses in the Trials."

I grinned. "I see."

"And," he added, his tone grudging, "You do scrub up well. Steven has done an impressive job turning a pig's ear into a silk purse."

"Thanks."

"My brother and his wife have been overly dramatic on how much you will embarrass our house at the Trials. To be honest, with you in that dress and with your hair like that, I find I am not too ashamed to be seen with you."

"Gee," I said. "Don't go overboard."

"Well, as long as you don't move or speak a word, I think I'll be fine. And don't forget, I did tell my brother and his wife that you have a pretty face."

"I'm not going to stab you on the way home, Brackin. You don't need to butter me up anymore." I gnawed on my lip, looking out the window.

He watched me carefully. "So, what is bothering you now?"

"Nothing." *We really need to get that damned journal.*

He rolled his eyes. "Little Daffodil, just tell me. Perhaps I could help. It would benefit me to get you out of my life as quickly as possible, you know."

The pervert makes a good point. On impulse, I decided to tell him. "Do you think you could get my journal back?"

"Pardon?" He frowned. "Your what?"

"The thing the Watch Commander confiscated. He took it and locked it in his office drawer."

"Oh." Brackin's expression cleared. He sat up straight and put his hand in the breast pocket of his jacket. "You mean this thing?" To my astonishment, he pulled out the journal, still double-sealed in the Ziplock bag.

I snatched it from him. "Oh my gosh! Brackin! How the *hell* did you get this?"

He shrugged. "You were upset when the Watch Commander took it, so I went back to the barracks after my brother finished shouting at me and demanded it back."

Running my fingers over it, I saw it was still sealed. The blue marble charm was with it, rolling around inside the bag. "And he actually gave it to you?"

"Daffodil." Brackin pouted. "I don't underestimate you, but you surely underestimate me. I might be the spare to the Dukedom, but I'm still Lord Brackin Pesh of Gloom. When it benefits me, I can throw my weight around. I merely bullied the Watch Commander a little and threatened to tell everyone how lax he'd been, having not spotted that explosive shale in the wall much earlier. He gave up the journal for my silence."

I can't believe he got the journal back for us, my brain said, sounding deeply unsettled. *I feel all warm and fuzzy all of a sudden.*

"You said it was private and personal, so I thought it might give me some clues as to why the hell you are here in my realm," Brackin added.

I smiled. Brackin was a piece of shit, but at least he was an honest piece of shit. "You didn't open it, though."

He grimaced. "I didn't know how. I confess I was concerned that if I broke that clear seal, you'd know it was tampered with, and then you'd kill me when you found out I was trying to read your private and personal notations."

"Aha." I giggled. "Foiled by a Ziplock bag, huh?" The relief almost made me giddy. Now, I could find Romeo, give him the journal, and we could go home.

I just had to slip away from the guards. Brain-Daphne bared her teeth. *Stabby stab stab.*

"So..." Brackin nudged me and pointed at the journal. "What is it?"

"None of your business."

"Come on, Daffodil. I did you a favor and got it back. Please allay my fears and tell me it doesn't contain a spell to blow up the Kingdom, because I'd feel rather put out if you committed an act of terrorism and didn't give me time to escape."

"Fine." I exhaled. "It's not a spellbook, it's just a journal. And it's not mine. It belongs to someone else."

"Aha. Who?"

"*That's* none of your business." I slipped the journal, still in the Ziplock bag, into my thigh harness.

CHAPTER
TWENTY-FOUR

B rackin stopped pouting as soon as the carriage rolled into the palace gates.

The palace was exquisite. A million giant slabs of pitch-black obsidian glittered in the starlight, shining with an overwhelming intensity. Dramatic spires reached into the night sky and soaring arches pointed towards the heavens. Every window was lit with candles and lamps, throwing warm light—violets, golds and soft reds, the colors of sunset and dusk. Fireflies twinkled like stars, bright against the dark stone.

Despite the jaw-dropping grandeur, the palace struck me as oddly familiar. I smiled when I realized it reminded me of a giant version of Romeo's gothic church. His heritage had never abandoned him. It seemed he'd always been a Prince of Dusk.

We followed a convoy of other carriages inside the gates, joined the loop of vehicles waiting to disgorge their guests and finally stopped outside the main entrance. Brackin got out first, then held out his arm so I could climb out of the carriage. I arranged my dress, holding the slit together so I wouldn't flash my vagina at everyone, took his arm, stepped out, and looked up at what felt like a mile of steps leading to the entrance.

"It's all a bit flashy, isn't it?" Brackin commented. "Overloads the senses."

"You don't like it?" I assumed Brackin would adore something like this.

"It is fine, I suppose." He shrugged. "I prefer Gloom." We started to walk up the steps. "I suppose, in essence, I am a humble man."

I let out a snort, then realized he was being sincere. "I never thought of you as a humble man, Brackin." *I barely think of him as a man,* my brain added.

"Come, now, Daffodil. I know you have a low opinion of me." He screwed up his face. "I suppose I deserve it. I was rather cruel to you when you were younger."

"That's a bit of an understatement. You kept me as a *slave*, Brackin!"

"I preferred to think of you as an unpaid employee."

My fingers twitched towards my blades. *Scumbag.*

He waved his hand. "And anyway, you had a place to live and food to eat."

"You threatened me with violence to keep me in line. You literally threatened me with torture and mutilation if I ever thought about running away!"

"Hyperbole," he scoffed. "Honestly, I was shocked that you actually believed I was capable of all the things I threatened you with. I never once beat you, Daffodil, and I never laid a finger on you in any other capacity."

Because we don't have feathers, you fucking pervert.

"And," he continued, "in my defense, you literally stabbed me."

I scowled at my feet. The split made walking in my

gown relatively easy—I wasn't at risk of tripping. "I'm not letting you off the hook, Brackin. I was just a lost little girl, and you took advantage of me. I spent six months working for you, and I was terrified the whole time."

"And look what you have become now, Daffodil!" He grinned at me. "I dare say that any hardship you endured because of me, well, it made you what you are today."

I let out a heavy sigh. There was a reason I'd chosen Brackin Pesh to get me here, rather than any of the other fae warlords or mage masters I knew. Firstly, he was a coward, and I knew I didn't have to hit him hard to beat him into submission. Second, well... he really was the best of a bad bunch. "There's no getting through to you, is there?" I sighed.

"Not even a little." He smiled widely. "Now, focus. You will need your wits about you if you are to survive the slaughter."

Brain-Daphne was already onto it. She'd clocked the sentries up ahead, guarding the door—five of them in full battle armor. Three more guards in elegant courtier tunics and capes carefully scanned each guest as we walked up the stairs and made our way into the palace. Only their eyes moved, but I caught the scent of a whole variety of strong fae magic I vaguely recognized. We were being monitored for threats.

The rules of each Bride Trial were different. "Am I allowed weapons?" I asked Brackin.

"Only if they are concealed. It would be considered hostile and rude to have them on display," he murmured back. "See that woman in the yellow dress?"

Brain-Daphne had already scanned her and marked her as a possible threat. She walked ahead of us, a few couples in front—tall, at least a head taller than me, lithe and graceful, with that telltale muscle contour in her arms that you only get from a lifetime of martial arts training. Her honey-colored hair was scraped back off her face tightly, highlighting her exceptional bone structure—high cheekbones, huge sapphire-blue eyes, a swan-like neck, and pointed chin. She didn't look much older than me, but as a high fae, she was probably eighty years old already. "I see her." The yellow dress she wore was a mass of ruffles. Brackin wasn't lying about this being the fashion. And there were plenty of places to hide weapons.

"That's the favorite to win the Trials," Brackin murmured in my ear. "That's Princess Nyla of the Spring Court, the youngest daughter of King Aranbold."

I looked at her and her escort carefully. "That's not the King with her, though."

"No. The King is very old and not able to travel quickly enough should the Scorch descend. He remains at his court. Nyla's escort is her older brother, Prince Aranbold, the heir to the throne. Prince Aranbold's aunt was Queen Carissa, the former Queen of Dusk."

I nodded, remembering. "I suppose they want to get their princess on the Dusk throne to extend their power."

Maybe this is the cause of the imbalance, my brain pondered. *There seems to be an excess of Spring brides marrying into Dusk families. Light spilling into darkness.*

There always had been, though. All the High Fae aristocracy were related; they weren't different species. They didn't just worship nature—they *were* nature. Queen Maeve and Queen Titania were sisters, but they changed themselves to suit the Court they chose to rule and embodied opposite seasons.

The common fae had their own preferences, of course, just as some humans preferred to live in the mountains and others liked the beach. But they always blended into their surroundings rather than force their surroundings to change around them.

That was why it was odd that Lady Pesh had suddenly painted the town walls in whitewash to make it brighter, and why she'd forced springtime watercolors on the dark-paneled walls. It was like she'd regressed. She should have naturally assimilated to the shadowy tones of the twilight realms years ago. Fae were like chameleons; they naturally blended into their environment.

There were always exceptions to this rule, though. The Beast of Bakkanon was one. He forced his surroundings to bend to him, wiping out whole species and devouring the magic of anyone he deemed inferior. He wanted purity and enforced it by sucking the life out of entire ecosystems. That was why the balance between the Wastes and the Wilds had been thrown out a few years ago. The weight had been tipped in favor of Order instead of Chaos, and it had a ripple effect all throughout the universe.

Oi. Bitch, focus.

I snapped back to attention. My brain was pointing out the whiff of ogre behind me. I shot a glance over my shoulder and spotted a female ogre coming up the steps behind me, escorted by a grim-faced, high fae man with very blonde hair and blue eyes.

The ogre's complexion wasn't the usual green. They'd cast a glamor to give her a beige tone but left everything else the same—the rubbery skin, the thick brow bone, the short tusks protruding out of her heavy bottom jaw. She was small for an ogre, only a head taller than the man next to her, and she wore the fluffiest bright-green dress I'd ever seen in my life.

Brackin saw me looking and rolled his eyes. "The Duke of Dew thinks this is a good strategy."

"It *is* a good strategy," I murmured back. "An ogre has a

great chance of surviving the bloodbath." I caught Brackin's eye. "Don't forget that a troll almost took the hand of Prince Witchinghour eight years ago, my Lord." The troll candidate was the only female in that Bride Trial that wasn't crushed to death by rolling logs in the cross-country race. "She was the only one left, so she won the Trial by default."

"That's right," Brackin chuckled. "I forgot about that. The prince threatened to kill himself if he was forced to wed her. They ended up wiping out the village that sponsored her so he wouldn't have to go through with it." Brackin shot me a strange look of approval. "I forget how knowledgeable you are on our customs, Daffodil."

"It's hard not to be knowledgeable, considering how much you lot gossip."

When I was stuck in Faerie, I made it a point to always pay attention to the gossip. While I'd never been near the ballrooms and palaces of the Royal High Fae, I knew almost everything there was to know about them. You could argue that servants knew more about the aristocracy than they knew about themselves.

We walked, following the line of guests as it snaked through the massive arched doorway and into a large entrance hall lit up by an enormous glittering candelabra lining the walls and a chandelier hanging low from the vaulted ceiling. The proportions of the palace were outrageously opulent. I felt like I was in a fairytale.

It was definitely a fairytale I didn't belong in, though. I couldn't ignore the pointed stares and the raised eyebrows of everyone around me. With my sensitive wolf-ears, I could hear the other guests in line gossiping about me, and there was nothing complimentary to be said. Despite Lady Pesh's hopes, it seemed that news of my candidacy had already spread.

I listened as the sniggers, scornful snorts, and sly murmurs drifted over to me.

"... I cannot believe it's true! I thought it was just a cruel prank... Gloom really has entered a mortal changeling... can't understand why they would bother, she's only a shapeshifter, she'll be dead in a heartbeat... sleeping with Lord Bron's little brother, I think, and it's a scam of some sort...I heard he did it deliberately to embarrass Lord Bron, you know how he is... Scandalous, that dress, very calculating on her part... I remember Queen Talia wearing something similar when she rode out to conquer the Witchinghour rebellion... very striking, though, not sure if it's supposed to impress the Court of Dusk or insult it..."

The line of guests wove left, down a grand corridor, and through an onyx archway. In the distance, a herald announced each guest as they entered. Guards stood to attention, lining the hallway. Guess there really was no escape.

My heart pounded in my chest. Romeo was here somewhere... upstairs in the suites or maybe out in the courtyard, watching the giant crescent moon as it rose in the night sky. Goddamnit, I wanted to find him so bad.

I just needed to get through the ball. "Have you got any info on any other candidates besides Nyla Aranbold?" I whispered to Brackin.

To give him some credit, he wasn't leaning away from me. He took my arm in the same way the other sponsors did and guided me forward as if he weren't ashamed to escort me. "Oh, I suppose it might help you, wouldn't it?" He pursed his lips, thinking. "Princess Nyla is the favorite to win. She's the most cunning and vicious, and she's the most suitable match for the prince, so if there is more than one candidate left standing, everyone says that the King and Queen will choose—"

I cut him off. "I don't care who the favorite is."

"Ah, good point, Daffodil. You're right, Nyla will be targeted for elimination by the other brides."

I rolled my eyes. "Just tell me about the other candidates."

He rattled off a handful of names, some that I recognized as minor princesses from the other main Inbetween courts—Spring, Dawn, and Autumn, or noblewomen from the larger towns, covering the whole of the Inbetween. "There are several you should watch out for, Daffodil," Brackin whispered. "The other favorites are Lady Sybell from Nightfall, a niece of King Ronus, and Lady Brisa of the Frost Vale."

I flinched. Lady Brisa came from a large territory that was too close to Winter for my liking. The High Fae that dwelled in places that embodied the extremes of the seasons tended to be more magically powerful than the others. They were more of a force of nature, which is why Asherah, a princess of the Winter Court, was so powerful.

Brackin saw my expression. "Yes, Lady Brisa is full of magic and an accomplished spellcaster; that's why she's a favorite."

I exhaled slowly. "I just have to get through tonight."

"Tonight?" Brackin raised his brows. "You're not continuing into the Trials?"

"Not if I can help it."

He pouted. "I thought this was the whole point, Daffodil. I assumed you wanted the hand of the prince."

I almost laughed out loud. "Oh, I do."

He shook his head. "So then why—" He saw my face. "You know what? I don't think I want to know." He squeezed my arm. "Please, if you could reassure me of one thing, Daffodil..."

It wasn't like Brackin to say please. "What is it?"

179

"You're not here to destroy the Kingdom of Dusk, are you?"

I rolled my eyes. "No, Brackin." We moved forwards a few steps, closer to the entrance of the ballroom. He didn't look reassured. "I promise you I'm not going to do anything to destroy your Kingdom, Brackin."

"You can hardly blame me for asking. Things are so precarious as it is," he muttered, not looking at me, "I know I can be flippant, but I have been deeply unsettled of late. Gloom is my home, and it's not feeling quite like home anymore, if you can understand that. The Scorch rampaging through our lands, and people are losing faith in the King and Queen. It will only take a spark, Daffodil, and the whole court will be on fire."

Goosebumps rolled over my skin. "And then the scales will tip over completely."

"Exactly."

We stopped at the entrance to the ballroom, watching as Princess Nyla of the Spring Court was announced by the herald. A smattering of oohs and ahhs echoed out into the hallway. I couldn't see her face from the back, but I caught the arrogant tilt of her head, the tightness of her shoulders, and the grace with which she floated forward into the ballroom.

She thinks she's got this in the bag.

Brackin let out a worried breath. "I just hope that the Bride Trials will fix whatever corruption is lurking within the Court of Dusk."

The courtier at the door was glaring at me with open hostility. He wrinkled his nose as we stepped forward to be announced. "A changeling, Lord Brackin? I was hoping the rumors weren't true. I couldn't imagine why you would seek to make fun of the Trial like this."

Even the Herald's eyes widened when he saw me. He

looked down at his scroll, then back up at me. After a moment, he huffed out a breath and took another deep one.

"Presenting, Lord Brackin of Gloom, and his candidate for the Bride Trials, the Little Daffodil!"

We walked forward. The entire ballroom turned to stare at us.

Let the games begin.

TWENTY-FIVE

You could have heard a pin drop.

Any other time, I would have enjoyed walking into a fairytale ball. I would have relished the sight of the palace ballroom, the opulence and grandeur of it all, the high ceiling and glittering crystal chandeliers, the shining dark marble floor, the shimmering onyx walls contrasted with old-gold candelabra and flickering lights. I would have loved taking in all the guests, each one a perfect vision—dressed in stunning flowing gowns and structured tunics, dripping in gold and precious gemstones. But, for a brief moment in time, nobody moved.

Hundreds of pairs of eyes fixed on me, most of them bewildered, confused, or openly hostile.

Take a picture, bitches; it will last longer.

Brackin lifted his chin and tugged on my arm, leading me into the ballroom. The crowd parted as we walked through. "This is why I don't come here," he muttered under his breath, keeping a pleasantly blank expression on his face. "These courtiers are like sheep. They're all waiting for someone to decide how to treat us before they act."

I heard murmuring as the Dew candidate behind us—

the ogre—was announced. Her name was Lady Bork. I could even feel her heavy footsteps vibrate through the marble floor as she thumped into the room.

"She's not getting near as icy reception as what I got," I said wryly.

"Her candidacy is not shocking," Brackin replied, steering me around the crowd. "Everyone expects one duchy or another to enter a hardier candidate. But you, my dear, don't make sense. Nobody can see the merit of entering a mortal changeling."

A server in a royal scarlet and black suit, carrying a tray filled with sparkling fae wine, walked towards us. He saw me, his eyes went wide, and he did an abrupt about-turn and walked the other way. "Would it help if I told them I'm not a changeling?" I said.

"I'm not sure anything will help you, Daffodil." Brackin had to steer me around an elderly couple who glared at both of us with open hostility, refusing to move.

Out of the corner of my eye on my left, I watched Lady Bork stomp to the wall of the ballroom and pick up a delicate chair by its leg. Her sponsor still held onto her arm, and, trying to keep his expression blank, hissed at her under his breath. "Not yet. Bork, I told you, not yet!"

Brackin wisely steered me away from her.

"Let's just keep doing laps until this whole thing is over," I said under my breath.

That's actually a good plan, my brain said approvingly. *It's harder to hit a moving target.*

"You are expected to speak to the other candidates, Daffodil," Brackin said. "At some point, you're going to have to interact with someone." He swiped a glass of overly bubbly fae wine off a passing server and downed the whole thing in one gulp. "The whole point of this ball is to get to know the other Brides and size up the competition. Murdering each other stealthily is secondary."

"I can say hi in passing." My eyes had already found where the other candidates were gathering in the far corner of the ballroom. The favorite, Princess Nyla of the Spring Court, was already there, talking to a shockingly thin young woman with platinum hair who was dressed in a glittering light-blue gown. I narrowed my eyes. "Is that Lady Brisa from Frost?"

Brackin followed my gaze. "It is. They could be forming an alliance, Daffodil. That is another strategy available to you, you know. You could pledge your support to another competitor in exchange for protection during the Trials and gain a political alliance when the bride is crowned."

"I don't think anybody needs my support," I said dryly.

And we're not sticking around that long. Are we?

I didn't answer her. "Let's just keep moving."

It was a good plan, so we stuck to it. We were on our third lap of the ballroom when my senses prickled. Suddenly, alarm bells rang in my head so hard I could barely concentrate.

It's poison, my brain said cheerfully. She'd efficiently been processing everything my senses picked up on. *Steel needle shaft, the smell of a river reed, and a dot of bogtoad scum. Someone in here has a blowdart and a dozen poison needles.*

Bogtoad scum was so lethal, once it was in your bloodstream it killed within seconds. I'd have to keep my eyes on whatever Bride was packing the blowdart. I kept my expression pleasantly blank, let my eyes roam around the ballroom, and searched the guests, taking in the two-dozen or so beautiful young fae women dotted around the room.

I didn't have to guess which ones were candidates for the Bride Trials. They all were. Every single other pretty girl in the Kingdom would be staying home tonight rather than come here and risk being mistaken for a candidate and murdered quietly.

It took me a minute to locate the source of the vile poison scent. It was coming from a new arrival—an ethereal-looking woman with pearly skin and silver hair. I turned my head to face Brackin and nodded towards her. "Who is that?"

He looked. "Lady Winnara, the candidate from Gale."

Gale. Blowdart. Figures. "Keep an eye on her," I said.

"Little Daffodil, I am trying to keep an eye on all of the candidates." A muscle in Brackin's pointed jaw clenched.

Lady Winnara of Gale floated gracefully over to join the other candidates in the corner where Princess Nyla of Spring seemed to be holding court.

We continued our loop of the ballroom. A few moments later, the first bride fell. On the far side of the ballroom, a short, curvy woman with very pointed ears crashed to the floor.

I hadn't caught the sound of a blowdart being fired, nor smelled the poison on the needle. My brain bared her teeth. *What took her out?*

"Did you see what happened to her?" I asked Brackin as the dead bride was carried out quietly.

"No. The King and Queen haven't even arrived yet." Brackin sounded worried. "This ball is going to be such a bloodbath, there won't be any competitors left."

A few moments later, I caught a waft of freshly spilled fae blood, and another bride was scooped up before she collapsed. Her sponsor, a muscular dark man from a town called Harvest, carried her out of the ballroom without a word.

The crowd murmured amongst themselves. There were no screams, no cries. It made my gut churn.

We expected this. This is the whole point. Kill without being caught. Show off your stealth, your intelligence, your grace, your ruthlessness. Show what you will do for the crown.

It was still sickening.

Brackin and I kept moving through the crowd. I stepped more deliberately now, keeping my senses on high alert, always making sure there were bodies blocking me from any other bride in the room. An orchestra by the entrance to the ballroom began to play, and some of the older guests started to dance. People chatted, laughed, and tossed back their hair. Brackin and I kept walking, deliberately not catching anyone's eye.

The scent of bogtoad poison suddenly blossomed in the air. I flinched. My eyes found Lady Winnara quickly; she was facing away from me. A second later, another bride collapsed.

"How long do we have to stay here for?" I murmured to Brackin.

Brackin unhinged his jaw with difficulty. He was grinding his teeth. "Until the King and Queen leave."

"They're not even here yet."

"I know," he hissed. We started another loop of the ballroom.

After another minute, Bork the ogre hitched up her dress and stomped over to a pretty girl in a pink dress and smashed a chair over her head. The girl collapsed.

The crowd backed away, their faces outraged. Murder was fine but they weren't going to tolerate bad manners.

"Lady Bork," her sponsor hissed. "I said, not yet! And not like that!"

She shook him off and stomped back into the crowd, while he tugged at her arm, trying to stop her. "And I told you; you're supposed to be quiet about it!"

The tension in the ballroom thickened. There was nothing we could do. Brackin and I continued our loop of the ballroom, avoiding all eye contact, never stopping or even pausing.

A horn sounded, and almost everyone flinched at the noise and turned towards the doorway. The herald cleared his throat and announced the arrival of King Ronus and Queen Talia.

Every guest stopped their conversations immediately, turned towards the entrance, and cleared a path down the middle of the ballroom. The women sank into deep curtsies, and the men bowed at the waist, while the King and Queen walked through the crowd towards the dais at the back of the room where two enormous, bejeweled thrones sat empty.

I curtsied, my heart thumping in my chest wildly. Staying still right now felt like a game of chicken. Would any of the brides break protocol and attack now? I sank even deeper, keeping as low as possible, while straining my eyes to catch a glimpse of the King and Queen as they walked past. Both of them looked exactly like High Fae Royalty from the Winter side of the Inbetween—poreless skin in a pearl-white color, enormous wide eyes with pitch-black irises, and sculpted high cheekbones and proud straight noses. King Ronus's long silver hair betrayed his age—they said he was almost a thousand years old. Queen Talia's raven-colored hair had a thick streak of silver at the front, but they both still looked regal and very handsome.

King Ronus reached his throne, turned around, and waited until his Queen had settled beside him before he sat down. I watched them both carefully from underneath my eyelashes. Both of them were keeping their expressions carefully blank, but I focused on a handful of things—the miniscule crease between Talia's eyebrows, the hardness of Ronus's jaw, the thin lips, the intense, meaningful stare they exchanged.

They were both very worried.

I suppose they had good reason to be. They were both old, in a room full of scheming courtiers, and two-dozen homicidal fae women vying for their grandson's hand in marriage. And I could only imagine how much resistance their new heir had given them.

Romeo. My own brain gave a shiver of longing. *Can we just hurry the fuck up and get this over with so we can find him already? I'm going to eat him like a corn cob. I'm going to suck him dry. I'm going to ride his face like I'm a cowboy and he's a mechanical bull.* She ran through a whole reel of very dirty— and quite unsettling—things she wanted to do to him when we found him. I had to work hard to keep my expression blank.

King Ronus waved his hand. "Carry on." His voice rolled through the room like thunder.

I waited another few seconds before I straightened up, enjoying a second of cover before Brackin and I continued our circuit. He took my arm and led me back through the room, weaving through the couples randomly, changing direction here and there so nobody could predict our movements. Brain-Daphne went back to work, zeroing in on threats, processing suspicious scents and sounds.

A tall woman—statuesque, with very pale skin and raven-colored hair pulled back off her face—in a billowy, ruffled blood-red gown stepped in my path. She looked right at me.

I stopped walking. I had to or else I would have crashed into her. Brackin made a movement left, as if trying to pull me away, but I planted my feet. Running away now would only make everything worse.

I had to face one of them eventually. Better this one than Lady Bork, who was over near the entrance trying to smack another Bride in the face with a silver tray while her sponsor dangled from her arm.

I met the raven-haired woman's eye calmly. Here we go.

Nightfall Court, Brain-Daphne whispered, processing her appearance, coloring, and scent. *I bet this is Lady Sybell, the Nightfall candidate, niece of the King. Her pulse is thrumming like a hummingbird. She thinks we're easy pickings. I can smell silver and leather in the folds of her gown. She's got a dagger hidden in there.*

Lady Sybell of Nightfall stared at me for another three seconds, then arched a perfect eyebrow. "Daffodil, was it?" Her scarlet lips curved into a frown of disapproval. "What kind of a name is that?"

I paused for a full five seconds before speaking. High Fae manners were convoluted and complicated. Offence was carefully given and easily taken, and her opening shot was so rude she might as well have slapped me across the face and flipped me off.

We know exactly how to handle this bitch.

"Dayannavan, my Lady." I smiled at her, dropped my eyes, then lowered myself gracefully into a deep, perfect curtsey.

Ha, ha. Go fuck yourself, hoe.

"My path forward is blessed now that it has crossed yours," I continued smoothly, rising to my feet slowly.

This was how a lady greeted another lady for the first time. I made it slow, loud, and deliberate, just to rub in how rude she'd been.

Her nostrils flared as she registered the fact that I was insulting her, but she couldn't do anything about it. "Dayannavan," she said through gritted teeth. "I am Lady Sybell. May our paths cross many times."

I waited another five seconds. A whole lot of eyes focused on us now. The crowd pretended to talk and dance and drink, but they were paying careful attention to Sybell and me. We were putting on a great show. Everyone had witnessed how rude Nightfall's competitor had been to another Bride, who had responded—surprisingly for an outsider—with perfect manners and exceptional grace.

The gossip would spread through the courtiers. It might even make its way to the Royal couple. Lady Sybell had fucked up and she knew it. She might as well have snatched a lute from a musician in the orchestra and tried to knock me out with it, like Lady Bork was trying to do in the corner of the ballroom right now.

"A pleasure, Lady Sybell," I finally said, still smiling calmly. "I was announced as Daffodil, but it is my sponsor's pet name for me."

My sponsor had already dropped my arm and was hovering five paces to the left, shielding himself with a silver serving platter while trying to pretend he was admiring the decorative handles. I wasn't expecting much from Brackin, but to give him some credit, he hadn't run away yet.

Lady Sybell inclined her head, a faint smile on her lips. "And it is a pretty pet name, for such a pretty pet."

Ooh. Bitch.

It was a cheap point. I chose not to rise to the bait. "My real name is Daphne Ironclaw. I'm a shapeshifter from the mortal realm."

"A shapeshifter?" Lady Sybell's lips twitched, like I'd said something silly, and she was trying not to laugh. "You know you are not allowed to appear in any other form for the duration of the Trials, though, don't you, Daffodil? If we were allowed to appear in another form, then Princess Ember would turn herself into a giant *cait sith* and eat all of us. Your dual nature will not help you survive. I am sorry to inform you that you must stay as you are." Her eyes sparkled. She didn't look sorry; she looked delighted.

"Oh, I'm aware of the rules of the Trials." I kept my expression pleasant. *And we're not planning on sticking around, anyway. As soon as those royal butts are out of those blinged-out thrones, we're blowing this popsicle stand.*

Lady Sybell, seeing that I wasn't gasping in horror at the fact that I wasn't allowed to compete as a werewolf, realized her shot had missed the mark. She carefully schooled her expression, her midnight-blue eyes flickering as she thought about her next move. I could almost hear her train of thought. *Is this wolf girl really that stupid? Or is she hiding something?*

I caught the moment she decided I was stupid. A smug look softened her sharp eyes. "I am glad you are aware of the rules." She moved her arms to her back, pretending to clasp them behind her, and took a step closer to me. The ruffles of her enormous scarlet dress brushed mine.

Brain-Daphne growled. *Her hand is in her dress. She's going for her dagger.*

Lady Sybell's smile grew snake-like. "I would hate to see the guards fill you with arrows in the very first event. That is what happens when you break the rules, you know."

I nodded at her. "Oh, I'm aware."

"I'm glad you have studied our customs, Lady Ironclaw—"

"You flatter me, but I'm no lady," I told her.

Lady Sybell's lips tightened for a fraction of a second. I'd taken her next cheap shot out of her hands before she could even throw it. Everyone was listening. She wanted to rub it in that I wasn't high fae, and I wasn't even part of the aristocracy in my own realm. Lady Sybell was trying to correct the mistake she'd made earlier—she didn't have to be polite to me, because I was just some changeling wretch.

I leaned closer and gave her a conspiratorial wink. "Just between you and me, Lady Sybell, I'm not even the ruler of my own household. I have an Alpha at home who keeps me in line."

Where is that horny fucker, anyway?

"Is that so?" The skin around her eyes tensed. She was trying very hard not to glare at me. The longer this interaction went on, the more she lost face.

Not so easy picking after all. She's going to make her move in three, two, one...

"Then perhaps you could use a guiding hand here." Lady Sybell's face split into a huge grin. "I shall help you. Let us be friends, Daphne Ironclaw," she simpered and held out one arm, inviting me to step in and hug her. She kept her left hand in her pocket.

Finally, some action.

I smiled back happily, stretched both arms out, and stepped towards her, going in for the hug. I made it as tight as possible, just to piss her off.

Lady Sybell's skin was freezing cold, but as a lady of Nightfall, I had braced myself for it. Moving stiffly for a high fae, she hugged me back with her right arm, shuddering slightly. The voluminous ruffles of her dress buried both of us from the chest down and hid her surreptitious movements, but I could hear what she was doing perfectly. As I hugged her, she gripped her silver dagger and slid it out of her hidden sheath...

"It is so nice to have a friend!" I said loudly, right in her ear, unsettling her. I squeezed her with my left arm and dropped my right arm, sliding it into the ruffles of her dress. With a quick twist and split-second timing, I plucked the dagger out of her hand, reversed my grip, then drove it straight into her back.

She flinched. I hugged her tighter, using all my strength to hold her in place.

You missed her kidney.

I wasn't trying to kill her, I whispered internally. I don't want to kill anyone. This isn't war; it's just a game. And... I feel weirdly ashamed about using lethal force right now. I don't know why.

Hmm. Yeah, I noticed that. Brain-Daphne knocked on the iron-hard core of certainty within me. *I thought we'd feel more confident with this inside us now. Childhood trauma?*

All our shit is childhood trauma.

Yeah, Brain-Daphne sighed. *Well, at least we got some action. Twist the blade for me, would you?*

I decided to give it just a little tweak. Lady Sybell jerked in my arm. I let go of the dagger and hugged her even harder. "I'm so glad I met you, my Lady of Nightfall." I kissed her cheek and stepped back.

Her eyes were wide, and she looked horrified. The smell of blood bloomed between us, but her scarlet ruffled dress hid everything—including the knife sticking out of her back.

I took another few steps back and dropped into another deep curtsy. "I have taken up enough of your time this evening, my lady."

Her mouth trembled for a second, then, realization dawned on her face. I'd bested her, and now, I was letting her go.

She nodded once, turned very stiffly, and hurried away through the crowd.

TWENTY-SIX

T exhaled with relief. So did Brackin. "Whew," he said, tossing the tray to a passing server. "That was tense. You did well, Daffodil." He grinned at me. "I've never seen anyone from Nightfall retreat like that."

"That was nothing." Someone was clapping; it distracted me. I couldn't see who it was, though. The crowd had tightened around us since Sybell ran away.

I moved left and spotted an odd-looking high fae girl with startling coloring—hair the color of cream, beige skin, pale gray eyes, and vivid rosy, red cheeks. She grinned at me happily and clapped her hands together joyfully.

I smiled back, a little confused. Was this another bride? She seemed too young. Judging from the angle of the points of her ears and the wideness of her eyes—sometimes the only concrete markers of maturity among the fae—I'd guess she'd only just reached adulthood.

The girl wore a vivid pink and green ruffled gown, and it reminded me instantly of Marie, my vampire ward. Marie, the mad genius, loved to wear clothes that made your eyes hurt. The strange fae girl laughed, turning to watch as Lady

Sybell stumbled away through the crowd, while putting pressure on the stab wound.

The girl turned, dipped a lightning-fast curtsey, popped back up, and spat out the obligatory greeting "Dayanna-van-my-lady-my-path-is-blessed-now-that-it-has-crossed-yours." Her face split into a happy grin. "That was awesome."

I murmured the obligatory greeting back. Brain-Daphne was on high alert. *This tiny one is packing more knives than a sushi chef. There's a mini crossbow strapped to her right thigh. And, judging by the shape and smell, she's padded her bra with a curse-grenade in each cup.*

So, she was a Bride. She seemed far too young. I shot Brackin a look, but he'd already backed away.

"I'm Ember," the girl said, holding out her hand for me to shake. "For that little show, I think I'll give you a free pass."

I let out a little huff of surprise, while Brain-Daphne checked her outstretched hands for weapons. "*Princess* Ember? Of Sandstone?"

"That's me." She used the common tongue, not the normal, flowery High Fae.

So, this was the former Queen's daughter. She'd only been a child when her stepfather, King Monton, and her baby half-brother were killed. I gulped, reached out, and shook her hand. Her grip was surprisingly strong.

Brain-Daphne gnawed on her lip. *I'm not sure how to handle this one.*

I didn't know either. Judging by the expression on Brackin's face, he wasn't going to be of any help. He seemed wary but not scared like he was of Lady Sybell.

Ember was young—probably about sixty in fae years, around fourteen in human years, while all the other Brides would be the equivalent of my age or older—but it would be stupid to think she wasn't a threat. In fact, it would be smarter to be incredibly wary of her.

I gave her a tentative smile. "Are you a candidate for the Bride Trials, Princess Ember?"

"Sure am." She shot little finger-crossbows at me and made a *swoosh swoosh* noise. "But don't worry, I'm not here to win the heart of the new prince. I'm not fond of men." She wrinkled her nose. "Their dangling parts are disgusting. Women are much more desirable."

Brain-Daphne giggled. *She's not wrong.*

"I suppose you don't have to be fond of men to become Queen of Dusk," I said cautiously.

Princess Ember made a face. "I don't want to be the Queen of Dusk, either. It's too dark and cold here. I like it at Sandstone, but my Uncle Redfoot is proving astonishingly hard to kill."

Was she joking? I wasn't sure. I hesitated, trying to remember what I knew about her. Ember's mother, Queen Carissa, was brought up in Sandstone, a region very close to the Summer Court. She had Ember with her first husband, a nobody, with no title. He died soon after Carissa gave birth to Ember. Carissa's older brother, the Duke of Sandstone, quickly arranged for her to be sent to the Court of Dusk to try and catch the eye of the new King Monton. It worked, because Carissa and Monton were married, and Monton became baby Ember's stepfather.

The Duke of Sandstone was running the same play with Ember, apparently. "Were you, uh, forced to enter the Trials, my lady?"

"Oh, no," she said, chuckling. "I entered myself. Uncle Redfoot eagerly escorted me, though." She winked. "Between you and me, I think he's hoping to be rid of me."

This girl was bizarre. Did she have a death wish?

I wouldn't blame her if she did. She'd been through a ton of trauma. She would have witnessed her stepfather and baby brother killed, for starters. And, according to the gossip the servants of House Pesh had fed me, Queen Carissa had a mental breakdown after she was kicked off the throne of Dusk. It was possible Ember hadn't had anyone decent to parent her since.

I licked my lips. "Then, uh, why are you here?"

"Revenge," Ember said, her expression twisting into a snarl. She tossed her glass behind her and clenched her fists. "I've got so many scores to settle, I had to make a list. That snotty bitch, Nyla, changed the decorations for my coming-out ball and ruined everything, so I'm going to gut her like a fish. Brisa of Frost is on my hit-list because she keeps sucking up to Uncle Redfoot. And I've got a score to settle with Saoira of Autumn, too. I've been forced to listen to too many of her lectures when Uncle Redfoot makes me visit her Court. She's a stuck-up know-it-all, but she's too crafty to let her guard down when she's at home, so I can't get her there. Here, at the Trials, I've got all the opportunities I need to finally take her out."

Woah. I took in the wild look in Ember's eye, the way she clenched her little fists, and the determined set of her jaw. *Childhood trauma, check. Murderous impulses, check. Looks like Princess Ember here is a sweet little psychopath.* Brain-Daphne sighed fondly. *She reminds me of me.*

Yeah, she does.

Suddenly, I was worried about Princess Ember. This poor girl had no idea what she'd gotten herself into. She thought she was a badass, but she was going to get murdered.

I remembered having fantasies of revenge when I was

little. But Chloe swooped in right when I needed her. She tempered my worst impulses, trained me how to use weapons properly, and taught me a lot about restraint, forgiveness, and mercy.

If Ember's mother was incapacitated, and her uncle was a cold bastard, Ember might not have had anyone to do that for her. For a second, I wondered if I should do something. Maybe I should suggest that she back out of the Trials now and save herself.

I opened my mouth, but Ember spoke first. "Well, I best be off and mingle." She sighed. "See who else I can kill tonight. I'm going to leave you alone, though. You're a fish out of water, Daffodil, and I can sympathize." She nodded thoughtfully. "I know exactly what that's like. How it feels to not belong somewhere."

Suddenly, she looked so sad, my heart throbbed. "Princess Ember, I'm sorry—

"Don't worry about me, I got it all figured out." She shot me an unhinged grin. "And I'm sure you'll figure it out one day, too, Daffodil."

A crash sounded from the other end of the ballroom. Lady Bork was trying to pick up a harp and smash it over another bride's head.

"I'm going to leave Lady Bork alone, too," Ember added. "I hope she survives to the end. She's hilarious. Imagine if this new heir was forced to marry her. Now that's a wedding I'd be happy to attend."

Suddenly, the floor rumbled beneath my feet. *On guard.* Brain-Daphne nudged me. *Something is happening.*

Brackin moved cautiously in from my left, took my arm, and bowed at Ember. "Your Highness, please excuse us. I must present Gloom's candidate to the King and Queen before the party breaks up."

"Knock yourself out," Ember said, taking a whole tray of finger food off a passing server.

"Nice to meet you, Princess Ember," I said. "If you need help with anything, please let me know. I'd like to have some friends."

She waved at me happily while stuffing pastries in her mouth.

"You'd probably be best to stay away from that one, Daffodil," Brackin murmured in my ear as he led me away. "Apparently, she is wildly unstable and will not behave. I heard that her uncle keeps trying to have her swapped out for a changeling, but the Enforcers of the mortal realm keep throwing her back."

Now I felt even worse for her. "She didn't try to kill me, Brackin. She was probably the friendliest person I've met since I got here. Delusional, yes, but she was nice to me. What happened to her mother? Queen Carissa should be looking after her."

He pursed his lips. "She retired to the desert in Sandstone, apparently, and is spending her days in rest and contemplation. According to gossip, her heart broke when she was forced to give up the throne in favor of Ronus and Talia, and she lost her appetite for the machinations of the royal courts."

The floor rumbled softly beneath my feet again, causing a tingle of fear to rush up my spine, and I forgot what I was going to say. Goosebumps rose on my bare skin. My eyes darted around the room; something was happening, but my senses couldn't gather enough evidence to figure out what was going on.

The atoms in the air tingled dangerously, as if a bomb were about to explode somewhere. But there was no whiff of fuel, nor the toxic waft of a curse.

Maybe all the tension was catching up with me. My

teeth began to chatter. "Please tell me we can get out of here soon, Brackin."

"That's why I'm going to present you now, rather than wait any longer. So we can get out of here the second the royal couple leaves," Brackin muttered. His shoulders were tense, too.

We approached the dais, waiting in line behind another couple—a silver-haired fae woman carefully holding up the candidate from Bloom. There was a deep gash in the girl's head. Blood poured down her back, staining her pink gown scarlet. She was clearly struggling to stay conscious.

I've forgotten how vicious the Royal Courts are in Faerie. That girl should be in a med bay, not standing here in front of the King and Queen, trying to stay conscious enough to remember royal etiquette.

Her silver-haired sponsor bowed deeply to the King and Queen, introduced herself as the Duchess of Bloom, her granddaughter as a candidate, and made her apologies for the girl's appearance. The royal couple nodded, giving tight smiles. The woman carried Lady Bloom away. We were next.

Suddenly, a rush of adrenaline surged through me, and my heart began to thump in my chest so loudly, I could almost hear it.

Girl, what? What are you doing?

I didn't know. Why the hell was I panicking? Why were my goosebumps getting goosebumps? I wasn't scared of King Ronus and Queen Talia. I'd met powerful fae royalty before. I literally fought Asherah a few weeks ago, and as a Winter princess, she was far stronger and more unhinged than any of these nutjobs.

Except Ember, probably.

Brackin pulled me forward towards the dais and cleared his throat. "Lord Brackin of Gloom, Your Majesties." He bowed deeply. "May I present the Bride Trial candidate for Gloom, the Little Daffodil."

With enormous effort, trying to ignore my legs shaking, I pulled myself together, sank into a curtsey and held it, knowing I wasn't allowed to rise until they acknowledged me.

The heavy weight of both pairs of eyes settled on me. The temperature suddenly dropped.

No, you're not imagining it. Something is going on; I can feel it too. It's not them, though, I'm sure of that.

Neither the King nor the Queen said anything; they just inspected me. The silence stretched on, almost unbearable. Someone to my left let out a smug chuckle. I heard the whispers rustle through the ballroom like leaves skittering in the breeze. "...I knew they would take it as an insult... Lord Pesh will be thrown out of Gloom for this, mark my words... probably stripped of his title... miracle the girl's still standing..."

Brackin's legs shook. I froze in my curtsey and waited, but my brain panicked. *Why are we in fight or flight?* Adrenaline flooded my system, priming me for action. *They're not going to kill us. Probably not, anyway. Is it them? Or something else?*

A crash came from just outside the entrance, then, I heard raised voices. Shouts and screams of pain.

There! Brain-Daphne screeched in my head triumphantly. *Something is going on. A fight? A rebellion? A coup?*

I glanced up under my eyelashes and saw the King and Queen staring above my head, looking confused and worried. They weren't paying any attention to me anymore, but I didn't dare turn to see what they were looking at.

Suddenly, I knew. A soft exhale left my lips.

The herald sprinted the length of the ballroom, dashed

around me and Brackin, and bounded up the steps. He had a black eye, and his shoulder was dislocated, his arm dangling limply by his side. "Your Majesties, Lords, Ladies, and Gentlemen." His voice shook, and he waved a trembling hand towards the entrance. "May I present his Highness, the Prince of Shadow."

TWENTY-SEVEN

He walked up behind me, cutting through the crowd like a furious thunderstorm. Every person in the ballroom scuttled back and dropped their heads, bowing and curtseying. I didn't dare turn around, but I could feel him as intensely as if he were touching me. He knew I was here.

"Zarayan," Queen Talia said softly. Her eyes followed him as he approached us, so I knew exactly where he was.

Move, bitch! my brain hissed.

Oops, yes, I better get out of the way. Her Majesty would be pissed if I blocked her view of her grandchild. Still bent in my curtsey with my head down, I did a smooth little shimmy to the side, backing into the crowd. Brackin wisely did the same. Nobody else moved or said a word, but I heard several women let out soft sighs. One even moaned, before catching herself.

Fuck off, you horny bitches, my brain snarled. *Stop looking at my man.*

I took a deep breath. Now that he was here, in the same room as me—now that I could feel him, alive and well—I was a lot calmer. I'd found him, and I could take him home. Everything was going to be okay.

Don't do anything rash. We still gotta get out of the city before we can use the World Key, babes. If we put one foot out of line, we'll end up in the dungeons, and Romeo will be forced to marry Lady Bork.

My warlock walked slowly through the crowd. Nobody moved. I shivered again as he got close, and his essence rolled over me. Gods, I missed his dark-chocolatey fireworks scent. He smelled explosive and dangerous, seductive and safe, all at the same time, and I loved it.

When he moved into my line of sight, I had to bite my lip to stop myself from launching forward and tackling him to the ground. Romeo was dressed so simply—black leather trousers and boots, silver belt, and a black shirt with the sleeves rolled up to his forearms. His forearm muscles bulged; his fists were clenched.

Oh shit. My brain gave a whistle. *He's big mad.*

He was. A prickle of fear rolled through me as I realized I'd never seen him so angry before. His eyes glittered silver. His fists were shaking. He didn't look at me as he walked past, but I felt the weight of his attention.

He wasn't focused on anything else except for me.

The second he realized I was here, he came—breaking protocol and risking both our lives. And now he was forced to tread very carefully so I wouldn't get hurt. I watched as the muscle in his jaw ticked.

I think we're in trouble.

The King shifted in his throne, leaning forward. "I thought we explained that your presence was not required here tonight, Zarayan." He spoke in perfect English, which surprised me. The fact that Ronus spoke in a language Romeo could understand was a concession I didn't expect.

Romeo stopped in front of the dais and rolled his

bottom lip through his teeth in a devastatingly sexy gesture. This time, I heard several moans coming from around the ballroom, both masculine and feminine voices.

Is that... is that witch magic I can smell pouring off him? He's doing something, but I can't tell what it is. And am I the only one who can tell he's on the verge of exploding into violence?

"You did, grandfather." Romeo's voice was a low rumble of thunder. "But I had a thought that I could not get out of my head. It is something I wish to discuss with you both." He tilted his head, feigning casualness. "Will the ball continue without you?"

I crossed my fingers, hoping they'd take the bait and leave with him, so I could get out of here.

There was a beat of silence. "Those who wish to stay may stay," Queen Talia said, directing her voice out over the crowd. She stood up and held out her hand. "Otherwise, we shall see you all tomorrow at the first Trial."

King Ronus took her arm. "Lead the way, grandson."

The whole room stayed frozen as they walked out of the ballroom together.

CHAPTER
TWENTY-EIGHT

Brackin took my arm. "We should go."

"Yeah, we should." My head was spinning in every direction possible, both fear and relief swamped me in equal measures, making it hard to concentrate.

Tricky wards everywhere, Brain-Daphne muttered, taking over. *Stay in the palace but find somewhere quiet. Once we leave the palace grounds, we won't be able to get back in, and he might not be able to leave to find us.*

Brackin plastered a confident expression on his face and led me through the crowd. "Running away from the ball so soon isn't going to look good for us, Daffodil. But we've already pushed our luck too far tonight."

A tiny part of me—the part that wasn't screaming for me to run after Romeo—noted the whispers and stares. Although, when we got closer to the entrance of the ball-room, I saw a couple of other candidates casually being escorted out by their sponsors, too. Lady Bork was still in the corner by the orchestra, trying to wrestle instruments away from the musicians so she could use them as weapons.

It didn't matter to me since I'd be getting out of here soon, but my heart nudged me to reassure Brackin. "Don't worry," I whispered to him. "All the brides will leave right now too, I guarantee it. Lady Bork's sponsor has abandoned her. She's making a fool out of herself and anyone she targets. Nobody is going to want to stick around to deal with that, not with the royal couple already gone."

"That's a good point, Daffodil." He shot me a look of grudging admiration as we hurried past the line of guards at the door and made our way down the enormous hallway. "You surprised me tonight. You have a far better grasp of Court politics than I ever imagined."

He's about to be a whole lot more surprised. Get rid of him, or Romeo will kill him. You saw the look on his face when he saw us, my brain hissed.

Halfway down the corridor, I tugged on Brackin's arm. "I need the bathroom."

He pulled me back. "It will have to wait, Daffodil. We need to get out of here."

"It can't wait. It's urgent."

"Dear girl, you can pee in the carriage for all I care." Brackin's voice broke into a desperate shriek. "Perhaps it is the tension of the ballroom catching up with us, but I sense danger in the air. We must go."

Brackin was more intuitive than I thought, and he wasn't wrong. I could feel the atoms in the air tingling. The shadows around us lengthened, growing dimmer, and tendrils of darkness reached out for us as we walked down the hallway.

He was coming. And he was furious.

We emerged from the hallway and made our way into the cavernous entrance hall of the palace. I took a deep breath, trying to calm the pounding of my heart, and made my move. "No, it can't wait, sorry, Brackin. Wait for me outside the palace gates, okay?" I wrenched my arm out of his, turned, and power-walked towards the powder room underneath the staircase without looking back.

Hasty footsteps behind me indicated Brackin was going to chase me, but I put on a burst of speed and hurried past the two female guards at the door before he could catch up with me. They wouldn't let him in.

The shadows in the powder room flickered as I walked in. Romeo knew exactly where I was. I took a deep breath and looked around, reaching out with my senses.

Two other ladies were in here, one combing her hair at a vanity in the corner, and the other doing her business behind ornate stall doors. My heart hammered; I was surprised they couldn't hear the thumping in the quiet. Feigning a casual confidence I didn't feel, I walked over to the mirror in the middle of the powder room and pretended to fuss with my hair.

After a minute, the woman at the vanity stood up, nodded at me gracefully, and walked out.

My pulse spiked.

Shadows surged, swallowing me in darkness. I closed my eyes and surrendered.

TWENTY-NINE

"Daphne." The voice growled at me within the ice-cold darkness. The shadows caressed me gently, sliding over my skin as he pulled me through nothingness. "I could *kill* you..."

Conflicting sensations and feelings devoured me, leaving me senseless—lightness and intense pressure, ice-cold void and overwhelming body heat, fear and relief, sorrow and joy. The darkness held me so tightly, for a second, I wondered if it would ever let me go.

It was overwhelming. I couldn't speak; words wouldn't form. I held my breath.

After a long moment, the darkness retreated. He pulled back, no longer touching me, and pushed me out of the shadows. My body moved back into solid matter.

I reached out to hold on, but he was gone again, back into the darkness. My heart gave a whimper.

He really was furious. Once I was solid, I opened my eyes and watched the shadows slip away into the corners. He had brought me to a jaw-droppingly luxurious royal bedchamber. His bedroom. We were alone, and I could smell his silence charm near the door.

Romeo was still here; I could feel him. He had retreated back into the shadows to get hold of his temper. I swallowed roughly. "Is this your room? It's nice."

The stone floor beneath my feet rumbled.

I licked my lips nervously. "Not your normal style, obviously," I stammered. Best get this over with. I followed my heart and walked slowly towards the far end of the room, a spot where the candlelight didn't touch. "You're more of a minimalist. Clean lines, natural colors, simple masculine finishings."

"You came so close to dying tonight." Romeo's voice echoed out from the darkness. "Too close. I can't..." I felt rather than heard him take a deep breath. The storm was still raging within him. My presence, for once, was doing nothing to calm him down.

I think we made it worse, actually. That's why he's so mad.

"Romeo..." I shook my head slowly. "I don't understand. Please. I know you're mad that I came here. Can you just look at me?"

The shadow split open, and Romeo walked out, sinister and ominous like a thundercloud. His eyes glowed silver. He reached for me. "Daphne..." His voice shook.

"I'm sorry." I looked up into his furious, brutally handsome face, and exhaled a long, slow breath of relief. "I know you're mad, and I know you—"

He lunged, grabbed me, pulled me into his body, and kissed me.

The feel of his mouth on mine was a little death all in itself—it was hard and desperate and almost violent. I melted, surrendering completely, letting him take the lead, and lost myself to the feeling of my warlock finally holding me again. One huge, hard hand slid up the back of my neck, and he held a fistful of my hair, holding me in place so I couldn't move. His other arm wrapped around my waist and lifted me until my feet left the floor. He took two steps backwards and pushed me against the wall. I wrapped my legs around his waist, and he ground into me.

Oh, gods. Oh, my gods.

I let out a moan against his lips. Gods, I missed this. I missed *him*. The juxtaposition was almost ridiculous. It was like I'd tripped running through a nightmare place where everyone hated me and wanted to kill me, and I'd fallen headfirst into a heavenly realm, a place where I was loved and cherished and wanted, a place where I knew I'd be absolutely ravaged until I was satisfied into unconsciousness, a place where everything was exciting and dangerous but so safe and calm.

That heaven realm existed, and it was right here between us, between me and Romeo—our own little bubble of perfection.

A desperate need consumed me. I had to feel him on my skin, I needed him inside of me, and I needed it *now*.

We'd already waited too long. I didn't want another second to pass. I didn't want to go to my death without knowing what it felt like to have this perfect, god-like man touch every single inch of me.

As if he read my mind, he put me back on my feet and his hands found the edges of my gown. He ripped it apart at the seams. I tugged at his shirt. Thankfully, it was flimsier than mine, but I still tore it to shreds getting it off his body. His pants disappeared.

Was that me, or him? It didn't matter. All that mattered was that I was here, with him, with the man I loved. He dipped his lips to my throat, laying a trail of kisses, his hands roamed around my naked body, squeezing, brushing over my nipples—the sensation so intoxicating, so shocking, I cried out loud.

Suddenly, I was airborne. My lover picked me up, and,

never letting an inch of space between us, he lay me on the bed behind me.

The hardness of his body... the heat... his mouth, his tongue...

Reason left me. All that remained was ecstasy. Desire consumed me, and I allowed myself to be devoured.

CHAPTER

THIRTY

Hundreds of years later and still too soon, Romeo pulled back. He'd made me scream and whimper, I made him groan and shout, and it still wasn't enough. I could stay here forever. If I died now, I'd die happy.

But neither of us were stupid. We didn't have the luxury of time right now.

And we should probably do some stretches before we let him hammer us like that again, my brain said sleepily.

Romeo's huge fists clenched around my shoulders. "You shouldn't have come here."

"I know you're mad—"

"Daphne, I'm not mad. I'm fucking terrified." His silver eyes had darkened, but I could see the fear lingering in the depths. "You have no idea how close you came to dying tonight."

I blinked. "Which time?"

His face froze. *I think that was the wrong thing to say, babes.*

"Sorry." I licked my lips. "Let me rephrase. Who was going to kill me?"

"Me," he growled. "It would have been *me* that killed you, Daphne." The muscle in his jaw clenched compulsively. "The dais in the throne room is rigged with offensive spells. I've been putting this together for months. I can't get out of this damn palace without a whole garrison of guards following my every move. I needed a big distraction so I could escape. I agreed to the Bride Trials, to the ball, to *everything*. It was all part of the plan to get my revenge on my asshole father and get the fuck out of here. Tonight was supposed to be the night I escaped."

"Oh." I hesitated. So that was what he was doing in front of the dais, when I sensed the magic pouring off him. He was deactivating his offensive spells.

Despite the harshness of his words, I saw the conflict in his eyes. "But you don't want to kill them—"

"I want to kill *someone!*" He turned his head away from me and swore viciously. "I needed to get out of here and return home to you; I was willing to do anything. I begged Ronus and Talia, but they didn't understand. They kept saying I could go home and visit soon, but it just made me crazier—I know time works differently here, and it might be centuries before they let me go home. I was desperate, Daphne! I was so angry and confused, it drove me insane." He turned his head back to face me, reached out a shaking hand, and cupped my cheek. "I let it make me crazy, and I almost *killed* you."

So this was what the Oracle was talking about. Romeo was going to do something that would lead to the destruction of Faerie. If he'd killed the King and Queen and escaped in the resulting mayhem, there would be nobody to put on the throne of Dusk. The closest heir was probably Princess Ember, and based on our brief interaction, I had my doubts about whether she should even be allowed out in public at all.

An unbalanced Kingdom needed a strong hand to guide it, and with the royal couple gone, the unbalance would get worse. The Scorch—whatever it was—would continue to rage, burning the whole of Dusk to ashes, and the damage would spread. The light would taint the Winter side of the Inbetween until the harsh rays destroyed everything.

I leaned closer and buried my face in the nape of Romeo's neck, inhaling him. "It's going to be okay," I whispered, running my hands over his tense shoulders, trying to get them to relax a little. "We're going to be okay. You didn't kill anyone."

"I could have killed *everyone*. I've never been off world before. I'm alone here; I'm out of my depth. I got scared."

"So you decided to blow up a whole kingdom to get home to me?"

He let out a grunt. "Yes. Of course."

"You must have known I'd come looking for you."

He gave me a crooked smile. "Oh, I knew you would. You're insane. I prayed that you wouldn't, but I knew you would try."

"I wanted to come much sooner," I said softly, stroking the line of his jaw. "It's been two weeks, and I've been fighting *everyone* to get here."

"You put yourself in danger. Not just from me. This place is a viper pit." He exhaled a rough breath. "I'm still so mad at you."

"I know."

"You put yourself in danger for me. You almost died. I could have killed you." He bent his head to kiss the nape of my neck.

I shivered. Gods, he felt good. "That's kinda contrary of you, but I understand. When did you realize I was here?"

"Right before I fought my way through the guards to get into the ballroom" he said, kissing a spot below my earlobe.

215

"I've been checking the crystal on my necklace every day for six months, waiting to see it twitch in some sort of direction. And tonight, just before I triggered the curse that would blow that entire ballroom up, I pulled out my necklace just so I had something comforting to hold onto, only to find it glowing purple. You were in mortal danger."

Oops.

"I panicked and put the crystal on my palm. It swung in the direction of the ballroom." His voice dropped an octave, rumbling through me. "You can't imagine what that did to my nervous system. I was about to pull the trigger, and I realized that you—the person I was trying to get home to— were right in the kill zone."

There was something else in his tone. He wasn't just relieved he'd stopped because of me. I took a shot in the dark. "You didn't want to do it, did you? You didn't want to kill them all, I mean."

"I told myself I did. My whole life I've waited for a chance to get even with the guy who ruined my mom, only to find that he was already dead. I want someone to pay for it. If not my bio father, then his parents. I feel like I owe it to the little boy I used to be."

I caught the reluctance in his tone. "You don't hate them, though."

He hesitated for a moment. "No. I mean, they're ridiculously entitled, of course, because they're Faerie royalty. They stole me without warning, brought me here, told me I was heir to the throne, and it was my duty to help restore the balance to the Kingdom. They said it all like I didn't have a choice, and I assumed I was a prisoner. But as time went on..." He blew out a breath. "Daphne, I've been so conflicted. I've been so confused."

Tell me about it.

"I hated these people so much," he continued. "I hate my biological father, and I despise the high fae. They take what they want, and they don't care who they hurt in the process. They don't care about anyone but themselves. I've just been biding my time, playing along, doing whatever they wanted until I could kill them all and come home to you."

I rubbed my thumb over his bottom lip carefully, marveling at the softness of his skin. "And at some point," I said, "You realized they're just doing their best to hold the Kingdom together."

"Yeah." Romeo nodded. "This whole time I've been making the offensive curses and planning my assault, and I started hating myself. I've been tearing myself in two trying to justify committing mass murder. I know why Ronus and Talia took me. They didn't know I existed until now, they had no idea one of their sons knocked up a witch, and they don't really care about the circumstances of my birth. They stole me because they're desperate. But I still hate them for what happened to my mom." He squeezed his eyes shut. "I don't know what to do."

"I have something that might help." Wriggling out of his arms reluctantly, I slid out of bed and picked up the tattered remains of my gown. I wasn't even sure how he managed to unbuckle my harnesses without me noticing. "I mean, it might make everything worse, and you might hate the High Fae even more than you did before..." I found the Ziplock bag near the unbuckled harness, and I held it up to him.

He glared at the clear plastic bag. "What is it?"

"A journal. Prue gave it to me; she insisted you need to read it." I opened the seal, took the journal out of the plastic, and held it out to him. "Careful. It's old."

He took it, ran a finger over the bright paper notation

tabs sticking out of it, opened it, and frowned. "It's in High Fae script."

I dug the blue marble out of the bag and handed it to him. "Yeah, Prue gave me a charm which explains everything—"

The words died on my tongue as I realized something; Romeo's mom wouldn't write her diary in high fae.

This wasn't her journal. It was his father's journal.

Romeo realized it at the same time I did. He put the charm down on the bed, handed me the journal, and took a deep breath. "Will you read it to me?"

I swallowed. "Are you sure?'

"Yeah."

My hands shook a little as I opened the leather book. The pages were yellowed and cracked with age. Carefully, I flicked through to the first page Prue had marked with a bright orange tag and began to read out loud, translating the script into English as best I could.

FORGET *everything I wrote until now. I am a fool, an unbearable idiot, and reading back on my selfish tantrums fills me with shame. But in fairness, how could I have known? Yesterday, this realm was gray and boring, pointless and stupid, and I could not wait to return home to my pleasant distractions and amusing diversions. But today I met her.*

I PAUSED AND GLANCED UP. Romeo had gone very still. "Go on," he whispered.

I NEVER DREAMED *such a creature could exist, not even in any pantheon of the gods. How could I? She is charm, beauty and grace incarnate. From the very first moment she slapped my face for being appallingly rude to her, I confess I was lost, irrevocably changed. My whole universe has been tipped on its head. This mortal realm is now vivid and bright, filled with color and shine, and the thought of returning home fills me with dread. Gwendolyn, my Gwendolyn. I have lost my heart to her.*

ROMEO HADN'T MOVED. I flicked to the next tab and scanned it quickly. It was more of the same, more breathless declarations of love and descriptions of how wonderful Gwendolyn was. "It goes on for a while," I explained. "The next few months of entries, in fact." I kept flicking through, being careful with the pages, and turned the page to the next tag. I read the next part out loud.

MY LOVE HAS DECIDED she will not come home with me. I will not press her on it; in fact, I understand her reluctance. Even though she would make the most excellent princess that Dusk has ever had, and even though she would shine like a star in the night sky, I want to keep her all to myself. This mortal realm— however much I loathed it before—it is where I shall stay, and as long as she will stay with me, it will be paradise.

I PAUSED AGAIN and glanced up. Romeo's eyes had gone silver like mist.

"Are you okay?" I asked.

He swallowed. "Keep going."

I flicked to the next tag and kept reading.

. . .

THIS HEAVEN HAS EXPANDED; ecstasy has multiplied. Gwendolyn carries my child. I had no idea such happiness could ever exist. But with this pure joy comes an equally pure terror—I cannot lose her. I will not lose her. So, despite my misgivings, I know I must venture back to Faerie to procure the items I need to help her ease this pregnancy. I do not want to leave her, but if our child is to be born safely, possessing all the might and magic I know he will have, I must. While I am home, I suppose I should let mother know there is another Winterbourne on the way—

I GASPED. "Winterbourne. Wintermade. I didn't... I mistranslated it. I never made the connection..."

Romeo's expression was unreadable. "Please keep going."

With shaking hands, I turned the pages of the journal to a red tab and quickly scanned it. My heart thumped in my chest almost painfully.

MY LOVE IS GONE. I don't know where. Nobody will tell me anything, not her wretched father or her vile stepmother. Everyone who knows her says the same thing—she just disappeared. I was not gone for long, barely a month of mortal time. I heard rumors she tried to follow me to Faerie, but I have traveled the length and breadth of both realms to try to find her, and she is nowhere to be found. I have scried for her and begged seers to give me answers, but nobody can See where she is. My Gwendolyn. The sun is gone from my life. All is cold and bleak.

I TURNED to the next tab. The date indicated several months had gone by. Before, the pages of the journal were filled with elegant dashing script. Now, there were one or two sentences in blunt, painful writing.

MY SON SHOULD HAVE BEEN BORN *by now—nine mortal months have passed since my Gwendolyn told me the news. My precious bride, my perfect son. I have lost them both, as well as the will to live. Every breath I take without my wife and son causes unendurable pain. I would take my own life but not for the tiny flame of hope within me that somewhere, somehow, my Gwendolyn is still alive.*

THE REST of the journal made me want to howl. The pain and despair practically screamed from deep within the journal. I read the last tabbed entry out loud. "This one is dated almost a hundred years ago, Romeo."

I HATE THIS WRETCHED REALM; *I despise everything about it. But I will not leave, no matter what my parents demand of me. I will stay here forever until the fates decide to grant me a connection to my beloved Gwendolyn. A link, a sign, a signal. A tiny touch of her presence. I will see her again, somewhere, somehow.*

I PICKED up the blue charm, unfolded Romeo's fingers, and dropped it into his hand. "I think you need to listen to what Prue has to say now."

He held the ball in his hand for a minute, then whispered a word. Silver magic poured off his fingers. The ball began to glow, and a translucent image of Prue appeared in the air between us.

Her expression was unusually solemn. "Now you

know," she said simply. "Your father was Prince Salozar Winterbourne. I realized it as soon as I saw your face. You look a lot like him."

Romeo took a shaky breath in and watched the image of Prue.

She continued, "I first met Salozar when I became the Enforcer of D.C. He was infuriating, an absolute asshole to deal with... until I punched him in the face. Something changed in him then." Prue shook her head, her eyes twinkling. "It was like he'd been brought back to life. Suddenly, he was a whole different person. It wasn't until after he died and I read his journals, that I understood why. I'd given him a connection to Gwendolyn, who'd slapped him the first time they'd met. Over a hundred years had gone by and he'd never given up looking for that connection. I gave it to him; I reminded him of his love for her. He fell in love with me because of it, and all the bitterness and hatred in his heart evaporated."

I glanced at Romeo. He stood still, just listening.

Prue paused for a second on the recording. "Salozar was no angel. In fact, for most of his life, he was the opposite. He was one of the Beast's generals before he grew a conscience and snuck off here to hide in the mortal realm, which is when he met your mom. His heart broke into pieces when he came back and found her missing. Fifty years after your mother disappeared, the anger and bitterness had warped him to the point where he hated the mortal realm with a passion, so much so he even conspired to destroy it at one stage. But he didn't leave, not for long, anyway. He always loved her, and he loved you. He was no angel, but he was the bravest, most extraordinary man I've ever met."

Tears welled up in Prue's eyes, she dashed them away. "You know what he did. He sacrificed himself to stop the Beast of Bakkanon from destroying our whole world.

222

Salozar endured the worst torture you could possibly imagine and still showed up, dying of iron poisoning, crawling on broken legs to the spot where the Beast was trying to come through. He dragged himself through cursed flame just for the chance to hold that asshole for the precious seconds I needed to kill him. Salozar Winterbourne gave his life willingly to stop a genocidal maniac from devouring the mortal realm. Your father died a hero." Prue's voice broke. A sob shook her shoulders. She'd loved Salozar back—not in the same way as he did, but in her own way. And his sacrifice had been extraordinary.

She paused, wiped her cheeks, swallowed, and continued, "He always loved your mother, and he never abandoned her. He never stopped looking for her. Maybe Gwendolyn reached out from beyond the grave and used my fist to punch some sense back into him, I don't know. Prince Salozar Winterbourne was your father. I wish he could have known you, Romeo; he'd be so proud of you. And I'm so glad that I knew him."

THIRTY-ONE

Romeo and I held each other for a long time. Both of us cried. Romeo shed tears for his father, and for the angry, hurt little boy who didn't know the truth. He said goodbye to the kid who was filled with the rage that anyone would abandon his mother and let her die on the street.

Salozar never abandoned her. She just got lost off-world like I had and came back over a hundred years later.

"I should have realized," I whispered, wiping his wet cheeks with my thumb. "Your name. Zarayan," I pronounced the word a little differently than he normally did. "It's a high fae term of endearment. It means 'my beautiful boy.' Your mom insisted you be called that, because Salozar would have called you that. And I'm not going to give you a lecture on high fae nomenclature, but you're literally named after Salozar's father, Ronus."

"I don't know what to do now," Romeo finally said, his voice rough. "I guess I already got all the revenge I needed to get. Marcus Jupiter was the one who turned Salozar away when he came looking for my mom. Wesley Jupiter was the one who turned my mom away and let her die on the street a hundred years later. All the Jupiters are dead."

I stroked his massive shoulder. "We could go home."

Ha. We're not going home, babes. You already know it; I already know it.

Silence fell between us for a minute or two. He took a deep breath and exhaled roughly, a frustrated sound. "Everything was much simpler when I was just going to kill everyone here and come home. This just makes everything more complicated."

A smile pulled at my lips. "You like your grandparents."

He paused for only a second. "Yeah. I do."

"They're trying to save their Kingdom. They want to figure out what's wrong with the Inbetween and why it's unbalanced."

He pulled back to look at my face; his eyes twinkled. "I don't even know why we bother talking. You already know everything I'm thinking."

"Because I've been thinking the same thing." I quickly briefed him on what the Oracle had told me. "If this unbalance in the Inbetween continues, it might eventually destroy the whole of Faerie. The Queens of Summer and Winter won't help because they're selfish, arrogant and insane, even though the unbalance would eventually destroy them, too."

"We don't have to help—"

"The unbalance will spread to neighboring realms. It will affect us. We're still dealing with a surge of authoritarianism from when the Beast was on the rampage. If Faerie falls, then we'll be next."

"*You* don't have to help," Romeo said more pointedly. "In fact, I'd be happier if I could just wrap you in bubble wrap and send you home."

"I'm not leaving without you." I smiled at him. "And you can't make me."

He grimaced. "I knew you would say that. Look, you've already saved Faerie once by stopping me from, you know"—he waved his hand—"killing everyone in the palace in a senseless, desperate rage."

I nodded graciously. "You're welcome."

"You've brought me the answers I needed to bring me comfort and help me make the right decisions. Killing the entire Court of Dusk never felt right, I'll admit that. This decision feels right. Ronus and Talia need me. And"—he paused and shrugged—"considering that my own father died saving my world, I should probably stay and help them save theirs."

I gave him a brilliant smile. I was so happy to be here with him. "So, I will stay too."

His eyes narrowed for a second. "Logically, I know you're far more experienced in surviving this realm than I am. I'm going to keep repeating that to myself whenever I get the urge to murder anyone that looks at you."

"That sounds like a plan. So, talking of plans... What do the King and Queen need you to do?" I booped him on the nose with my finger. "If you say, 'get married to a fae princess and have a baby,' I'm sorry, I'm no longer on board with that plan."

"Ronus and Talia aren't holding the Bride Trials to find me a wife," Romeo explained. "It's just an excuse to gather all the aristocracy of the Inbetween together in one place. They're doing it to figure out who killed King Monton and his young son and to flush out the cause of the Scorch."

"Huh?" I shook my head, confused. "I thought Monton and his heir died in a hunting accident?"

"No, they were murdered. There was no accident. The hunting party were using bows and arrows, and their bodies were found full of crossbow bolts. In their beds," he emphasized, "mid-morning, while they would have still been asleep."

I whistled through my teeth. "They kept that quiet."

"It was Queen Carissa's idea to keep the assassination a secret. She was trying to keep the Kingdom from dissolving into chaos. If the throne was weakened, then it would give one of the other royal courts an excuse to swoop in and take control or make war. Ronus thinks it was one of the other courts, trying to take over the Kingdom of Dusk."

"Oh." I gnawed on my lip. "I suppose it makes sense that it's the one enemy if the Scorch appeared around the same time. There's only one thing that unsettles a kingdom more than the murder of a regent, and that's a giant terror threat like the Scorch." I thought for a moment. "Are there any suspects in Monton's murder? In human murder cases, it's usually the spouse or a family member, and if Carissa wanted the assassination kept quiet..."

"Queen Carissa wasn't there at the time," Romeo replied. "She stayed in the palace. And we don't think she would have hired an assassin to do it because she loved him, and she didn't want to rule Dusk by herself."

I made a face. "That's what a murderer would say."

"No, Ronus is sure. Monton's death affected her badly; she was a wreck afterwards. She didn't want to stay here in the City of Dusk after he died. She wanted to go back to her family home in the Kingdom of Spring. But Ronus talked her into staying. He was next in line, but he was very reluctant to take the throne. Dusk is a huge responsibility."

"Huh." I lapsed into silence for a moment. "That makes me hate him less for stealing you away, I guess. A bad ruler would want the power and wouldn't care about the responsibility. A good ruler wouldn't need the power, and they'd take the responsibility seriously." I gave him a smile. "You're a lot like your grandfather."

Romeo gave me a lopsided grin, then became serious again. "He figured Carissa had already been ruling by Monton's side for long enough. They'd done a good job, and everyone was used to her. But then a week after Carissa announced she would rule Dusk by herself, she had a breakdown and ran away."

"She ran away?"

"Yeah. According to Ronus, the vultures were circling, eyeing the throne, and a lot of the aristocracy were lining up potential new grooms for Carissa, and she became suspicious and paranoid. When she ran away, Ronus and Talia were forced to step up, but even before then, they'd been noticing little hints of the unbalance in their own duchy of Nightfall. And not long after that, the Scorch was spotted for the first time. It's been rampaging ever since."

"Hmm." I thought about it. "It does sound like it's all linked."

"Ronus is sure someone from one of the other royal courts killed Monton and tried to replace him with one of their own through marriage to Carissa. And when she ran away and Ronus and Talia took the throne, they pivoted, systematically killed off Ronus and Talia's remaining heirs, and created the curse of the Scorch to weaken the Kingdom of Dusk. But it's not weakening the kingdom fast enough. We think their plan is to have one of their daughters win the Bride Trials, marry me, kill me off, then they'll stop the Scorch. Finally, they'll have complete control of Dusk."

I gnawed on my lip again. "I don't think the Scorch is a curse, though. It feels more powerful than that. Almost like... like a god. A little god, mind you, not a big one, but still god. Maybe they summoned the Scorch. It feels like an entity rather than a construct, if you know what I mean."

"No." Romeo's eyes hardened. "Please don't tell me you've already seen that thing, Daphne."

"Okay." I wiped my expression clean. I didn't have to tell him anything he didn't want to hear. I sandwiched my lips together.

He let out a gruff sigh and pinched the bridge of his nose. "Daphne... The Scorch is literally the plague of the Inbetween. Nobody knows what it is. Ronus and Talia have been trying to kill it for at least a decade. You've been here, what, two days? And you've already tried to fight it?"

"Of course not, Romeo." I rolled my eyes. "I wasn't trying to fight it. I was running away from it."

A growl rumbled from his lips. "Daphne..."

"Relax, Romeo. I survived, and I'm fine. Dwayne tried to pee on it," I added, trying to lighten the mood. "Geese don't even pee, but he managed it."

He sat up. "Dwayne is here?"

"Yeah." I shrugged. "Somewhere. He's got his own mission in Faerie." *The less said about that, the better.*

Romeo shook his head slowly. "I'll never understand your relationship."

"Dwayne trusts me to handle myself. And I'm going to stay out of his business, too, because *wow*." I whistled. "He's insane. Anyway," I said, sitting up on the bed a little straighter, "back to the plan. I understand why your grandparents are holding the Trials now. Someone wants to conquer Dusk, and we need to find out who it is, because their lust for power is going to destroy this entire realm."

"Exactly. The Bride Trials are the perfect way to get everyone together and figure it all out. All the main courts have sent either their rulers or heirs, so our enemy will definitely be here somewhere. Because of the Scorch, we're all locked in the City, and nobody can leave. Ronus and Talia will be focusing on Prince Aranbold of Spring, and King Rayna of Dawn. They've been Dusk's traditional enemies, and we've been at war before."

It had been a thousand years since the last war between them, but he was right, they were traditional enemies, and nobody held a grudge like the High Fae. "Princess Nyla of Spring is the favorite to win the Trials. They would have been training her for this since birth."

"And Glorina of Dawn's odds are almost just as good. Both their kingdoms have the might and resources to pull off a royal assassination, but I don't know who would have enough magic to create the Scorch. Or summon it," he added. "Ronus is having their most trusted advisors work the aristocracy during the Trials to see if they can find anything suspicious. Once the dates start, I'll be able to get a feel for which of the brides might be more interested in conquering Dusk rather than ruling it with me."

"And I'm going undercover with the bride candidates." I nodded thoughtfully. "Just like Miss Congeniality."

"I'm sorry." Romeo paused for a second, then blinked. "What?"

"It's a movie," I explained. "A hard-ass female FBI agent goes undercover at the Miss USA pageant to investigate a terrorist threat they think was made by another contestant—"

"No." Romeo cut me off. "I mean the part about you going undercover with the bride candidates."

"That's what the FBI agent does in the movie, Romeo," I explained patiently. "She goes undercover as a contestant and makes friends with all the other girls to try and figure out which one is going to detonate a bomb at the pageant. There's a makeover montage and everything. I've already done that part." Romeo was looking at me funny. "It's a great movie," I added, a little defensively.

"I'm sure it is," he said. "But it's not going to work. You'll have to stay in the background for this one, baby."

"But—"

He put a finger over my lips. "Just listen to me. First, I'm worried about what Ronus and Talia would do if they knew you were my girlfriend. They seem compassionate, but if they feel like you're going to fuck up their kingdom..." He grimaced and pulled me into a hug. "You know what the High Fae are like."

I did figure Romeo's grandparents might not take too kindly to the idea of me, considering all their plans for the future hinged on marrying their heir off to whoever could help secure their Kingdom.

"Sure," I said. "I know they're not going to like me, and it's best that they don't know I exist or else they might kill me and just hope that you eventually get over it. I do get that, Romeo. But—"

"And you can't enter the Trials, anyway. It's not an open invitation. You have to be chosen by one of the ruling families to compete. The aristocracy always plans three generations in advance. Some of them have specially bred and trained their princesses from birth to win these things."

"Oh. I, uh." I wriggled out of his arms awkwardly. "I already entered."

His face went blank, and he leaned back on the bed. "No, you didn't. I saw the registration list before the ball."

"I was registered under my nickname." I cringed. "Little Daffodil."

"What? What the *hell?*" Romeo lurched upright. "You entered the Trials? Is *that* why you were at the Commencement Ball?" He gaped at me in horrified silence for a

231

moment. "Oh, gods, you did, didn't you? Of course you did. But... *How?* How the hell did you do it, Daphne?"

"I hit up an old enemy and forced him to bring me here. I didn't actually want to enter the Bride Trials. It was my only way into the city," I admitted. "They were only letting candidates and their sponsors inside."

"Your sponsor?" He stared at me, aghast. "That greasy asshole that was standing next to you in the ballroom?"

"Lord Brackin of Gloom," I said. "He used to be my master. Now, he's my sponsor."

"Daphne!" He gripped my arms. "I could *kill you!*"

"Yes," I sighed. "That seems to be a common theme of the evening."

"Most of the candidates die!"

"I know. Deep breaths, babe. We'll get through this."

He turned his head away from me, inhaled through his nose, and started muttering under his breath. "Logically, I know you're far more experienced than I am at surviving this realm. Logically, I know you are far more experienced than I am..."

I grinned. "That's it."

After a moment, he turned back to face me. "So this is how it's going to go down? I'm going to be sitting beside the King and Queen, watching you battle to the death with a dozen bloodthirsty fae princesses?"

"Well, I know you don't want to hear it, baby..." I leaned forward and kissed him lightly on the lips. "But it wouldn't be the first time."

CHAPTER

THIRTY-TWO

The first Bride Trial was a classic woodland hunt. In theory, it sounded simple. The first candidate to bring back the head of the nominated target would win the Hunt Trial and gain the favor of the Crown of Dusk.

In practice, the brides would be hunting each other as well as whatever poor woodland creature they chose.

"We are down to only thirteen candidates," Brackin announced. He'd finally gotten over his outrage at being abandoned by the palace gates for two hours and was now filling me in on everything he knew, while I got ready in the servants' quarters of the Pesh residence. "We began with thirty. Two candidates died on the way here, victims of the Scorch. Another five dropped out once they got here and saw who the other candidates were, and ten Brides died last night at the Commencement Ball."

Steven fussed around me, adjusting the buckles and buttons, taking my coat in a fraction at the waist, all while she force-fed me the fae version of a grilled cheese—two massive hunks of sourdough bread soaked with butter, filled with stretchy, creamy cheese, and toasted over a hot grill. It was astonishingly delicious and possibly the best way to carb load for the Hunt event of the Bride Trial. Although the mention of so much senseless death did make me lose my appetite a little.

"Ten," I whispered. "Wow."

"The brides all knew what they were getting themselves into," Brackin said, helping himself to a handful of snacks Steven had laid out on the table for me. "Most of them were brained by Lady Bork after we left." He pursed his lips. "You should be glad of her, Daffodil. At least there's one bride in the Trials that is more embarrassing than you."

"Thanks, Brackin."

He picked up a handful of hard, little, round grains off the tray, closed his fist around them, and shook his hand sharply. Gunshot cracks came from within his closed hand. He opened it to display yellow puffed grain. "The horn will blow in an hour." He shoved the snapcorn in his mouth and chewed with relish. "You must hurry, Daffodil. I know you don't know the meaning of the word," he added snarkily. "But I would like you to try."

"I said I was sorry." I beat him to the snack tray and picked up my own handful of snapcorn, pouring it carefully in my crossbody bag. I'd forgotten how loud snapcorn was, and it might come in handy later. "I didn't mean to keep you waiting last night, Brackin."

I meant it. I assumed he'd go home. It was oddly touching when I snuck out of the gates and found Brackin still waiting for me. He'd ranted at me the whole way home, and once we got there, I endured another shrill scolding from Lord Bron and Lady Pesh, who were both outraged to see me still alive.

"Your apology is *not* accepted. I waited for over two hours. I thought you must be dead," Brackin said moodily. "It was most uncomfortable. I expended considerable emotional energy keeping you alive during that ball, you know, and I was worried it was all for naught."

"You did a great job," I said absently, checking myself in the mirror. Steven the brownie had done a great job on my outfit, too, fashioning offcuts and leftovers into equestrian gear. Luckily for me, she'd served fae crocodile filets for dinner. She'd somehow managed to process the hide overnight and used it to make a riding coat and breeches. The leather scales on the outside were almost as hard as Kevlar, and soft and warm on the inside. Their muted brown and gray tones would help camouflage me in the woods.

Brackin eyed my outfit critically. "You won't be noticeable. The other brides will be wearing their pastels, trying to stand out so the royals can see them better from the towers."

"The other brides will be trying to kill each other," I said, pulling my hair up into a high ponytail. "It seems silly to want to make yourself a visible target."

"Yes." Brackin looked doubtful. "The King and Queen will choose the winner in the end, though, so you should want to make yourself look as good as possible."

"I'm not trying to win, Brackin, I'm just trying to survive."

He frowned. "I wish you would tell me why."

"Not happening." I pointed a finger at him. "Stop asking."

He huffed out a sigh. "I suppose it would be a good idea to survive as long as you can. Tomorrow is the Diplomacy and Talent Trials, which will be less violent, so you should be okay. But the day after is War Games. That's bound to be a bloodbath."

War Games were like our version of Capture the Flag

but using live rounds. "What are the rest of the Trials going to be?" I asked.

"If you survive past War Games, the next day is Close Combat, and you'll be fighting each candidate one-on-one."

Close Combat trials weren't supposed to be a fight to the death, only to submission, but a good amount of the brides would be aiming to strike killing blows. Deaths were explained away as the incompetence of the victim.

"If you survive that, Daffodil—and it's doubtful—after Close Combat, they've scheduled the Compatibility Trial. You'll get to meet the Prince of Shadow for the first time and go on a date, which might be nice." Brackin's grin faltered. "He might kill you too, of course. It's been known to happen."

I don't want him to kill me. I just want him to give me the little death again. Ha ha. La Petite Mort. Get it? It's French for orgasm, Brain-Daphne explained.

I got it. Thanks, brain.

"And to wrap things up," Brackin continued. "There's the Death Race Trial."

"Oh, great," I muttered. "A giant murderous agility course to finish things up."

"They leave that for last because it's the most expensive Trial to set up. And there might not be any Brides left by then." Brackin glanced at his watch again. "We must go."

Steven helped me do up my boots and ordered me to practice whipping my Orion blades out of the hidden sheaths—sewn in the back of my riding coat—a few times before she would let us leave.

"You're a genius, Steven," I said, grinning.

She gave me a hug for luck, and Brackin took my arm. He led me outside to where our horses were waiting. I'd been hoping my gelding would be more relaxed with me on his back, but he still skittered a little. We rode with Brackin's two footmen to the City gates in silence, where a whole garrison waited to escort us to the woods to the west of the Kingdom of Dusk.

"The Scorch has been seen in the east, near Bloom," Brackin explained as we rode through the gates. "So you do not have to be concerned it will interfere in the Hunt today, Daffodil. I assume the King would call off the Trial if it had been sighted any closer."

It was a beautiful afternoon. The light streamed soft and orange through scattered puffy white clouds hovering above the horizon, turning them pink. We followed the crowd as it snaked down the road, leading to the thick woods a few miles outside of the City. I inhaled the fresh air gratefully, relishing the scent of fertile soil, squashy green moss, and fat green leaves on the trees.

A few of the brides rode up ahead. I could spot them easily, even from a distance. Like Brackin said, they were all wearing pastels—even Lady Bork, who was riding on a small rhino rather than a horse, which might not have been able to take her weight. The rhino's little legs were moving so fast they were almost a blur.

The favorite, Princess Nyla of Spring, stood out like a beacon in a bright yellow riding coat and cream breeches, trotting along gracefully on a beautiful white mare. Lady Brisa of Frost rode next to her wearing pearl-toned colors, with her platinum hair pulled into a tight roll on the back of her head.

Brackin noticed them too. "Lady Brisa and Princess Nyla have formed an alliance after all. I assume Frost will be supporting Nyla's bid for the crown."

"Two other brides are shadowing them. Who are they?"

"Ladies from minor courts," he said. "Nobody of importance. It's a miracle they survived the ball last night, in fact.

Their odds are terrible, and they obviously know it. They must be looking to ally themselves with Nyla, too."

"She's formed her own girl gang. Great."

"Oh, she's not the only one, Little Daffodil. The other two main princesses—Saoira from Autumn and Glorina from Dawn—they're gathering supporters, too. It looks like Lady Bloom has gotten over her concussion, and she's sticking with Glorina of Dawn. Lady Winnara of Gale was seen bowing to Princess Saoira, so she's obviously pledging her allegiance to Autumn."

I chewed on my lip nervously. Those were the main suspects—Saoira, Glorina, and Nyla. They were doing what they'd been trained to do—making alliances and gathering supporters to help them in their bid for the throne. But one of them came from a family that had gone too far. One of them was responsible for King Monton's assassination and for the Scorch. I just had to figure out which one was power crazed enough to do it.

A high-pitched voice let out a shrill hunting cry from behind me. "Out of the way, cretins! Coming through!"

Little Princess Ember of Sandstone galloped past, her massive pink stallion shouldering the other horses as it shot through the crowd. I was happy to see Ember had survived the night. She was so young, and so volatile, the others were sure to see her as easy pickings. I leaned over to speak quietly to Brackin. "What do you know about Princess Ember? Did her uncle force her to enter?"

"He talked her into it." His lips thinned. "Or so says the gossip of the court, anyway. Duke Redfoot never has been quiet about the fact he considers her a burden. Entering Ember in the Bride Trials was a win-win for Redfoot. If Ember wins the trials, he'll be rid of her. If she dies, he'll be rid of her."

I figured as much; I hadn't been convinced by Ember's

blustering talk of revenge. It was far more likely her asshole uncle had manipulated her into entering. That poor girl had nobody decent to take care of her. I'd have to keep an eye on her.

We rode for a mile or two. Eventually, the crowd poured into a clearing in the middle of the woods, right in front of three massive wooden towers. The tallest one in the middle had been draped with flags in the royal colors of Dusk. Brackin and I rode to the front, gathering with the other candidates.

I lingered at the back of the pack. Lady Sybell of Nightfall, resplendent in a scarlet riding coat, glanced over her shoulder and shot me a look of pure loathing. Two other brides turned to see what she was looking at, saw me, and whispered and giggled behind their hands. Lady Meena from Bloom, her head heavily bandaged, moved her horse further away from me.

Brackin turned to me. "Best of luck, Little Daffodil. Try not to die."

"I'll do my best."

He rode out of the crowd and headed towards the viewing tower to the left, where some of the smaller houses' sponsors were gathered. He left his horse at the bottom with his footmen and climbed up. Most of the aristocracy would be watching us from up there.

I looked up at the royal tower. King Ronus sat on a high-backed throne. Queen Talia was next to him, her hand resting gently on his arm. Romeo sat on Ronus's left, leaning forward, elbows on his knees. His eyes bored into me. I felt a throb of something wild deep in my core.

Some of the higher-ranking aristocracy were up there with them—I recognized Prince Aranbold of Spring, the Queen of Autumn, and King Rayna of Dawn. Most likely, it was one of them conspiring to overthrow Dusk. I understood why Ronus had gathered them all there.

My eyes drifted back to Romeo, hungry for him. His forearms were bulging. He looked so tense. I gave him a wink. Relax, baby. I got this.

King Ronus waved his hand. A herald blew a horn, cleared his throat, and announced the first event of the Bride Trials. "The rules of the hunt are simple," he bellowed over the gathered crowd. "Our candidates will hunt the Golden Stag. You may use any weapon you can carry."

Most of the brides had bows and arrows strapped to their backs, some had crossbows and extra bolts. All of us had at least one short sword. I had a bow, a quiver of arrows, my Orion blades, and some snacks in my crossbody bag. Ember was weighed down by at least six other daggers and a whole belt of throwing knives.

"The first to bring back the Golden Stag's head and present it to our Prince will be declared the winner of the Hunt Trial." The herald paused and glared at the brides. "It must be the *actual* Golden Stag—the King of the Woods. If anyone attempts to transform another candidate into a stag, paint her gold, and cut off her head, she will be disqualified."

My horse skittered under me. He wasn't happy to be here. Mine was the smallest horse out of all the competitors —most of the brides had huge mares or massive stallions. I patted him on the neck. "Relax, buddy. We're going to do fine."

The brides in my line of sight were baring their teeth, getting ready to gallop away. Every single one of them pulled on their horses' bridles roughly.

"At my horn, the hunt will commence!" the herald bellowed.

I checked in on Brain-Daphne. Do we have a plan?

Sure, she replied cheerfully. *Kill everyone else, climb the tower, throw the big guy in a body bag, and fuck off home.*

"Good plan," I muttered.

The herald lifted his horn to his lips and blew. The candidates let out undulating cries, whipped their horses, and galloped off into the woods.

My own horse skittered sideways, trying to turn around and go the other way. I yanked helplessly at the reins. We spun in a circle. He did *not* want to go any further into the woods.

The crowd of common folk behind me laughed and jeered. Some of the aristocracy in the towers tittered, watching me instead of the brides in the woods.

"Come on, buddy," I said to my horse. "You're embarrassing me." I managed to get him facing the right way. I was about to kick my heels into his side to encourage him into the woods when I heard a man's voice shout from the tower on the right. "Daphne? Sweet Daphne, is that you?"

I glanced up. The man was huge—seven feet tall, barrel-chested, with a great bushy black beard that touched his navel. I recognized him. My mouth dropped open. "Lord Fandoine?"

"Daphne!" he shouted, rushing to the railing. "My wife! My lost wife!"

Damn it.

I lost control of my horse again, and he spun back around to face the other way.

My brain nudged me. *Uh, the hunt? The other competitors have a head start on us, babes. We have to go. Ignore him.*

I couldn't. Everyone was looking at Lord Fandoine now. Great. This was just great. My past was coming back to haunt me.

Lord Fandoine let out a mournful howl and gripped the railing so tight, it splintered under his huge fists. "Sweet

241

Daphne, my beautiful wife! I never thought I would see you again!"

What the hell was I supposed to do? Fandoine was making a scene, Romeo was watching, and he was looking even angrier than before.

"I better take a minute to clear this up," I muttered under my breath.

Hurry up. We're losing time.

I took a deep breath. "Lord Fandoine, I'm not your wife," I shouted up to him. "I didn't consent to be married to you, remember? You locked me in a tower. I ran away the night before the wedding!"

"My Sweet Daphne!" He roared. "My love! Why did you run?"

I took another deep breath and yelled up to him again. "Because you're a bloodthirsty warlord, and you locked me in a tower?"

"This is our custom, Sweet Daphne!" he shouted back. "A cultural difference, that is all! I thought I explained that to you!"

This was going nowhere. I tried again. "Look, I don't want to hurt your feelings or anything, but honestly, Lord Fandoine, I really didn't *want* to marry you!" I shouted up to him. "That's why I ran away!"

He wiped the tears that were pouring down his face and soaking into his bushy black beard. "But I have missed you every day since. I am but a savage beast, and nobody has been able to soothe me like you!"

My horse turned in a circle again. "I'm... uh... kinda busy here, Lord Fandoine! But my answer was no then, and it's no now. You need to learn the concept of consent!"

"No!" he roared back. "I tried, but I don't understand it! Please! My precious wife!" Lord Fandoine took his hands off the splintered railing, clenched his fists, and howled as if his heart would break. "My Sweet Daphne!"

My brain nudged me. *Doll, there was no getting through to him back then, and there's no getting through to him now. Let's just go.*

This was so embarrassing. King Ronus had a confused frown on his face. Queen Talia looked at me, arching one perfect eyebrow ever so slightly. Everyone was watching me —except Romeo, who was glaring over at Lord Fandoine like he was going to rip his head off.

I hesitated for a second; Fandoine looked really distraught. "You'll get over me! Maybe try some therapy!" I shouted up to him. "Take up a hobby. Like... uh... knitting."

Babes, are you actually trying to embarrass us even more?

"My Sweet Daphneeeee!"

I swore under my breath. "I should just go, shouldn't I?"

Yes, you idiot. Go.

My cheeks burning with shame, I managed to wrench my horse around in a circle, and we cantered off into the woods.

CHAPTER

THIRTY-THREE

"Okay, shake it off. We've got this," I said to myself as we entered the gloomy woods. It was late afternoon now, and the sun had already dipped below the tree line. I could hear feminine screams and shouts echoing around me. From the sounds of it, only a few were tracking deer, trying to find the Golden Stag. Most were squaring off against each other. The carnage had already begun.

I urged my horse in the opposite direction of most of the screams. "Okay." I took a deep breath. "We don't have to win the Hunt Trial," I said to myself. "We just have to stay alive. I don't think we're going to be able to make any friends right now, so we'll have to shelve the whole Miss Congeniality idea, and hope that Romeo and his grandparents are getting some good intel from the sponsors while they watch us."

We'll keep our eyes and ears open, though.

"From a distance, sure. The other brides are attacking each other as well as hunting the Golden Stag, so we head in the direction it's least likely to be. Now, what do we know about the Golden Stag?"

It's a trophy animal. It's gold, and it's a stag.

"Thank you, Captain Obvious. But seriously, give me something here." Movement in the distance caught my eye, a scarlet riding coat vivid and bright among the trees. It was Lady Sybell of Nightfall, moving at a smooth canter, holding herself very stiffly. She was probably still injured from where I'd stuck the knife in her back.

More pastel colors flickered in the distance, not far from Lady Sybell. I stayed low in the saddle, kept my horse to a slow walk, and watched.

Sybell put on a burst of speed, drew out a throwing knife, and hurled it at a pink figure darting through the trees. Whoever the bride was—I couldn't see—she fell off her horse and landed on the ground. Sybell whipped her horse, thundering off towards the fallen Bride, and stomped her into the dirt.

My stomach churned.

Yeah, you probably should have twisted that blade in her back a little harder, Brain-Daphne muttered.

I led my horse away as quietly as possible. I'd never hesitated to kill before, as long as someone deserved it. Lady Sybell would get no more chances from me. All this unnecessary carnage made me feel sick, and strangely, a little ashamed.

Yes, something is clearly wrong with us. Anyway, back to the task at hand, Brain-Daphne said cheerfully, trying to distract me. *The Golden Stag is a magical beast, the king of the woodland fauna. The legends say he used to be a fae man blessed with transformational abilities, and he deliberately chose to change himself to a Stag forever and become the caretaker of the woods. He will magically reappear in the woods even after he's been shot to death and mounted by those bloodthirsty assholes. He is swift as the wind, with huge antlers and, uh, its gold, obviously. And—*

245

She fell silent as we saw another rider up ahead—a woman with a yellow coat. She lay face-down in the mud with three arrows sticking out of her back. The back of her head was bandaged. Lady Bloom.

This shit is getting heavy.

I swallowed roughly. Yeah.

I kept moving. I stayed low in the saddle, my senses on high alert, and headed further west. The brides had spread out through the woods now, and it was almost impossible to completely avoid them. Once, I froze in the saddle as a herd of deer rushed across my path. Only a second later, Autumn and Gale thundered past, chasing them.

I kept riding, crossed a river, then crossed back further upstream, moving in a wide loop around the woods and heading back towards the towers.

Sharp voices drifted towards me. Through the trees, I could see a massive pink stallion without a rider. His reins were looped around a broken tree branch, holding him in place.

That was Princess Ember's horse. I pulled my gelding to a stop behind a sourberry bush and listened carefully.

"That bolt almost hit me," a woman drawled. "It is lucky for you that it didn't, Ember."

"Fuck off, Nyla." Princess Ember's tone was shrill. "I'm allowed to—" Her words cut off abruptly.

I urged my horse forward a little, my heart in my mouth. Princess Nyla, still sitting on her huge white mare, gripped Ember by the throat, holding her six feet off the ground. "You squeak like a baby rat," Nyla drawled. "Like a pathetic, annoying baby rat who thinks she's someone important. Perhaps you should consider changing yourself into a baby rat permanently." She tilted her head. "I must confess I didn't think you'd survive this long, baby rat. Perhaps it is time I put you out of your misery."

Ember's face was turning purple. She writhed in Nyla's grip.

Nyla let out a pretty laugh and pulled her closer. "Sad, pathetic little Ember. You were *so* close to the throne of Dusk. Monton even made you a princess, which is more than what anyone else would have done. And then he died and left you with nothing." She smiled. "What does it feel like to know that I will be taking your inheritance?"

Ember mouthed like a goldfish, her face turning blue. She kicked her feet desperately. Her fingernails scraped at Nyla's wrist braces.

Nyla was going to choke her to death. Lady Brisa of Frost and the two other minor brides flanked her, giggling behind their hands.

Should we...?

Yeah, we should.

I urged my horse forward, not bothering to hold my bow or draw any arrows; I was a terrible shot, anyway. Instead, I dug into my crossbody bag and pulled out a handful of snapcorn. Galloping into the clearing, I tossed the snapcorn at their horses' feet.

The explosions cracked like gunshots. The horses jolted. Nyla's mare reared up, and she dropped Ember in the dirt so she could hold on. The other horses let out terrified whinnies and bolted out of the clearing, the brides screaming in rage.

I slid off my horse and rushed over to Ember. "Are you okay?"

Princess Ember took a few deep breaths. "Yes." Her color rapidly returned to her version of normal—white skin, pale eyes, vivid, bright-red cheeks. She blinked up at me, bounced to her feet, and grinned. "Thanks, Daffodil! Now I'm *really* glad I haven't killed you yet." Bounding like a rabbit, she jumped on her stallion. "Gotta go. I got a stag to bag. Catch you on the other sideeee!"

I watched her race at breakneck speed through the trees on her enormous horse. My brain let out a snort. *That girl is nuts.*

"And not in a good way," I muttered. Nyla was right—it was a miracle she was still alive.

THIRTY-FOUR

I got back on my horse and kept moving. The screams and shouts seemed to be coming from everywhere now. The brides had stirred up all the woodland creatures, and they were scattering in panic. I spotted Lady Bork thundering through the trees on her rhino, chasing a tiny squirrel. I swung my horse around and went the other way.

It was getting dark. All the Trials were held at dusk—it was traditional, and dusk went on for hours, anyway—but it made it damned hard to see anything in the thick of the woods. Even with my enhanced eyesight, it was getting difficult to find a clear path, let alone hunt anything.

Brides thundered back and forth, flashes of pastel in the distance, chasing ordinary, terrified deer.

A few moments later, I stumbled upon another body lying in the dirt—one of the minor ladies who I'd seen with Nyla. There was a knife sticking out of her back.

What happens if nobody finds the Golden Stag?

"I don't know," I answered out loud. "I guess we keep going until we tap out or die. Tapping out of a Trial means you're out of the competition completely, and most of them would rather die, I think. The shame would follow them around forever. Like Brackin said, we all knew what we were getting ourselves into."

Goosebumps rose on my skin. "That's weird." I hitched up the sleeve of my riding coat and rubbed my bare arm nervously, trying to get the bumps to go down. "It's not getting colder."

No, Brain-Daphne sounded worried, too. *It's getting warmer.*

A punch of danger hit my senses out of nowhere—the zingy scent of metal and the bright flash of a blade.

I moved just in time, twisting in the saddle. A throwing knife shot through the space where my torso had been a split-second earlier. The blade buried itself in my horse's neck.

He screamed and reared up. I tumbled off his back and landed on the ground, rolling to a low crouch. I spun on the balls of my feet, pulled out my Orion blades, and watched Princess Saoira of Autumn gallop away, laughing as she rode.

Turning back, I saw my horse bolt off into the distance.

"Damn it." I was screwed without a horse.

Brain-Daphne was still freaking out. *I think the lack of a mount is the least of our worries.*

"What do you—" Finally, I smelled it.

Smoke.

Oh, no.

A horn blew in the distance—three sharp toots. It was the emergency signal. The herald was calling us to retreat.

I froze for a second, my eyes flicking around the woods. Visibility had improved. It wasn't getting darker anymore. It was getting lighter.

Three more sharp toots cut through the silence,

sounding a little further away already. The royal party was retreating to the City.

The faint smell of smoke hit my nose again.

I took off, running through the trees, bouncing over the squashy moss and sliding in the loose pine needles. A handful of figures appeared in the distance, riding fast. "It's the Scorch!" one of the brides screamed. "We must get back to the city gates!" The pastel riding coats all disappeared into trees.

I kept running. There was no way I was going to be able to keep up with them, but I had no other options. They were all too far away, so I couldn't catch them to knock one of them off their mounts and take it for myself.

I lifted my head and checked the sky. It was lighter in the north.

I don't like this, Brain Daphne grumbled. *We have to head due east to get back to the gates. If it's coming from the north and heading south as fast as I think it is, it will cut us off.*

"Then let's run faster." Pushing all the energy into my legs, I bounded through the trees, moving into the fastest cross-country gait I could manage. My heart thumped in my chest. I tried not to think. The smell of smoke grew stronger and stronger.

Movement flickered through the trees up ahead—a little doe, bounding through the woods on delicate legs. She veered closer, running parallel to me. Another deer joined us, bouncing on the pine needles. Another popped out, then another, and another.

After a few minutes, I found myself running in the middle of a herd of young deer, does and bucks, frantically trying to escape the coming smoke, which now smelled like it was coming from everywhere.

My eyes snapped towards the skyline again—I spotted

the flare of light, moving quickly from north to south. *It's cutting us off. It's too late. We're not going to make it back!*

I ground my jaw. Goddamn it. The sky in the north was blazing orange—the trees were on fire. These woods were damp; it wouldn't burn for long, but I couldn't run through it right now or I'd get torched.

The deer running with me would burn to death, too. And if I got any closer, the Scorch might sense me and chase me.

"No," I said out loud, calling out to the deer bounding beside me. "Not this way. We can't go this way; we'll get burned."

They're deer, Daphne. They don't speak English. They're probably not going to understand you.

I didn't care. I knew I was right. I had to turn around. Mentally, I reached out and hugged that iron core of confidence within me.

Brain-Daphne hugged it too. *Yeah, of course we're right. The Scorch is probably going to run in a full circle around us, fencing us in, but yeah. Let's go.*

I yelled at the deer. "Come on, little buddies, we're going this way!" I changed course a little, veered left, heading south instead of east. "Come on, follow me!" Sweat dripped from my forehead. My breath came in ragged pants, but I kept running.

A young buck tried to push me back on track, but I held out my hands as we ran, guiding him south. The rest of the herd followed us. After a minute, I veered again, taking us back the way we came, heading west, directly away from the City. The Scorch had cut us off from the Kingdom of Dusk. All we could do was head deeper into the west and hope it didn't encircle us.

The heat grew intense. I shot another look into the sky and saw the beacon of light right behind us. I sent up a silent prayer. Please keep going straight. Don't chase us. All these little animals will die.

We'll die too, genius.

I was going to say something to reassure her, but a sudden gust of wind from the east pushed a wall of smoke over me, and I coughed.

Can you smell that?

"Yeah," I choked out.

Not a god. That's active fae magic.

There was too much to worry about right now. More woodland creatures had joined our pack—a small family of bears ran alongside us now. I glanced behind me and saw the beacon of light moving south in a straight line and let out a moan of relief.

It wasn't over yet. It could still circle around. If it was hunting people—and now I was sure that's exactly what it was doing—then it might sense me and swing back.

"We need to take cover," I panted. Up ahead, I spotted a tiny fawn sitting in the middle of a clearing, shaking like a leaf. I ran over, scooped him up, and kept running.

Water, Brain-Daphne pointed.

"Good idea," I puffed. We ran towards the river, heading to the spot I'd bookmarked earlier, a rocky outcrop flanking a fast-moving stream. It had smelled faintly of guano—bat poop. There had to be a cave somewhere. We would find shelter there.

I followed my nose and found it quickly—a ragged black hole in the side on a rocky outcrop over the river.

"Come on, team!" I shouted at the creatures around me. "Let's go!" Without hesitation, I ran inside the cave.

Thankfully, all the animals followed me.

CHAPTER

THIRTY-FIVE

T hesitated just inside the entrance and reached out with my senses, trying to check for danger. The deer didn't bother, they streaked past me, bolting straight inside the cave. The bears ran after them. Little squirrels and other rodents squeaked and chattered as they ran past me.

I took a few more steps further into the cave. The air in here smelled like water and only faintly of smoke. There must be air vents in there somewhere. I could hear water trickling, too.

My eyes adjusted quickly. The cave was huge, extending much further back than I thought. A tunnel curved to the left, and a small underground stream flowed right through the middle of the cave. Most of the deer had stopped around it, bending their heads to drink.

I hugged the trembling fawn to my chest and stroked his soft hide gently. "It's okay, buddy. We're going to be safe now. We're just going to wait it out in this nice cave, and we'll be fine." I knelt down at the stream and put the fawn down carefully, arranging his front legs underneath him so he could bend down and drink. The poor thing was so exhausted he could barely move.

Uh, babes... Brain-Daphne was suddenly nervous again. *Our eyes adjusted way too quickly for my liking...*

I glanced up. Over the lapping sounds of the stream and the rustling of dozens of animals, a slow clip clop echoed around the cave.

Uh oh.

A soft glow appeared from around the corner. Clip clop, clip clop. I held my breath.

To my utter astonishment, the Golden Stag stepped out from the tunnel.

He was huge, the size of a moose, with giant antlers that stretched up towards the roof of the cave. His hooves were bigger than dinner plates. Slowly, he walked into the middle of the cave and stopped. All the other animals froze and watched him.

"What do we do?" I whispered. I'd never seen a Golden Stag before, but he looked exactly how the stories described him. Majestic and glorious, like the King of the Woodland creatures. His hide was the perfect shade of old-gold, and it glistened even in the dim light of the cave. His deep amber eyes were ancient, all-knowing.

Wow. He's a handsome gent, isn't he? Brain-Daphne gave a whistle. *Do something, babe.*

"Hello," I said stupidly. I waved at him.

Yeah, that was perfect. Good job.

The mighty stag stared at me. I felt like his eyes were reaching directly into my soul.

I licked my lips. "I'm, uh... I'm Daphne."

The Golden Stag watched me for a long moment, then, his eyes fell on the fawn by my feet. The fawn turned his head, looked at him, and gave a little squeak.

The stag turned back to me. Moving slowly and deliberately, he lowered his head, stretched his front legs out, and bowed at me.

For a long time, nothing happened.

Welp, this is awkward. Say something else. "Hope you don't mind that we crashed your hiding spot," I stammered.

He stayed where he was, as still as a golden statue, deep in his bow.

I think he's thanking you for saving his people.

"Oh." I swallowed. "Is... Is that what you're doing? Are you thanking me?"

The Golden Stag lifted his head, met my eye, and bowed again, a deep nod. Just then, I felt the whisper of words in the back of my mind. Yesss...

I gasped. "I think I can hear you," I breathed out. It was similar to how Dwayne dumped words in my head—just far more subtle. A faint brush of communication, rather than a word-punch to the frontal lobe. I suppose the Golden Stag was close to a god, too. A god of little woodland creatures. "I *can* hear you." I grinned up at him. Gods, he was beautiful. Majestic. Those eyelashes were so long and thick you could use them as a broom.

The stag blinked and tilted his head, still watching me, and I felt that soft rustle of words again. You saved my kinnn...

"Oh." I shifted on my feet awkwardly, then dropped a little curtsey. "It was nothing. Don't, uh, don't mention it."

He drew himself back up and slowly walked closer towards me. What was he doing now?

Moving his mighty snout closer to me, he bent his knees and knelt down until he was only inches away. Then, he turned his head to the side, showing me his mighty neck. Words rustled through my head again. I owe you my lifeee...

"Seriously?" I frowned. "Are you exposing your throat to me?"

Take ittt... Take my headdd...

I exhaled a shocked breath. "Are you *kidding?* Wow. No, I'm not going to do that. What the hell?"

Owe you my lifeee... Saved my kinnn...

Oh, good gravy, he was serious. I wagged my finger in his face. "Come on, now, Your Majesty. That is silly."

Take my headdd... Owe youuu...

"Stop it. You're being ridiculous," I scolded him. "I'm not going to take your head just because I did you a favor."

He hesitated for a second, then nudged me in the shoulder with his snout. It grows backkk...

I took a deep breath. "This is insane. Look, Your Majest—"

The rustle of words in my head cut me off. Terranceee...

I stared at him. He stared back at me. For a long time, I was speechless. "Your name is Terrance?"

He cocked his head. Yesss...

"Look. Terrance. I appreciate that you are, uh, apprecia-tive of me saving your deer buddies over there. But there's no need for me to take your head as payment."

Growsss backkk...

"Yeah, you said." I held up a finger and pointed at him. "But it must hurt a bit when you get filled with arrows and die, right?"

He glared at me stonily.

"It does, doesn't it?"

He dropped his gaze to the cave floor and nodded sadly.

"Well, I don't need your head. I don't want your head. And despite the fact we were sent out here to hunt you so we could present your head to the Prince of Shadow, I don't think Romeo would want your head either!"

The Golden Stag—Terrance—turned back to face me and narrowed his eyes, glaring at me. Owe youuu... Must give somethinggg...

Goddamn these noble forest gods. I huffed out a sigh. "Well, instead of your head, do you think you could give me a ride?"

THIRTY-SIX

The Scorch was gone by the time we made it out of the forest. It had cut a wide path straight through the woods from north to south. A beacon of light shone in the distance, but it was far, far away now.

I exhaled gratefully as the Golden Stag ran through the line of still-smoldering trees at an eye-watering pace. I hugged his neck and breathed in his musky, woodsy scent, grateful that his hooves didn't burn on the ground. Soon, we were out of the torched section of woods and on the road back to the City of Dusk.

Holy guacamole, this is a smooth ride, Brain Daphne stretched out, enjoying the softness of his broad back

He swung his huge antlers to the side, as if tossing his head back. Shock absorbersss...

Night had fallen now—a crescent moon hung in the sky, casting only a faint glow. There was nobody on the road. In the distance, I could see the City gates firmly shut. The sentries would be on high alert, looking to see if the Scorch would come back.

A section of wall near the gates was black with char.

Looks like the Scorch tried to ram the city walls, my brain noted.

A tingle ran down my spine. It was lucky we'd told the Watch Commander to get rid of the shale-heavy stone there.

Terrance put on a burst of speed as we got closer to the gates. From the City, we must look just like a comet soaring through the sky. For a worried second, I thought they might think that Terrence, with his golden glow, was a threat just like the Scorch. But then, I heard a shout coming from the wall, and the gates cracked open.

"Are you sure you want to do this?" I asked Terrance. "You don't have to go in, you know. You could just drop me outside."

The Golden Stag turned his head as he ran so he could catch my eye. Owe youuu...

I grimaced. "Fine. Let's go then."

He slowed down a little and trotted proudly through the crack in the gates. Inside, the common fae packed the streets. The crowd gasped as I rode in. They all stared.

A path cleared in front of me. A few of the commoners fell to their knees.

It had only been an hour or so since the royal party abandoned the hunt and retreated back to the City, so some of them might have only just gotten there. We kept moving forward.

Further inside, it was pandemonium. I tried to ignore the gaping people around me and scanned the crowd up ahead.

The royal party had obviously been escorted inside the gates first, so they were further up the road. I could see the royal banners a quarter of a mile up ahead. My eyes adjusted, focusing on them. A garrison of soldiers surrounded the aristocracy.

Most of them were still on their horses. The brides sobbed dramatically as they were reunited with their families and sponsors. Advisers and courtiers fussed over the royals, fanning cheeks and offering water. A red-faced man was holding Ember by the collar. "Let me back out there," she squealed. "The hunt's not over yet!"

I sagged with relief when I saw him. Romeo charged through the crowd, ignoring the guards who were trying to hold him back. He had my crystal on the palm of his hand, and he was watching it intently.

Someone screamed. "The Golden Stag!"

Moving simultaneously, every single royal and member of the aristocracy turned towards me. The guards stiffened.

Silence gripped the City, broken only by the clip clop of the Golden Stag's hooves.

Terrance trotted proudly down the road, huge, glowing, looking every inch the King of the Woodlands. He nodded his head towards Romeo. Is that himmm..?

"That's him," I said. My heart pounded. "That's the Prince."

Romeo finally looked up and saw me coming towards him. An expression of pure relief crossed his face. The guards around him stopped trying to hold him back, and they pushed and shoved the courtiers out of the way, making some room around him. King Ronus and Queen Talia strode forward and came to stand at Romeo's side.

They all watched me in silence as I rode towards them. I had to resist the urge to wave. The Golden Stag stopped a few feet away from the royals and bent his knees so I could slide off his back.

I hit the ground, straightened up, patted his neck, stepped in front of him, and dropped into a curtsey in front of the King and Queen. "Your Majesties."

The royal couple stared at me, eyes wide, shocked into silence. Romeo's face was priceless.

I curtsied again in Romeo's direction. "Your Highness." I waved my hand upwards. "I present to you the head of the Golden Stag."

The king and queen gaped at me.

I smiled awkwardly. "It's, uh, still attached to his body. I hope that's okay."

CHAPTER

THIRTY-SEVEN

"**H**is name is Terrance. You don't have to keep calling him the Golden Stag."

Romeo brushed my hair back, trailing his fingers lightly through my scalp. "Baby, I don't think I can call the King of the Woodland Creatures *Terrance.*"

"But that's his name," I said weakly. Romeo's hands were doing magical things to me. It was hard to concentrate on the conversation right now.

"Okay... Well, you'll be happy to know that *Terrance* is now safely back home in the western woods."

"I'm glad." I wriggled against Romeo's bare chest and sighed happily.

After I presented him with the Golden Stag and he'd declared me the winner of the Hunt Trial, things dissolved into anarchy. Some of the sponsors insisted the Hunt Trial had been called off, and I hadn't actually killed the Golden Stag, so I couldn't be the winner. Prince Aranbold of Spring was particularly vocal and even went as far as calling me a cheat. Romeo's guards had obviously gotten used to him quickly, because they were already holding him back to prevent him from punching Prince Aranbold in the face.

Eventually, after a lot of yelling, the royal advisors put their heads together, and the herald made the announcement. Technically, the Hunt Trial wasn't called off; the woods were just evacuated. It was never specified that the Stag had to be killed, nor did his head have to be separated from his body. So, I was declared the winner.

Brackin took me home, white as a sheet. He was still in shock. Lord Bron and Lady Pesh wouldn't even look at me. Nobody knew what to think. I had won the first Bride Trial —but in an unfathomable manner, under totally bizarre circumstances. Nobody could get their head around it.

Hours later, after Steven the Brownie stuffed me to the brim with soup and the most delectable vegetable dumplings, the shadows in my little dormitory lengthened and Romeo stole me away. He took me back to the palace to his private bathroom and locked the door.

Now, soaking in hot, fragrant water with a glass of red wine in my hand and leaning back against the bare chest of the most handsome man in the universe, I felt so relaxed and happy I could fly.

We had serious things to talk about, though, and not too much time to do it. Romeo's guards checked on him regularly and would alert the King and Queen if they got suspicious. We'd already spent too much time locked in here.

I dived right in. "Do you have any leads on who killed King Monton yet?"

"Just the same suspects as before," Romeo replied wearily. "Prince Aranbold is an arrogant ass. The Court of Spring is ambitious as hell, and so far, they've been the most vocal about wanting to put Princess Nyla on the throne. King Raynor of Dawn is more subtle, but no less pushy. The Queen of Autumn is very charming, and very manipulative. All of their advisors are working every single courtier in this kingdom, drumming up support for their candidates. It could be any one of them." He paused and exhaled heavily. "But honestly, I don't think any of them would actually cross the line to regicide. It just doesn't make sense."

I didn't think so either, but I wanted to hear it from him. "Can you elaborate for me?"

"You'd have to have a good reason to assassinate a king. There was a very clear line of succession—Monton's son, then Carissa, then Ronus—so none of them killed Monton for a shot at the crown."

"Unless they could convince Carissa to marry one of them."

"She never showed any intention of doing that, though. It would be the longest of long shots. And besides, you commit murder when you're cornered, not just on the off chance you could eventually put one of your people on the throne."

"Okay." That seemed like a good train of thought to jump on. "Were any of them cornered?"

"I checked. None of the other royal courts had beef with Monton at the time he was killed. So there was no concrete motive. The only person who raises any red flags is the Duke of Nightfall. He's Ronus's little brother, Gorman. He's a bloodthirsty son of a bitch, a total snake. Gorman is the type of guy who would smile at you while stabbing you in the back."

The irony didn't escape me. "Lady Sybell's father," I murmured.

"That's right. Gorman was an earl of a small town on

the edge of Autumn, and he made no secret that it wasn't enough for him. He became Duke of Nightfall when Ronus took the throne of Dusk. Nightfall is a warrior duchy—they have a huge army, they're traditionally very aggressive, and they pride themselves on their abilities in combat, which all suited Gorman perfectly. Nightfall rode with King Ronus to try to stop the Scorch years ago. Gorman was the one who sent Ronus's other sons in with a battalion to stop it. Of course, the heirs conveniently died. And Gorman was apoplectic with rage when Ronus told him he was trying to talk Carissa into staying on the throne."

I nodded. "So, Gorman could have killed Monton just so Ronus would take the throne of Dusk and leave Nightfall for the taking."

"Exactly. We don't have any proof, of course, and Ronus hates to think that his baby brother is behind all this, but we're keeping an eye on him. Lady Sybell could have been put in the Trials to take me out. If I die, Gorman is next in line."

I sighed. "Court politics gives me a headache." I downed the rest of my wine and cut straight to the chase. "I think you should keep an eye on the Duke of Sandstone, too."

"Redfoot?"

"Yeah. I don't think Princess Ember had any choice in entering the Trials. And I don't think Carissa had a choice in coming here to seduce Monton all those years ago, either. I think Redfoot forced them into it. Their family is magically powerful, aren't they?"

"They are," Romeo confirmed. "Carissa wielded strong elemental magic, and I suspect Redfoot has the same abilities. But, again, I can't imagine how they could summon something as devastating as the Scorch. And that's the other reason I'm doubting the Duke Gorman of Nightfall.

He had the means and motive to kill Monton, but he doesn't have any magical power."

I gnawed on my lip. "I think the Scorch is a person, Romeo. A high fae person, I mean. Like the Golden Stag." I drained my wine, put my glass down on the side of the bath, and nestled back into Romeo's warm chest, acutely aware that our time together was coming to an end. I could hear his guards outside the door, muttering to each other about coming to check on him. "Terrance used to be a man," I continued. "But he became a small god because of his devotion to the woodland creatures. I get the feeling that the Scorch is something similar. I caught a whiff of active fae magic when it was rampaging through the woods. It's someone's innate personal magic."

Romeo murmured, his lips at my temple, "You're probably right, because you seem to be right about everything. I know that some high fae can transform into animals, and they can turn other people into animals, too. But the Scorch also burns hot like lava. That would be transformational *and* elemental magic. Nobody in history has ever possessed both kinds of magic at once, and the power needed to express that kind of force for as long as the Scorch has..." He blew out a breath. "It's unfathomable."

I hesitated for a second. "Aunt Marche didn't have the power to cause the Suffocation," I whispered. "A curse did that. The feedback loop between the Agreement and the death magic inside of her... that's what did it."

He let out a sad rumble. "You're right."

"It could be another feedback loop caused by a curse. Maybe... the god of cows was cursed by the Summer Queen to burn hot like the sun? Or maybe it was the other way around. Maybe a high fae from the underworld with lava powers got transformed into a mad cow."

267

Romeo raised his eyebrows. "That's possible. It's a good theory, anyway."

"You broke Aunt Marche's curse. Do you think you could come up with something to undo a curse like that?"

He shifted underneath me and wrapped his arms around me again. "They've tried similar things before. Nullifying charms, freeze spells..."

"But have they tried a charm to undo a curse?"

He frowned. "I don't know. But it doesn't matter anyway; every single thing they throw at the Scorch burns up and disintegrates before it hits."

"Hmm. I see the problem."

His arms tightened around me. "I'll see what I can come up with. In the meantime, we've got bigger problems."

I grimaced. "Oh, gods, what now?"

"Lord Fandoine."

"Oh." My cheeks instantly warmed. "He's, uh, he's—"

"*And* Lord Asternay."

"Oh no." I sat bolt upright in the bath, splashing the water. "Lord Asternay is here too?"

"You didn't hear him screaming your name at the City gates earlier?"

I did wonder why I was let inside the gates so quickly. Damn, not Lord Asternay. I slid down into the water, trying to cool my flaming cheeks. "I was a little busy."

A deep rumble came from Romeo's chest, almost a chuckle. "How many fae warlords did you say locked you in towers and tried to marry you against your will?"

"Twenty-three," I said in a little voice. "Look, don't get the wrong idea, Romeo. I never led anyone on. You do a guy a favor, and sometimes he's so grateful he insists on marrying you."

Romeo laughed. "What did you do?"

"I saved Lord Asternay's favorite niece from getting

eaten by a vicious cait sith in the grasslands. Lord Fandoine was about to raid a neighboring village, but as I travelled past it, I could smell a plague of spellsickness a mile away. The villagers were all zombies," I explained. "I saved Lord Fandoine's whole war party. He was... grateful."

He chuckled softly. His hands slid downwards. "None of this surprises me at all." His cool breath tickled the nape of my neck. "I know exactly what you are, Daphne Ironclaw."

THIRTY-EIGHT

I looked up at the city wall and grimaced. The mob gathered to watch the War Games Trial was enormous. It seemed like every single person in the City of Dusk lined the walls. The crowd stretched out in both directions, as far as I could see. The royals and aristocracy were gathered in the watchtowers on either side of the gates. I could feel their eyes on me.

Brackin stood next to me. He glanced up at the wall and nudged me. "Your fan club has grown, Daffodil."

"Stop," I muttered. "I'm trying to ignore them."

"I don't know why you would do that. They were the only ones who cheered for you yesterday." Brackin pursed his lips, still looking faintly embarrassed. "Your abysmal showing in the Trials yesterday seems to have made no dent in their devotion to you."

I exhaled wearily. Lord Brackin was right; yesterday had been an absolute disaster.

The Court of Dusk had held two Trials in one day—Diplomacy first, then the Talent Trial. I managed to undo all the goodwill I'd accumulated in winning the Hunt by absolutely bombing out in both of them.

For the Diplomacy Trial, the courtiers decided to hold a large debate. All the candidates were seated at a round table, and the brides were directed to argue their position on one question—what would you do to secure the safety of Dusk?

I was never any good in group discussion, and I was uncomfortable from the very beginning. Early that afternoon, based on my win of the Hunt Trial, Lady Pesh decided to get involved. She ordered Steven to put me in a fluffy pink pastel dress for the Diplomacy Trial. The dress clashed with my hair, squashed my breasts up, and itched like hell.

To make things worse, when we were brought in to be seated in front of the crowd, I was thrown off further by the appearance of Lord Fandoine and Lord Asternay. The two fae warlords had been joined by four more of my former captors—all big brutes, rulers of small towns deep in the Inbetween who, at one point or another, tried to force me to marry them. For some inexplicable reason, all six of them stood together in the crowd, and all called out to me. Occasionally, they cried. It was excruciatingly embarrassing.

During the debate, I quickly got overwhelmed. I was stuck at a round table, trying to get a word in edgewise while eight razor-sharp, witty, hyper-intelligent princesses made interesting points about the safety of the Kingdom. I couldn't get a word in, and I couldn't decide what I should say, anyway. I just sat there with my cheeks burning with embarrassment.

I was so far out of my depth, it was humiliating.

After a while I gave up trying to say anything and just listened to the princesses, hoping to get some clues as to who might be behind the Scorch and King Monton's assassination.

All of the princesses proclaimed their desire to see the

unbalance corrected and the Scorch destroyed—except Ember, who said that she much preferred sunshine to the gloomy shadows of Dusk, but as soon as she was allowed to, she was going to head out and kill the Scorch herself. The other brides rolled their eyes at her, and she hissed like a kitten and clenched her fists.

Then, Princess Saoira of Autumn took over the debate. I remembered that Ember had said Saoira was a know-it-all who loved to give a lecture, but even I wasn't prepared for her long, passionate speech about the importance of nature and keeping the balance in all things.

But, eventually, the Princess of Autumn worked her angle and delicately suggested the Scorch was a curse inflicted on Dusk for not doing a good job at keeping the balance in the first place. Choosing her words carefully, she insinuated that the unbalance began because King Monton chose to marry Carissa of Sandstone, which was too close to the Summer Court. Saoira argued that despite outwardly adapting quickly, Carissa had brought too much light to the Kingdom of Dusk. She made the point that the new Prince of Shadow should choose someone from the Winter side of the Inbetween as his bride, and the unbalance would be corrected.

The Summer-side brides all glared daggers at her. Someone even threw one, but I didn't see who it was.

The only one with less to say than me was Lady Bork, who had no idea what we were even talking about, and took the opportunity to put her head down on the table and have a nap. The debate concluded, the advisors put their heads together, and Saoira of Autumn was declared the winner.

But my shame had only just begun.

The Talent Trial was after supper. Too late, I realized I hadn't even thought about what I was going to do.

I had no talent. Not unless you count sniffing out things like a dog, and there was no way in hell I was going to willfully humiliate myself like that.

The whole thing ended up exactly like an awful nightmare where you get ushered onstage to perform something in front of a huge audience, but you're naked and unprepared.

With growing horror, I watched in the wings while the brides showed their talents. Nyla of Spring sang an exquisite folk song, Brisa of Frost played the harp, Glorina of Dawn danced a ribbon-dance. Ember showed off her weapons skills, getting one of her trembling grooms to hold up vegetables so she could shoot them out of their hands. Lady Bork stomped around the stage, picking up whatever she could get her hands on so she could throw things at the other brides—a lectern, Brisa's harp, even the herald himself.

Eventually, the herald called my name. One of the Courtiers shoved me onstage, and I did the only thing I could think of.

I started to breakdance.

I started with the robot, did a little toprock, a couple of turtle spins, and hopped to my feet. The crowd was silent. Deathly silent.

For some unfathomable reason, I kept going and tried some other moves. I hit the Dougie, did a Billy-Bounce, and a few booty-pops.

To make everything worse, Dwayne chose that *exact* moment to crash through the window of the ballroom. He landed on stage next to me and started to beatbox.

The beat didn't help. The crowd watched us, completely silent, with horrified expressions on their faces, as I did the two-step, the running man, the humpty, a little popping-and-locking, ended up with a thirty-

273

second burst of vigorous krumping, and finished with a B-Boy freeze.

The following silence almost deafened me. It was broken by Romeo, wheezing from his throne on the dais at the other end of the room. He was trying to hold in his laughter so hard, his face had turned purple.

Even the Lords Fandoine and Asternay were subdued, but after a moment, they started clapping and shouting at me, telling me that if I came back to their villages now, I wouldn't have to endure such public humiliation ever again. Dwayne vanished the second I was ushered offstage by a courtier, and I hadn't seen him since.

I flushed red now just thinking about it.

It wasn't that bad, Brain Daphne said cheerfully. She was busy taking in every single detail of the massive arena outside the City gates. *I think our dancing was awesome. It was probably just a case of knowing your audience. We would have killed it on the mean streets of Brooklyn, babe. Or at the Olympics.*

I wrenched my focus back to the Trial at hand—the War Games trial. Today, the competitors would be divided into two teams and play a bloody, high-stakes game of Capture the Flag in a magically enhanced, specially designed arena.

The more-than-a-mile-long battleground sprawled out in front of us. Some sections of it were hidden by mist and fog. Two house-sized replicas of the palace sat on either end of the battleground, one bathed in orange light and the other in red—the colors of Dusk.

The trial was simple. The brides had to work together to get from our assigned palace—red or orange—and make our way through magically-enhanced terrain and get to the other team's palace. The trial would end once the palace was occupied by the invaders. The King and Queen would choose the winner based on how the brides conducted themselves during the trials.

"I count almost twenty lords in your fan club," Brackin said, pointing up at the wall. A group of big men with beards, armor, and axes stood together and waved lavender-colored handkerchiefs at me. "Is every one of your old masters so beholden to you?"

"I'm not sure if beholden is the word," I muttered. "And no, because you're not."

Lord Brackin tossed back his dark hair. He had regressed back into his pirate-like outfits—lots of leather and billowy shirts. "At least I stayed to support you yesterday," he sniffed.

"You got so drunk afterwards I had to carry you home!"

"I had to drown my shame," he said haughtily. "Anyway, Daffodil, this trial should involve lots of stabbing, which is very much in your wheelhouse. Let's just hope you apply yourself better today."

I took a deep breath and sighed it all out. "At least there's a bright side to bombing out yesterday. Lady Pesh gave up on me. I don't think I could have handled more pastels." I pulled one leg up behind me, stretching my quads.

Steven had put me in an aymander skin jumpsuit. It was figure-hugging, matt-black, moisture-wicking, and flame resistant. It was also ridiculously sexy. When I bent to stretch my calves, the warlords on the wall above me began to sob and shout louder. "Daphne! My wife! My beautiful Sweet *Daphneee!*"

"You'll be happy to know I have researched this Trial thoroughly," Brackin announced. "And I have information to impart to you, Little Daffodil."

I glanced at him, a little shocked. "You did research?"

"Well. To be more specific, I went to the tavern for

lunch today and happened to meet one of the goblins who worked on the construction of the battlefield. I bribed him with a few coins." He cocked his head, eying me meaningfully. "You're welcome. And the goblin let it slip that the terrain down there has been spelled to replicate the harshest aspects of Faerie environments. There's a Summer section and a Winter section, a Wastes, and a Wilds."

"Oh." I turned to look at the battlefield. "Is that why some of it is misty and other parts are too bright to look at?"

"Yes. Although the visual impairment will lessen for the spectators once the Trial begins. You will have to trudge through the untamed jungles of the Wilds and navigate through the harsh glare of Summer, but the spectators up there will be able to see you clearly. Although," he added. "The Winter section is apparently giving them a little trouble. My goblin informant mentioned that the blizzard enhancement ballooned out of control this morning, and they're having trouble figuring out what's wrong with it."

"Fabulous."

"All this to say, Daffodil, that the variation in seasons will make the brides uncomfortable. They have little time to adjust, they're not used to working as a team, so all of them will want to get this over with as quickly as possible." He looked me in the eye. "Do you have a plan?"

"Sure." My plan was to go full Miss Congeniality, turn on the charm, and try and make friends with my teammates so I could ask some questions and figure out who was trying to ruin Dusk. "Survive."

"Okay." Brackin patted me on the head awkwardly. "Just do your best, because I think I will miss you if you die, Daffodil."

That asshole is actually growing on me, Brain-Daphne let out a sniff.

The herald blew his horn. I punched Brackin in the shoulder for good luck and made my way over to a platform by the watchtower where the other Brides had already gathered.

They had hurried to the platform because Romeo was there. One of his grandparents had obviously bullied him into wearing the royal attire of a high fae prince—black pants and tunic with leather and scarlet detailing—and he looked jaw-droppingly sexy. The brides giggled and waved at him. Lady Bork blew him a kiss. A big wad of spit flung out of her mouth along with it, but it landed just short of Romeo's feet, so he didn't have to navigate a potential diplomatic disaster and dodge it.

"Welcome to the War Games Trial!" the herald bellowed. "His Highness, the Prince of Shadow, has decided on who will have the honor of selecting the teams."

The corners of Romeo's lip twitched ever so slightly.

"He has made the decision based on your performances at the Talent Trial yesterday—the best, and the, uh... most unusual showing. So, without further ado, please step forward... Princess Nyla of Spring and Little Daffodil!"

The crowd broke into polite applause and awkward chuckles. I cringed and walked forward. Romeo had told me he'd make sure I had the opportunity to choose my team so I could get closer to some of the suspects, but I thought we were just going to draw straws or something.

Nyla floated up to the platform and curtsied to Romeo. I walked up, spread my arms wide, extended my middle fingers, and dropped into my curtsy, keeping my hands where he could see them. "I am honored, my lord," I said, flipping him off with both hands.

"The honor is mine," he managed, before he had to turn his head away. I saw his shoulders shaking with silent laughter.

277

"As winner of the Talent Trial, I will make my selection first," Nyla declared, her entitlement both breathtaking and a little impressive. Even the herald nodded in approval. It was what a Queen would have done. Nyla nodded at the brides below us. "I chose Lady Brisa of Frost."

Brisa moved to stand in front of Nyla.

I cleared my throat. "Lady Sybell of Nightfall."

Sybell's eyebrows shot up—she hadn't expected me to pick her, but since her father was our number one suspect, I wanted to get closer to her. She grimaced and moved to my side.

Nyla lifted her chin. "I select Princess Glorina of Dawn."

I expected that—it was becoming obvious Glorina didn't have a chance of winning the trials. Nyla was probably going to use this opportunity to talk her into forming an alliance.

I thought quickly. I needed Princess Saoira of Autumn. Her lecture at the Diplomacy Trial made me suspect that her family was far more manipulative than anyone thought, and I wanted the chance to speak to her. But if I chose Saoira now, Nyla would definitely choose Ember next. Nyla wouldn't choose Lady Bork—she was a total liability, completely uncontrollable.

And, if Nyla chose Princess Ember, she could kill her in an instant just to get her out of the way. We were allowed to kill our own teammates. It wasn't even frowned upon. This Trial wasn't about teamwork; it was about conquest.

I think you're right, my brain muttered. *Nyla's giving Ember the evil eye right now. She's pissed that Ember survived the Hunt.*

I made a snap decision based on my gut feeling. "I choose Princess Ember of Sandstone."

The crowd muttered a little. Whispers reached my ears

—everyone thought I was an idiot. Ember bounced over to my side.

Nyla frowned. I'd thrown her off. She'd expected me to choose Princess Saoira of Autumn, too. She waved her hand. "I chose the Princess of Autumn."

Saoira looked pissed to be chosen second-to-last but floated over to stand with Nyla's team.

I smiled at Lady Bork, feeling a little bad for her. On impulse, I decided to address her using the ogre tongue. "Gungh bonnk hugh gunk*kaaah* hunk, Bork!" I smacked my chest with my palm, then punched my fist towards her.

She frowned. "Bungh hurggh ogrekahh?"

I punched my fist towards her again, letting her know that yes, I did, in fact speak ogre. I was rusty and I mangled the vowel sounds, but she got the gist of it.

The herald, his eyes shooting back and forth between us, suddenly cleared his throat. "The War Games Trial will begin on my horn. Candidates, please take your places!"

I hopped off the platform and joined my team. Lady Sybell stalked off first, snarling under her breath. "Did you choose me to join your team as some sort of revenge, Daffodil?" She waved her hand at Lady Bork and Lady Ember, walking alongside me. "You have picked the worst of all the candidates and lumped me in with them. I have never been more insulted in my life."

This whole Miss Congeniality thing really isn't working out for us, is it?

Ember was pissed, too. "I wanted a shot at Nyla," she whined. "And at Saoira. It would have been easier if I was on their team; I'd be able to take them by surprise. Stab them in the back, you know?"

She needs a reality check. "Both of them would kill you faster than you can blink, Ember. You saw the way Nyla was looking at you."

279

"She won't kill me." Ember tossed her head. "She's not powerful enough. She's got no magic, did you know that? Her father—my uncle—is embarrassed of her. All the Aranbolds have elemental magic. My mom had the most." Ember scowled. "It's too bad that my mom chose to be a traitor." She stomped off.

"A traitor?" My instincts screamed at me. Did she just tell me that Carissa killed King Monton? I hurried after her. "Ember, wait—"

But Lady Bork reached out a massive hand and tugged me backwards. "Grunkk bork gruga hughf grugg?"

"No," I replied in her own language. I couldn't run off to chase Ember; Lady Bork was holding the back of my jumpsuit. "No, I'm not being blackmailed, Lady Bork. I entered the trials of my own free will. Hang on." I turned to look up at her and frowned. "Are *you* being blackmailed? Is that why you came here?"

She shrugged her massive shoulders. "Grukag huff boff boff gurgh."

I gasped. "Lord Dew said *what?*"

"Grukag boff."

I shook my head. "Oh no, my Lady. For one, I can tell you that the Duchy of Dew doesn't have the resources to drain the Swamplands. He's just the earl of a small town, not a kingdom. Secondly, if they even tried to raid your village, you guys could squash them into a pulp, couldn't you?"

She lowered her head. "Gurgh hoffag borko hugf."

"Oh, no." I shook my head again. Suddenly, I felt desperately sorry for her. "No, Lady Bork, I'm sorry, but Lord Dew has lied to you. He doesn't have an army. I do know he's very good at illusion magic, though. He probably showed you a projection of an army with millions of soldiers." I jerked my head back at the City behind me. "The

Kingdom of Dusk has the biggest army out of most of the Inbetween, and even they don't have a million soldiers. And I can tell you right now, Dusk has no intention of going to war with the Swamplands."

Lady Bork's eyes narrowed. "Bufguv gorvgh?"

I felt so bad for her. And I felt ashamed. I could have had this conversation with her much earlier. "Yes, it sounds like he tricked you. He probably just wanted the strongest candidate he could find. I'm so sorry, Lady Bork."

Lady Bork stopped in her tracks. I shot a look towards the rest of my team. Ember had already reached the staircase leading over the wall into the battlefield. Sybell threw herself over the wall without looking back.

"Come on, Daphne, let's go!" Ember yelled at me. "We've got a Kingdom to overthrow! The horn will blow soon!"

Lady Bork scowled at the ground for a minute. Then, she reached out, grabbed me, lifted me up, and pulled me into her chest.

She hugged me so hard, I felt my back crack. "Grufgh huff grolll," she rumbled. She licked the top of my head, dropped me, turned around, and stomped away.

CHAPTER

THIRTY-NINE

Lady Sybell was so angry, two bright red spots had appeared on her cheeks. She swore under her breath as we made our way to the ramparts at the top of the model castle. "I have never been more embarrassed in my life," Sybell seethed. "For some reason, you decided that now was the best time to get rid of the only valuable member of our War Games team." She glared out over the battlefield.

There wasn't much to see—just barren dirt, blinding lights, and lots of mist in the distance. "I am left to wage war with a child and an imbecile," Sybell muttered, grinding her teeth.

The herald blew his horn once. Ready.

My brain nudged me. *Come on with that Miss Congeniality charm, girlfriend. We need to get her to talk.*

"Don't be so pessimistic," I said to Sybell, smiling at her. "It was a strategic selection. There are three overambitious princesses in Nyla's team; they're bound to fight amongst each other. Lady Bork was just as likely to kill us as anyone else, so I've removed that element of uncertainty from this

282

Trial. And don't forget," I added, unable to resist. "I disarmed you and stabbed you with your own knife at the Commencement Ball. So if I'm an imbecile, what does that make you?"

She bared her teeth at me.

I said charm her, not antagonize her!

The horn blew again. Set.

"Relax, Lady Sybell," I continued. "We're the underdogs, but if we win, everyone is going to think it was because of you. Because, y'know, I'm an imbecile and Ember's a child. You're the most high-profile candidate on this team."

"Hmf." She looked a little mollified. "You make a good point, Daffodil."

On my other side, Ember produced two daggers out of nowhere, clutched them in her little fists and shook them wildly. "Let's do this!"

The horn blew again. Go!

Ember let out a little scream of excitement, hopped off the wall, and started to run. Sybell grabbed her by the collar and dragged her back. "Not so fast, little princess. We need a plan."

Good, good. She's sinking into the role that you pushed her into. Good job.

Sybell's dark eyes flashed. "There aren't enough of us to have someone stay back and defend our castle, so we all have to go. We should stick together, cover each other's backs, and rip out our enemies' throats as a team."

"Rip throats," Ember nodded. "Got it."

We bounced down the steps of the mini-castle, and I quickly filled them in on what Brackin had told me about the terrain. "From the looks of it, we're about to enter the Wastes section."

"Easy," Ember said, bouncing down the last step to the

ground. "The Wastes is just nothingness. We'll be through in a jiffy."

"Don't underestimate any of the terrain," I told her. "The goblins have recreated everything about the Wastes. Unless you've been there, you won't understand how it feels.

Sybell snorted. "You haven't been in the Wastes. Nobody goes there."

"I have, actually." Just briefly, and only because I got lost. "I get around, Lady Sybell." *Poke her!* "I think you should seek to understand and experience every part of the land you wish to rule."

She ground her jaw and kept walking.

We reached a long section of dry, flat earth that seemed to stretch on forever. "You're going to feel some anxiety, Ember," I said. "Prepare yourself."

Sybell stalked forward, grimacing. "I have no intention of ruling the Wastes. I only wish to prove my father wrong."

"Oh, curse on the gods." Ember's footsteps faltered on the bare ground. "You weren't lying, were you? Suddenly, I feel so depressed." Her lip wobbled. "I want to go home."

I felt torn; Ember was upset, but Sybell was spilling her guts. We kept walking. I turned to Sybell. "What do you mean, prove your father wrong?"

"This is disloyal of me, but I will tell you, as you will most likely be dead by the end of this, Daffodil." Sybell swept back her hair. "But I see the imbalance in Nightfall, and it breaks my heart. Nobody else has any plan to stop it. My father does not care. I believe if I win the trial and marry the Heir, I can push the King and Queen to do more to stop it."

That's food for thought. Let me think about that for a second...

"It's so cold and desolate," Ember said in a little voice, distracting me. "I hate it here."

I wrapped my arm around her shoulder. "We'll be through it soon."

"It goes on forever," she whimpered.

"It doesn't. It just looks like it. It's a quarter of a mile at the most, Ember." And it was nothing compared to the writhing, furious tendrils of darkness trapped inside me. In fact, I felt curiously insulated against the misery of this faux-Wastes. I had the personification of misery inside of me. The fact that I was its permanent captor made me feel more confident.

"Let's jog," I said. "We'll get through it quicker, and I bet you anything the other team will be racing to ambush us in the mists of the Winter section. Go on, Sybell, what were you saying?"

"I only want to rule Dusk so I can make the changes we desperately need," she said, her voice hard with conviction. "I plan to appeal to the Winter Queen to help redress the balance. And if she won't help, I shall make laws to forbid bright paint and summery colors in Dusk, just for a while, and see if it makes a difference. Perhaps the Scorch will move East and haunt brighter places if ours is darkened." She grimaced. "My father thinks I'm a fool for trying. He expects I will die in the trials. But I must do something. For the good of the whole of Faerie."

Is she for real?

I didn't think Lady Sybell was lying. She sounded like she was being genuine. While Saoira of Autumn had given a big lecture on keeping the balance, the only idea she put forward was getting a Winterside princess on the throne, which was a totally self-serving idea.

And Sybell wasn't lying about her father. It sounded like he didn't believe in her, and she was determined to prove him wrong. Duke Gorman still might have murdered his brother, but he didn't have the magic to create the Scorch. And Sybell had nothing to do with any further plans to conquer Dusk. I mentally scratched her off my suspect list.

After a minute of sad, depressed jogging, Sybell trudging in front and me pulling Ember behind me, we suddenly shot out into blazing sunshine. It was so harsh, we had to shield our eyes.

The entire section of the battlefield had been designed to look like a beautiful summer courtyard—leafy topiary trees scattered amongst white stone and marble statues and archways dripping with roses. The sun blazed down on us, bouncing off the white marble. Lady Sybell shuddered dramatically, slunk towards the nearest archway, and huddled in the shade. "This is almost worse than the Wastes."

Ember's tensed little shoulders sagged instantly. She inhaled and breathed out a string of imaginative swear words. "This is just like Sandstone. I love the sunshine." She breathed out. "You know what? I should probably pull out of this competition now. Knowing my luck, I'd win and be forced to marry that big oaf, and I'd have to stay here in Dusk."

Her odds of winning were even worse than mine. "You'll get used to it again, Ember," I said.

We moved through the courtyards and plazas. I made a note of every good place to duck and cover, and anything that could be picked up and thrown as a weapon. The other team would be heading this way very soon. "You had to adapt to Dusk when you were a kid, didn't you? When you lived here with your mom?"

A dreamy expression floated over Ember's face. "When we first came here, mom used to use her elemental magic to make sunshine for me because I missed it so much. I wish I had elemental magic like her."

"She sounds lovely."

Her little face screwed up in a scowl. "She's not. She abandoned me. She chose them over me, and she abandoned me. I fucking hate her."

Holy shit.

I mouthed for a second. "Who? Who did she choose, Ember?"

But Ember had trotted off, moving further into the Summer Courtyard. "Look over here!" she shouted. A heavy fog blanketed the end of the summer section; she rushed over to examine it.

We need to pursue this. It sounds like her mom was beholden to someone else. She might have run off with whoever killed Monton.

I agreed. Ember was pissed at her mom. We were so alike, Ember and me. My mom had done some awful things to me, too. She abandoned me, and she chose the Ironclaw pack and her own safety over me, too.

Lady Sybell was already gliding towards the foggy end of the Summer Courtyard as quickly as possible. "Oh, it's much cooler here." She drifted into the mist.

I could hear voices, whispers in the wind. The other brides were there. Just as I thought, they were going to ambush us in the mist.

I shot forward and grabbed Ember's hand before she rushed in. "Careful," I whispered.

CHAPTER
FORTY

We moved into Winter. My eyes struggled to pick out details of the new terrain. It was absolutely freezing cold. The icy mist whirled around us, slowly retreating as we moved further into the next section.

A winter wonderland lay before us. In the middle of the battlefield lay a small lake, frozen solid and ringed with willows, their bare swooping branches glittering with a million icicles. To the left of the lake lay a winter courtyard, dove gray stone walls covered in snowdrifts and hardy evergreen bushes trimmed into deeply unsettling shapes—serpents, griffins, roaring hedge monsters towering twenty feet high.

We moved further into the Winter section. Beyond the walls, there was a stone courtyard with a rose garden—delicate white blooms on long dark-green stems.

I couldn't see anything to the right of the lake. A blizzard blocked out almost all vision. It was deeply unsettling.

A whisper hit my ears, and suddenly, everything went to hell.

Arrows and crossbow bolts shot towards us from the

rose garden. An arrow sliced Sybell's arm before she could move. I pulled Ember down to the ground. She rolled and produced a little crossbow out from beneath her tunic, rolled again onto her tummy, and started firing. "Take that, you bitches!"

Sybell let out a battle cry, drew her knives, and charged forward. More arrows flew towards her as she ran into the courtyard; she battered them away with her blades and bared her teeth. "Face me yourself, Nyla, you hag!"

A flash of yellow told me Nyla was hiding behind the archway in the rose garden. She laughed out loud and jumped out, storing her bow. She'd run out of arrows already. She was a terrible shot.

Princess Saoira appeared beside her. Nyla turned to her and pointed at Sybell. "Take her."

Saoira's mouth twisted. "I'm not going to be your meat shield while you run off and take their castle, Nyla." Saoira took off at a run, not towards Sybell, but going right, heading around us.

Nyla swore. "If you sneak off to their castle, Saoira, I swear—"

Ember jumped to her feet and ran toward Saoira to intercept her. Nyla pulled a short sword out from a sheath on her back, ran towards Sybell, who pulled out her own sword from under her cape, and let out a scream.

Goddamnit.

I leapt to my feet. Razor-sharp ice suddenly whipped towards me. One cut my cheek. I turned to investigate.

Brisa of Frost wove through the frozen willows, shooting icicles at me.

I ran towards her, ducking and using my knives to shatter the icicles as they soared towards me. She kept up the assault, white hair whipping around in the wind, her pale gray eyes filled with spite.

Behind her, I watched as Ember skidded on the ice and tackled Saoira. They both went sliding into the blizzard on the right-hand side of the lake and disappeared.

Brisa of Frost was gathering more magic towards her. She was more powerful than I thought, especially here, in a familiar element. She manifested two long ice-daggers and charged towards me.

I needed to finish this quickly; I had to save Ember. I moved in close, ducked Brisa's first, second, and third swipes of her ice blades, waited for an opening, and punched her right on the point of her very pointed chin.

Her eyes went glassy immediately, and she was out before her legs even buckled.

Over in the ice garden, Sybell and Nyla were locked in an epic sword fight, leaping over stone walls and crushing the white roses. Nyla may have been a terrible shot, but she was an incredible swordmaster. She ducked Sybell's swipe, leaned back on the return, stepped in, and kicked Sybell in the chest.

Sybell went flying. She slid all the way over the frozen lake, into the blizzard on the other side, and disappeared.

Suddenly, my skin prickled, and a chime went off in my ears. Something was inside that blizzard. Something huge and terrifying.

There was no time to process the sounds and scents that were screaming for attention and no time to stop and think.

Nyla turned towards me, chest heaving. "You're dead, Little Daffodil!" Nyla screamed.

Glorina of Dawn ran up behind her and let out a triumphant laugh. "Kill her, Nyla! I'll go ahead and take the castle. We'll win this together!"

"Fucking coward." Nyla turned to Glorina, her mouth twisted in fury. "Why won't any of you stupid bitches just do what you're told!" She spun around and sliced at Glorina with her sword, ripping open her throat.

Glorina's eyes bulged, and her mouth went slack. Bright-red blood bubbled up and poured down her neck, staining her yellow tunic. With a huff of contempt, Nyla pushed her over into the snow.

Glorina slumped on the ground, dead. Nyla nodded once in satisfaction and lifted her head. She shot me a glare. "You can wait. I need to take care of that little rat, Ember." She stomped off towards the blizzard and disappeared inside.

We need to save her.

I shot forward to chase her, then stopped abruptly, skidding on the frozen ground. The blizzard suddenly pulsed. Someone—some*thing*—inside let out a multi-tonal, absolutely terrifying moan.

The chill up my spine had nothing to do with the cold.

I don't think we should go in there, my brain screamed at me.

We had to. Shielding my face with my hands, I held my breath and walked into the blizzard.

Several feet in, the ice storm cleared. It was suddenly eerily quiet. Too quiet.

Quickly, I realized I was in the eye of a storm. A blizzard tornado whipped in a huge circle around a castle made of ice.

I blinked. The brides were frozen on the lawn in front of the ice castle. Frozen solid in their fight-stances, like statues. Nyla, closest to me, had been swinging her sword towards Ember's head when she was frozen.

I glanced up. A scream froze in my throat.

An enormous, absolutely terrifying-looking swan was bent over the ramparts of the castle, her wings outstretched, her long neck writhing from side to side.

Hey. Dwayne was behind her, huffing and puffing. **A little privacy here, please.**

The swan's face morphed abruptly, the feathers on her cheeks and forehead disappeared, appearing more humanoid. The terrible, beautiful snow-white face screwed up in a grimace of pure pleasure—then morphed back to a giant swan again.

Immediately, I averted my eyes. Oh, shit.

You might want to get out of here, little one, I think she's going to come again.

CHAPTER

FORTY-ONE

Do something! Our freaking alpha is banging the Winter Queen in a secret ice castle right in the middle of the War Games battlefield, and she's freezing everyone where they stand!

Adrenaline swamped me. My pulse hammered, pushing me to act, to do something, to move. What should I do? What the hell do I do?

Uh... run away?

I couldn't leave the other brides. Every second that passed, the chances of them surviving diminished rapidly. If I could get them all somewhere warm quickly, they might be okay...

Keeping my head low, ignoring the terrifying squeaks and moans of the Winter Queen, I dashed forward, grabbed Ember, swung her by her coat, and flung her through the blizzard. Nyla went next, only because she was closest.

The swan Queen Maeve let out a deep grunt, then another, low but building in intensity. Panic shot through me. I darted forward, grabbed Saoira and Sybell by their frozen-stiff jackets, and hauled them both at the same time.

Was that it? Was that all of us? Glorina was dead, and

I'd knocked Brisa unconscious outside of the blizzard. I gritted my teeth, leaned forward, ignored the rapid grunts Maeve was making, pushed everything into my legs, and charged outside of the Winter Queen's shag pad, just as she let out a high-pitched swan squeak.

The snowflakes in the air around me shivered in mid-air. Frostbite chomped at my back.

I'd escaped just in time. I popped back into the Winter courtyard hauling Saoira and Sybell behind me.

We weren't out of the woods yet. It was freezing here; the brides wouldn't thaw. I had to get them over to the summer section. I let out a furious shout to the crowd outside, hoping someone would hear me. "If you guys can see me, you better send someone to help right now, or all these princesses will die!"

Could they even see me? I had no idea. Queen Maeve's blizzard was obviously hiding her and Dwayne. If anyone knew she was here, the herald would have called off the War Games trial before it even started.

I gritted my teeth and kept running, dragging Princess Saoira and Lady Sybell behind me. They had been frozen for the longest. I had to get them warmed up. A quarter mile of agonizing torture later, I'd pushed both of them out into the Summer courtyard and sprinted back to where Ember and Nyla lay frozen.

Lady Brisa is gone, my brain noticed, trying to keep my spirits up.

She must have regained consciousness and run off. I just had to get Ember and Nyla back to the summer court-yard, and they'd be okay.

I grabbed Ember by her frozen arm, took Nyla's leg, and pushed myself out of the Winter zone, and ran right into the warmth of Summer.

The sudden change from cold to hot felt like I'd been

plunged into boiling water. I kept moving, though, stomping my frozen legs, running from Ember to Nyla to Saoira to Sybell, rubbing their chests and slapping their cheeks gently, trying to shock them back to life.

A few moments later, the herald's horn blew, and the battleground was immediately filled with royal guards. Someone wrapped me in a warm blanket and carried me away.

CHAPTER

FORTY-TWO

Brackin fidgeted in his seat. "What do you think they want with us?" He glanced out the carriage window again nervously. It was late, only a few hours from dawn. The Close Combat Trials had finished hours ago, and the City was winding down for rest after two days of excitement. "Do you think I'm in trouble?" Brackin asked me.

"I don't know what they want with us, and yes, I think we're both in trouble." I was very nervous, too.

Brackin turned to look at me, his face desperate for reassurance. "But you won Close Combat. You won the trial today, Daffodil. That has to count for something. They didn't say anything about your conduct in the War Games trial yesterday."

My conduct in the War Games trial yesterday had spoken for itself. The whole City had watched me. They hadn't seen anything within Queen Maeve's blizzard, but they watched me haul four frozen-solid brides out of it. They all saw me drag Ember, Nyla, Saoira, and Sybell to the Summer zone to warm them up, rather than just leave them to die.

Sybell never woke up, though. Once her body thawed, they found several stab wounds in her back. It wasn't the ice that killed her, but I still felt terrible for her.

Lady Brisa of Frost won the War Games challenge. She obviously woke up soon after I knocked her out and took off down the battlefield to take our castle. She won, but nobody cheered for her. Everyone was too confused about what they'd seen. I'd gone in to save the other brides, while Brisa ran off to win the Trial.

My fan club—the mob of sobbing warlords waving lavender-colored handkerchiefs—all hooted and hollered about how smart I'd been. The other brides owed me a debt for saving their lives, and in the end, Brisa really won nothing of worth.

Once the frozen brides revived, they all told the same story, they'd been frozen by the Winter Queen in her swan form. Everyone assumed they'd hallucinated. The goblin engineers insisted that their spells must have been too strong, the magical version of a technical glitch.

I kept my mouth shut. Nobody would believe me, anyway. And I felt bad I underestimated Dwayne. He could shag anyone he put his mind to.

So, Brisa won, and the King and Queen retired to their palace alone to figure out what the hell happened at the War Games Trial.

Despite the uncertainty and all the rumors of a Winter Queen on the loose, today's Close Combat Trial went ahead as planned. The brides gathered in the ballroom of the palace and fought one-on-one, no weapons, on the hard marble floor.

Brisa died first. Nyla took the opportunity to punish her for her betrayal in running off to win the War Games by herself. Their Close Combat fight began, Nyla wrapped

Brisa up in a lock and bashed Brisa's head against the stone floor until her brains spilled out.

Nyla's frustration and rage had reached boiling point, and now I was sure that the Court of Spring had something to do with the attack on Dusk. If the Aranbolds were as aggressive and ambitious as Nyla was, then it had to be them. I suspected it might be what Ember had meant by her mother being a traitor—she'd had her own husband killed so she could run back to her family in the Kingdom of Spring. She'd definitely run away with someone.

The guards quickly cleaned up the blood, and Ember and I fought next. Ember, the little cow, tried to hit me with a couple of transformation spells before we began. I managed to dodge them. I quickly and gently wrestled her into a choke, but she refused to tap out.

With no other options, I put her to sleep. My fan club cheered and waved their handkerchiefs while I put my hands over my burning cheeks and tried to pretend they didn't exist.

Saoira and Nyla fought next. Saoira fought admirably, but Nyla was too quick and well-trained in combat. Saoira knew it and submitted after only a minute.

Unfortunately, Nyla was too deep in her bloodlust fog, and the guards had to pull her off. Saoira rose to her feet, wincing, and made several loud comments on decorum and keeping one's wits. "We are not savages, Nyla," she had said scornfully. "And this is just a demonstration."

I fought Saoira next, and she clearly forgot her own words, because she tried her best to kill me. I knew she would—she knew she had no chance against Nyla but assumed she could take a mortal girl easily. Unluckily for her, it only took me twenty seconds to knock her out.

Nyla and Ember were supposed to fight next, but I

offered to finish out my rounds and take on Nyla straight after Saoira. It meant that I had no time to recover, but it also meant that if I won, the Trials would be over, and Ember wouldn't have to die.

Nyla had sneered at me, told me to prepare for death, and launched herself at me. The fight lasted thirty seconds. I broke her jaw, choked her unconscious, and won the Close Combat Trial.

Now, three hours later, we'd been summoned back to the palace to speak with the royal family.

"You won the Trial," Brackin said, echoing my thoughts. "For once, you didn't embarrass me horribly. That's two trials you've won. Why would the King and Queen want to speak with me now?"

I grimaced, bouncing in my seat as the carriage turned onto another cobblestone lane leading to the palace. "I don't think it's you they want to talk to."

"Well, I should hope not, because I have done nothing wrong." Brackin suddenly turned and glared at me. "I suppose they were perturbed by the behavior of your warlord fan club." His eyes narrowed. "Was this your plan all along, Daffodil? Is this why you're here? Did you amass a group of your old admirers so they could provoke the new heir?"

Oh, gods...

A saucy look melted away some of his agitation. "Because clearly, *that* didn't work."

Immediately after I won the Trial, Romeo, hovering like a thundercloud behind King Ronus's throne, told the cheering rabble of warlords to hold their tongues. Lord Fandoine and Lord Asternay, overcome with emotion, shouted that Romeo didn't deserve a warrior goddess like me.

Romeo, of course, took that personally. He definitely had energy to expend. So, he asked the King and Queen permission to utilize the fight ring while it was still set up and challenged all the warlords to combat.

He beat the shit out of every one of them. Coldly, methodically, one by one—sometimes two or three at a time.

None of them lasted more than ninety seconds. My poor fan club were now nursing their wounds in a tavern.

Brackin gave a shudder of pleasure. "I stiffened considerably, watching that. The heir has extraordinary hands. Long fingers...." Brackin let out a sigh. "They would be perfect for tickling," he murmured.

"Brackin, don't take this the wrong way, but if you talk about the Prince of Shadow like that ever again, I will rip your throat out," I said.

He huffed out a chuckle. "I suppose you are in love with him, like every other female in this Kingdom."

The carriage slowed, then stopped. "We're here," he said. "Now, seal your lips, Little Daffodil, leave the talking to me."

I gathered up the train of my gown in one hand and hopped out of the carriage. Lady Pesh, back on board with my candidacy after my win at the Combat Trial, had tried to bully me into one of her gowns, a lemon-yellow puffball skirt. I was tired, and I'd lost all my patience with her, so I politely told her to back off.

She insisted. Lord Bron, who had actually shown up at the Combat Trial and watched me fight, ended up putting his hand over Lady Pesh's mouth, and dragged her out of the room.

Steven came to the rescue with a bolt of fae snakeskin and a mouthful of pins, draping and folding the black silky skin around my naked body and sewing me into it.

The result was an extraordinary masterpiece of drapery in a stunning, shimmering iridescent scaled fabric. The capped sleeves rolled off my shoulders, and the silky snake-skin dipped in a cowl between my breasts—just on the decent side of indecency—and flowed down my body, highlighting my waist and curve of my thighs, coming in before flaring into a long, majestic train. It was light as a feather, too. If the fabric were tougher, I'd wear this dress into battle. Hell, I'd wear it to the movies. Or to the market. I'd never felt more beautiful in my life.

A quartet of footmen surrounded us, and another four guards flanked them. They all guided us into the palace. Brackin, holding my arm as we walked, leaned closer to me. "I cannot tell if we are being honored or frog marched," he whispered.

I had no answers for him. We entered the palace and were immediately escorted into the throne room. It was smaller than the ballroom but no less luxurious, with a glittering chandelier overhead, the walls lined with candelabra, the flames of every candle casting a warm orange glow over the dark marble walls and floor.

The King and Queen sat on their thrones at the end of the room. Ronus wore a severe pitch-black tunic and trousers. Talia wore a black gown, high necked and long sleeved, with a scarlet sash across her chest. They both stared at me with stony expressions as we approached. Romeo stood next to Talia's throne, his face carefully blank.

I stopped in front of the thrones and curtsied. Brackin bowed deeply and cleared his throat. "Lord Brackin of Gloom, Your Majesties. I am honored to be called to your presence. May I pre—"

But King Ronus held up his hand. "You can dispense with the formalities, Lord Brackin."

Brackin shut his mouth. We stood in uncomfortable

silence for a whole minute. The King and Queen glared at me.

Brackin broke first. "If I may, Your Maj—"

"You may not, Brackin," Queen Talia snapped. Her sharp eyes rested on me. I met her gaze and read everything in her expression.

Ah, fuck.

Queen Talia inhaled through her nose. "Who are you?"

Brackin made a flourish gesture with his hand. "This is the Little Daffodil, my Queen, she is Gloom's candidate in the Bride Trials—"

"Brackin." Her voice was like a gunshot.

He flinched.

She flicked her eyes towards him. "Take several steps to the left."

After a moment, he awkwardly shuffled away from me.

"Now, perhaps you will understand I am not talking to you. Close your mouth, and do not speak again. Do you hear me?"

Wisely, Brackin nodded.

Queen Talia returned her razor-sharp gaze to me. A tiny sigh left her lips. "At first, I assumed Gloom was insulting us, introducing a mortal shifter girl to the Bride Trials. Then, when you won the Hunt Trial, I worried that you were part of the conspiracy to destroy Dusk." She paused for a second. I felt the air around her grow tense.

Please don't kill us, Brain-Daphne said in a little voice.

After a few minutes of silence, the Queen's shoulders slumped very slightly. She let out a tiny sigh, then turned to look at Romeo behind her. "Go and stand beside her," she said in perfect English.

Romeo's eyes darkened, and the line of his shoulders tensed. He walked down the steps and came towards me.

Our eyes met, and I melted. Even with all the danger

zinging through the air, I couldn't help the surge of adoration that pulsed through me. Gods, this man was absolute perfection. I'd never get used to looking at him. I'd never get over the look in his eyes when he stared back at me.

He walked to my side and reluctantly turned to face the Queen.

Talia sighed again. "I knew it."

King Ronus frowned and glanced over at her. "My love, please enlighten this old fool. I do not understand what is going on."

She waved her hand towards us. "I saw the look on Zarayan's face when she rode into the City on the Golden Stag. I assumed he was in awe of her bravery and her... unusual methodology. But I also saw the twinkle in his eye when he watched the Talent Trial. I saw the panic in his expression when she disappeared into the blizzard at the War Games trial. I saw the terror in his gaze as he watched her fight in Close Combat, and I watched his fear turn to something *quite* extraordinary when he challenged her rabble of admirers."

She paused, and her gaze turned a little frosty. "Despite all my efforts in making my grandson comfortable, I have not seen him so relaxed and satisfied as immediately after beating all those warlords into a bloody pulp." She paused and looked at Romeo again. "He is in love, and he has been hiding this from us."

Romeo didn't say anything. He didn't really need to.

The Queen's eyes fell on me again. "You came here for him."

I bowed my head. "I did, your Majesty."

Brackin let out a dramatic gasp and clutched his chest. "Daffodil!"

"Uh uh—" Ronus held up his finger. "Lord Brackin, take ten more steps to the left."

Brackin awkwardly moved a little further away from us. "Turn around."

Brackin shuffled around in a circle until he was facing the other way.

"Okay." Ronus took a deep breath. "Let us have the whole story."

FORTY-THREE

I t didn't take long to explain myself. It took me a little longer to explain the entire plot of the movie Miss Congeniality, which wasn't totally necessary, but I was nervous.

Thankfully, Talia and Ronus didn't freak out, in fact, Talia in particular was quite moved by the lengths I'd gone to in my effort to rescue my lover. They were also both touched Romeo and I had decided to stick around and help figure out who was trying to destroy Dusk.

"I won't even try to claim that you should have come to us earlier." She smiled at Romeo fondly. "If I hadn't seen everything she has done with my own eyes, I would not have believed anyone was worthy of you, Zarayan." Her lip curled slightly. "None of the Trial candidates are worthy, at least. But this mortal girl has run circles around the best this realm has to offer." She paused. "Except Talent. I think we can all agree that you need to do some work there, Daphne Ironclaw."

Romeo squeezed my hand. "I thought you were awesome," he whispered to me. "I saved it on a replay charm so I can watch it over and over."

Clearing my throat awkwardly, I changed the subject, first telling them my theory about the Scorch being a former High Fae, and quickly filling them in on what I'd learned about the brides and their motivations. "Nyla of Spring seems like she's becoming increasingly desperate and unhinged. According to Ember, she's got no magic, but the rest of her family is skilled in elemental magic. I can't imagine *one* person having enough power to curse a transformed High Fae or the god of cattle with some sort of eternal flame, but it's possible the whole lot of them got together and did it. It would take the entire family. If it's them, then Nyla must have elemental magic. They don't seem to give a crap about the imbalance in Faerie—definitely not like Sybell of Nightfall, anyway—so their end goal might be to turn Dusk into another Spring. Which, of course, would ruin us all."

"Saoira of Autumn is incredibly manipulative," Romeo said. "Her family has been working overtime with the nobles here in the city. Most of our courtiers and advisers think she's right; we should choose her as my bride and hope it helps redress the imbalance. As far as we know, there's no strong personal magic in their family. No elemental magic, no transformation magic. But they keep their secrets held firmly to their chests. It's possible they created the Scorch to scare everyone into only marrying within similar sides of the Inbetween."

"And finally," I said. "Princess Ember, as unhinged and psychotic as she is, dropped a few hints about her mother. She called Carissa a traitor and said that her mother abandoned her. I'm wondering if Carissa did have Monton killed."

Ronus shook his head. "But Carissa loved Monton desperately. I counseled her after he died, and she was devastated."

Romeo cut in. "Maybe she didn't love him. Maybe she loved someone else. Perhaps she killed Monton to break free from him, and her son died as an accident, so she lost her mind."

The King and Queen seemed unconvinced.

"I need to talk to Ember," I said. "She knows far more than we think. I bet you she knows what happened between Carissa and Monton. She'd know why Carissa broke down and ran away, anyway."

"She was only a child at the time. Six years old, by mortal standards. She would have no understanding of what was going on," Queen Talia said. "And as far as talking to her goes, her uncle has her under lock and key, so that will not happen until another Trial commences. And I would take everything she said with a grain of salt, anyway. It is common knowledge that the girl is totally unhinged."

I smiled at her, a little uncomfortable. People said that about me, too—that I was only a child, and I was totally unhinged. A sweet little psychopath.

Something told me that Ember had all the answers, though. "If I can only speak with her during one of the Trials, then I need to get her alone at some point during the Trials. And that won't happen at tomorrow's Compatibility Trial, since they are one–on-one dates."

"We were going to cancel the Compatibility Trial anyway." Talia turned and gave Romeo a smile. "At the request of your lover. Zarayan has been quite emphatic about not wanting to go on a date with anyone."

"Oh." I blinked up at him. "Good. Well..." I blew out a breath. "We need to get everyone to show their cards. Get everything on the table, if you know what I mean. The last trial, the Death Race—"

Talia had her eyebrows raised. "No holds barred, winner takes all?"

"That's what I'm thinking."

A smile curved her lips. "Are you sure you are up for it, Daphne Ironclaw?"

Romeo pulled me into his chest and wrapped his arms around me. I didn't need it—the iron-solid sense of conviction inside me gave me all the strength I needed—but the heat of his body made me melt inside. "I'm sure. That's why I'm here."

Romeo kissed my temple. The King and Queen watched us with fond expressions on their faces, clearly relishing the sight.

A little voice broke the silence. "Can I turn around now?"

CHAPTER

FORTY-FOUR

I t was a beautiful, sultry afternoon in Dusk, and the final Bride Trial was due to start in ten minutes. A one-mile-long giant murderous obstacle course lay outside the city gates, right where the War Games battlefield had been.

It was very quiet. As Brackin and I made our way through the streets, heading to the City gates, the lack of noise struck me as very odd. For a second, I wondered if someone had put a silence spell on the crowd. The tops of the gates were packed with people, but everyone was curiously, suspiciously still and quiet.

What's going on?

I was so unsettled by the silence, I answered my own brain out loud. "I have no idea. Maybe there's something we haven't anticipated."

I was prepared as I could be, wearing heavy steel-capped boots and a reinforced black aymander leather hooded jumpsuit treated with spell-reflectors. My hair was braided tightly on my scalp and tucked away, and my Orion blades were stashed in thigh-holsters, in easy reach. I was packing throwing knives, some first-aid potions and a length of reinforced rope.

I'd covered all my bases. But why was the crowd so quiet?

We walked through the gates, heading to the platform beside the start line of the Death Race. The other brides were already there with their sponsors. All of them were staring up, their mouths wide open, at the watchtowers where the royals would be settling in.

I turned around and looked up.

The tower to the right of the gates was festooned with the red and orange flags of Dusk. King Ronus and Queen Talia were there, sitting stiffly in their high-backed seats. Their expressions were tense. They were on-edge.

However, the tower on the left, which had held the other royal courts in previous trials, looked very different. It sparkled with snowflakes and had been draped with shimmery blue and silver flags.

Oh, shit. Brain-Daphne giggled nervously. *We forgot to tell them about Dwayne.*

That explained the nervous silence. The Winter Queen had come to watch the final Bride Trial. Queen Maeve sat in the tower on an enormous throne made of ice, staring impassively down at the course below her.

Do you think Talia and Ronus are going to kill us for this?

Possibly. Queen Maeve hadn't left the Winter Court in thousands of years. She wasn't just a royal; she was a force of nature, practically a goddess. Every Kingdom on this side of the Inbetween was beholden to her, so Talia and Ronus were forced to suffer her presence no matter what.

Brackin stared up at the tower, his eyes wide. "Oh, dear gods..."

Good grief, Maeve was huge in her human form—at

least eight feet tall, her white face glowing like the surface of the moon. She wore a high-necked, long sleeved silver gown that sparkled with a million diamonds. She was so glorious and terrifying, I couldn't even look at her directly.

Dwayne sat next to her on his own ice throne, although he was wearing a blue sweater with snowflakes on it, and sitting on a bearskin rug. He saw me, waved, and pointed. **That's her, pookie! That's my little girl. Go, Daphne! Team Ironclaw!**

The Winter Queen arched her eyebrow, staring down at me.

Don't look her in the eye!

I wasn't an idiot. I averted my gaze and dropped a curtsey.

She's a good girl, pookie. You'll like her.

Queen Maeve inspected me silently. Then, she turned away, apparently dismissing me.

I exhaled a relieved breath. It was the best response I could have asked for. She reached out her hand to stroke Dwayne on the head.

Brackin cleared this throat awkwardly. "Let's try and pretend she's not here, shall we?" He wove his arm through mine and walked with me towards the starting platform. I could see Princess Nyla up there already, looking fierce as hell in her fire-yellow combat suit, listening carefully to her older brother Prince Aranbold.

Princess Saoira was there, too, in skin-tight orange leather with reinforced black armor over her chest. She was stretching her legs and taking last minute instructions from the Queen of Autumn, nodding with a determined look on her face.

Ember stood with her arms crossed over her chest, looking sulky while turning her head away from her uncle,

Duke Redfoot of Sandstone. He was obviously giving her a lecture. Ember was wearing red, and she was so weighed down by weapons it would be a miracle if she even made it over the start line. I counted two mini-crossbows, a dozen throwing knives, two daggers on both sides of her thighs, and a short sword strapped to her back.

"Now, dear Daffodil," Brackin murmured in my ear. "Listen up. I spoke to the construction goblins again, and it is as the King and Queen said. I will run over the course now just to remind you of what they decided."

I remembered everything we'd spoken about, but Brackin had gotten weirdly protective, and we couldn't see any of the course from here—it was surrounded by a twelve-foot wall on all sides. The crowd above us could see everything, but for us, it was supposed to be a surprise.

I let him talk me through it. "After you go over the wall and drop into the course," he said, "there will be a long section of lawn. Beneath the surface of the lawn, they have planted a thousand snaptraps at random intervals."

Snaptraps were vicious, carnivorous flowers. Imagine a bear trap with roots, and you've got a fae snaptrap flower. That was fine; I'd be able to smell them early enough to avoid them.

"After the snaptrap field," Brackin continued, "You will come to a climbing frame, which you must climb to get to the swing-ropes. Here's the fun part—both the climbing frame and the swing rope are woven out of live slumber-snakes."

Slumber-snakes were lazy bastards, but if you pissed them off, they'd bite you, and their venom was worse than taking five Ambien and drinking a bottle of whiskey. The effects of the venom only lasted thirty seconds, though, and it wasn't lethal.

"Don't let them bite you, and don't fall off the climbing

frame," Brackin continued. "It is as high as the watchtowers. If you fall, you will surely die. Mostly because they put iron spikes beneath the climbing frame."

I nodded. "I got it." There was nothing more poisonous to the fae than iron, but not being fae gave me no advantage. If I fell from the climbing frame, it didn't really matter what kind of metal impaled me.

"Then," Brackin went on, "the mists of madness, as we discussed. The goblins worked all through the night to make the alterations."

The mists of madness were a quarter-mile section of the course made up of nothing but solid fog. The goblins were going to include magical enhancements to freak us out and muddle our senses so we wouldn't know what direction we were supposed to be going in.

The team that designed the course had protested this change, saying it was pointless having a section that nobody in the crowd could see. The King and Queen insisted, however, saying that the most exciting part of the War Games Battle was the point where we all disappeared in the blizzard. The mystery was a crowd pleaser, they said. It upped the tension and created a delicious anticipation to see who would make it out.

We'd included it to give a hidden space so the other princesses could show us their cards. The enhancements were designed to push them to the brink, and hopefully, Nyla or Saoira would snap and break out some heavy-duty elemental magic. Or confess to King Monton's murder. At this stage, I'd take either of them.

The whole plan was flimsy as hell, and I was wildly aware we were absolutely grasping at straws, but it was all we had. Ronus was convinced there would be an attempt on his life if the traitor's bride didn't win, so he was expecting an assassination attempt, too. We'd done everything we could think of to prepare ourselves.

The herald blew his horn.

"That's us." I smiled at Brackin. "Wish me luck."

To my surprise, he pulled me into a hug. "You don't need luck, Daffodil. You have hope. You *are* hope." He pulled back and gave me a watery smile. "You will save us all; I just know it." His lip wobbled for a second. He abruptly turned away and walked back to the gates so he could climb up and watch with the rest of the crowd.

I took a deep breath and walked up the steps to the starting platform and joined the other three brides. None of them looked at me.

"Welcome to the Death Race Trial!" the herald bellowed. "The rules are simple—the first to reach the end of the course alive will be declared the champion of the Bride Trials. In this race, there are no restrictions. Use whatever you will and do whatever you need to make it to the end. The King and Queen have waived their right to veto, so the winner of this challenge will take the hand of his Highness, the Prince of Shadow, and become his betrothed."

Winner takes all, no holds barred.

Out of the corner of my eye, I saw Nyla bare her teeth. She wanted it more than anything. Ember wasn't looking at the herald; she was glaring at Nyla.

Brain-Daphne whistled. *That girl needs therapy.*

She needed someone to guide her, that's what she needed.

The herald threw his head back and shouted. "To the start lines!"

Romeo caught my eye and mouthed at me, "I love you. Good luck."

I gave him a quick smile. I got this.

We spread out on the platform, facing the wall, six feet between each bride. A simple rope hung over the wall. That was our way in. The herald shouted, "On my horn, the Death Race will begin!"

A pulse of adrenaline shot through me, and my vision sharpened. The herald blew his horn.

The race was on.

CHAPTER

FORTY-FIVE

rincess Saoira was over the wall first; she was so
light on her feet. I fumbled the rope. For some
reason I wasn't expecting it to be as silky as it was,
and my hands slipped twice while I was trying to haul
myself up. I cursed myself. I'd fallen behind on the first
hurdle.

Shake it off. Let's go.

Ember's little legs flipped over the wall just before
mine, and we landed together on the soft grass of the other
side. She bent into a crouch, arms outstretched, surveying
the wide green lawn before us.

Saoira and Nyla were already skipping over the lawn
just a few yards ahead of us.

"Ember," I hissed.

She jerked her head towards me and glared.

I pointed at the ground. "Snaptraps. Be careful." I
pushed off from the wall and ran.

Hopefully, we'd all leave Ember far behind. With any
luck, Nyla would ignore her, choosing to just win the race
rather than go to the trouble of killing her. I bolted over the

grass, letting my nose sniff out where the snaptraps lay ahead of me.

I darted and weaved, avoiding the slightly bitter steel scent the snaptraps gave off. They were hidden very well, nestled right in the ground, but now and then I'd get a flash of silver between the emerald-green blades of grass, a hint of the snaptrap's razor-sharp teeth.

Saoira dashed over the grass to my left, a few yards ahead of me. The scent of ripe berries and summer wine drifted over on the wind, pulling my focus towards her. Saoira held her hands outstretched as she ran. A faint amber glow surrounded her fingers.

Saoira of Autumn *did* have magic. A botanical affinity, maybe? Whatever she was doing, it was helping her detect the snaptraps as she ran over the emerald lawn. She darted left and right, but nothing snapped at her at all.

On my right, Ember had fallen behind. She was being more careful with where she put her feet, hopping like a little kangaroo, then pausing and hopping again. A flare of hope surged in my chest. Please, let her fall behind.

On her other side, Nyla had pulled out the length of rope coiled at her side. I glanced at her, realizing it wasn't rope—it was a whip. A long, golden whip with a leather handle.

Damn, my brain whistled, *I wish I thought of that. She looks badass.*

She really did. Nyla unfurled the whip, swooping and cracking it along the grass ahead of her. The snaptraps in her path leapt up, biting their teeth together. She pulled the whip back, tugging it easily through the gaps in their fangs, and hopped over the closed traps effortlessly. Whip, snap, pull back. She repeated the action over and over.

Brain-Daphne made a note to get herself a whip and practice using it immediately.

Nyla ran ahead of the rest of us. She didn't have to dodge anything; she just thundered across the closed traps until she was across. She slowed down and darted carefully through a short section of iron spikes and reached the climbing frame first.

I didn't focus on it until I was sure I'd cleared the snaptraps. To my left, Saoira was already there, a few paces ahead, weaving through the spikes and staying as far away from the poisonous metal as possible. I looked ahead. The climbing frame's ropes shivered slightly, moving very slowly, and coiled around each other. The slumber-snakes were woven together loosely. As I cleared the last section of lawn, Saoira placed her hand on the frame.

A slumber-snake hissed and bit at her.

She cursed and pulled back, shooting a glance up at Nyla, who was already halfway up the frame. Nyla pulled herself up on the snake-frame, not even trying to be delicate about it. The slumber-snakes hissed and snapped at her. None of the bites seemed to affect her.

Nyla's wearing bokleather, my brain whispered. *It's impenetrable.*

Saoira must have missed the memo. Nyla's suit covered her whole body, including a hood and mask. The slumber-snakes bit at her, but their venom wasn't getting through to her at all.

Saoira only hesitated for a second. She pulled out a vial from her jumpsuit, opened it, swallowed the contents, and started to climb.

My brain processed the scent of the potion. *Broad spectrum anti-venom,* she whispered. *Guess that's one way to do it. She better climb quickly before it wears off.*

I pulled my own hood and mask up, covering everything except my eyes, and started to climb. My pulse pounded in my ears. The iron spikes below me smelled stronger than usual.

It's on purpose, remember? It's supposed to freak the brides out. If we lose focus for a second, we fall and die.

A flash stole my attention away—a fizz of magic. A dozen snakes hissed loudly, and above me, Nyla lost her footing. She recovered quickly and swore. "Ember," she roared, "I swear I'm going to fucking kill you when this is over!"

I glanced down and saw Ember at the bottom of the climbing frame between two iron spikes, pocketing her sling. She'd been shooting curses at Nyla, hoping she'd fall. She chuckled, tugged her own hood over her head, and started to climb behind me, quick as a monkey.

Go. Just go. She'll be okay, and Nyla will focus on winning the race.

A second later, I was almost at the top, neck and neck with Saoira, when Ember let out a heartbreaking cry.

I glanced down and saw her face. Two tiny red fang marks stood out on the lily-white bridge of her nose, right between her eyes—the only exposed part of her body.

She'd been bitten. Her pale eyes went dark as her pupils dilated, then rolled back in her head.

Ember was going to fall. We were halfway up now—twenty feet in the air. Iron spikes littered the ground right below us.

She's going to die.

Her arms went slack. Shit.

Without hesitation, I pulled out my rope, fed it through the frame, secured it, and pushed myself sideways in an arc, swinging downwards.

This would look a lot cooler if we used a whip.

I caught Ember just as her fingers lost their grip. Holding on to the frame with one hand, I gritted my teeth, slid my rope free, and wrapped it around my body, securing Ember's little body to my back.

Gods, she was heavy.

I hauled myself up, using my legs to push up and my arms to pull. The slumber snakes lashed out at me, biting over and over again, but mercifully, none hit any exposed skin.

Ember started to stir just as we reached the top. "Wass-appening?" she slurred. On the platform on top, I rolled her off my back and undid the rope. "Wassgoingon?" She blinked.

I looked out; Nyla was already at the end of the platform, tugging the rope swing free. Saoira wasn't far behind her.

We can still catch up.

I coiled my rope up quickly. "You should stay here, Ember," I said quickly. "Stay alive, okay?"

Ember shook off the last of the venom and scrambled to her feet quicker than I expected. "You saved me." She beamed. "Thanks, Daffodil!" She held out her arms and ran in for a hug.

Her knife went straight into my back.

CHAPTER

FORTY-SIX

The pain was excruciating. Completely paralyzing. A million thoughts exploded in my brain all at the same time—me and brain-Daphne screaming, at each other, together. *She stabbed me. Ember stabbed me! How... what... It must be an accident, she couldn't have meant to...*

Suddenly, the pain compounded, blocking out all reason, all comprehension. It was a million years before I could understand what had just happened. She'd twisted the knife in my back. *Ember twisted the knife in my back!*

The psychotic little princess bounced back, grinning. Her hands were empty. She'd left her dagger in my kidney.

"Sucker." She chuckled.

I couldn't move. I couldn't even breathe. *But... but she's not... she's not...*

Ember moved quickly, kicked my knee and shoved me at the same time. I whirled around and stumbled, falling off the platform.

"Say hi to the Underworld for me!" Ember's voice was triumphant.

I fell, my body limp and helpless, sliding and flopping

down hissing ropes of the climbing frame. My brain screamed at me. *Do something, catch hold of something, we're going to fall, we're going to die!*

My fingers snagged a silky snake rope and held on.

Good. Good. Hold it. Breathe.

I took a breath.

We need to get this knife out of our back, because it hurts so bad I can't think straight. Get it out, and heal the wound. Grab the handle.

With enormous effort, gritting my teeth against the unbearable agony, I twisted my arm around my body and found the handle.

Spelled blade. I should have known. That bitch spelled her blades so they'd penetrate our impenetrable leather. Now, pull.

I screamed out loud as I tugged the knife out of my back. Snakes hissed and spat all around me, snapping little fangs at my arms and legs. I dropped Ember's knife. It clanged loudly when it hit the iron spikes below me.

Okay, good. Healing potion.

I fumbled in my breast pocket. My hands shook. I used my teeth to pull out the stopper and downed it.

Now wait. Hold on and wait just a moment. Let the wound heal and we'll climb back up.

I concentrated on my breathing for a moment. The pain was diminishing quickly, and I could finally think a little clearer. "Ember stabbed me," I breathed out.

Yeah. She stabbed some fucking sense into us, too, Brain Daphne snarled.

She did. I'd been blind, but I saw it all clearly now. All the clues. All the things Ember had done, all the things she'd said. The crossbow, the weapons, her lust for violence, for petty revenge. Her uncle's attempts to keep her quiet and have her die quickly. Her mom, her magic.

Ember killed her stepfather. She killed King Monton.

She was only six years old at the time, so everyone dismissed her, but when I was six, I killed my own mom.

Ember did it. I was sure of it. "I can't believe I didn't see it sooner. How could I not see it?"

Suddenly, despair and hopelessness surged through me. I felt that iron-hard core of certainly, that righteous sense of conviction... crumble away.

I let out a whimper. My fingers, still holding the snake-rope of the climbing frame, began to shake. "How could I have been so wrong? Again?"

The darkness within me suddenly stirred for the first time since I got here. A tentacle waved at me. Join us. Come back and join us.

Fuck, no! In my mind, Brain-Daphne charged in with a dustpan and broom and scooped up pieces of certainty and piled them back into a little mound. *Nope, we're not doing this. We're not omnipotent, babes. We don't have to be right about everything. We can be wrong.*

Despair surged again. "We saved Ember's life," I mumbled. "So many times. She... she.."

We got it wrong, and that's okay. Everyone makes mistakes. We can only make the best decisions with the information we've got.

"But it was Ember all along. All the signs were there, right in front of me, and I chose to ignore them because she reminded me of *me*. I underestimated her, just like everyone underestimates me. This whole time, we've been trying to invent scenarios and make up motivations and decipher complicated court politics and jam pieces of the puzzle where it wouldn't fit..." A sob left my lips. "I thought she was a sweet little psychopath, just like me."

But that's just it. We needed this, Daphne, she said gently. *This is it, the final self-realization. You were never a psychopath.*

I exhaled a small breath. But...

323

Never. She is, though. You never *were.*

I sat with it for a minute.

My brain was right. I was nothing like Ember.

I never had been. I'd only ever lived to serve others. Sure, I killed people. Lots of them. In self-defense, to save innocent people, to save the world. I never killed for power, though I never hurt anyone just for revenge, not even once.

And if I was right about Ember...

She only served herself. She really was a psychopath, and I'd never been one.

Ember was the anti-Daphne. The Wario to my Mario. The monstrous me of my childhood and final boss I needed to defeat in my journey of self-realization.

I'd never realized I carried so much shame around the things I was forced to do to survive as a kid.

Forgive yourself, my brain whispered. *That's all you have to do.*

I obeyed her. A lightness filled my chest.

Good, good, let the hope flow through you, Brain-Daphne cackled. *And just in time, too, because we've got a race to win. You can't lose Romeo to that psychopath now.*

FORTY-SEVEN

Thanks to Romeo's healing potion, the hole in my kidney only took a minute to seal up. I felt the strength flow back into me as I hauled myself back up the climbing frame. I jumped to my feet, ran the length of the platform, and looked out over the course.

A short field of sharp iron spikes ended in a deep, black pool, a hundred feet long. At the far end of the pool, I could see a flash of Nyla's yellow jumpsuit. She was already out.

Saoira and Ember wouldn't be far behind her.

I reached out, grabbed the rope, and swung myself out over the spikes, down, then up....

I let go at the top, cleared the spikes by a few yards, did a little spin in the air for the sake of the crowd, who oohed appreciatively, and dived into the water.

The water wasn't as dark as it was from the surface. I could see clearly, which wasn't good, because the water was filled with kelpies. The murderous, red-eyed water horses charged back and forth, but most of them galloped through the water in a circle just up ahead. One charged towards me, though. It opened its mouth and bared broken-looking jagged teeth.

I swam close. I punched it in the snout, kicked my feet, and swam on, powering through the length of the pond. Most of the kelpies kept swimming in a circle, up ahead and a little to my right.

My instincts nudged me. I veered towards the circle of kelpies.

Strangely, there was a little goat in the middle of them, flailing its legs and thrashing its head. The goat was drowning.

That was it. I was out of air. I pushed to the surface, took a deep gulp, and dived again.

A passing kelpie snapped at me. I punched that one, too. There was no reasoning with these bastards. Kelpies were mean to the core, and they enjoyed watching sentient creatures drown. That's what most of them were doing right now, watching this pretty little speckled goat slowly drown in the dark pond in front of them. I could hear them whinnying in delight as the goat thrashed helplessly in the water.

I could just swim on, but I wasn't Ember. And the goat was on the way, so I wouldn't lose any time. I swam towards the goat, punching and kicking kelpies out of my way. Coarse manes brushed against me, jagged teeth snapped, and hooves kicked out, but I kept going, grabbed the little goat by the scruff of its neck, pushed to the surface, and took another breath.

The goat coughed, inhaled, and bleated pathetically. Now that we were out of the water I could smell the magic surrounding it more clearly.

Fae transformation magic.

I ground my jaw. "Saoira."

The goat bleated again. It *was* her. Motherfucker.

I gnashed my teeth. It was all there, right in front of me

every step of the way. I just didn't want to see it, because I hadn't forgiven myself.

Okay, babes, can we shelve this self-reflection until later? If any more of those watery bitches bite us, we're going to be black and blue.

Holding goat-Saoira firmly by one little horn, I powered through the rest of the pond and hauled us both out. She bleated and trembled next to me.

My fingers twitched towards my pocket, where I had Romeo's anti-transformation charm, the one I'd asked him to make in case the Scorch showed up again. I couldn't use it on Saoira, though; Romeo had wrapped the charm in a casing of tungsten—the metal with the highest melting point—so it had a better chance of reaching the beast before it burned up.

There was nothing I could do for her that her family couldn't, anyway. I bent down and, unable to resist, patted Saoira on the head. "This will all be over soon. Just stay away from the edge of the lake, okay?"

She lowered her head sulkily but didn't protest.

"Sorry," I said. "I've got an *actual* sweet little psychopath to catch up with."

I sprinted off, heading to the foggy wall up ahead, and charged into the mists of madness.

CHAPTER

FORTY-EIGHT

T couldn't see a thing. The solid wall of mist covered everything in front of me. Even the air tasted sinister —a hint of smoke, a touch of blood, a taste of a sacked city after barbarians had been through, a waft of bloated corpses buried in a mudslide.

I shut my eyes and took a deep breath. Carefully, I separated the real things I could smell and hear and taste and mentally tagged the flavor of the magic that pushed the fake stuff towards me.

It became clearer. The grass under my feet was real, the stone wall fencing us in was real. A quarter mile ahead, I could smell the red and orange ribbons of the finish line. They were real.

The rest was fake.

Voices echoed all around me. "... shame to your family... worthless, an embarrassment..."

The goblin madness magic was at work. Reaching out with my hands, I kept walking, trying to stay in a straight line.

"... murderer... you'll burn in hell...shame... how could you do this to your people..."

My brain chuckled, wiping imaginary sweat off her brow. *It's a good thing we already did that self-realization exercise earlier.*

"Ha," I agreed out loud. "Bad timing on Ember's part. She should have stabbed me in here."

The goblin madness magic was designed to latch on and amplify any negative feelings. If I'd raced in here feeling anxious or uncertain, soon, I'd be buried in my despair.

But Ember wouldn't be feeling anything, because she was an actual, proper psychopath that didn't care about anyone other than herself. This was a mistake, this challenge. It was an advantage for Ember. But that was okay. I was allowed to make mistakes.

My ears twitched; a real sound floated towards me. A scream of agony. Not Ember.

Nyla.

I bolted forward. The mist cleared in front of me. I found them quickly.

Nyla was on the ground, screaming in agony, holding a bloody stump of a leg. Bright-red arterial blood spurted. I sniffed. It was real.

Ember laughed, her little voice sounded so merry and carefree, but now, I could hear it clearer. There was nothing more sinister than the sound of a child's laughter. She skipped into the clearing, heading towards Nyla, juggling two glowing-red curses in her hands.

She saw me, stopped, and grinned. "Daphne! You made it!" Her smile was so bright. So unhinged. She jerked her head towards Nyla, who was still screaming in agony on the ground. "Do you want to finish her off with me?"

My hands shook. "Ember..."

A tendril of darkness writhed within me, and suddenly, I could hear one of them.

One of the evils within me spoke.

The words died in my throat.

I remembered their voices, whispering, hissing, sneering. For thousands of years, they pinched and bit me as we were all squished together in a tiny urn. I knew why they were speaking now. I saw Ember for what she was, so they finally noticed her, too. They stirred, nudging me, stroking me.

I'd forgotten what they sounded like, and for a second, hearing them shocked me to my core. Hoarse, unctuous, so seductive, the voice of the evil echoed right through my head.

This could be a good thing, they said. Being like Ember. Taking whatever you want. It would make you more powerful, you know, and you want to be powerful, don't you, Hope? If you were powerful, then you could save more worlds. You could save them all—

I marched over and punched Ember in the face.

CHAPTER

FORTY-NINE

I used my Orion blade to cut my rope in half, using one piece to tie Ember's hands behind her back, and the other to quickly make a tourniquet for Nyla.

Ember hissed and spit. Blood poured from her nose and rain down her chin. "Let me go, you son of a bitch whore!"

Nyla was pale; she'd lost too much blood. But, as soon as I was done tying up her leg, she started dragging herself through the mists towards the finish line.

You gotta admire her commitment.

I hauled Ember to her feet; she spat in my face.

"Classy," I told her, shaking her roughly. "Let's go." I dragged her along through the solid fog, passing Nyla. I'd give her the honor of finishing the Death Race under her own steam. I followed my nose, moving in the direction of the scent of the finish line ribbon. "It was you all along, wasn't it, Ember? You killed King Monton."

"Of course," she spat out. "That fucker refused to take me hunting. Said that girls couldn't shoot. Well, I showed him, didn't I?"

She didn't give a shit. "How did you do it?"

"Dressed up like a page and hid in with the footmen."

She let out a bark of laughter. "Plugged him full of bolts when he was asleep."

"Is that right?" My voice was toneless. I dragged her forward.

"Nobody will believe you, you know," Ember cackled. "Nobody thought I'd be able to hold a crossbow, but I've been shooting since I was a toddler. I'm sixty years old now and everyone thinks I'm still a baby, because I'm not eighty like you old bitches."

"You killed your own baby brother."

"Half-brother," she snapped. "And he deserved it. Whiny little bastard. He took all of Mom's attention."

"Oh, yeah. Your mom." I ground my teeth, trying to insulate myself against Ember's aura of pure evil. We just had to make it to the finish line, and I had to get Ember to confess to everything while I could. The goblin magic made it hard; I kept having to remind myself that the smell of rotten corpse and woodsmoke wasn't real. "Tell me about your mom, Ember? Why is she a traitor?"

"Because she abandoned me!"

I shook her roughly. "But not because she ran away though, right? You mean before that. She betrayed you before that."

"Are you a fucking imbecile? Yes, she betrayed me! After I killed my idiot stepfather, she chose to keep the throne instead of taking me back to Sandstone where we belonged. With Monton and that whiny brat gone, we could have just left straight away. Gone home. But Mom chose them."

I knew, but I needed her to say it anyway. "Who is *them*?"

"The people." Ember's face twisted in hate. "The people of Dusk. She said she had to stay on as Queen so the City would stay safe and secure. She didn't care that I hated

Dusk. I hated the cold and the dark. She didn't want to take me home to Sandstone. She didn't fucking care!"

"So what did you do, Ember?"

She dissolved into mad laughter.

I shook her. "What did you do?"

Wait... babes. I think the smoke smell is real.

I sniffed and examined the air. Oh, shit.

Ember's insane laughter echoed around the mists. "I made her useful, that's what I did. Eventually, we'll turn this Kingdom back to the light, even if I have to burn it to ashes first."

CHAPTER
FIFTY

Okay, this is it. One more little burst of being an absolute baddie, and we're done.

I bolted through the mists, dragging Ember behind me. The orange and red ribbon of the finish line was right there, just up ahead. Ember laughed like a maniac. "Nobody will believe you."

"That's where you're wrong, you little psycho," I said cheerfully. "The whole course was rigged for sound. King Ronus and Queen Talia heard every word you said."

Her expression flipped immediately, and she started to scream and thrash. "No! No, you fucking little toad, you pathetic stupid—"

We charged out of the mists into the dim light of late afternoon, and the smell of smoke bloomed. I dragged Ember, kicking and screaming, all the way to the finish line ribbon. The crowd above me roared when they saw us.

Then, I paused. Nobody was perfect, and I was allowed to be petty. I pushed Ember over. She landed face first in the dirt. I ran through the ribbon, tearing it with my hands.

Romeo appeared at the top of the wall before me. I

pointed at him, shook the finish line ribbon, and shouted, "Dibs!"

For a fraction of a second, the fear on his face vanished, and he let out a bark of slightly hysterical laughter. "It was never in doubt." He turned serious immediately. "Baby, you have to get out of there. The Scorch is coming!"

"I know!" I shouted back. "We have to stop it, Romeo!"

He hesitated. "I don't know if—"

"I do! I'm sure, Romeo. Your spell will work; I know that now."

"How are we going to do it? She's going too fast, and she's burning too hot." He leaned over the wall and gave me his hand. I grabbed it, and he pulled me up onto the wall surrounding the Death Race course as if I was weightless.

The smell of smoke intensified. From here, I could see a flare of orange on the horizon. Even while I watched, it grew bigger and bigger.

The Scorch was coming straight for us.

I shot a look behind me toward the Kingdom of Dusk. The crowd gathered on the wall was starting to panic, scattering and trying to get down and move deeper within the City. In the watchtower, King Ronus and Queen Talia looked down on us, their expressions filled with fear. The courtiers behind them were all shouting at each other.

In the other watchtower, the giant Winter Queen was nuzzling Dwayne's neck.

I turned back to Romeo. "We need to slow the Scorch down. Can you do something?"

He furrowed his brow, looking out towards the rapidly growing orange spark on the horizon. His breath was rough in his throat. "I can try. But one of us needs to throw the charm."

I licked my lips. "I'm a better aim than you."

"Daphne—"

"And I heal faster, too, remember? All I have to do is get close enough to hit her with the charm, and I'll roll away—"

Dwayne's words dropped into my head, but he wasn't talking to me. **Pookie, do you mind if I give my little girl a hand down there?**

The Queen's reply echoed through my connection to Dwayne, but I couldn't decipher it. I could only feel it. It felt like when you accidentally got your tongue stuck on a frozen metal pole. A hint of panic, a tingle of pain.

Thanks, baby. I'll be right back, I promise. Then we can try that thing with the ice pops if you want.

The Winter Queen gave a laugh. My whole body broke out into goosebumps. Romeo shivered. "What the hell was that?"

"You don't want to know," I muttered, shooting a worried glance to the east. The orange glow was getting too big; she was coming faster than I realized. "You don't have to worry. I've got a ride. We can hit her from above. Dwayne to the rescue."

Dwayne jumped from the watchtower and swooped down, growing bigger as he flew. The remains of the crowd started to scream. He landed on the wall next to us like a great dragon in a high fantasy film.

I turned to kiss Romeo. It was too quick, and almost painfully so; my heart begged to hold on to him. He held me for a moment, and I could feel his reluctance to let me go, too. "Ask Dwayne to drop me a mile away," he said. "I'll set off a lava spell right in her path and run for the trees. She'll hit the lava, and it will slow her down."

Hopefully she wouldn't sense him and chase him. I didn't say it, though. This wasn't the time for doubt.

He bent his head, resting his forehead on mine. "Don't get too close."

336

"I won't." I kissed him again, forced myself to let him go, and backed away.

Dwayne held out his wing, and I climbed it to get up on his back. "Thanks, sir."

That's why I'm here, baby girl.

I didn't point out that this was not why he was here. Dwayne lurched, charging forward on his giant feet, flapped his mighty wings, and took off into the sky. Immediately, he circled back around, swooped down, dangled his leg, and let Romeo grab on. Riding on Dwayne was like being tossed in a giant laundromat dryer; I sent up a silent prayer that Romeo was holding on tight.

We rose up higher into the air. The ball of orange light grew brighter and brighter. She really was coming straight for us.

If she hit, it would mean the end of Dusk. Nothing would survive that heat, that fury, that anguish and despair. We had one shot.

I roared into the wind. "Slow down and drop Romeo on the road here! Nice and slow, Dwayne!"

You got it. He turned his wings, flapping outwards and slowing to almost a stop. His feet brushed the ground. I held my breath until he'd soared away again, and I could see Romeo standing on the road, safe and well.

Dwayne banked, and we flew in a slow circle overtop of her, a mile up.

Heat brushed my cheeks. She was just like the sun. Like a miniature version, blazing away, scorching the earth wherever she raged. Ember had asked her for sunshine, so she'd given it to her.

I looked down on the road and focused on Romeo. I could feel the atoms in the air trembling with the weight of the magic he gathered. A minute passed, then thirty

337

seconds more, and a thunderclap split the sky. A pit of bubbling bright-orange lava appeared in the road.

Romeo turned and ran off into the woods.

I sent up another prayer. Please, keep him safe.

The Scorch was coming fast, shooting up the road. I could see her clearly now—a bright white cow with massive horns. The look in her eyes made me want to destroy the world myself. She'd been caught in a loop of absolute horror for over a decade now. For her, there was no escaping the pain.

Showtime. "Bring us down just after the lava pit! Try and get me as low as possible, Dwayne!"

Are you going to pee on her?

"No, sir!" I pulled out the anti-transformation charm.

Do you want *me* to pee on her?

I exhaled. "No, it's fine. I got it."

This was it. One last thing. One last thing and Romeo and I could go home...

Dwayne shrank a little as we flew, then, a little more. The heat was too much. His wings started to smoke.

The white cow was lost in her panic and didn't see the patch of lava in front of her. She tore straight into it.

I held my breath.

Her momentum slowed, just a little, as the boiling rock swamped her. It only lasted a second, then, she was out of the lava.

Dwayne dipped his wings, swooping low. The tips of his feathers burst into flames.

Now!

I lined up my shot and threw the spell.

The whole world shook when it hit her.

CHAPTER
FIFTY-ONE

The smoke cleared slowly.

I walked through it, following the sound of a woman's sobs. She lay in the road, her naked white body smudged with dirt. Butter-yellow hair covered her face.

Her desperate cries broke my heart.

I didn't know if she would ever recover from this. But now, at least, I could see exactly what had happened.

Ember, the selfish little psycho, never adapted to Dusk in the way the Fae were supposed to. She didn't want to, and she didn't try. Like the Beast of Bakkanon, she tried to make the world fit around her, to bend it to her own will.

She did everything she could to bring in more light. She demanded her mother use her elemental powers to summon some sunshine for her, over and over and over again. And Carissa indulged her, because Ember was her child, and she loved her and wanted her to be happy.

That might have been where the imbalance began, with Carissa secretly giving in and bringing too much bright sunshine to a place that was meant to symbolize the end of the day. But it wasn't enough for Ember.

I knew Ember killed her stepfather in a fit of selfish and jealous rage, hoping to make Carissa take her back to Sandstone. I knew that Ember had a tantrum when Carissa told her they'd be staying in Dusk instead of returning home.

The rest was just guesswork, but I understood how fae magic worked, and I understood how curses worked. Ember would have begged Carissa for some sunshine to soothe her, so Carissa summoned it all over her body. Then, Ember used her own magic, turned her mother into a cow, and told her exactly what she'd done, just to hurt her. Ember told Carissa it was she who'd killed Carissa's beloved husband and son.

It was just like blood magic. Carissa's unendurable suffering at having her own daughter do this to her... the pain fueled her elemental magic and made Ember's transformation spell stick. Panic, betrayal, anguish, fear; it was all a feedback loop that made the Scorch.

But now, the spell was broken.

I walked over and knelt next to her. "Queen Carissa."

She lifted her head. The pain in her expression almost broke me.

"I'm so sorry," I whispered.

There was nothing else to say.

CHAPTER

FIFTY-TWO

Queen Talia embraced me warmly. "I should be angry with you, my dear. You are taking my beloved grandson away."

I hugged her back. "I'll fight you for him."

She laughed and squeezed me tighter.

It felt like the entire City had come out to say goodbye. We gathered on the grass outside the gates, waiting for the royal mages to work the magic to send us home. Crowds of courtiers and common fae surrounded us on all sides. A group of bruised warlords stood a safe distance away, waving lavender handkerchiefs, sobbing and wailing like their hearts were breaking.

Next to me, Romeo hugged King Ronus. There were a lot of gruff manly emotional noises coming from them.

And, a lot further away, near a shimmering cloud of snowflakes, there was another noise I wished I couldn't hear. Dwayne was saying goodbye to Queen Maeve. I tried to ignore it and focus on saying goodbye to Talia. I liked her a lot.

After a moment, Talia pulled back and looked me in the

eye. "It is astonishing how much a mortal wolf girl could be just like me." She smiled. "Please come back soon, Daphne Ironclaw."

"Apparently, I have to." I grinned at her. Technically, according to fae custom, Romeo and I were betrothed, and I was now the future Princess of Dusk. And, according to all the long, loud proclamations from the herald, one day I'd be Queen.

Talia laughed. "There is much life left in these old bones, my dear girl. It will be a hundred years before you can push me off my throne."

I smiled. "I'm glad for that."

The sucking noises became impossible to ignore. Both Talia and I glanced over to where the giant, terrifying Queen Maeve stood, holding Dwayne to her breast. He nuzzled her white neck and nibbled her ear. **Miss you, pookie.**

I tried to block out Queen Maeve's response. It felt like frostbite in my ears. Talia's smile wavered as we watched them. "Are we doing the right thing?"

I knew what she was talking about. Ember was crouched in the dirt a few feet away, her lips frozen together and her hands still bound. Her pale eyes were hot with fury. She glared at us as if her eyes could kill, and she wanted us all dead.

Queen Maeve had declared that Ember was hers to take. I could understand it. Maeve's domain was many things— sleep, winter, death, night, but also, she was destruction and annihilation. Ember was like a wrecking ball. I could see why Maeve had decided Ember was hers.

The Winter Queen was taking Ember back to her court, where she'd serve out an undisclosed term of service as restitution for upsetting the balance of nature in Faerie.

"I don't think we have a choice," I said to Talia. "But for

what it's worth, you can't ever tell Carissa what happened to her daughter."

"I agree," Talia said quietly. "Carissa has suffered enough."

Romeo and Ronus walked over to join us. "Carissa will live out her days in peace and solitude," Ronus said. "I'll make sure of it."

A strange shattering noise, the sound of ice cracking, cut through the air. My breath suddenly turned to vapor. We turned to look.

Queen Maeve—still wearing her glittery blue gown—had turned back into a giant swan, her black eyes hooded, her head weaving seductively from side to side.

Dwayne had his wing up Queen Maeve's skirt.

"Dwayne," I hissed. "Stop fingering the Winter Queen!"

Oh. Sorry. He withdrew his wing. **Okay, pookie, I gotta run. I promise I'll come visit soon.**

The Queen, still in her swan form, nuzzled him one more time and withdrew. She swung out one of her wings and scooped Ember up underneath her. Then, the Winter Queen let out a tinkling squeak, spread her wings, and took off into the sky.

We all let out a sigh of relief when she disappeared. Talia took my hand. "Despite the terror of her appearance, it seems hosting Queen Maeve here for the briefest amount of time has already redressed the balance here in Faerie. She has not left her Court in generations. I noticed that even Lady Pesh is wearing Dusk colors again." Her eyes met mine. "You are a miracle, my dear. Your methodology is most unusual, but you saved us all."

Ronus kissed my cheek one more time. "Come back soon."

"We will," Romeo said.

Magic prickled a few feet away from us. The royal

mages had opened the portal. A shimmery circle of pure blackness appeared in mid-air.

"Wait, wait!" Brackin ran forwards, weighed down by suitcases. "I shall go first, your highnesses. I shall ensure the way is clear!"

I gave him a little bow. "Of course, Diplomat."

Brackin deserved his own reward for the part he'd played in saving Faerie. I'd misjudged him. Just like I misjudged Troy, and Ember, and probably a lot of other people who betrayed me.

But I wasn't responsible for their actions. I was only responsible for mine.

Brackin was a kinky, selfish slimeball, but in the end, he did have his people's best interests at heart. Gloom wasn't his to rule; that title belonged to his brother, and Gloom didn't really suit him, anyway. He needed more excitement.

With that in mind, I suggested that Ronus and Talia give him the post of Fae Diplomat. So, he was coming with us and heading to an open Diplomat post in Tijuana. I hoped he would find some fellow tickle enthusiasts there.

Brackin held his head high as he marched into the portal and disappeared.

The King and Queen moved back from us. Ronus bowed, and Talia curtsied. "It is an honor to know you, Daphne Ironclaw."

I curtsied back. "The honor is mine."

Romeo took my hand. "Ready to go home, baby?"

I smiled up at him. "I'm ready to go wherever you are, my Prince of Shadow."

EPILOGUE

The first thing I did when I got back was try to call Lennox Arran. I needed to talk to him about Myf, but the bastard was dodging my calls.

I wasn't going to give up. Myf had been in the back of my mind the whole time we'd been in Faerie. I knew it wasn't my fault—I'd done my best, just like I always had—but I knew I'd neglected her. Now that Romeo was back, and there were no monsters threatening the safety of Philadelphia or anyone trying to kill me, I was determined to make it up to her.

I sat upright in bed, adjusted my super-cozy flannel pajama top, and dialed Lennox Arran's number for the fiftieth time. Romeo walked back in the room with a pizza box in his hand as the phone rang. The smell of garlic and cheese almost annihilated my frustration. Romeo gave me a sexy smug smile and put the box down in front of me.

"My Queen," he murmured.

"Stop that," I mouthed. I was never going to get used to it, and I didn't really want anyone finding out about it, either. Judy would have a heart attack.

Hmm. Maybe we should tell everyone...

Less than two days had passed in the mortal realm while we'd been gone. I hadn't even missed any work, since Monica had given me a few days off. Romeo and I had walked out of the portal, straight back into the grounds of Romeo's church, and into the very enthusiastic arms of his covenmates.

They were all ecstatic to have him back. Cole even cried a little.

All we'd done since we got home was lay in bed and eat. The food in Faerie was fine, of course, but there was nothing in any realm in any universe better than quattro formaggi pizza and a big bottle of cola.

Now, I just had to get Myf to come home. Damn Lennox Arran, he might never let her go.

The phone clicked, and I listened to his vain, bombastic greeting on his voicemail. Before it finished, I hit the cancel button, then threw my phone across the room in a huff.

Romeo caught it with one hand, sat down on the bed next to me, and pulled out his own phone. "Let me try. The Alpha Shifter has to answer for the High Priest."

I frowned and dug a piece of cheese pizza out of the box. "It might be a mistake getting you involved, though. Myf is a shifter; she's Lennox's responsibility—"

"So you've said a million times." He unlocked his phone. "I don't have to get involved, Daphne. I'll just get him on the line, and you can talk to him." He hit a few buttons and put it on speaker. The phone rang.

The line clicked. "What do you want, High Priest?" Lennox sounded annoyed.

I grabbed the phone. "Lennox."

He let out a hiss of exasperation. "Daphne, I *don't* want to talk to you!"

I knew why. I'd humiliated him badly when I beat him up in front of his pack. And, even worse, I'd dropped the biggest ick-bomb ever—we were most likely half-siblings. Lennox had been publicly hitting on me for years. He'd almost waged a war to force me to be his princess. Now, we were both grossed out and embarrassed by it all.

"Just for a second. Please," I begged him. "It's about Myf."

Lennox paused. "Who?"

I frowned. "What do you mean, who? Myf, my roommate."

"Oh, the pretty redhead? Yeah, what about her?"

I mouthed like a goldfish for a second. "Isn't she there?"

"No." He sounded sulky. "Why would she be here?"

I glanced at Romeo. He furrowed his brow, then got up, and left the room. I turned back to the phone; it gave me no clues as to what was going on. "There's no grumpy Welsh redhead living in your compound?"

"No. I'd know if she turned up," Lennox said. "I liked her. She had some fire behind her eyes."

A creeping chill spread from the base of my spine. I swallowed. "Okay. Thanks anyway. Let me know if she shows up."

"I'm not letting you know shit, Daphne." Lennox cut the call.

I stared at the phone, confused. I'd read the note Myf left a million times. The pain in her words was engraved on my soul.

I found someone who cares about me. Someone who cherishes me, and he's going to take care of me from now on.

If she wasn't with Lennox Arran... Who the hell was she with?

After a minute, Romeo came back into the room with Micah, who was carrying a laptop. "Myf's not answering her phone," Micah said, "but since it's on our shared network, we can trace it."

I glanced at Romeo. "Brandon gave the phone to her," he explained. "She was using an old analog phone because she was paranoid about getting tracked down by the People of the Claw. We gave her one of ours to use. I didn't think to track her sooner because we assumed she was at the compound with Lennox."

I took a breath; it felt too shallow. My chest was getting tight.

Micah nodded at me. "Dial her number again. I'll ping her."

Why was I suddenly so scared? With shaking hands, I picked up my phone and found Myf's number. Every time I'd tried before, I didn't even get a dial tone. I assumed she'd switched it off. But this time, it connected and rang.

Once, twice. The line clicked.

A man answered. "Ah. The little box."

My heart stopped.

The voice was familiar, but not. It was high-pitched and cold as the grave. That voice haunted my nightmares, and now, it was impossibly, incomprehensibly loaded with power.

I began to shake.

"Are you looking for your dragon, little box? Because she's with me right now." He chuckled humorlessly. "And I'm taking good care of her."

It was Christopher Jupiter.

TO BE CONTINUED

Also by Lauretta Hignett

Go back to the start with Imogen Gray series:

Immortal Ghost (freebie prequel novella)

Immortal

Immortal Games

Immortal World

Immortal Life

Immortal Death

Then follow Sandy in the Foils and Fury series:

Oops I Ate A Vengeance Demon

Dancing With The Vengeance Demon

Dating With The Vengeance Demon

Dying For My Vengeance Demon

Then go on to Prue's story with Blood & Magic:

Bad Bones

Bare Bones

Broke Bones

Blood & Bones

Burned Bones

Bitter Bones

Head on into Chloe's series, The Waif in the Wilds:

The Waif in the Wilds (freebie prequel novella)

Vicious Creatures

Fractured Gods

Ravenous Beasts

Savage Daemons

Duck Duck Motherf*cker (freebie epilogue novella in Dwayne's POV)

And then Daphne's story in the Hidden City Supernatural Sleuth:

The Wolf Vs The Vampire

The Wolf Vs The Warlock

The Wolf Vs Santa (Holiday Novella)

The Wolf Vs The Shifter

The Wolf Vs The Witch

The Wolf Vs The Monster

And detour into a new universe with Susan in Welcome to Midlife Magic:

Susan, You're The Chosen One

It's Called Magic, Susan

Susan, Break The Curse!

You Can't Fight A Prophecy, Susan

Printed in Dunstable, United Kingdom